Joy Dettman was born in country Victoria and spent her early years in towns on either side of the Murray River. She is an award-winning writer of short stories, the complete collection of which, *Diamonds in the Mud*, was published in 2007, as well as the highly acclaimed novels *Mallawindy*, *Jacaranda Blue*, *Goose Girl*, *Yesterday's Dust*, *The Seventh Day*, *Henry's Daughter*, *One Sunday*, *Pearl in a Cage*, *Thorn on the Rose*, *Moth to the Flame*, *Ripples on a Pond*, and *The Tying of Threads*. *Wind in the Wires* is Joy's fourth novel in her Woody Creek series.

Also by Joy Dettman

Mallawindy
Jacaranda Blue
Goose Girl
Yesterday's Dust
The Seventh Day
Henry's Daughter
One Sunday
Diamonds in the Mud

Woody Creek series
Pearl in a Cage
Thorn on the Rose
Moth to the Flame
Ripples on a Pond
The Tying of Threads

Joy Dettman

WIND IN THE WIRES

PAN

First published 2012 in Macmillan by Pan Macmillan Australia Pty Limited
This Pan edition published in 2013 by Pan Macmillan Australia Pty Limited
1 Market Street, Sydney

National Library of Australia
Cataloguing-in-Publication data:

Dettman, Joy.

Wind in the wires / Joy Dettman.

9781742611952 (pbk.)

A823.3

The characters and events in this book are fictitious and any resemblance to real
persons, living or dead, is purely coincidental.

Typeset in 12.5/16 pt Adobe Garamond by Midland Typesetters Australia
Printed by IVE

My heartfelt thankyou to Emma who tolerates my idiosyncrasies and to my readers who supply the fuel which keeps my nose to the grindstone

PREVIOUSLY IN
WOODY CREEK

Gertrude Foote (Granny), town midwife and small property owner, was once wed to **Archie Foote**. She is the mother of **Amber** and grandmother of **Sissy** and **Jenny Morrison**.

Vern Hooper, farmer, sawmill boss and leading Woody Creek citizen, is **Gertrude's** half-cousin and her long-term lover. He has three offspring, **Lorna**, **Margaret** and **Jim**, a childhood friend of **Jenny**.

George Macdonald, mill owner and farmer, and his wife, **Maisy**, are the parents of eight daughters and identical hell-raising twin sons, **Bernie and Macka**. When a drunken prank goes badly awry, **Jenny**, a schoolgirl, is found to be with child. For her good name's sake, a hurried wedding is arranged by **Amber** and **Norman Morrison** together with the parents of the twins.

Jenny has other ideas. Fifteen, alone, afraid, her childhood dream of becoming a famous singer ripped from her by the twins and **Margot's** birth, Jenny escapes to Melbourne, where she meets

Laurie Morgan, a redhead who looks like Clark Gable. He is kind. He takes care of her, buys her pretty thing – and takes advantage of her confused innocence. **Georgie** is conceived.

Jenny returns to the ever dependable **Gertrude**, her life in tatters. The town has lost respect for her, as she has for herself. When she learns that **Sissy** is engaged to **Jim Hooper**, it may well be the straw that breaks the camel's back. **Jim** is **Jenny's** friend and one of the few in town who still looks on her as the girl she had once been.

By accident or design, their friendship develops into much more. Then **Jim** breaks his engagement and joins the army. Seven months later, **Jimmy** is born. **Jenny** is eighteen and the mother of three illegitimate children, **Margot**, **Georgie** and **Jimmy**. She vows to never again become pregnant.

Vern learns of his grandson and is determined to claim the infant. **Jim** hasn't been back to Woody Creek. **Jenny** won't reply to his letters. His family tell him he has a son and he wants to see him before he is sent overseas. To escape **Vern's** threats of court, **Jenny** flees to Sydney and to **Jim** with their ten-month-old son, her tiny **Georgie** left in **Gertrude's** care.

Elsie, a light-skinned aboriginal who calls **Gertrude** 'Mum', lives with her husband **Harry Hall** on Gertrude's land. They have the care of several children: their own, **Elsie's** niece and nephew, and **Margot**, who **Jenny** has had little to do with.

Vern and his daughters refuse to contemplate a marriage between **Jenny** and **Jim**. He has bought her a wedding ring. She has taken his name at the Sydney boarding house, but at eighteen will require **Norman's** permission to marry. Since Georgie's birth, she has had no contact with **Norman**, **Amber** or **Sissy**.

In Sydney, she is singing again at clubs and parties, and when Jim is reported missing in action, she takes on day work at a clothing factory where she meets **Lila**, also married and a mother. Jenny is living an exemplary life, waiting for news of **Jim**.

Come New Year's Eve, 1943, she is in the club pianist's car, on her way home, when disaster strikes in the shape of five drunken American sailors.

Ten months later, **Jenny** leaves **Amberley**, a comfortable boarding house, to return to a life of constant labour on Gertrude's small property and to live in **Gertrude's** two-and-a-half-room hut. She carries with her a guilty secret.

Gertrude must never know a third daughter was born to **Jenny** – **Cara Jeanette**, given at birth to Amberley's childless landlady, **Myrtle Norris** and her husband **Robert**, a high-school principal. **Cara** may well be Jenny's secret for life, but to **Myrtle** and **Robert** she is a cherished only child.

Vern Hooper and his daughters haven't given up. They will not have their son and brother wed to a little trollop who can't keep her pants on. They allow **Jenny** to believe that **Jim** is dead, and again threaten to take her son.

Ray King wants to marry Jenny. She doesn't love him, but he has a house in the city, and to have any chance at life, her children need to have a father.

Then **Amber Morrison**, who has never been quite sane, murders her stationmaster husband **Norman** in his bed. For twenty-one years, **Jenny** has believed **Norman** to be her father. The night of his funeral, she learns the truth of her birth.

Archie Foote, singer, poet, physician and Gertrude's philandering husband, is her natural father. **Juliana Conti**, an Italian woman who died in childbirth, is her mother.

She tells **Ray King** she will marry him but will never have another child. He wants her, not children. He doesn't want her children. The marriage has little chance of success. She loved **Jim Hooper**. She promised him when they said goodbye never to remove his ring. When she marries Ray, she moves **Jim's** ring to her right hand.

The war has been over for months when she learns that **Jim** is alive and in a Melbourne hospital. She takes **Jimmy** there to meet his father, but **Jim**, a prisoner of the Japanese for two years, has lost a leg and some say his sight and his mind. He does not appear to recognise, or even see, her.

After a violent episode, **Jenny** leaves **Ray** and once again returns to **Gertrude**. **Vern Hooper** is growing old and infirm, and still has only the one grandson, who he will not allow to be raised as a bastard in Woody Creek.

He gains custody of six-year-old **Jimmy**, and before **Vern's** death, **Jimmy** is adopted by **Margaret Hooper** and her husband **Bernard**.

Ray has formed an association with **Florence**, a young and inexperienced girl. She has two children to him, **Raelene** and the retarded **Donny**. In 1951, **Ray** comes to Woody Creek with his two motherless babies, where **Jenny**, still mourning the loss of her beloved son to the Hoopers, finds a focus in **Ray's** babies. A relationship is forged, though never again as husband and wife. **Jenny** cares for **Donny**, and grows to love the doll-like **Raelene**.

In 1958 **Gertrude** dies, then less than a week later, **Ray** is crushed beneath logs at a mill. Unable to manage the now seven-year-old **Donny** alone, **Jenny** delivers him to a Melbourne home for disabled children then finds employment in Frankston, with **Vroni**, an old friend.

Charlie White, the elderly town grocer, has a daughter **Hilda**. He hasn't seen or heard from her in many years. He is known as the meanest man in town, though not by **Georgie**, who has been working for him since she turned fourteen. The **Fulton family** are **Charlie's** long-term tenants and good neighbours. **Miss Blunt**, the town draper and dressmaker, is another of **Charlie's** tenants. He owns half-a-dozen rental properties in Woody Creek.

Jack Thompson, the young constable, is falling in love with **Georgie**, who in 1958 is eighteen and a stunningly beautiful redhead.

Teddy Hall, middle son of **Elsie** and **Harry**, is involved in an odd relationship with **Margot**, a plain and frumpish girl.

Back in Melbourne, **Florence**, **Raelene** and **Donny's** natural mother, sees **Ray's** death notice in a newspaper. She contacts **Jenny**, stating that **Ray** stole her children and that she wants to see her daughter.

Against her better judgement, **Jenny** takes **Raelene** to the city to meet **Florence** and her husband **Clarrie**. She chooses the wrong day. It is the Saturday of the football grand final. Flinders Street station is crowded. She sees a familiar head, well above the crowd. It can't be Jim? She calls his name, and he turns, and **Jenny** runs to him.

PART ONE

PART ONE

THE OLD HOUSE

Trees of the walnut family were once an important component of the vast temperate forests of Asia and North-eastern America. The walnut's dense clusters of flowers are inconspicuous, the meat of its hard shelled nut highly nutritious, but it is for its timber the tree is valued and used extensively in cabinet making.

Georgie Morrison found that piece of information while glancing through her new set of encyclopaedias – near new, she'd found them in a box at the tip while dropping off a load of shop rubbish. Georgie wasn't proud – or not about her reading material; she owned shelves full of second-hand books. *In their natural habitat walnut trees reach great heights and girths*, the encyclopaedia said. Granny's tree was no giant of its breed. Planted by her father, along with a dozen more, he may have dreamt fine dreams of furnishing his mansion with a walnut cabinet and table. Who knows what a dead man dreamt? One tree had survived to maturity. No mansion had ever risen on his acres.

For most of Georgie's life the midsummer sun had set each night behind that tree, its dense canopy of green doing what it could to protect the western wall of Granny's house from the worst of summer's ire. Its limbs were naked in July of 1958, when she'd packed her earthly bags – but if there was a place out there behind the walnut tree, behind the sunset, then as sure as that tree produced its annual bags of walnuts, Granny was up there milking her heavenly goats and thanking God she hadn't lived long enough to see the abomination Bernie Macdonald and his working bee had made of her cosy little home.

Her kitchen hadn't survived the onslaught. Its small window, which for eighty-odd years had offered morning light to that long and narrow room, was gone. The timber floor had been replaced by cement – and not enough depth of cement. Already it was crazed by cracks. The green curtain, hung for Georgie's lifetime in the lean-to doorway, was gone, as was the lean-to. A door had been hung in the green curtain's space. It refused to close.

That long room no longer served as a kitchen. It had donated its iron chimney and stove to the new kitchen. A dark place now, a connection now, forcing three groups of unrelated rooms into a marriage from hell.

The door which refused to close gave entrance to a brand-new laundry and bathroom, their floors eighteen inches higher than the cement floor. Continue through and one more step up and you entered the old bathroom, which had made the transformation to third bedroom, a walk-through bedroom, and Georgie's preferred entrance to Ray's old bedroom, now a newly baptised kitchen. Split-level homes might become the latest fad in a year or two. That house, a hotchpotch of many levels, was before its time.

Shakey Lewis had been more or less responsible for the design. A champion footballer in his heyday, a builder too, though a lot of water had passed under the old bridge since then. It was well known in town that he couldn't name a hammer until the pub opened, that he shook too hard to hit a nail on the head before midday. By midafternoon Shakey was at his best; he'd designed the new kitchen in the afternoon, and given what he'd had to work with, he'd made a reasonable job of it – apart from his addition of a pair of large second-hand windows, set into its west wall, perfectly positioned to look December's afternoon sun in the eye. Then he'd positioned a new stainless steel sink beneath those windows, perfectly positioned to reflect the sun's glare.

Today its dazzle was blinding and no curtain to draw against the glare. No Jenny to sew the curtain. The night of Ray's funeral she'd delivered Donny to Melbourne and signed him into the care of strangers at a home for retarded children. He was Ray's son, not Jenny's. Ray had been able to handle him, Jenny couldn't, not alone.

Christmas Day tomorrow and that cloudless sky didn't bode well for the roast chicken and steamed pudding dinner. The chooks who had donated their lives to Christmas could have been the lucky ones. Today, their sisters were panting in the shade. The bitumen newly crowning Forest Road was melting. A paddock away from it, Georgie could smell the tar.

They'd done a lot of work on that road since the floods of July – or since a Melbourne blow-in had opened his caravan park for business. Charlie White, grocer and Georgie's employer, swore the caravan park's owner had bribed the council to bitumen that road and erect a sign where two roads forked.

Forest Road, Caravan Park. 4 Miles, it read.

Forest Road? It was a wending, winding bush track that had found a vocation, that's all. It would never be marked on road maps. It didn't go anywhere. Woody Creek was barely a flyspeck dot on Georgie's new road map of Victoria – which she'd use when she could afford to buy her own ute.

The old ones had named the town for the creek that twisted through a red gum forest like a snake with a belly ache. Forest Road twisted at its side – a busy track since the caravan park opened for business.

City campers might like roughing it, but they liked their grog cold, liked to plug in their caravan's refrigerator and flick a switch. More bribery, Charlie said. Light poles now ran alongside Granny's front fence, and a month back the electricity company had fixed a meter box onto the wall beside the front door, beside Jenny's tin plate plaque, beside the house name, painted by Georgie on a length of leftover floorboard: *The Abortion*.

Flick a light switch and a globe lit up to highlight that painted board. Flick those switches indoors and naked light globes displayed every flaw.

No globe necessary at six o'clock, or not today. Outside those twin kitchen windows, the sun clung to the sky like an aggressive kid clinging to his weary mother's teat. The new kitchen was white hot – and white. Three four-gallon tins of paint donated to the fundraising committee, intent on rehousing the widow of Ray King, had been slapped onto that kitchen. Its walls were white, its ceiling, its cupboards, its doors were white.

There was plenty of cupboard space, unmatched, donated units, forced by Shakey Lewis's screw and nail into one before being wed into a unit by white paint – and a red gum bench top. In some not too distant year, those boards would warp and crack, though not today. Today that bench gleamed red, offering some relief from white.

As did Granny's old black stove, set midway down the southern wall. During its many years of life that stove had rarely seen the light of day. Georgie had never noticed the pattern on its oven door. It was on display now, as was the battered kitchen table, and Granny's old dresser, which in some future year may be classified a genuine antique. Today it only admitted its age.

The kerosene refrigerator, purchased five years ago, didn't flinch from the light. It stood opposite the stove, beside the bathroom door, a block of green, its burning wick adding heat and the odour of kerosene to the kitchen.

Plenty of space in that room, space enough to seat a crowd, and only Georgie in it – until Margot entered in search of her comb.

'Did you move my comb from the bathroom?'

'Nope.'

Margot would only use one comb, white, coarse toothed, purchased for her by Maisy Macdonald, her grandmother.

Bloodless, squat, chunky, born of rape to fifteen-year-old Jenny, then deserted by her. For the first year of Margot's life, Elsie and Harry had raised her. She still spent most of her time with them, on the far side of the goat paddock.

Today her white hair hung limp, still damp from the shower. She'd turn twenty in April. She might have been fifteen or thirty. There was something lacking in Margot. Always the runt of Jenny's litter of three, her growth spurt had begun late and ended prematurely. She had the Macdonalds' height, though less of it. She had Bernie and Macka Macdonald's stumpy hands, their broad jaws and pale purple eyes. Never pleasant eyes to look into, Margot's were less so today. She was excited.

Georgie wasn't. She'd agreed to go to Molliston with Jack Thompson, to stay overnight at his parents' hotel and have Christmas dinner with them tomorrow. Didn't want to go. Couldn't get out of it now.

'Okay. I'm off then,' she said and walked out to Charlie's old ute.

*

Margot watched the dust and feathers fly as Georgie drove up the track to the open boundary gate, then she walked through the house to continue her search for her comb.

The best part of the renovation was the east side. The working bee men had moved half of a farmhouse to the site, a sitting room, a tiny passage, bedroom and a veranda. Those two rooms were furnished like other houses, the sitting room with a couch and matching chairs, stored for years in the Macdonalds' shed. Ray's bedroom suite was in Margot's bedroom. It was supposed to be Jenny's room – if she ever came back. She wasn't getting it. Its door had a key.

Margot loved looking at the house from the east side. It looked like a proper house; it even had a cane chair on the veranda.

No one approached from the east side, or entered via the east side door – not by day. Teddy Hall crept in that way by night then locked the bedroom door behind him. He and Margot did what they liked in that bedroom. And tonight they'd have all night to do what they liked in it.

The first time Teddy had done it Margot hadn't thought he'd be game enough to do it again, but only two days later she'd gone out to the shed to get wheat for the chooks and Teddy had walked in. There was no lock on the shed, no door on it, and it had been about half past five and still light.

'What do you think you're doing over here?' she'd said.

'What do you think I'm doing?' he'd said, then he'd taken the basin from her hands and they'd done it on the bag of wheat and all the time he'd been doing it he'd tormented her.

'Mum's milking the goats. Why aren't you yelling out for her, dobber?'

She hadn't wanted to, that's why. Nothing exciting had ever happened to her. Never in her life had she done one single thing that everyone hadn't known about. No one knew about her and Teddy, and they never would either.

'You're like opening up one of those crates of donated junk Bernie Macdonald dumped down here,' he'd said last Saturday night. 'It looks like there's nothing worth having in you, but dig down deep enough and you're full of surprises, aren't you?'

People who were addicted to drugs hated those drugs. Teddy said he was addicted to sex. She was too. She still hated him, but she took him anyway.

Perhaps in the dead of night Granny's ghost stood at a window shaking her head at the goings-on in Ray's double bed. Perhaps on the darkest nights when Margot heard a tap-tap-tap at the window, it was Granny, tapping out a ghostly warning. Margot had heeded few of her warnings.

*

Georgie had. She still missed Granny and knew that she continued to walk her land at night. Every time the light globe in the
old kitchen had to be replaced, she knew Granny had been about.
'Who needs their electric lights when we've got that old moon,'
she used to say.

Granny had never trusted electricity. Had never trusted cars
either. She'd named anything faster than twenty miles an hour
speeding. Georgie was behind the wheel of Jack's car and touching
fifty on straight sections of the road.

Until ten minutes ago she'd never driven further than the
outskirts of Willama. Tonight Jack had let her drive through that
town. They were out the other side now, and heading into territory
unfamiliar to Georgie.

'Did you go to the Willama high school, Jack?'

'I was thirteen when the war ended,' Jack Thompson said.

That war supplied timing for many things. Everyone said it
– before the war, since the war. Georgie couldn't remember it,
other than the day it ended. She knew they'd still been fighting
when Jenny had come home from Sydney with Jimmy. He'd been
three at the time, so it must have been in 1944. She remembered
staring at the big girl, who Granny had said was Georgie and
Margot's mother. She hadn't looked like a mother.

Later she'd learnt that Jimmy had a father and he'd been killed
in the war, which could have been the first time Georgie had asked
about her own father. 'He's in Sydney,' Jenny had said. He'd been
in jail at the time. She hadn't told her that.

'Why did you join the cops, Jack?'

'Dad was a cop,' he said.

Probably locked up mine, Georgie thought, wondered what he'd
think if he knew Jack was taking the daughter of Laurie Morgan,
the redheaded water-pistol bandit, home to eat Christmas dinner.

For weeks she'd done her best to wriggle out of meeting his
parents, and was beginning to wish she'd wriggled harder. But
he'd taught her to drive, and they were mates – and her hanging

around with him could have been saving him from a life sentence of Woody Creek. A few of the town girls gave him the eye – not that he was anything special to look at, he was single, that's all, and single blokes were thin on the ground in Woody Creek. Most of them left school and left town.

'Keep your eyes skinned for roos along this stretch,' Jack warned. 'They're in plague proportions out here.'

She shouldn't have been driving his cop car. He'd probably get into strife if someone dobbed on him, though he didn't seem too worried about it.

Since he'd given her a licence in October, she'd been driving Charlie's '47 Ford ute around the town. He'd bought it cheap after his daughter left home with his sedan and a trailer load of his best furniture. No one would bother to steal his ute. About the best anyone could say for it was it had four wheels and a motor that usually went. The cop car was almost new; she loved driving it.

Jenny had said in one of her letters that she'd driven a car from Melbourne to Geelong when Georgie had been a peanut in her belly, that the sniff of petrol must have got into her bloodstream. It probably got into it before that. Laurie Morgan had stolen cars along with pretty much anything else.

Didn't want to think about her water-pistol bandit tonight. Didn't know why she was – except for Jack's father being an ex-cop. If he'd been a cop in 1939 he could have helped in the arrest. Jenny had said that there'd been six or more police at the Geelong station when they'd caught Laurie.

'How long has your family lived in Molliston, Jack?'

'I was born there. My parents have been there since the twenties – not together. Mum lost her husband, Dad lost his wife – and then there was me.'

'I can't work out why anyone who managed to get away from one tin-pot little town would move back to another one,' she said.

'I get to see more of my folks. They're no spring chickens.'

'If not for Charlie's broken arm, I'd be in Frankston now.'

'He's not your responsibility, Georgie.'

'I know that.'

'Is your mother planning to stay down there?'

'She's got a job. She won't get one if she comes back here.'

'I thought she got her husband's insurance from the mill accident.'

'She says it's for Raelene and Donny, not for her.'

'She's his widow,' Jack said.

'She didn't live with him, not since '47. He lived with us and we looked after his kids.'

'Does she pay much for Donny's care?'

'I don't think she pays anything.' She didn't pay rent either. She worked for a friend at Frankston, and lived in two rooms behind her health resort, a three-minute walk from a beach – and she wanted Georgie to move down there with her.

She might too – if she could talk Charlie into trusting someone else in his shop. In March she'd be nineteen, and since a few weeks before her fourteenth birthday she'd been standing behind Charlie's counter. She'd managed the shop single-handed for the three weeks he'd been in hospital and the old folks' home.

He wasn't her responsibility, but he was more grandfather than employer. He called her Rusty; she called him Charlie; and since his broken arm, he'd been paying her a full adult male's wage – which could have been another reason why she wasn't in Frankston. She was stuffing money into the bank, and if she continued stuffing it in, she'd be able to buy her own ute soon. In Frankston, she'd be lucky to get a job that paid half of what Charlie paid.

He was a problem. If he'd ever had any fear of authority, old age had discarded it. Since she'd started working for him, he'd been helping himself to any large note that landed in his cash drawer – taking back some of the money he'd lost during the depression, he said. It hadn't concerned her until she'd started doing his bookwork. She did what she could. His ute'd had phantom brake linings last month.

If Jack knew how she balanced those books he wouldn't be taking her home to meet his parents – who would read more into her agreeing to have Christmas dinner with them than she meant for them to read. Didn't know why she had agreed, except this Christmas would be only the second of her life without Granny, and without Jenny, too, she couldn't face the bedlam of Christmas with Elsie and Harry and their horde. They were like family, but had been more Granny's family. She had raised Elsie.

Shouldn't have agreed to go. She liked Jack, liked the way he'd adopted Charlie since he'd broken his arm. He'd tracked down Hilda, Charlie's daughter, had found her widowed and living in Sydney with her daughter and son-in-law. The son-in-law told Jack that they'd try to get down to Willama. They hadn't, but one of them had spoken to the hospital and asked them to find a place for Charlie in the old folks' annex.

He might have been old enough – he was pushing ninety – but he didn't consider himself old enough and had spent his days absconding, so Georgie kidnapped him and brought him home to his corner in the storeroom. Until the plaster was removed from his arm, Jack had taken him over to the police station to help him shower.

A good bloke, Jack Thompson. Had she been older, she might have liked him a lot more than she did.

'That's Dad's old station,' he said, pointing left as they broached the top of a hill and were too suddenly in the centre of a town.

MOLLISTON, POPULATION 450.

Just a tiny town, perched on top of a hill. Woody Creek had a larger population. Woody Creek land was flat. The town had space to sprawl. No sprawl in Molliston. Shops and houses clustered around a massive old gum tree growing on top of the hill. Georgie slowed to stare, then to circle the tree. No hotel.

'Where to?'

'Down the hill,' he directed. 'We're a good mile out.'

'The drunks sober up on their way home?'

'That's the idea,' he said.

Miles Away

A time of family, Christmas. Finding staff willing to work through the holidays wasn't easy. Jenny had nothing better to do, and was so grateful to Veronica Andrews and her doctor partner she would have worked seven days a week for them without pay.

She'd known Vroni in Armadale, as a card-playing friend, and later as her saviour when she'd aborted two of Ray's babies. She'd already had a daily battle to feed the ones she'd had – and she'd had no intention of tying herself to Ray with babies. Vroni had saved her life again by offering her a job and accommodation in the servants' quarters behind the guesthouse – or saved her from Woody Creek.

In a bygone era, there had been five servants' rooms built alongside a big old kitchen. Vroni's doctor had turned two of them into one and set up a modern surgery there. He'd turned two more into comfortable bedrooms, and one into a modern bathroom. A few of his city colleagues recommended a week of sea air to a frantic female patient, or to the frantic mother of a patient. Every week or two a guest arrived in a taxi, feeling so unwell she was placed in isolation, out the back, where within a day or two she was feeling much better.

Jenny and Raelene, Ray's seven-year-old daughter, lived in the western bedroom, beside the old kitchen. They used the bathroom when there was no guest in isolation, used Vroni's when there was. Jenny delivered meals to those special guests, made their beds, and was compensated well for her tight mouth.

She'd thought nothing of living beside an abortion clinic until she'd run into Jim Hooper at Flinders Street Station. She thought about it now – but if not for Vroni, she wouldn't have been at the station to run into Jim. It was Vroni who had talked her into allowing Raelene to meet Florence Keating, her natural mother.

Natural? Mothers nursed their kids through chickenpox, measles, sore throats, multiple colds. Mothers tucked their kids into bed at night, kissed them, changed the sheets when they wet the beds. They didn't turn up seven years later and start calling themselves the natural mother.

'Like it or not, kiddo, you need to pacify her or you'll end up in court,' Vroni had said. 'Raelene knows you're her real mother.'

Maybe she did, but she liked being treated like baby Jesus at the Keatings'. Jenny had left her with them for two hours in October. The Box Hill station was on the same train line as Ringwood, where Jim had told her he was living in a caravan behind Nobby's house, an old army mate Jenny had met in Sydney the week she'd spent there with Jim and ten-month-old Jimmy. Nobby and his wife, Rosemary, had greeted her like a long-lost friend that first afternoon. Jim had kissed her hello; the visit had started out so well. It hadn't continued well.

The night, at Flinders Street Station, when she'd sighted Jim's head above the crowd, she'd thought Jimmy might be with him. He'd told her then that Jimmy was with his sister Margaret. She'd told him in Ringwood that she wanted to see their son.

'I'm not in touch with them, Jen,' he'd said.

'But you see Jimmy?'

He hadn't seen Jimmy since 1947. Margaret and her husband had adopted him a few months before Vern Hooper's death. She'd done the wrong thing, then, she'd opened her mouth and let her tongue loose, but it had been like losing Jimmy a second time.

'How could you let her adopt him? He's our son. I gave him to you. I thought he was safe with you.'

And he'd withdrawn from her, had folded in on himself. She'd watched it happening, had seen his eyes grow distant, seen his big Hooper hands begin to tremble.

She'd seen Nobby's reaction too, Rosemary's.

He wasn't well. At the station she'd thought he was. She'd got out of there fast, left without a word to anyone, afraid of what she'd done and hating him for his weakness and for allowing his dithering bitch of a sister to get her hands on Jimmy. Hated the Hooper name that day.

In the taxi Nobby's house had been minutes from the station. It might have been a ten-minute walk if she'd known where she was going. She'd got hopelessly lost, had been late picking up Raelene and for two weeks after Ringwood she'd felt . . . adrift.

Then Nobby turned up at Frankston. He'd done most of the talking. He'd told her how he'd found Jim, where he'd found him, told her of Jim's years of shock treatment, how his memory had been shot to hell by their electricity.

'I thought he was well,' she said. 'He'd seemed well at the station.'

'Our team had just won the premiership, Jen. He's coming good. Most of the time he's good. He runs my timber-yard office.'

'How could he not have even seen his son since '47?'

'We thought the same thing a few years back. We tried to put him in touch with his family. He won't have a bar of them.'

'Is he all right now?'

'As right as rain. The day you took off I got him on the booze. He likes a drink and it's better for him than pills, or me and Rosemary reckon it is. He told me he wrote his last will and testament in '47, leaving Jimmy and his money to you, then he tried to hang himself with his dressing-gown cord. He said his sisters and old man let him think his boy was with you – until his old man kicked the bucket. The sister had adopted Jimmy by then.'

'How long has he been with you, Nobby?'

'Anzac Day '55.'

'I saw him at a Melbourne hospital a year after the war ended. He didn't know me. Where was he between then and when you found him?'

'Hospitals. He doesn't remember much about any of them. He was living behind a Chinese restaurant when we found him.'

'His father would have left him money.'

'He wouldn't touch it if he had. He told us once he had his own money. If he has, he's got no interest in it. It's like he's doing a bit of a balancing act on a tightrope right now, Jen. He still crashes off it from time to time, but these days we've worked out how to get him back up.'

'Bless you, Nobby,' she said. 'I'll stay away.'

'Don't you even go thinking about doing that. For a week after he saw you at the station, he was damn near doing cartwheels on his tightrope. He knew it was you when the taxi pulled up out front that day, and he lit up like a beacon.'

'I can't . . . I never could walk on eggshells, and not about Jimmy.'

'He blames himself for losing your boy. Back during the war he used to say that you and Jimmy were the best things that ever happened to him. I was with him over there until I took a bullet in my leg. Most of us when we got letters from home would rip them open where we stood. He'd take off with his. He kept them on him too. We'd be sitting in a hole, no light, no moon, and he'd have his photos out, looking at them on a pitch black night, reading your letters in the dark. He loved you, Jen, and still does.'

'I've never taken his ring off. Even when I was married to Ray, I never took it off. I would have waited the rest of my life for him, and his family knew it. They let me think that he was dead.'

Nobby had offered to drive her to Ringwood that day, to drive her home. She'd shaken her head. He'd kissed her cheek when he was leaving and told her to come around for dinner on Sunday.

She hadn't planned to go back, not that day. But she'd lost Jimmy first, and she'd known Vern Hooper and his daughters. Margaret hadn't been able to keep her hands off Jimmy when he'd been five months old, and the Jim she'd seen at that city hospital wouldn't have had a chance against them.

She'd gone back on a Sunday in late November. Florence had wanted to give Raelene a little birthday party. She'd left her with them and found her way to Nobby's house. It had been a good day. She hadn't mentioned Jimmy or Woody Creek, not that day. Jim remembered the ring. She'd removed it, and he'd taken it from her hand to look at the engraving, *Jen and Jim, 1942*. He'd reached for a pair of glasses so he might see it more clearly.

'They suit you,' she'd said, and they did, they made him look like a professor. He'd never been the best-looking man in Woody Creek. Too tall, and not enough flesh to cover his bones. His cheekbones looked sharp, his long jaw as sharp. Didn't know why she loved his face, but she did. And maybe he did still love her.

He'd walked out with her, walked to the corner, and would have walked further if she hadn't told him to go back. He'd lost half of one leg in the war and his limp was bad.

She'd asked no questions about his missing leg, had tried not to look at his shoes, tried not to see Vern in his limp, in his face. His father had that same long jaw. Not Jim's eyes though or his mouth, not his gentle ways.

She'd see him again tomorrow. Today she was playing carol singer cum waitress; Vroni playing hostess, not nursing sister; her doctor partner playing pianist instead of abortionist; and the guests all legitimate and over forty, other than a fourteen-year-old girl down here with her parents and wanting pudding and custard, not fruit salad, for sweets.

'I don't know why you wanted to come to this place,' she said as Jenny continued on with her tray, leaving the family to argue about Christmas pudding.

Jenny watched her from a distance, her mind flitting to another fourteen-year-old girl eating Christmas dinner with her parents at Amberley.

*

Cara Jeanette, born to Jenny in '44, handed at birth to Myrtle Norris, had turned fourteen on 3 October. She was eating roast chicken with all of the trimmings at a trestle table, in a Traralgon backyard, barely a hundred miles from Frankston as the crow flew.

She'd never heard of Jenny King or Jenny Morrison. She didn't know she could blame her for her frizzy yellow-gold hair and atrocious fingernails, though this year she had become aware of how little she resembled her parents and cousins.

Her best friend, Rosie, was adopted. For a time, Cara had been convinced Myrtle and Robert had adopted her, which would explain why she looked different, but she'd asked and they'd said no, and whether she was or not, it wasn't her biggest problem. A mother who looked and thought like her grandmother, and who refused to let her grow up, was her biggest problem.

Rosie, who was barely five months older than her, was allowed to wear makeup. And her mother had bought her a pair of boys' black jeans. Cara had asked for a pair for Christmas and she'd got a new tennis racquet – a good one, but still boring. Uncle John and Aunty Beth gave her a gold necklet, which she might wear when she was about thirty. And Gran Norris! She'd knitted her a purple and blue striped sweater, the most despicable thing anyone had ever set eyes on, which Pete, Cara's youngest cousin, named the Purple People Eater.

Since she'd unwrapped it after breakfast, Pete had been singing 'Purple People Eater', and by the time the table was set for dinner, he only had to look at Cara and threaten to open his mouth and she got the giggles.

He was thirteen, and not even one of those thirteen-year-old boys who suddenly take it into their heads to start growing. He looked about twelve, if he was lucky, and he was far too young for her to be giggling with. They'd always done it, though. Way, way back before Robert had got his job in Traralgon, way back when they'd eaten Christmas dinner around Amberley's huge parlour table, when there had been a million reasons to giggle, or no reason at all except it was Christmas and there were presents. Myrtle and Aunty Beth had always separated them at the table. They'd been separated today, and poor Pete given the chair on Gran Norris's left.

'You've got a purple bruise on your arm, Gran,' he said.

'She's got that cupboard too close to her bed,' Gran accused. Cara bed, Cara's cupboard. She'd been evicted from her room for Gran.

Uncle John and his entire family had driven down from Sydney yesterday. He and Beth had six kids, the two eldest already married. Paul, who had two little kids, had towed Uncle John's caravan down. It was parked on the front lawn. The rest of the cousins were in tents on the back lawn. Uncle John and Aunty Beth were in the spare room.

It was fun, like being away on one of their family camping holidays, except for Gran, who didn't approve of camping holidays, or Christmas dinners eaten in backyards.

She'd turned ninety this year and had been dying for as long as Cara had been alive, and no one was allowed to forget it. She'd brought along a shoe box full of pills to prove how close she was to death.

'I'm ninety years old and expected to sit all day in a car for the pleasure of sharing my dinner with swarms of flies.'

'And us, Gran,' Pete said. He'd driven down with her and had had his fill of complaints before they'd got to Goulburn, so he said. There were a lot of miles between Goulburn and Traralgon.

Gran spent her life complaining or demanding, often doing both at the same time. Cara should have been the one complaining. She was the one who had lost her bed. Not that she minded sleeping in the tent with Pete, though the fun of queuing up to go to the toilet was wearing thin, with Gran on it for half an hour at each sitting. Two or three times a day one of the cars had to make a trip to the public toilets.

There were nineteen chairs around the trestle tables – kitchen chairs, outdoor chairs, fold-up camp chairs, and a high chair borrowed from next door for the baby, who was wearing a half-decent white cardigan that Gran had knitted. She'd knitted Pete half-decent socks, and the Purple People Eater for Cara. It was a statement, like saying, That will nark you, girl.

Gran liked Cara's dad better than Uncle John. He didn't see as much of her so didn't talk back like Uncle John. She liked John's kids better than Cara, who didn't talk back, but didn't kiss her every time she saw her either. She had whiskers on her chin, and smelled of camphor – and so did the Purple People Eater.

'When are you bringing your family home where they belong, Robert?' Gran carped.

Home, Amberley, where the dining-room table would have seated nineteen at a pinch. Traralgon's table was hard-pressed to seat six, and no room to move around it when it did.

They'd never go home now. The school principal was retiring sometime next year and Robert, the vice principal, might get his job. If he did, they'd be stuck here forever.

Cara eyed her father, mentally betting every penny of pocket money for a month that he hadn't brought them down here so he could be a vice principal, which he'd said was the reason.

She'd asked Monica, her second oldest cousin, if she knew anything about Robert and Myrtle adopting her. Monica was plenty old enough to know the family history. If she knew, she was in on the conspiracy. Pete would have told her if he'd known. All he'd said when she'd asked him was that he wished someone would adopt him. Since Monica had married and moved out, Gran Norris had sold her house and moved into Monica's room.

'Be thankful for small mercies,' Pete said.

In a way she was. Had they still been living at Amberley, they would have copped Gran. John was too much like his father for Gran's liking.

He must have been. He looked nothing like Gran, or Robert. John was taller, broader, bald, which made him look older. Robert's hair was thinning on top, though not obviously – unless you were looking down on him. He had a male version of Gran's features, back when she'd had features. John's features were heavier. Everything about him was heavier – except his wife. Aunty Beth was skinny. Having all of those kids, running around after two grandkids, and now Gran Norris, had worn her down to skin and bone.

'Dragging your family miles away from home to this,' Gran said, back on her hobbyhorse and determined to ride it to death.

'You're in a purple old mood today, Gran,' Pete said, and Cara, her mouth full, slid from her chair and ran for the house, where she spat meat and potato into the bathroom washbasin, then stood attempting to gain control of her giggle. Her giggling reflection didn't help.

Rosie said she was good-looking. Dino Collins said she was the best looking sort in town. She looked heaps better when she sneaked on a bit of Rosie's lipstick and eyeliner. Since Rosie, life down here had been okay. And Dino wanted to be her boyfriend. 'Hands off. She's mine,' he said if any of the other boys started mucking around with her.

His name was James, but they all called him Dino because he looked a bit like James Dean. Most of the boys had nicknames. They called Tony Bell 'Ding-dong'.

'Cara!' Myrtle called from the kitchen.

'Coming.' She was supposed to be the hostess – or waitress. She washed her hands, raked a comb through her curls, then went outside with a tray of Christmas pudding, Myrtle behind her, carrying a second tray.

Pete got the largest serve, and Steve, four years Pete's senior, complained.

'He needs it to grow on,' Uncle John said.

'If that girl keeps growing, she'll be looking down on the lot of you before she's much older,' Gran said.

Always 'that girl' to Gran, never Cara – and in the real world, she wouldn't even be considered tall. The Traralgon backyard wasn't the real world. Myrtle and Beth might have measured five foot three. Uncle John's two girls were no taller, unless they wore high heels. Gran might have stretched to five foot before she started shrinking. There was no more room for shrinkage. She'd become a hobbling, carping Egyptian mummy.

'It must be this good healthy country air, Mum,' Uncle John said.

'Why don't you stay down here for a month or two, Gran,' Pete said. 'You'll probably grow six inches.'

'Where's my cup of tea,' Gran carped.

Cara made a pot. She took it with cups to the table. Myrtle poured, then Cara had to carry Gran's cup inside. She'd had enough of the filthy flies. There were no flies in Sydney – so she said.

'Put it in me bedroom,' Gran said. 'And get me me pills and some water.'

Never a please, never a thank you polluted Gran Norris's mouth. How she'd produced her father and Uncle John, Cara didn't know.

Laughter growing in the backyard, Cara wanting to be a part of it, and here she was, fetching and carrying for Gran. She untied Gran's shoelaces, placed her shoes against the wall. She opened her shoe box of pills, then stood waiting, just in case a bottle top required a stronger hand than Gran's. It wouldn't, or not until Cara tried to walk away.

A major production, Gran's pill popping. Lids removed one at a time, a pill or two poured from each bottle to be placed in a row on the bedside table, then the lids replaced, the pills counted, the bottles returned to the shoe box.

Robert took pills when his war-injured knee played up. He went to the bathroom, tossed a couple into his mouth and washed them down with a mouthful of water – and was rarely seen doing it. Gran took hers one at a time, the glass placed down between sips. And she talked, about her various pills, her variety of ills, forcing Cara to wait, just in case she needed more water.

She'd lived in Sydney all her life, had wed a fool of a man, then taken in lodgers when he'd left her to raise his two sons alone – which was probably where Robert had got the idea to turn Amberley into a boarding house. Cara didn't know how Robert's father had died, if he'd died or just run for the hills. Knowing Gran, he'd probably run for the hills.

Today she asked, between the laxative and the tiny pill that was supposed to keep her tranquil and didn't.

'When did Dad's father die, Gran?'

'Your father was fourteen year old when I was left on me own.' Two pills went down, and Cara still didn't know if he'd died or run. 'Another woman would have taken him out of school and put him to work, and for all the thanks I get for educating him, that's what I should have done. I worked my fingers to the bone to keep that boy in school, and what does he do to me? He joins up before he's old enough to be in that filthy war, that's what he does.'

Probably saw it as the lesser of two evils, Cara thought. 'What did he die of – my grandfather?'

Gran humphed before replying. 'The Norrises were all weak in the chest. I told your father he wouldn't last a week in the trenches, then his fool of a brother tries to go with him. Fifteen year old, John was. I put a stop to his games. I went down there and dragged him home by the ear.'

'He was in the second war.'

'In the home guard,' Gran scoffed. 'He never went further than Newcastle. Your father was overseas for years.'

'How long was he overseas before I was born?' Cara asked, just a fishing sort of question. She wasn't expecting it to hook a soul-swallowing shark.

It was weird how you could question people until you were blue in the face and end up learning nothing, then, when you were least expecting it, out it came. The shoe box was in Cara's hands. She'd been on her way out the door when Gran put her cup down.

'They sent him over there in '42 and he didn't set foot back on Australian soil until 1945,' she said. 'You could have knocked me down with a feather the day she walked in with you. And she was too old to be taking you on, and I told her so. I said to your mother the day I first set eyes on you. What a damn fool thing to go and do with Robert thousands of miles away dodging bullets. Not that she ever listened to me.'

'Where did she get me?' Cara's heartbeat thundering in her ears, muffled her own words.

Gran flicked a bird-claw hand towards the heavens. 'God sent you. All the churches had those homes for the unwed, and by God there were plenty of them around during the war.' She lifted her cup, sipped and spoke over the rim. 'We all knew they'd been talking about adopting before the war, but she never said one word about doing it while your father was away. Mind you, not that I saw her from one year's end to the next. While Robert was over there, I saw your mother at Christmas and Easter if I was lucky. And she only lived half an hour away from my house. Too busy with her lodgers to worry about how an old lady was getting along.'

The cup was down again, and empty this time. Cara's stomach threatening to get rid of Christmas dinner, she picked up the cup and walked fast to the kitchen where she stood over the sink, swallowing her need to vomit while staring through the window at the crowded table. Her mother – not her mother – laughing at something Uncle John had said – not her Uncle John. Not her cousins either, not even Pete.

And she was going to howl because Pete wasn't her cousin, howl and vomit at the same time. She'd asked her parents. They'd looked her in the eye and said no, they hadn't adopted her.

'Liars.'

Every nerve in her body wanted to run out there and call them liars in front of everyone.

Knew she couldn't. Knew she'd have to hold it inside her until those tents came down. And they wouldn't be coming down until after New Year.

She poured a glass of water, drank it down. Washed her face, wiped it on a tea towel, remembering so clearly the day she'd asked them if she was adopted.

'Liars.'

A DIFFERENT CHRISTMAS

*T*here was something about Molliston, something about its air. The more of it Georgie breathed, the more relaxed she became. By midafternoon she was calling Jack's mother Katie and walking with her around the veranda, admiring her pot plants while Jack and his father sprawled on chair and couch, sleeping off Christmas dinner.

Their home was a hotel. It sold beer but didn't smell of beer. If you walked within ten yards of Woody Creek's hotel veranda, the smell of stale beer was enough to give you a hangover. Jack's parents' hotel smelled of wet soil and greenery. She'd never been here before, but she felt she'd known that veranda and those pot plants a hundred years ago.

And the bar room. In Woody Creek, women weren't allowed in the bar and few would want to go in there. Georgie had tasted her first glass of wine in Jack's parents' bar room, at a rough-cut bar where a hundred years of people had leant and she'd known that she'd sat there in some past life, which was totally weird when she didn't believe in past lives.

Granny had. Maybe she'd been here, or maybe the aged smell

of the rooms reminded her of Granny's house – before the renovations. The west side of the hotel veranda was vine-covered like Granny's hut's west wall had been, and the dark hotel kitchen with its tiny high window smelled like Granny's old kitchen.

The day a scorcher, they delayed their return trip until after nightfall. The sun long gone down had forgotten to take its heat with it. Every window of the car was open, but not a breath of breathable air entered.

'What are you thinking?' Jack asked.

'That you must have had a normal life.'

'What's normal?'

'Molliston is, and your parents. Everything is normal.'

'Woody Creek isn't?'

'Is it?'

They sighted half-a-dozen kangaroos, missed one by inches. They smelled half-a-dozen who hadn't been as lucky. Kangaroos were a rare sight around Woody Creek and, if sighted, usually ended up on a dinner plate or as dog's meat. Woody Creek farmers didn't tolerate the roos.

The town was sleeping when they drove in, the streetlights glowing over empty streets. As Jack pulled into the police station's drive, Georgie opened the door and was out of the car before the motor died. She'd left Charlie's ute parked in front of the shop, and while Jack locked the sedan, she walked over the road, smelling Woody Creek air and feeling lonely, or jealous, or something.

He followed her. And the ute's driver-side door refused to open.

'What's wrong, Gina?' he said. Jack had introduced her to his parents as Georgie. His father, a little deaf, had called her Georgina. This morning Katie had shortened it to Gina – but Georgie wasn't tolerating it in Woody Creek.

'This door is, and don't call me Gina.' She walked around to the passenger door. It opened. He followed her, but she slid in, slid across the bench seat and behind the wheel.

'I had a good time,' he said.

'Me too. Thanks.'

She got the motor going, but he hadn't closed the door. She turned to him, waiting for him to close it. Knew he probably wanted to kiss her. His was a kissing sort of family. Katie had kissed her when they were leaving, his father had kissed her and told her he'd always had a soft spot for good-looking redheads.

They thought she was Jack's girlfriend. And she wasn't. Maybe that was what was wrong with her, maybe tonight she wanted to be his girlfriend. Maybe she wanted to be Gina – or someone other than Georgie Morrison.

'See you,' she said. He closed the door, which took two slams to click it. She backed out, whacked the gear stick into first and drove towards home.

Home? It wasn't, not any more. Charlie's shop was about as close as it got to home these days. She slept in Granny's old bedroom. The working bee had ruined it with windows but she'd tacked old blankets over them to bring back the dark to that room.

Had to admit she liked electricity. Would have liked to see a bit of it shining as she drove down the track. No light left on to greet her.

The lights had been on at Jack's hotel when they'd driven in and his parents sitting on their front veranda waiting for them. They came out to the drive to greet Jack. And he was so beautiful with them. Men didn't kiss men, or not where she came from they didn't. He'd hugged and kissed his father, swung Katie off the ground, and while Georgie had watched the two of them, his father had kissed her.

Granny had been free with her hugs and kisses. Jenny hadn't been a natural hugger, but she'd been a smiler, a handholder. One of them would have heard her ute, would have come out with a lantern. Snarly bugger Margot couldn't even leave the front light on.

I'm going to Frankston. I'll tell Charlie to find himself a junior to train, then I'm going – and his daughter will have him back in the old folks' home the following week.

She'd sent a couple up to assess him before Christmas. He was antique but still one step ahead of the crowd. He'd asked them to drive him home.

He lived in his storeroom but owned a house. He owned three side-by-side identical houses. During the floods, when Granny's land had been a lake, Georgie had moved into Charlie's house – Jeany's house, he called it. He'd had a wife once. He'd lived in his house with his daughter until five years ago. Mrs Fulton, Charlie's long-term tenant and neighbour, now kept an eye on Jeany's house. That city couple's assessment wouldn't have been what Charlie's daughter was hoping for.

Georgie pulled on her handbrake and turned off her head-lights, and in the instant before the light died she caught a flash of running man. Again her twin beams sprayed their light, but whoever she'd seen had gone, or gone to ground. She slid across the seat and was out running across the paddock towards the road. She knew this land better than any prowler, and if he was heading back to town, she'd cut him off.

No movement on the road. No sound of movement. She stood amid the trees, waiting for him to creep out from behind one. He'd been heading towards the goat paddock, towards Elsie's house. He could have gone east towards the bush, or cut back south towards Flanagan's land. Or gone to ground beneath Elsie's house. There was three feet of space beneath it and plenty of stored junk to hide behind.

She walked down Elsie's gravelled drive where she felt for the rake, always leaning against the fence. Armed then, she circled the house, expecting movement from every shadow. No movement, except for Teddy, standing in the dark of the back steps.

'What are you up to?' he asked.

'I saw someone running this way. Have you got a torch handy? He's probably under your house.'

Teddy brought two torches. They checked beneath the house, checked the road again, checked the trees on the far side of the road and Granny's shed – then Teddy turned off her ute's headlights. He had a better relationship with motors than with people.

She stood in the yard when he left, watching him disappear into the dark. That was when her mind started asking questions. How long had he been standing on the back steps? If he'd been standing there when she'd driven in, he would have seen the prowler as he ran towards him. She squinted, attempting to visualise the running man. Light shirt and movement, that was all she'd seen.

Teddy's shirt was grey. Had he been taking a short cut home? Then why hadn't he said so?

Because he'd been up to something he shouldn't have been up to. Drinking or raiding Joe Flanagan's orchard, no doubt.

*

Myrtle told Cara she could invite two friends to their New Year's Eve party. She invited five: Rosie, Henry Cooper, who everyone called Coop, Ding-dong Bell and his girl, and Dino Collins. Myrtle invited three neighbours and their families. Robert invited two teachers and their kids. With Aunty Beth, Uncle John, the cousins and in-law cousins, the house was packed solid, as was the veranda.

It was almost midnight before Robert noticed her talking to Dino Collins. When he did, he took her arm and led her inside, into his bedroom, where he closed the door.

'I don't want you to have any more to do with that Collins boy, poppet.'

'Why?'

'You'll need to trust me on this,' he said.

'What's he done?'

'He's not fit company for a fourteen-year-old girl,' Robert said.

She knew Dino had been expelled from school, way back near

the start of the year. All the kids knew. No one knew why, or if they did, they wouldn't say.

'Your Uncle John is asking the boys to leave. Remain in here until they've gone.'

'Rosie will go with them!'

'The Hunter girls are here, and more fit companions.'

Mrs Hunter taught history at the high school and her daughters were bigger pains in the bum than their mother.

'If I had a bed, I'd go to it,' Cara snapped.

'Hop into ours,' he said.

The tents were pulled down the following morning, the cars and trailer loaded, then at nine they all left in convoy for the return trip to Sydney. Gran got the last word. She always got the last word.

'You get your family back home where you belong, my boy.'

Cara stood with her parents waving them out of sight around the corner, and as the caravan disappeared from view, her heartbeat quickened. Now she'd tell them that they were a pair of liars.

Now. Tell them what Gran had said.

Except Robert put his arm around her and kissed her nose. 'Always nice to see visitors arrive, poppet, but maybe nicer to see them go, eh.'

That was honest. They went inside and the house looked, felt larger. The backyard looked huge, and a mess, the lawn a checkerboard of flattened, sickly yellow-green where the tents had been, of grass worn down to dirt and too-long grass elsewhere.

They worked that morning, Robert mowing, Cara and Myrtle stripping beds, tossing sheets into the washing machine, sweeping, washing floors while the machine laboured. Two or three times Cara almost told her mother what Gran had said. When she helped make up her bed with clean sheets, she tried to say something. Didn't, just wiped Gran methodically from every surface of her bedroom.

Then at one-thirty Rosie came around.

'Coop and Dino want to meet us at the milk bar,' she whispered.

'I can't, Rosie. Dad said I'm not allowed to go near Dino.'

'Chicken.'

No one wanted to be called chicken, and if she didn't have Rosie to hang around with, she'd have no one. She went to the milk bar, and the boys weren't even there, so they shared a chocolate milkshake and she told Rosie what Gran Norris had said.

'Promise not to tell anyone.'

'Spit my death and hope to die,' Rosie said.

At fourteen, secrets are easily shared, promises easily given. They have as much substance as the froth sucked noisily from the bottom of a milkshake container. At fourteen, her father's warning was treated like so much froth and bubble, sucked down and forgotten by the time Dino and Henry Cooper came in. Coop a panel-beater apprentice and always broke, Dino fed the jukebox and they practised rock-and-roll steps.

TENANTS

*T*here are good tenants, then there are the other type. For sixty years, Charlie White had been collecting rent from half-a-dozen properties; he'd known a few of both types. These days he considered himself an expert, swore he could pick a good tenant from a bad by the way they kept the inside of their cars.

The Hoopers had been lucky. Every Sunday, instead of going to church, their tenants were out washing and vacuuming their car or mowing lawns. Vern's garden looked like something out of a magazine. Joe Dolan had kept the garden, to the east of Charlie's house, looking nice – until he'd dropped dead of a heart attack at fifty-four and his wife moved in with one of their city sons.

Mrs Fulton rented the house to the west of Charlie's. Charlie didn't like many, and trusted less. He liked and trusted Mrs Fulton, and when she complained about the new tenants he'd put into the house to the east side of his, he listened, not that there was much he could do about it. He'd given them a twelve-month lease.

He bathed and shaved at home, but rarely slept there. Always woke up there feeling lonely for Jeany. He didn't wake up feeling lonely in his storeroom bed.

He'd ridden home to clean up for Christmas, to spend Christmas Eve in Jeany's bed, and found out what Mrs Fulton had been complaining about.

The rowdy buggers had started arriving around nine and they'd kept on coming, loud Melbourne louts, in cars, on motorbikes, and they'd brought their dogs with them. A man with poor hearing can tolerate a barking dog – if it doesn't spend all night doing it. A man with poor hearing can tolerate a wild party next door – if the revellers go to bed at midnight. The party had continued until morning, when it moved out to the street, where two maniacs roared motorbikes and the rest of the party yelled encouragement while their dogs howled.

Someone had rung Jack Thompson. He'd been out of town. The party continued into Boxing Day when someone called Jack again. He'd moved a few of them on.

Charlie had waited until a few more left, then he'd gone next door to give the noisy coots their marching orders. The male tenant waved his lease in Charlie's face and told him to piss off.

Which he'd done, though not quietly.

He'd returned to his storeroom and hadn't gone home again until New Year's Eve, which was a repeat of Christmas Eve, with fireworks. Not a soul in the street got a wink of sleep. Then the following morning, all hell broke loose, or the tenants' guests' dogs had. Three big ugly buggers attacked Bobby, Mrs Fulton's fox terrier, and the mongrels ripped him to shreds.

Mrs Fulton, her son Robert, plus Charlie and half-a-dozen more, spoke to Jack Thompson.

'You said they're paying their rent, Charlie. I can do something about the dogs and the noise, but as far as I see it, you've got no legal cause to evict them.'

'Their dogs killed Bobby,' Mrs Fulton said.

'There was a girl running around the yard last night, stark naked,' Charlie said.

'A landlord can't dictate how his tenant chooses to live, Charlie.'

'A bloody tenant can't dictate how I live either, but that's what they're doing,' a neighbour said.

'There were a few parties in town last night,' Jack said.

'Half of Melbourne was at theirs, Jack,' Robert Fulton said.

'We had cars from one end of the street to the other. We couldn't get out our own bloody drives,' the neighbour said.

'I can't charge a man for having a party,' Jack said. 'You need just cause.'

'They're wrecking my bloody house!' Charlie said. 'That's just cause enough for me.'

When he'd signed that lease, that house had manicured lawns, front and rear, flowers, shrubs. The lawns were bum-high grass, empty bottles and rubbish. He'd paid a fortune for new floor coverings before moving the tenants in, bought three new roller blinds. No blind at all now at the kitchen window or on the broken front window.

A quiet week followed; the new tenants kept their heads low until the long weekend in January when the cars, bikes and dogs arrived again.

Charlie waited until they went to bed, sometime after dawn, when he walked next door, armed with a tape measure. He was there to measure up the broken window – not that he had any intention of repairing it, he wanted to get a look in through it. He measured – and while so occupied, a dirty great mastiff's head came through the hole, its face in his face, and that ugly bastard looked big enough, hungry enough to eat him.

There wasn't much left of Charlie White, but what there was backed off fast to the front door where he knocked until he raised his bleary-eyed, towel-clad tenant.

'No dogs inside the premises,' Charlie said. 'It's in the lease.'

'Piss off, you geriatric old bastard, or I'll let the bloody dogs out,' the tenant said.

It was the 'geriatric' that did it. It hurt. That 'geriatric' decided Charlie.

He bought a long garden hose that week, and a cigarette lighter. He didn't smoke and never had. He rode his bike around to the garage and asked Roy, the garage chap, to fill up his can with sump oil.

'The best thing I know for eradicating noxious weeds,' he said.

In the pre-dawn hours of a Sunday morning, after what might be termed a tame Saturday night party by his tenants' standard, Charlie crept next door, turned the electricity off at the mains, connected his new garden hose to their tap, checked the backyard for dogs and, when he didn't see any, got down to business.

A man who had lived as long as Charlie White had learnt how to make a lot of smoke with very little fire. He'd gathered together a ragged pair of longjohns, an old shirt with a collar that cut off his circulation, a couple of worn-out singlets, and newspapers, which he'd rolled tight, screwed into wicks, then wrapped in the singlets, shirt and longjohns.

The kitchen window hadn't been closed since the new tenants had moved in. He dipped a singlet into his bucket of sump oil, lit the wick and, once it was burning well, pitched his first smoke bomb through the window. Working fast then, as fast as a bloke with one gammy arm could work, he lit two more. One went in through the rear door, one through the broken front window. The last of his smoke bombs, his longjohns, he pitched in through the front door, then he closed the door and stepped back to the garden tap to await the desired results.

Their dog must have smelt the smoke. It started barking. Charlie gave it time to wake the house. It woke its mates. Charlie wasn't here to do murder and with no sight or sound of the tenants, the hose turned on full bore, he dragged it up to the front door and opened it. Acrid smoke gushed out.

'Fire,' Charlie yelled.

Given the guidance of his voice one dog exited, sneezing, shaking its head. Two of its mates followed it out.

'Fire,' Charlie bellowed, dragging his hose indoors, spraying in the direction he'd tossed his wicks.

They came, one by one, two by two; he counted five, and washed a sixth from his mattress.

A hose in a house, in the hands of a determined old coot, could spread a lot of water in the time it took for Jack Thompson to get there and turn off the garden tap. Most of the neighbours were out on the street, smelling smoke but seeing no fire. The rest emerged when the fire truck arrived, its bell ringing.

Jack found a partially burnt singlet on the kitchen floor. He sniffed it before pitching it out the window. 'Don't think you're fooling anyone, Charlie. What you've done here is illegal and dangerous.'

'But bloody effective,' Charlie said, armed now with a dipper of water, which he brandished as a bare-bummed bodgie came in looking for his trousers, his *HATE* tattooed hand occupied in covering up his genitals; he wasn't looking for a fight.

'They've got a lease,' Jack argued.

'If it was in here, it's water damaged,' Charlie said, tossing his dipperful into a food cupboard, then pitching what he'd saturated out the window.

The ceilings were dripping, the floors awash, the sink over-flowing. Jack turned off the tap. Charlie found another one in the bathroom.

You can't wrestle a dipper from a near ninety-year-old bloke when he's only got one good arm. Jack gave up and went out to the street to offer the homeless, half-clad mob a pair of dripping jeans and a bed for the rest of the night in his cell. They wanted their car keys. Charlie had them.

'Give them up, Charlie.'

'They're too drunk to drive –'

'Give them their keys, Charlie, or you'll spend the night in my cells.'

A soggy lease went into the lavatory pan before the tenants and their guests got their car keys, minus Charlie's house keys. Two cars and a bike took off to someplace, hopefully to a far place.

*

On Granny's land, they knew nothing of Charlie's war. Civil war had broken out down there.

All Georgie's fault. She'd spent too many of her formative years with Charlie, and the rest of them with Granny – other than the two she'd spent in Armadale in Ray's house, which had taught her that few men could be trusted.

For weeks she'd been tossing her prowler theory around in her mind. The night of Charlie's war, she decided to prove or disprove her theory. Hooked a couple of lengths of fine wire, at ankle and calf level, across the east-side front door. As a second front, she set pots, pans and jam tins in a row on the veranda, then sat on Norman Morrison's old cane chair to await results.

Four o'clock when Teddy attempted to creep out. Tripped on the wires; fell headlong into the pots and pans and the noise of his landing might have woken Granny from the dead.

It woke Harry, and Harry, barefoot, clad in sagging jockey briefs, a gangle of bony limbs topped by rusty hair in need of a cut, wasn't a sight to be tangled with. Nor was Lenny, Teddy's cousin-brother, a big, blond-headed bloke with a punch on him like the kick of a mule.

Georgie, who sat on Teddy until they came, gave him up to Harry and Lenny then went into Margot's room to haul her out of bed and frogmarch her out to the kitchen.

Elsie came, dressing-gown clad, carrying Harry's trousers. Teddy sat, nursing one arm, Margot stood *ahzeeing* while Georgie gave leash to a tongue, which until that moment she hadn't known she possessed.

MARGOT'S INDIGESTION

A ninety-year-old man grows weary when he misses out on a night's sleep. At eight in the morning, Charlie crawled into Jeany's bed. If he moved in the next twenty-five hours, he didn't know about it.

On Granny's land, civil war raged for most of Sunday. Georgie got to bed late and couldn't sleep when she got there, or not until the early birds started dancing on the low tin roof.

The rooster didn't wake her. Couldn't believe her watch when she finally opened her eyes. No time for breakfast; she dressed, grabbed her keys and ran, and found two customers champing at the bit when she got to the shop.

Charlie usually unlocked if she was held up. No time to think about him: Denis Dobson, on her heels, was gasping for a fag.

She saw light coming in through from the storeroom's rear door, which meant Charlie had risen. Flicked on the light switches, then reached for the cigarette shelves for a packet of Turf.

Nothing on those shelves. Nothing on the tobacco shelves.

'Looks like you've been done over,' Denis Dobson said.

'Charlie!' Georgie ran for the storeroom. Back door hanging open on one hinge. 'Charlie!' She damn near tripped on a carton that shouldn't have been there. 'Charlie! Where are you?'

He wasn't in his bed. Not in the lav either. No Charlie tossing crates around in his backyard.

Her customers lived in town; they knew about the fire and Charlie's war with his tenants. Jack knew. He roused Charlie from slumber and drove him to the shop. Unshaven, uncombed, his fly undone, Charlie didn't give his empty shelves a glance as he scuttled by Georgie, Jack and four customers, who tailed him to his storeroom, where he got to his knees beside his bed, not to pray but to reach beneath it.

'Checking on your chamber pot?' Maisy Macdonald asked.

'Thieving, wrecking bastards,' Charlie panted as he rose from bony knees with difficulty. 'It's them.' He sat on the bed, a hand on his heart, panting for breath. 'What did they get, Rusty?'

'Cigarettes, tobacco, the bag of change. Lollies, biscuits. It's hard to say what else yet.'

They hadn't got Charlie's biscuit tin. That was all he cared about. Insurance would cover the rest. He had fire insurance on the ruined house too, though it could be safer not to put in a claim for damage he'd done.

*

A bad end to January. February was worse. The leftovers of a cyclone that hit Queensland cut across country to Woody Creek. It had done untold damage up north. In Woody Creek, it blew trees over, blew down powerlines.

Things got worse for Charlie. Georgie told him she was going down to Frankston, that she'd spoken to Emma Fulton who had worked at the shop when Charlie's wife had been alive.

'She said she'll give you a hand until you can get someone else. There's a dozen kids in town who'd kill for the job, Charlie.'

He tried bribery, spent a handful of his ill-gotten gains on a bunch of brewery shares in Georgie's name. He'd stopped her from leaving him once before with shares, or guilt.

'I don't give in to blackmail,' she said, then she picked up the phone and rang Jenny.

'Have you got room for me, Jen?'

'I'll set up a bed in the kitchen,' she said.

And it sounded like home, and she wanted to go home to Jenny and Raelene.

She might have gone, too, if her war and Charlie's hadn't met head-on in Willama. The tenants, living in a caravan at the Willama caravan park, were arrested, along with two Willama locals and Teddy Hall. They were charged with being in possession of stolen goods.

Teddy hadn't been in on the robbery, Georgie could vouch for that. He hadn't left the house until Monday morning when Harry, who had confiscated his car keys, had given them up so Teddy could go to work. They hadn't seen him since. They hadn't known where he was until Jack drove down and told them.

The cops altered the charge against Teddy to the purchasing of known stolen goods. Harry and Lenny bailed him out.

'I didn't know they were old Charlie's, did I,' Teddy argued. 'And all I got was a dozen lousy packets of the things.'

'Get in that car.' Harry, white-faced beneath his freckles, watery blue eyes shooting sparks and Teddy knowing those sparks hadn't been caused by a few lousy packets of cigarettes. Knowing, too, that he'd been safer in the cell, he stopped arguing and folded himself into the back seat.

'She wouldn't leave me alone, Dad.'

'You keep your mouth shut or I'll shut it for you,' Lenny said.

'My ute's down here somewhere. We have to get it.'

'Ronnie is driving it home – and it's his ute,' Harry said. Teddy had been gone for less than a week. A lot can happen in a week.

Chunky, dumpy, snarly bitch Margot, clad in her frumpy skirts, her baggy shirts and cardigans, her sandals and ankle socks, ate like a horse. Weight ran in the Macdonald family. She'd been complaining of indigestion since Christmas. Elsie had been dosing her with liver salts.

No one looks for the unexpected, but give them the whisper of a hint, and their minds will leap to the obvious conclusion.

Ronnie beat them home. A redhead like his father, and as tall, he was in the sleep-out bedroom he shared with Teddy, packing his clothes. He was off to Mildura to his girlfriend before Harry changed his mind about the ute.

'He's not taking my bloody ute,' Teddy said.

'He'll take it if I tell him he can take it,' Harry roared. 'You've broken your mother's heart.'

Elsie had been bawling off and on since the night of the civil war. She was still doing it. Georgie was to blame. Teddy had been in love with her since she was twelve years old and they'd rafted down the creek on an inflated truck tyre, determined to ride it down to the ocean. They'd ridden it out to Monk's place.

And she'd done this to him.

'She's having a dear little baby, Teddy,' Elsie bawled.

If he'd known that, he wouldn't have stopped in Willama.

'It's mine and your daddy's grandbaby, Teddy.'

'It's not all my fault, Mum. I'd stop going over there and she'd threaten to dob on me.'

*

A man doesn't sell his soul easily. It took two days. He wouldn't sell it to silence his mother's bawling, or for her dear little grandbaby; but he'd do it for his hotted-up ute.

'You make him give me back my keys and you can do what you want.'

A wedding was what they wanted, and wanted it done fast. By the look of Margot's belly when it was stripped down, she could have been five months pregnant. Lenny drove into town to ring up a Willama parson, who said he could do it after church on Sunday.

Elsie stopped crying to unpack Ronnie's case. They'd need his suit. Teddy didn't own one. She wanted Harry to drive in and ask Maisy to ring up her girls and see if one of them had something nice they could lend Margot for the wedding.

It was Margot who saved Teddy's neck – or his soul.

'Ath if I'm marrying a blackfeller,' she said.

That was the day Margot became indigestible to Harry and Lenny. That was the day Georgie received a phone call from Jenny, a call that delayed her retirement from the shop. If Margot was going down to Frankston, then as sure as hell Georgie wasn't.

When you can't go, and you can't stay, you look for sanctuary. Only Jack. She spilt the whole sorry story to him that night – except the bit about the doctor Jenny knew who might be able to do something about Margot's indigestion, and about Elsie, howling again because Jenny was plotting against her dear little innocent grandbaby.

'I'm living in bedlam, Jack, then I go to work to more of it. We made a loss last week – and we didn't. He helps himself from the cash drawer and I can't stop him.'

'That's not your responsibility, love.'

'It is. I do his books.'

Jack got rid of one of Georgie's problems. He drove Margot to Frankston, wedged between Harry and Lenny in the rear seat, *ahzeeing*. Georgie sat at Jack's side, pleased to be at his side.

She walked on the beach with him that day, after Veronica Andrews and her doctor partner had shot Margot in the backside with a horse needle to shut her up.

They walked for miles, Georgie picking up shells and lacy seaweed, crawling over rocks.

And in a rock pool, Jack found a treasure, identified by another beachcomber as a nautilus shell. A delicate thing, perfect and white, which the identifier wanted to own. Jack gave it to Georgie and told her he had put in for a transfer back to the city.

'I thought you'd be down here, love.'

He asked her to marry him on their walk back to Jenny's rooms.

'I wish I was ten years older,' she said. That was all she said.

*

The chap renting Vern Hooper's house received notice that his lease wouldn't be renewed and that he'd be required to vacate the property by the end of March. Two more families received identical letters. The Hoopers were selling up in Woody Creek.

There were few rental properties in town. Most who owned a house lived in it; Charlie owned three and two of them were vacant. He hadn't slept in Jeany's bed since the robbery. When Hooper's tenant approached him, though Charlie wanted him, he shook his head.

'The last lot buggered it,' he said. They had. Every door was dog-raked, one of the kitchen cupboards had been dog-chewed. The floor coverings needed replacing again. One of his smoke bombs had singed the floor. His hose had done its own damage.

'Your insurance ought to cover it,' Hooper's tenant said.

Charlie scratched his head and eyed him. There was still a stink of sump oil in that house. He hadn't put in an insurance claim. Maybe he ought to chance it. He wanted Hooper's tenant.

'Give me a day or two to think it over,' he said. Or to think something over.

Until his last tenants had gone feral, he'd considered renting out Jeany's house. He thought about it that day.

February ended no better than it began, and March came in, looking no better than February. Two days into the month and work began on building Sydney an opera house, which would likely cost the taxpayer countless millions. And what did the average taxpayer need with an opera house? Charlie couldn't turn his radio off fast enough when one of those screeching opera-singing sopranos opened her mouth.

He received two letters that day. One made him happy – the insurance company had paid up for the robbery. The second letter killed his pleasant mood. It was from the taxation department.

2 March 1959
To whom it may concern,

Your thieving city bodgies have already done over my business this year. It might be to your advantage to put off your own raid until next year when, with a bit of luck, I might be in a better position to pay for your bloody opera house.
Yours bloody sincerely,
Charles W. White, Justice of the Peace

They didn't reply, not by letter. One of their numbers men replied in person, a chap of thirty-odd, heavy dark-rimmed glasses, dark suit, couldn't crack a smile to save his life. For two days he took over the bottom end of the counter, demanding invoices. Charlie gave him a few cardboard cartons full, half of which were prewar, a few of which may have been pre first war.

Before the tax accountant retired defeated, he learned of the hidden costs in running a country grocery store. Potatoes went rotten, mice got into bags of oatmeal, power wires blew down in storms and goods went off in freezers. He learned, too, that it was a dangerous game to make a move on the person of Georgie Morrison. He departed for home with one arm of his heavy-framed glasses held together by a bandaid, and none the wiser about Charlie's habit of filching big notes from the cash drawer, or about his clutch of share certificates, impaled on a wire spike and hung behind the storeroom door beneath a vintage moth-eaten tweed overcoat.

'You need to stop now, Charlie,' Georgie warned.

'It's my hobby, Rusty,' he said. 'You can't take an old chap's only vice away from him.'

'Take up chain-smoking instead. It helps,' she said, and lit one to prove it.

'You need to do something about that empty house, Mr White,' Mrs Fulton said. 'Another one of your windows got broken last night, and we heard kids running around in your own backyard.'

'I'm getting around to it,' he said.

'You need to clean up behind your shop, Mr White,' the bank manager said. 'You've got a mouse plague out there and they're getting into the bank.'

'They won't eat much,' Charlie said.

'I need to know what you're planning to do about your vacant house today, Mr White,' Hooper's tenant said. 'Bill Roberts just offered me his place for six months.'

Everyone knew why. Lila Roberts, a Sydney tart, wed to Billy Roberts, had taken off towards Sydney with a juvenile. Her husband was moving to the west, placing a continent between them. Their house was a dump. It didn't deserve Hooper's tenant. Charlie deserved him.

He offered him a ten-year lease on Jeany's house, then gave it to him rent-free for six months, on the understanding that he'd do what he could next door with both house and garden.

Went home then for the last time, just to see what Jeany thought about what he'd done. At times he swore he heard her at night, saw her shadow in the passageway.

'What do you reckon, Jeany love? Did I do the right thing? They'll look after her for us.'

She wasn't talking tonight.

He had a habit of nodding off when he sat still. He nodded off on Jeany's couch, and woke to her singing, her voice as clear as it had been thirty years ago.

'*Charlie is my darlin', me darlin', me darling . . .*'

She wouldn't be calling him her darling if she hadn't liked what he'd done. Wouldn't call him darling if she ever found out what he'd done in Willama when her daughter had him locked up in the old fogies' home. Some things wives need to know and some they don't.

'*I dream of Jeany with the light brown hair, floating like an angel on the hot summer air,*' he sang.

JIM HOOPER

*H*e'd lost her son and lost her again. Lost them both a long time ago.

He'd hung on over there for her and Jimmy. Every morning when he'd opened his eyes to another day, he would lie there gathering the threads of who he was, who he'd been, then weave them into some life form that might make it through to nightfall. He'd survived those little yellow bastards for Jenny and his boy.

They'd carried him out of that camp, the bones and ulcers of him. They'd brought him back. The first faces he'd known had been his father's, Lorna's and weeping Maggie's. He'd wanted Jenny and Jimmy, had asked for them.

'She didn't wait for you, son. She wed Henry King's stuttering lout,' Vern'd said.

That was when he'd run out of threads to hang on to. That was the day he'd tossed in the towel.

He lay on his caravan bed on a Saturday morning in April, searching for guts enough to get up off his back, to get his leg strapped on. No work today. No reason to get off his back, so he lay there, turning the pages of his life, flipping by most of them since the war. They were blank anyway.

Forty-six had gone missing. In '47 they'd brought Jimmy to his hospital ward and he'd shaken his son's hand, and learnt that his father and sisters planned to raise him. Powerless, useless, but aware that he had to stop them getting their hands on his wide-eyed boy, he'd worked out how that night. He'd written his last will and testament, stating that he wanted his son raised by Jenny, wanted his trust fund transferred to her and Jimmy. He'd woken two of his ward mates to sign as witnesses and make it into a legal document. Left it folded on his pillow and went to the bathroom where he'd made a noose from his dressing-gown cord.

He hadn't done it right. He hadn't done much in his life that had been right. The cord had stretched, or he'd been too long. Only had one foot to stand on, but he couldn't stop it from reaching out for purchase to save his useless neck.

They'd moved him to a secure ward with a locked door and no dressing-gown cord. Plenty of supervision and good powerlines. They'd strapped him down, taken his dentures, fitted him up with a crown of thorns and crucified him.

For how many years? He'd lost track of '48, '49, '50, '51.

Woke up in '52. Someone must have told him his father was dead, that he was going to his funeral. If they had, he hadn't heard them. He'd stopped listening by then.

They crucified him again for the big day, made him pliable enough to walk out to a car, to get in. Someone's. He'd noticed the suit he was wearing before he'd noticed Lorna, noticed Ian Hooper, his cousin behind the wheel – and Maggie – in that order. Maggie had always come last.

He'd noticed the city buildings on the way through town, and the road, and the road noise. Noticed a lot of things that day.

Heard the parson extolling the virtues of the great, the all-powerful Vern Hooper. Seen faces from the past coming at him at the cemetery. He'd expected to see his son there. Lorna would have demanded he be at his grandfather's funeral.

He'd asked about him.

'Bernard stayed home to look after him,' Ian had said.

Jenny had married Raymond King. Jim remembered that much. No matter when he woke up, where he woke up, he always remembered that much.

'Bernard?'

'Maggie's husband, Jim,' Ian said.

That was the first he'd heard of Maggie catching herself a husband. Maybe he'd been pleased for her, but what were they doing with his boy?

Too hot at the cemetery, he'd walked out to the shade with the family accountant and when he'd opened his car, Jim had got in, into the front passenger seat. They'd tried to get him out.

The offer of a cold beer at the Farmer's Arms Hotel had got him out. That's where he'd learnt how he'd signed his boy over to his mother, who in turn had signed him over to Vern.

'Your sister and her husband adopted him a few months back,' the accountant had said.

'Pass the parcel,' Jim had said.

'A prize worth winning, Jim.'

He remembered that. And the cold beer.

They'd delivered him back to his locked ward where previously there had been no world, no time. He couldn't lose time after the funeral. It had got a grip on him.

Six weeks later they'd moved him to a place with a bush garden and trees and hills outside that garden. He'd found an onion bulb in a pile of garden refuse, found a broken terracotta pot, and planted it.

It had become his clock of seasons. He'd given it sun and water by day and carried it to his room at night. Watched it shoot up a tiny green spear that grew into many spears; watched it bud, watched the bud become a stalk of purple-blue flowers. A nursing sister named it Hyacinth.

In '53 he'd watched that cycle again.

No lock on his door in that place. No crown of thorns there. A tall fence, a locked gate, though not always locked.

In '54 two green shoots had pushed free of the dirt, before he'd seen Lorna walk through the gate, briefcase in her hand. Hadn't wanted the calm of that garden place defiled by his sister. He'd left his pot in the garden and walked out that gate, no aim in mind other than to stay outside until she went away, without her signed papers.

He'd limped downhill and had been leaning against a white post, looking up that hill, aware he couldn't make it back, when a car had pulled up beside him.

'How far are you going, mate?'

'How far are you going?' he'd asked.

'Richmond,' the chap had said.

That was where he'd dropped him, in a busy street, the wind biting through to the bone. It had felt good. For a time it had.

His age, his limp, must have marked him as a serviceman. A Salvo had fed him breakfast. He'd washed dishes for the Salvos, wiped down their trestle tables. They'd got him a job plucking chickens behind a Chinese restaurant.

He'd plucked a lot of chickens. They'd called him Chicken Man. Looked a bit like the Japs. Hadn't smelt like them.

Anzac Day of '55 he'd stopped plucking chickens and walked down to watch the parade and count the dead. Paddy blown to smithereens; Bull, head on him like a bull, and the little yellow bastards had aimed for his head. Basil, Martie, Tomo –

All gone.

Then one of the dead called his name. 'Hoop!' They'd all called him Hoop. Chicken Man had wanted to march with the dead.

'Hoop? That's not you, mate?' A chunky little bloke had broken ranks to push his way through the crowd. 'Stone the bloody crows,' he'd said. 'We thought you were dead, Hoop.'

Too tall, Chicken Man, head always above the crowd. Too easily seen.

Nobby had seen him, Nobby who'd been bought an early ticket home by a bullet through the leg. 'Artie's marching, Dave, Kracka. We were only talking about you an hour ago, and there you go, rising from the dead.'

He'd arisen that night. Drank a lot of beer. Woke up in a bed, his leg off. Woke to the noise of squabbling boys – and Nobby, offering him his leg.

He'd tried to go.

'You can't go without a bit of breakfast, mate,' Nobby had said.

'Have a bite of lunch with us, Jim,' Rosemary had said.

He'd told them he had chickens to pluck. They'd showed him an old caravan down the bottom end of a naked backyard.

'It's yours, mate. You can give us a hand to do something about the mud.'

A brand-new house sitting in the middle of a moonscape of clay and mud, but something clean and unsullied about it.

Something healing about earth, the feel of a clod breaking up in the hand. He had two legs from the knees up. He'd spent a lot of time on his knees, his hands in the earth.

There's magic in a seed. A shrivelled speck, smaller than a grain of sand, given earth, sun and water, will get its head out of the dirt and a few months later reward you with a blossom. A rose cutting, snipped in June from a neighbour's garden, will bud up and bloom by November.

He'd been content on his knees, until they'd found Ian Hooper's number in the phone book.

'You need to get in touch with your family, Jim.'

They didn't know his family.

'What happened about Jenny and your boy, Jim?'

'Collateral damage,' he'd said.

By '56 he'd been driving down to the timber yard with Nobby to load trucks, stack timber, learning to tell one length of wood from the next. In '57 the chap who ran the office smashed his car into a tree. Nobby was no office man. Jim might have been. He might have been a lot of things.

It was the office chap's injuries that made him aware that strapping on an artificial leg each morning wouldn't have sounded too bad to the office chap who came out of hospital with his two legs, but unable to make either of them move. He didn't return to work. Jim had stayed on in the office.

A good year, 1958, a good year for the Collingwood Football Club too. A smashing good year for Nobby and his oldest boy, one-eyed Magpie supporters. Enthusiasm rubs off. All winter Jim had gone with them to the Saturday matches. When their team got into the grand final, there was no way they were going to miss that game.

And they'd won.

Waiting for the train that night and she'd come running through the crowd calling his name.

It had been like being sucked back to that other time. Like the missing years, like every year between their saying goodbye at the Sydney station had been wiped out. He'd been twenty-two again, and whole for a time – until she'd come out to Ringwood.

In the light of day, those years had come rushing back – and they hadn't stood still. He wasn't twenty-two. She wasn't eighteen. You can't wind back time to where you lost it. And she hadn't come out there looking for him, but for Jimmy.

Told her where he was. Told her he'd lost him. Hadn't expected her to come back.

She had, in November. Not the same though. His Jenny had opened her mouth and let it rip. The new Jenny measured, then filtered each word before she let it out.

Still beautiful. Older, but still beautiful.

She'd come on Boxing Day, then again halfway through January.

And he hadn't seen her since. And he knew why. Rosemary had told him why. She'd given Jenny Ian Hooper's phone number.

He and Maggie had always been as thick as thieves.

MARGOT'S LITTLE MISTAKE

A pril. Saturday, 11 April. Jenny never came out to Ringwood on a Saturday, but a woman had rung, asking if she'd arrived there yet.

And at three she did. 'I hope I'm not interrupting your day,' she said.

Rosemary told her she'd taken a call from a Veronica Andrews, that Veronica had said she'd call back.

'Did she say what she wanted me for?'

'All she said was that you were dropping Raelene off to spend the night with her mother, then coming out here.' There was a question in that statement, and Jenny answered it.

'Her mother lives in Box Hill. I split up with Ray in '47 and he got together with a seventeen-year-old kid. She had Raelene and Donny to him, then in '51 he turned up at Granny's with both kids. I've raised Raelene since she was three weeks old and now her mother wants her back.'

Wound up tight that day, chain-smoking, watching the phone. 'I shouldn't have let them put Ray's death notice in the papers. That's how she found me.' Unfiltered Jenny that day, unabridged

Jenny, impatient for the phone to ring, lighting a new cigarette from the last.

'They're threatening to take me to court over her. People have been threatening to take me to court since I turned eighteen.' Looked at Jim when she said it, accused him for his family, sucked in smoke and blew it out. 'Sorry, but I've just about had enough. I've got my oldest –'

And the phone rang and Jenny sprang up to take the call.

'What?' she said. 'Margot? . . . Jesus, Vroni.'

Jim had known Margot and the other one as toddlers. One redhead, one white.

The phone was an open door away. He heard, 'Ambulance.' He heard, 'What the hell did she think she was doing?' He heard, 'I'll get a taxi now, Vroni. I'll come straight to the hospital.'

The phone down, she returned to the doorway. 'Would you have a taxi number handy, Rosemary?'

'We'll drive you down,' Rosemary said.

'I'll grab a taxi. Thanks though.'

They found a number. Rosemary rang it, and Jenny picked up her bag and walked out to the gate to wait. Jim followed her, stood with her, wishing he had two legs and a car, watching her count the coins in her purse, finger a ten-shilling note, find another, crumpled.

'Have you got any idea what it might cost to Frankston?'

'I don't use them,' he said. Nobby drove him to work, drove him home. Always dependant on someone. Nothing to give anyone. He had money. He took his wallet from his hip pocket, removed a five-pound note and offered it.

'Thanks,' she said. 'I'll post it back.' Looked up at him then. 'Remember that other five-pound note?'

'Your talent-quest money?'

Shook her head. 'That time when you wanted me to send you a photograph of Jimmy, when you were stationed up near Darwin. I kept posting the fiver back and you kept posting it back to me. Before Sydney.'

He remembered.

'It's too late, isn't it?' she said.

'To find Jimmy?'

'That too,' she said. 'Lorna doesn't even know where he is. I meant for us, to find us, Jen and Jim, 1942.'

'I'm a screwed-up mess, Jen.'

'Righto,' she said, nodding, nodding for a while. 'That's that then – though I'd love to know what gives you the right to believe that you're more screwed up than the rest of us.' She slid his five-pound note into her purse. 'Maybe it's a money thing?'

Filters definitely not working today. He had to swallow it, lumps and all – or spit it out and walk away.

He swallowed it. 'The old man bought me a special dispensation at birth, Jen.'

'Margot's got one too, though I don't know who paid for hers. I didn't.' She breathed deeply as she looked towards the south, the direction a taxi would come from, then to her watch. Took a packet of cigarettes from her pocket, struck a match. 'I wish someone had bought one for me, or I could curl up in some dark hole and say, "Take this cup away from me". No one else wants it, that's the trouble.' She got the cigarette lit before the flame died, and blew smoke towards the sky.

'Margot has got a severe case of indigestion. She shoved my vegetable knife in to the hilt to let the air out.'

'What?'

'The little fool got herself pregnant to Teddy Hall, one of Harry and Elsie's boys. She doesn't want to be pregnant so she's not. I've had her down with me since February and she's driving me stark raving crazy – her and Raelene both. Vroni told me to shout myself a day off, let Raelene go to her mother for the night and she'd keep her eye on Margot.

'Her doctor partner decided to make Margot listen to the baby's heartbeat. When he finished with her, she picked up the vegetable knife and shoved it in.'

Taxi coming. He opened the gate and she walked out to the kerb. 'Thanks for the loan.' That was all she said.

Only one way out of Nobby's street. Jim leaned on the gate, watching the driver start his three-point turn, knowing that he loved her, why he loved her – because she'd never curled up in a dark hole and given up, and never would. While he'd been hiding from life, she'd been out there living it. Knew he could survive anything if she was beside him.

The taxi completed its turn. She glanced his way, raised a hand. He was raising his hand in a wave when the hand changed its mind and the wave became the universal sign for 'stop'.

Out the gate then. She wound down the window. He opened the door, and she moved over to make room for him at her side.

*

They saw the infant as it was being transferred to an ambulance for the ride to Melbourne. Just a glimpse of a squirming scrap with stick-thin limbs and a wrinkled old face – more monkey than human.

'Margot is in recovery. She'll be fine. The baby is struggling. Its best chance is in the city. It's a girl,' Veronica said. 'Pleased to finally meet you, Jim. Now, I have to get back. Do you want to hang around here for a while, kiddo? They might let you see her.'

'I'll grab a lift back with you, Vroni.'

The women walked to the car, side by side, Veronica filling in the hours Jenny had been away, Jim limping behind them. Had Jenny got into the front seat, he would have asked for a lift to the station. She'd got into the rear seat, with him.

'Feel like joining us for dinner?' Veronica asked.

'Another time, thanks Vroni.'

'Nice meeting you, Jim. I've heard a lot about you,' she said. 'Have a good night.' Gone then, into the main building.

Jenny led the way around the west side of the guesthouse to her rooms. No lock on her kitchen door, not much worth locking in.

Plenty of space, though. She filled an electric jug, plugged it in, took half a bottle of milk from a vibrating refrigerator.

'You said Jimmy was born early. Did he look . . .?'

'He was a Hooper,' she said, as if that said it all. She sawed two slices from a crusty loaf, uneven slices. She looked at one, then tossed it into the bin. 'Granny used to say that Hoopers had a bad habit of killing their mothers. He got stuck coming out. Doctor Frazer had to drag him out with forceps.'

She sniffed and sawed off another slice of bread, little better than the last, then with her shoulder swiped at a leaking tear.

'I wasn't allowed to see him for days, and when I did, his head still looked like a bruised egg. He was scratched, one of his eyes was swollen shut. And he was the most beautiful thing I'd ever seen in my life. And he's mine, not your bloody sister's.' And she tossed the loaf from her, tossed the knife and opened the fridge.

He stood watching her, the table between them, Jimmy between them. He'd always be between them.

'I'm sorry, Jen.'

'Me too,' she said, wiping her eyes with her fingers. 'Granny knew. The minute she saw his hands she knew there'd be trouble with your father. I don't think she believed he was yours until she saw his tiny double-jointed thumbs. The first things your father looked at were his hands. If Margot's baby lives, the first things I'll look at will be its hands. Margot's inherited the twins' stubby paws – and I still can't stand to look at them, can still feel them all over me . . .' She sniffed, wiped her nose with her forearm.

'Will it live?' he asked.

'Ask Him,' she said, pointing with a packet of cheese towards the ceiling. 'He's running this bloody show.' She reached for her frying pan and dropped it. It bounced beneath the table. She picked it up and looked at its dented lip.

'Old when I bought it,' she said. 'Cheap. Good enough for me. All my life, second best has been good enough for me. I didn't wear a new dress until I nicked off to Melbourne and got run over by Georgie's father.'

'Sit down, Jen.'

'I don't want to sit down. I want a fried cheese sandwich.'

Turned on a small hotplate. Placed a knob of butter into the pan. 'Jimmy wasn't second best. You weren't either. Do you think I give a damn about your wooden leg and your screwed-up head? I wouldn't care if you had three wooden legs, a white cane, were cross-eyed, screwed-up, or otherwise buggered-up, you fool of a man, I love you, and . . . and I need you to hold me before I crack.'

He held her whether he was second best or not. He kissed her hair, then her face and she wanted his mouth. He got lost there, and when she pulled away from him, he wanted to bawl.

Men don't cry. And only the butter burning in that dented pan. She turned off the heat, placed the pan on the sink, then returned to his arms.

Narrow bed in the kitchen. Jimmy had been conceived on a narrow bed in Monk's cellar. Jim hadn't been with a woman before that cellar. Hadn't been with one since Sydney. Didn't know if he was man enough to be with a woman.

An artificial leg can't be removed without embarrassment, and when it was off, he couldn't hide the puny stump of scarred calf attached to his knee. Didn't want her to see his mutilation.

Be a man, his father said.

Fear of failure, desperate not to fail, Jimmy between them and Vern Hooper in his head –

'It's all right,' she said. 'I need you, not that. It's all right.'

And it was. She hadn't been with a man since Ray in 1947, and had sworn she'd never do it again. There was peace in the holding of Jim, in him holding her. They were Jen and Jim again. That was all that mattered.

A Convoluted Life

*H*e slept in her double bed that night, stayed with her on Sunday, held her hand when they caught the train back to the city and another to Box Hill, then he continued on to his caravan and she walked around to the Keatings' to claim Raelene – hoping to walk in on a tantrum but meeting a happy Raelene at the door, a Raelene wearing new red shoes.

'I hope you don't mind, Jenny,' Florence said.

'They're very pretty.'

'We had a lovely time. We'd like to do it again next week.'

'We'll talk about it, Florence,' Jenny said.

She spoke to Vroni about renting a flat that week. She had no argument with what went on in the neighbouring rooms – and what would continue to go on in back rooms all over the world while women were expected to spend their lives pregnant. Jim could never know about what went on next door. Like Granny, he'd consider it murder.

Too much on her mind that week to worry about the future. Margot to worry about, her baby. Raelene too. She was full up with her pretty bedroom in Box Hill and ice-cream in Florence's fridge and even ice-cream cones in a packet. No ice-cream in Jenny's elderly fridge. It melted.

Then Wednesday evening and another one of Vroni's specials moved in, and Jenny and Raelene had to walk over to the main building to use Vroni's bathroom and toilet, just for two nights, but for those two nights Jenny was on call, and the patient in isolation was a sixteen-year-old girl who enjoyed hitting her buzzer and disturbing Raelene, who was reaching an age where she resented the sick lady who wouldn't let them use their own bathroom.

Had to get a flat, or a house, or another job.

On Friday, Florence rang. She and Clarrie would be willing to pick Raelene up on Friday night and return her on Sunday.

'Do you want to sleep at Florence's house again, love?'

'They do things,' Raelene said.

'What things?'

'Shops and everything.'

The Keatings picked her up at seven. Jim came in a taxi on Saturday morning. She took him down to the beach and walking on sand wasn't easy for him, so they sat on sand and when he tried to get up he lost his balance and fell. She could panic or make light of it. She did the latter, laughed, and offered him her hands.

'I'm useless,' he said.

'Not entirely,' she said. 'Though beach walks might be out.'

They booked a room at a hotel and it was like being in Number Five in Sydney. They kissed and lay, his arm beneath her shoulder, her arm over him, holding him close to her, and talking, talking about everything under the sun and beyond the sun.

He told her how he'd attempted to drive Nobby's car two nights ago. 'I can't judge pressure on the clutch with a dead shoe,' he said.

He'd been driving since his legs had grown long enough to reach the pedals. When she'd been nine or ten, he'd driven halfway to Sydney with his father and sisters and Sissy.

'You'll get the hang of it.'

'I doubt it.'

'Then I will. I drove from Melbourne to Geelong once.'

They spoke of Sissy. Maisy still kept in touch with her. He asked about Jenny's mother.

'My natural mother died in childbirth.'

He knew nothing about Juliana Conti and Archie Foote. There was so much to talk about. She told him she'd sung at a city jazz club, then told him about Amber and Norman.

'You would have been back in Australia when she killed him. The newspapers were full of it,' she said. 'He was in bed asleep, and she bashed and stabbed him to death – then cleaned the house.'

'Insane?' he said.

'She always was. When it happened, she was judged unfit to go to trial and locked up in an asylum for the criminally insane. There was supposed to be some sort of hearing about her a while back. For all I know, they could have let her out.'

She told him that she'd spoken to his cousin, Ian Hooper, on the phone, that he'd told her Lorna had lost track of Jimmy and Margaret.

'He'd told me that after Margaret and her husband adopted Jimmy, they bought a house at Cheltenham and bought one for Lorna in Kew, but she refused to live alone in it. He said that Margaret and her husband had moved house several times in an attempt to lose her, and they finally succeeded last December. Jimmy was here when I came down to Frankston. He was here when I met you. He went to school at Kew until December. I rang up the school. They couldn't tell me anything.

'Ian said he writes to Margaret, posts his letters to her accountant and he passes them on. I wrote to her. She didn't reply. She would to you – if she didn't know you were with me, she would.'

He didn't want to write. She didn't push him.

Saw Margot on Sunday. Learned from one of the sisters that she was to be moved down to Melbourne for psychiatric assessment. And maybe she needed assessing – she still denied having that baby.

The Keatings brought Raelene home. She'd seen Jim at the station the night of the grand final. Hadn't approved then. Didn't want him getting into Florence and Clarrie's car. Florence and Clarrie belonged to her, and their car belonged to her.

*

The Keatings had offered him a lift back to the city. Taxis cost money. He'd accepted. And wished he hadn't once they were on the road.

'Have you known Jenny long?' Florence asked.

'Since we were kids,' he said.

'Are you thinking of marriage?'

'Not at the moment.'

'Our solicitor says that, given her situation, there's little chance of a judge awarding her custody of Raelene,' Clarrie said.

'That's Jen's business, not mine,' Jim said.

'We'd never cut Raelene out of her life,' Florence said.

'Her living conditions would go against her in court. Raelene has got her own room at our place, and Flo doesn't work,' Clarrie said.

'A bit of traffic on the road,' Jim said. Maybe they got the message.

*

The one constant in life is change. The following Friday Jenny came late to his caravan door. She'd received a letter from the Keatings' solicitor.

'They've picked their time,' she said. 'Margot is in a ward for disturbed patients. I'm thirty-four and a grandmother, and my only claim on Raelene is being married to her father and raising her for seven years.' She lit a cigarette and drew hard on it.

'Want to know why I raised her, Jim? Want to know why I changed Donny's backside until he was almost as big as me?'

He wanted to know. He'd been gone too long. Maybe he didn't want to know when she told him.

'I aborted two of Ray's babies – or Vroni aborted them. And the last one of them will still be on record somewhere. It went wrong and I woke up in hospital with a cop leaning over me in bed.'

'Why would you, Jen?'

'Because I couldn't stand him touching me. He never did again – or not in that way. Because I knew I was going to leave him.' She inhaled smoke and flicked ash. 'Flora, the woman who shared Ray's house, knew about the last abortion. Florence Keating lived with him in that house. She was bosom buddies with Flora Parker, and still is. Their solicitor has got a statement from her.'

'About the abortion?'

'Not yet. Just about Florence being a good mother and about Ray's abuse. If I fight them for Raelene, Flora will give them more.

'And you may as well know the lot while I'm about it. Vroni's partner does abortions three rooms away from mine. Want to run for the hills?'

'I wouldn't get far, Jen.'

They saw the baby the following Saturday. Elsie and Harry met them in the city and they went to the hospital together. It was still a poor wee mite of a thing, but it looked less monkey and a little more human, and they were allowed to touch it. Elsie, who planned to raise it, couldn't keep her hands off her grandbaby. She had a baby complex.

Jenny touched a fragile foot, a minute hand – which didn't look like a Macdonald hand, not that there was enough of it to tell. An old-man wrinkled thing with grabbing fingers, it grabbed for her.

They saw Margot, or the women and Harry saw her. Jim, who had seen the insides of too many psychiatric wards, remained outside. Harry was out in minutes.

'Christ,' he said. 'Christ, but I don't know what went wrong with that girl.'

He rolled a slim smoke, got it lit before offering his tobacco. Jim shook his head. He'd got out of the habit of smoking.

'Just between you, me and the gatepost, mate, I'm inclined to think they've got her in the right place,' Harry said. 'Christ Almighty.'

For the best part of an hour Harry rolled his skinny smokes while they waited for the women, who waited almost as long to speak to a doctor. And achieved nothing. Elsie attempted to explain how Margot had denied her pregnancy from day one, how she'd refused to marry her baby's father; Jenny told him Margot believed she'd let the air out of her stomach with the vegetable knife, and by the look on the doctor's face, if they hadn't got out of that place fast, he might have locked them in too.

Harry had left his car in Bendigo and come the rest of the way by train. With time to fill, the two couples ended up in a city car yard, where the men discussed the merits of V8s, and Jim's attempt to drive Nobby's Holden.

'Young Ted is a genius with cars. He'd work out a way for you to get around the clutch,' Harry said. 'You used to drive too, didn't you, Jen?'

'When I was fifteen. I didn't know what I was doing then and I'd know less now.'

'Get yourself a few lessons. Young Georgie has taken to it like a duck to water.'

'She seems fond of Jack,' Elsie said. 'We don't see a lot of her lately.'

The Halls boarded their train to Bendigo. Jen and Jim booked into a hotel for the night and on hotel paper, he wrote to Margaret.

> Dear Maggie,
> I ran into Harry Hall today . . .

In his youth he'd got on well with the younger of his two sisters, and seeing Harry had taken him back to those years of poker nights in Gertrude's kitchen, of dances, and balls with Maggie and Sissy. On Jenny's advice, he didn't mention her name.

Since '56 I've been working in the office of a timber yard . . .
You've no doubt twigged as to why I'm writing to you. I want
to see Jimmy . . .

They sealed his page into two envelopes, wrote *Margaret Hooper*
on the inner envelope, addressed the outer envelope to Vern's
accountant and posted it that night.

Then waited.

*

Margot spent six weeks in the psychiatric ward before those trained
to deal with problems of the mind tossed their hands in the air and
released her into her mother's care.

Jenny hadn't wanted her as a baby and didn't want her now.
Vroni picked her up and installed her in the isolation room, and
with her in there, Jenny needed Jim. He came on Friday night after
work and slept in the kitchen on Margot's bed. Raelene shared
Jenny's, but the Keatings picked her up on Saturday morning.

On Sunday, at noon, when Jack Thompson, Georgie and
Elsie arrived to take Margot home, Elsie said that dirty word. 'We
popped in to see your *baby* on the way through, love. The nurses
say she's doing really good.'

If Margot was sane, Jenny would eat her hat. She threw a
screamer. Elsie pandered, petted. Jenny walked away.

'Walk away from her, Elsie,' Georgie said, taking Elsie's arm.
'Start treating her like an adult and she might start acting like one.'

She sounded like Gertrude, so much like her, a ghost walked over
Jim's grave. He followed Jenny outside, and Jack followed him.

'Your father's house is becoming the louts' hangout,' Jack said.
'There was a *For Sale* sign up until a week or so back. Do you know
if it's been sold, Jim?'

'I'm not in touch with my family,' Jim said.

He knew his mother had left the bulk of her money to him,
and the house. He knew too that he'd signed Lorna's papers blindly.

Maybe it was time to find out what they'd done with his money – and house.

When they got rid of that lisping, bawling lump of a girl, he spoke to Jenny about Vern's house.

'It wasn't a part of Pop's estate. Mum's first husband built it, back before the first war. She left it to Pop for his lifetime, then to me. Margaret has received my letter. That will be why the house was taken off the market. They probably thought I was dead.'

THE WATER-PISTOL BANDIT

Mid-June and cold. They were halfway home and Georgie driving when a sleety drizzle set in. They'd stopped for a fast coffee at six and Margot had wanted fish and chips. Elsie gave in to her. They'd lost half an hour waiting for the meal to come, then waiting for Margot to eat it.

Elsie had been given three bottles of pills with Margot's name on them. She'd fed her two with her dinner. Georgie didn't know what they were for. Some sort of sleeping pill maybe. She was asleep now, her head on Elsie's shoulder, Jack's travelling blanket over her.

They spoke of the greasy roads, of Raelene, Florence Keating and her solicitor. Jack knew the law. He knew the court system. Given the facts, he believed that most judges would award Raelene to her natural mother. Florence and her husband were childless. Florence claimed that Ray had thrown his mother-in-law from the house and broken her wrist, that she'd gone with her mother in the ambulance, and when they'd returned the following day, Ray and the babies were gone.

The solicitor had obtained the hospital records of Florence's mother's broken wrist. Flora and Geoff Parker, who'd owned the Armadale house, had both sworn statements backing up Florence's story. They'd gone with Florence to report her kids missing.

Georgie didn't doubt that what they claimed was true. She had total recall of Christmas Day, 1951, of Ray pulling Donny out from beneath his riding jacket, then digging Raelene out of a saddlebag. He'd looked half-crazy, had been shaking so hard Granny had sent her across the paddock to get the bottle of medicinal brandy. At the time Georgie had been convinced that he'd murdered his kids' mother and buried her in Jenny's garden. He'd half-killed Jenny one night.

Granny had made the rules on her land. He'd obeyed them. There'd been a wildness in him, but most of it in his eyes when he'd looked at Jenny. He'd paid for the two back rooms to be built then had his bedroom furniture brought up on the train, expecting Jenny to share that new room. She hadn't. She'd moved Donny's cot out there.

Her eyes left the road for an instant to glance at Jack. He wanted her to marry him. For the best part of a year she'd been telling herself he was a mate, maybe her best mate, but not her boyfriend. She was close to understanding why a man and woman might want to share a bed. Knew she probably could with him.

He'd do anything for her. She hadn't asked him to drive down to Frankston. He'd been in the shop when Jenny rang, and while she was on the line, he'd said to tell her they'd be down on Sunday, as if he was already a part of the family.

Charlie liked him. Elsie and Harry liked him. Most did.

'Want a break?' he asked.

'I'm good,' she said.

Elsie was asleep before they reached Willama, propped against the doorframe, her coat as a pillow, Margot still dead to the world, her head now on Elsie's lap.

'Unless someone does something, she'll have Margot draped around her neck until the day she dies.'

'How come she calls her "Mum"?' Jack asked.

'Easier to say than "Elsie".'

'She's good with her.'

'Her own kids don't need mothering any more. Margot does.'

'What's going to happen when she brings the baby home?'

'Elsie's still imagining weddings and happy families. Did you hear what she wants to name the poor little coot?'

'Gertrude, for your gran.'

'Even Granny loathed the name.'

'What's your favourite name?'

'Not Gertrude.'

Just the road noise then, and the windscreen wipers' flap-flap, flap-flap. They were through Willama and heading into familiar country before Jack spoke.

'If you moved down to Frankston with your mum, I'd be able to see you.' He was being transferred to the city at the end of June.

'Charlie,' she said.

'Charlie is becoming a law unto himself. I should have charged him for what he did to his tenants.'

'You don't know the half of it.'

'He's not going to improve with age, love, and you're too young to have the responsibility of him.'

'So you keep telling me.' Silence again and more rain blowing at the windscreen. She sat forward and eased off the accelerator.

'I don't want to leave town with us up in the air.'

'I'm not cop's wife material, Jack.'

'I reckon you were made for the job, so do Mum and Dad.'

'I know me better than they know me.'

They were nearing the Mission Bridge when she asked if cops kept track of criminals after they'd served their time.

'A good percentage of them end up back in,' he said.

'Would it be possible to find out if a bloke locked up in 1939 was in or out?'

'It would be easy enough if he's in. What did he do?'

'Robbed banks, stole cars. You name it. Laurence George Morgan, the water-pistol bandit they called him. He got three years.'

'What's your interest?'

'He's a relative,' she said.

For three years she'd believed he was a movie star. Slept with his framed newspaper photograph beneath her pillow. Nagged Jenny to take her up to Sydney to see him. In Armadale she'd found out he was a thief, not a movie star, and she'd put him away. Since meeting Jack's father, Laurie Morgan wouldn't stay out of her head.

'What sort of relative?'

'Pretty close.' She shrugged then, and added, 'He's my father.'

'You're kidding me.'

'Told you I wasn't cop's wife material. I fiddle Charlie's books too. Do your parents want bank-robber grandkids?'

'Your mother is a receptionist at a posh health resort.'

'My mother had Margot at fifteen and two more by the time she was eighteen, and all to different fathers. Tell that to your parents.'

'They wouldn't care, and it's got nothing to do with who you are.'

'Your father probably arrested mine.'

'I'll ask him. Do you know where he was arrested?'

'Geelong. I think Sydney had a prior claim on him. He was tried in Sydney and locked up there.'

'Dad would enjoy tracking him down for you –'

'Don't you dare.'

'Want to hear one of my family secrets?'

'Your father took bribes?'

'Mum probably tried it a few times. You know how Dad calls the sunken room out the back "Katie's sly grog joint"? It was, back before the depression.'

'I don't believe you.'

'Ask her. She inherited the hotel from her second husband. He used to make apple cider out there. She was married twice before

Dad, and she didn't marry him until two months before I was born – when he threatened to arrest her if she didn't – or that's their story.'

They were home by nine, when, exhausted by her day, Elsie doled out another pill to Margot, a different pill, then sat beside her bed until she slept again. Georgie drank coffee in the kitchen with Jack, sat close to him and when he was leaving she walked out to the yard and kissed him goodnight.

The night before he left Woody Creek, she almost did more than kiss him. Stopped herself though. She had no intention of adding to the world's population.

*

It was close to midnight, five days after Jack left, Georgie had been reading in bed, attempting to read herself to sleep, when she heard thumping. A rhythmic thump, thump, thump, which sounded like Donny when he'd taken a fit. Margot was taking pills for something. Afraid she'd started taking fits, Georgie ran, as Jenny and Granny had run when Donny had started fitting.

She hit Margot's light switch running. And caught them red-handed, or red-faced, in bed, or on it, or Teddy on it and Margot on him.

'You pair of mindless rabbits,' she said.

'Piss off,' Teddy said.

'Pith off,' Margot echoed.

Born on a Kitchen Floor

Cara should have been home by half past ten. She tried to creep in at one-thirty, but the back door was locked and Robert and Myrtle were waiting for her. They caught her with her face painted and wearing Rosie's old jeans. Myrtle looked as if she'd been howling for hours. Robert, dressing-gown clad, thinning hair standing on end, looked furious.

'Where have you been until this hour?'

'It's none of your business, is it? You're not my father, so you've got no right to tell me what I can do.' She dodged around them, went to her room and slammed the door.

Robert opened it. 'You'll see how much right I've got,' he said. Then he told her she wouldn't be leaving the house for a month, other than to go to school.

Since Christmas Cara had known he wasn't her father. Until they'd driven up to Sydney at Easter time, she'd believed she was a stray pup they'd taken in and given a good home. She knew now that Myrtle was her mother and that she'd played around with someone while Robert was overseas during the war.

They'd gone to Amberley to check the fat manager's rent books and to have a new gas stove installed in the lodgers' kitchen. Left to her own devices for most of one day, Cara had checked out a few things with Mrs Collins, one of two long-term lodgers. She'd been a teacher, so Cara had woven a story about how she had to write an essay about being born during wartime. It wasn't a complete lie, except they'd written that essay two months ago. Anyway, she'd said that one of her New Australian friends was going to write about being born while her mother and grandmother hid from the Germans in a muddy gutter.

'Do you know anything interesting about when I was born?' she'd said. Mrs Collins had told her she'd been born at Amberley, in the kitchen.

'Your mother looked after the little boy of a young war widow, a singer who was working out of town. She arrived very late one night and found your mother in the kitchen, you in her arms.'

Which may have been almost as interesting as being born in a muddy gutter if it hadn't proved that her mother had cheated on her father while he'd been fighting the Germans – which was more or less what Sarah North, her first best friend, had originally said. Sarah hadn't said Myrtle wasn't Cara's mother, just that Robert wasn't her proper father.

And it was sickening seeing Myrtle pretending that butter wouldn't melt in her plummy mouth, and seeing Robert with his arm around her, when he knew she'd cheated on him. Cara hated her for it, and hated Robert for letting Myrtle make a fool of him.

She shouldn't have done what she'd done, shouldn't have done it on the way back to Traralgon, definitely shouldn't have done it in heavy traffic. She'd done it anyway. They'd been about ten miles from Amberley when the boiling inside her had bubbled up and spouted out of her mouth.

'So, who was it you were you playing around with during the war, Mum?' That's what she'd said.

Myrtle had swung around as if there were a rattlesnake in the back seat. Robert had sideswiped the car beside him and almost lost control of the wheel. They'd had to pull over to the side of the road and swap names with the other driver, who had been as mad as a hornet. His new car was scraped all the way down one side.

She could have caused a serious accident and killed everyone. The shock had kept her quiet for the next hundred miles, until they were out of the car in front of public toilets, which stank, so it was the perfect place to attack both of them.

'Mrs Collins told me, so you may as well admit it.'

They hadn't. They hadn't spoken to her or to each other. It was the worst trip of her life. They'd planned to stop in Albury for the night but Robert had just kept on driving and driving. They'd got to Traralgon after midnight.

And she'd nicked off the next morning while they were sleeping, had breakfast at Rosie's and stayed there all day. Then Dino Collins, who Robert couldn't stand, had come around. He was still after her – not that that stopped him going with other girls. It stopped Cara from going with anyone. He'd belted up Graham Jones from school, just for walking home with her one afternoon.

She hadn't let Dino kiss her until after the Sydney trip, after he'd given her a ride home from Rosie's on the back of his motorbike, which she only did to nark Robert, who hated motorbikes worse than he hated Dino Collins. He saw her kiss him too. That was the night they'd stopped giving her pocket money.

Everything had gone from bad to worse since. Robert drove her to school each morning, and as soon as he walked into the building, she'd walked out the gate. She'd gone riding once with Dino, only once. He'd ridden out to the bush and started kissing her, like shoving his tongue halfway down her throat while trying to shove his hand up her school uniform. She'd had to kick him to get away, and lucky she'd been wearing her school shoes. He'd roared off on his bike and left her to walk three miles home.

He was crazy. All of the kids knew it. They said it was because his parents had drowned or something when he was a kid and he'd had to live with an old bat of an aunty who had only taken him in because his parents had left him pots of money and she got some of it for looking after him. He'd told them that getting money out of her was like squeezing out her blood – a spoonful at a time – though it would have taken more than a spoonful to pay for his motorbike and his riding gear.

Cara spent a lot of time thinking about money, now that she had none to think about. On the days she wagged school she wandered around the shops dreaming about what she'd spend her money on – if she'd had any.

They'd still fed her at home, though she'd stopped eating with them. She ate in her bedroom, so Myrtle stopped tidying her bedroom.

Their cold war had turned into a hot war after the midyear exams. She'd failed Maths and Geography and she'd never failed a subject in her life, and it hurt enough without Robert getting stuck into her.

Then a few days ago Dino's aunty had kicked him out for trying to starve her ancient old cat to death while she was in hospital.

He came around to Rosie's on the Sunday and said he was going up to Sydney. And like a fool, Cara said she wished she could go up to Sydney, and all of a sudden they were all going up to Sydney.

'We'll need money,' Dino said.

'Cara has got piles of it in the bank,' Rosie said.

She had a huge bank account, and every week there was more in it, because part of the money from the lodgers' rent got paid into it – for when she went to university, Robert said. As if.

'I can't get it out without Mum or Dad's signature,' she said.

'You can copy it,' Rosie said.

Which she could. Myrtle's was easy. She'd forged it on absent notes for school, though doing it at a bank was more illegal than a note for a teacher. If she was going to do something illegal, it would be easier to take Robert's wallet and Myrtle's emergency five-pound note. Her handbag lived behind the sitting-room door and Robert's wallet, when it wasn't in his pocket, lived on the fridge with his car keys.

Except she wasn't a thief, and she might want to go to Sydney, but not if Dino Collins was a part of the deal.

He didn't even feel pain like normal people. She'd been at Rosie's the day he'd cut *HATE* into the knuckles of his left hand with a razor blade, then rubbed black biro into the cuts, which he'd said was how the crims in jail did it.

Rosie had wanted him to do Coop's name on her shoulder, in a heart. She felt pain. One cut, one bead of blood, and she'd changed her mind.

Cara went to school that week, except on Friday, after lunch. They were supposed to be leaving for Sydney on Saturday night and everything she owned needed washing. Since she'd stopped speaking to her parents, Myrtle had stopped washing her clothes.

'At least sort the lights from the darks, pet.' Myrtle stood at the laundry door offering instruction.

'You can do it if you like,' Cara snapped.

She didn't like, so Cara tossed the lot in, turned on the machine, then walked down to the bank with the best of half-a-dozen forged withdrawal forms.

And when she got there, she couldn't pass it over the counter. Ripped it into tiny bits and scattered the bits as she walked home.

She was ironing in the kitchen when Robert came in. He kissed Myrtle, put his car keys and wallet on the fridge and went to the bathroom to shower. Cara didn't speak to him. She hadn't spoken to him for a week.

And as if he'd care if she was there or not. A week after she was gone they'd both forget she'd ever been born. She was going to Sydney and when she got there, she'd go out to Uncle John's place and live with them.

The cases were stored in the garage. She found her own and carried it through the house.

'What do you need with that, pet?' Myrtle asked.

'I'm going to Sydney.'

'Don't start that foolishness again.'

'He's the fool,' Cara said. She fetched her ironing from the kitchen and tossed it into her case, shoved in the bits that hung over the edges and attempted to close it.

'Robert!'

He came from the bathroom, clad in trousers and singlet, his hair still wet from the shower. He didn't stand in the doorway with Myrtle. He walked into the bedroom, picked up the case, emptied what was in it to floor and bed, then returned to the bathroom to finish shaving, and he took the case with him.

'I'll go in what I'm wearing then,' Cara yelled.

'I wouldn't place my last ten bob on that,' Robert yelled back.

'You're not my father and you can't tell me what to do!'

'I wouldn't place my last ten bob on that either.'

She didn't have ten bob to bet with. She didn't have five bob. Hated Myrtle for cheating on him, hated him more for being fool enough to let her get away with it. Wanted to get Dino to cut *HATE* into her knuckles – and *THEM* into her other hand.

'Hang up those clothes,' he said as he walked by with her case, walked outside to the garage with it.

She picked up a handful of clothing and chased him, pitching pants and shirts at him. Myrtle collected the scattered garments. She was howling. Robert looked angry – and silly. She didn't often see his skinny old white arms sticking out of a baggy singlet. He was over sixty and he looked every year of it when he wasn't wearing a shirt and tie.

'Hang up your clothing then come out to the kitchen and help you mother with dinner.'

'I want my case!'

'Tell her, Robert.'

'Tell me what?'

'That we've got this crazy idea that you'll start coming to your senses in another year or two, and that we plan to be around to see it,' Robert said.

'What do you care what I do? She had an affair while you were in the war, and you took me in like you'd take in a stray cat –'

'A stray cat might have been easier to live with.'

'I've got a right to know who my father was.'

'You've just about cancelled any rights you ever had in this house.'

'This house stinks and so do both of you.'

'Your room stinks, as does your behaviour. Pick up your clothing and hang it up.'

'Who did you do it with, Mum? Or did you have so many boyfriends you don't remember which one he was?'

Myrtle's handkerchief was out, and like the fool he was, Robert put his arm around her so she could cry on him.

'I hate the way you crawl around her all the time. How can you crawl around her when she cheated on you?'

'Wash that muck off your face,' he said. 'You look like a racoon with conjunctivitis.'

He didn't care why her makeup was running. She returned to her bedroom to bawl on her pillow, then changed her mind, stripped the pillow slip from it and began stuffing clothing into it. Stuffed it full then pitched it at the closed door, because she had no intention of going up to Sydney with someone who thought he was a cross between Jimmy Dean and a skull and crossbones bikie, who ten miles out of Traralgon would be trying to shove his tongue down her throat. The only thing she liked about him was his cigarettes.

She had a packet in her school case. She dug it out, found a box of matches in the pocket of her school uniform, then stood before her dressing table, watching her reflection light up and blow smoke – and saw what Robert had meant about her eyeliner. Wiped it off on her school uniform, then replaced it with wider lines of black, added lipstick, one of Rosie's used-up lipsticks. She drew a beauty spot on her left cheekbone with an eyebrow pencil stub, also one of Rosie's.

They had noses like bloodhounds. Robert came to her door and slapped the cigarette from her hand. It flew, landed on the dressing table. He snatched it, mashed it into a pot of pancake face powder.

'Wash your hands.'

'They're not dirty.'

'If you plan to eat tonight, you will wash your hands. It's your choice.'

Braised chicken and mashed potatoes wasn't a choice. Braised chicken and mashed potatoes was blackmail. She washed her hands and slouched into the kitchen.

'Was my father one of the lodgers or someone from your church?'

'He was an eighteen-year-old American boy,' Myrtle said.

THE YOUNG WAR WIDOW

'*I*'m sick and tired of you both lying to me. As if an eighteen-year-old boy would be interested in a fat forty year old. As if an eighteen-year-old boy would even look at you without laughing.'

'I didn't give birth to you, Cara,' Myrtle said.

'It's too late to pull that. Mrs Collins already told me I was born on the kitchen floor at Amberley.'

That made them sit up and shut up. For ten or fifteen seconds the only sound in the kitchen was the peas hissing because the saucepan had run out of water. Myrtle lifted it from the stove, added a knob of butter, pepper.

'God sent an angel to my door –'

'Oh, yeah, and I'm baby Jesus – and now I'm really going to Sydney.'

'You were born to a twenty-year-old country girl who already had three children,' Robert said. 'A young war widow –'

Cara was halfway out the door. 'War widow' caught her attention. She turned.

'Sit down,' he said.

'While you think up a few more lies.'

'The boy's name was Billy-Bob. He was an American sailor. Jenny was one of my lodgers. After her husband was killed, she took work at a clothing factory,' Myrtle said.

'Mrs Collins said that she and Miss Robertson were in the kitchen minutes after you had me on the floor. She said I was wrapped up in a tea towel.'

'What she told you is the truth as she knew it, pet. Jenny and I deceived those dear women. You weren't born to me, but you've been mine since the minute of your birth.'

Mrs Collins had said the lodger had been a singer, not a clothing-factory worker. Liars need good memories, and Cara was about to say so, when Myrtle added, 'She had a little boy. I looked after him for her.'

Mrs Collins had said there was a little boy. It could have been true. And Cara didn't want it to be true. Her every word, her every action since Easter had been aimed to punish her plummy-mouthed, too good to be true, cheating fraud of a mother – who, if she wasn't her cheating mother, had no reason to put up with being punished.

'You probably found out I was talking to Mrs Collins and you bribed her with free rent to lie for you.'

'It's the truth, pet.'

'Then I'm nothing to you, to either of you?'

'Only everything,' Robert said. 'Sit down, poppet.'

'Stop calling me that – and you know what I mean. I'm not related to either of you.'

'We're related by love,' Robert said, reaching out a hand. She flinched from his touch. 'Had you been born to us, we couldn't have loved you more, and you know it.'

Silence then, a heart-thumping, wobbly sort of silence. Her legs were shaking. It was too ridiculous. Having a father called Billy-Bob was totally ridiculous – probably too ridiculous not to be true.

Myrtle having a lover had been more ridiculous. Even in an essay she'd tried to write, the part where Captain Amberley came home from the war and found out his wife had a ten-month-old baby had never been believable. And as if a man would fall in love with a baby his wife had cheated on him to get – unless he was a complete fool, which Robert wasn't.

If it was true, it changed everything. Even Amberley. That house had always belonged to her because it belonged to Myrtle, and before Myrtle, to Myrtle's father. She had no claim on it now. She was a bag of rubbish left behind in a vacated room, rubbish Myrtle had picked up and found a use for.

Cara turned away, walked away from braised chicken and mashed potatoes.

Robert rose to follow her.

'Leave her,' Myrtle said, and moments later, Cara came back carrying the heavy family Bible.

'Swear on it. Both of you.'

Myrtle took the book. 'You were born to a twenty-year-old lodger. Her name was Jennifer Hooper. She had a small son, Jimmy, and two daughters living with their grandmother.'

'I said swear.'

'I swear by Almighty God that what I've told you is the truth, pet,' Myrtle said and handed the Bible across the table to Robert, Cara's eyes following it. She knew what that Bible meant to her parents.

'Me too, poppet. I still have the telegram Mummy sent to me about her lodger. I swear,' he added then placed the book on the table, and Cara sat.

'If she already had three kids, why give me away?'

'Her situation was complicated,' Myrtle said.

'How?'

How could she explain Jenny Hooper's situation? Tell an already confused child she'd been born of rape. That was a truth which must never be told.

'Jenny had a brief association with an American sailor. I know little else about him, pet.'

'What was his other name?'

Myrtle shook her head. 'She mentioned only his Christian name, Billy-Bob.'

'She must have been a moll,' Cara said and Myrtle's serving spoon flinched at the word, spilling gravy.

'Rules alter in wartime.'

'What did she look like?'

Look in the mirror, Myrtle thought. Cara was Jenny around the eyes, the brow. She had her colouring, her hair. Taller than Jenny. At twelve she'd outgrown Myrtle, at fourteen she stood eye to eye with Robert, measured by the army doctors at five foot eight.

'You're very much like her,' she said. And perhaps in more than appearance. 'Eat your meal, pet, before it gets cold.'

Cara picked up her fork and used it, with her fingers, to break the meat away from the bone. Myrtle caught Robert's eye, willing him not to demand acceptable table manners tonight.

Is a child's destiny set in stone at birth? she thought. John and Beth had daughters. They'd given their parents not one moment of trouble, had met boys who fitted so well into the family. Until puberty, until high school, Cara had been perfection.

Perhaps they should blame themselves for Cara's rebellion. They'd disrupted her life when they'd moved to Traralgon, taken her away from a home she'd loved, from her friends.

'Stop staring at me,' Cara said.

'I was thinking of the night Jenny placed you into my arms. I didn't doubt that God had sent her to my door to bring me a priceless gift.'

'Now you wish she'd had me in a public toilet and flushed it.'

Robert placed his fork down to butter a slice of bread. 'Remember when you used to nag us daily for a black and white puppy? Imagine for a moment what it might have been like had you given up all hope of ever owning your own puppy, then along came a stranger and placed Bowser into your arms.'

'You would have made me give it to a lost dogs' home,' Cara said, mouth full.

She had Myrtle's voice, but Jenny's tongue. She had Jenny's hands – and perhaps her table manners.

'Imagine we'd allowed you to raise that puppy,' Robert said. 'That you'd loved it, fed it, cared for it for fifteen years, then one day, instead of greeting you with a wagging tail, it snarled and bit your hand. Would you stop loving it, or decide that poor old Bowser had a pain, that his bite was the only way he could tell you about it?'

'I asked both of you if I was adopted.' Cara's fork was down. Her plate was clean. 'You said I wasn't.'

'We didn't adopt you. Had we lied to you then, you would have asked more questions. We told Robert's mother we'd adopted you and have spent our lives lying to her,' Myrtle said.

'You would have had to adopt me somehow to get my birth certificate.'

'You were registered as our daughter. Mrs Collins and Miss Robertson believe I gave birth to you. To this day they believe they witnessed your birth.'

'How?'

'Your mother wandered around Amberley with a cushion tucked beneath her pinny,' Robert said.

'She did not!'

'I did,' Myrtle said.

'That old maroon cushion she won't give up,' Robert said.

'You didn't.'

'Did so,' Robert said.

Like the old game Robert's shadow puppets had played on Amberley's parlour wall, back when Cara was four or five, the two old hens arguing over who had laid that egg.

'That's why your mum won't throw the raggedy old thing away,' Robert said.

'It fits my back,' Myrtle said.

'How could you do that?'

'I did,' Myrtle said, then told the tale of Jenny, a prisoner for three months in their private rooms at Amberley, how the passage door was never opened, how Jenny had stitched long tapes to that old cushion one morning then chased Myrtle around the parlour table with it, singing her own words to *Greensleeves*.

'She sang?'

'She sang beautifully.'

That's when Cara knew it was all true, and when Myrtle sang Jenny's ditty, indelibly imprinted in her mind.

> *There was a landlady named Myrtle, who lived in a shell, like a turtle,*
>
> *Until one fine day, she decided to play, and Myrtle the turtle proved fertile.*
>
> *Oh, Myrtle the turtle was glowing, her stomach was definitely showing.*
>
> *The lodgers aghast at her colourful past, each week watched it growing and growing.'*

Myrtle couldn't hold a tune to save her life. Her off-key song was more convincing than ten thousand words. She couldn't make a rhyme to save her life either.

For an instant Cara saw beyond her mother's butter-won't-melt-in-my-mouth facade, saw a forty-year-old woman so desperate to have her own baby she'd been willing to look ridiculous for months, to do something more illegal than forging a signature at a bank – and just to get a baby.

'Is that why you called me Cara Jeanette, because she was a Jeanette?'

'She was a Jennifer, Jennifer Carolyn,' Myrtle said. 'She chose your name.' Myrtle reached out a hand, not touching Cara's but placing it fingertip to fingertip. 'I suggested Cecelia, for your grandmother, and she said she had a sister Cecelia and that I wasn't saddling you with that name for life. I have always believed that she chose Cara Jeanette so she might leave you her initials.'

'Turned-around initials,' Cara said, then looked down at her mother's hand. A small, plump hand with perfect almond-shaped fingernails. She looked at her own hand, longer and with flat, atrocious fingernails.

'Did I get my rotten fingernails from her?'

Myrtle smiled and nodded. 'When she saw your tiny hands for the first time, she said, "God help her, Myrt. She's got my rotten fingernails." She was intrigued by hands. Do you remember Mr Nightingale? He was our minister until you were six or seven years old?'

'That tall one?'

'Very tall. He had incredibly long, fine fingers,' Myrtle said. 'Spider-hands, Jenny named him. She told me one day that his hand dissolved into spider legs when she shook it. I recall a Sunday afternoon, shortly after I had begun wearing the cushion, which I dared not wear to church. He became –'

'You gave up church to get me?'

'I did. Mr Nightingale became concerned and he called on me one morning to see if I was well. An unmarried man, I had invited him to lunch on occasion, and had no choice but to invite him inside. His eyes fastened onto my cushion –'

'Where was Jenny?'

'In the bedroom. If we had someone at the door, or at the rent hatch, she hid in the bedroom. I can see Mr Nightingale's hands now, his long fingers near dancing against the leg of his trousers, counting. He knew your father was overseas and how long he'd been over there. Then Jimmy began slapping at the bedroom door, calling Jenny.'

'Jimmy. He's my brother,' Cara said.

'He was a delightful little boy.'

'Were his hands like mine?'

'I don't believe so. Jenny once said that had he not inherited his grandfather's double-jointed thumbs, she would have been better off.' Myrtle's hand had crept forward to cover Cara's.

'You didn't call a doctor or anything for her when I was being born?'

Myrtle shook her head. 'She was foolishly brave. I recall standing at the kitchen door, too afraid to enter, the wireless playing at full volume – Joseph Schmidt singing "A Star Falls From Heaven".'

'What if she hadn't kept her word, and you were wandering around with the cushion up your dress? How did you know she wouldn't change her mind?'

'I knew Jenny.'

'What was her other name?'

'Hooper – though, I doubt she was married to her tall soldier. When he was reported missing, she wasn't informed through the official channels. Her grandmother sent a telegram, addressed to Jennifer Morrison.'

'Where was she from?'

'Woody Creek. It's a small town in Victoria.'

'Daddy should have told me when I asked the first time.'

'How do parents tell a child they have taken her illegally, signed documents dishonestly?' Robert asked.

'You could have told me at Easter time when we were driving home.'

'You were not being very pleasant when we were driving home,' Robert said.

Cara took Myrtle's hand and turned it palm up, placing her own beside it. 'They don't even look related. I'm an alien.'

Robert placed his own hand on the table. 'We're all from different planets, poppet, but we've done well enough together for a lot of years.'

'We did before we came to this town. I hate it here, hate everyone here.'

'You don't know enough people to make that statement.'

'I don't want to know anyone else. I want to go home.'

'We will when I retire.'

'That's years away.'

'Not so long, not once you get to my age,' he said.

'What did Dino do to get expelled from school?'

'Who?'

'Dino Collins – James Collins.'

'He's trouble, poppet. That's all you need to know.'

'It isn't. I'm almost fifteen. Tell me why he was expelled.'

'It was to do with one of the young female teachers,' Myrtle said.

'Was it about sex?'

That word was never used in Myrtle's house. She flinched from it, but replied. 'He molested her, Cara, and if not for the school cleaner, it may have been worse than it was.'

'And that goes no further than this room,' Robert said.

'Why protect him if he did something like that?'

'I want your word on it.'

Cara shrugged. 'Take me up to live with Uncle John and Aunty Beth until you retire.'

'That's not an option,' he said.

'I can't go back to school here.' She looked at the clock. Quarter to seven already. She'd told Rosie she'd see her at half past seven to finalise their arrangements for tomorrow. She'd told her she'd get the money from her bank account too. Rosie would hate her for not getting it, and hate her more when she told her she wasn't going to Sydney. They'd all hate her.

'I want to live with Uncle John and go to school with Pete.'

'Your home is with us, poppet.'

LIKE RIDING A BIKE

*D*riving a car is a little like riding a bike. Once learned it is never forgotten. A skill becomes rusty when unused for twenty years. Only surface rust; it brushed off easily enough. The road rules had altered. Back when Laurie had taught Jenny to drive, she'd learnt two road rules. Don't hit anything, and it's a good idea to give way to the man on the right. Vroni, self-elected driving tutor, presented her with a book of rules. A hard taskmaster, Vroni.

Then another letter came from the Keatings' solicitors, and on the same day the hospital rang. Margot's baby was ready to go home.

On the Friday, two weeks into July, Vroni at her side, Jenny picked up Raelene from school then she drove all the way to Box Hill, where Florence couldn't look her in the eye. No time to waste then, Vroni at the wheel, they continued on to the hospital.

'Fifty per cent of Maisy's grandkids have got pale purple eyes. She'll know who that baby belongs to the minute she sees it,' Jenny said.

'Is the other grandmother still planning to raise her?'

'I haven't heard from her. I think she's got her hands full with Margot.'

The baby's eyes weren't purple. It didn't have the Macdonalds' stumpy hands. It was bald. Margot had been bald until she was eighteen months old. Probably end up with her snow-white hair, Jenny thought, but something had to be done about it, so she did it. By five, Vroni was fighting her way through peak-hour traffic, home to Frankston, Jenny in the rear seat, the hospital-scented bundle in her arms.

The hospital had supplied them with a sample of baby formula. They bought a large tin of it at the chemist's shop, bought two dozen napkins at a department store, three tiny singlets, three flannelette gowns, three bunny rugs.

'Three enough?' Vroni asked.

'One on the baby, one on the clothes line, one sicked on,' Jenny said, her arm aching beneath the small weight, her eye on a cane carry basket. They bought the basket too, and half-a-dozen feeding bottles.

Two women with a new toy, one of them childless and, according to her, barely knowing a baby's backside from its elbow. The other's motherhood skills a little rusty. They were still fussing with the baby when Jim arrived in a taxi at eight and Vroni left them to it.

He read the solicitor's letter while the baby slept in her basket on the table. They went to bed in a room smelling of baby. And were shocked awake at five-thirty by a tremulous siren.

Saturday disappeared in the sterilising of bottles, the changing of that minute backside, the washing, the making up of bottles of formula and in the watching of baby lips sucking life from that teat.

The Keatings brought Raelene home on Sunday evening, and Florence, uncommunicative in Box Hill, wanted to hold the baby, to smell the scent of her, and to drip tears for the infants she couldn't conceive, while Jenny told her a tale of a Woody Creek mother, and of a baby born early.

'How many children has she got?'

'Seven,' Jenny said.

'Some people have all the luck, don't they. I'd sell my soul to have one. What did they name her?'

Elsie had named her Gertrude, though Jenny couldn't bring herself to admit it, not to Florence.

'Trudy,' she said.

'That's pretty.'

It was a definite improvement on Gertrude.

Jim got a lift back to Box Hill with them. Raelene wouldn't have a bar of him or the baby.

'Why do you have to look after her?'

'Because her mummy can't look after her yet, like Florence couldn't look after you when you were tiny.'

'She can now, and I want to live at her house, not here.'

'The baby will be going soon.'

'And him too?'

'No,' Jenny said. 'Not him.'

No driving lesson that day. No school, no work, and the sky threatening to rain on a clothes line full of napkins. Day gone before Jenny saw daylight, and Jim arriving with the rain.

'On a Monday night?'

'I don't want him to come here again,' Raelene said.

Jenny did. Tonight she needed him.

There's something about grandchildren. They're not yours, but they're somehow connected into your bloodstream. Deny it you may, but they know. They see your face, and their silly little gummy mouths open in a gaping twisted smile. You know it is only wind, or your logic knows. Your heart doesn't. It starts to melt.

Not by any stretch of the imagination could Trudy be called a pretty baby. Some were. Raelene was. She'd looked like a kewpie doll with her mob of black curls – Florence's kewpie doll. Her behaviour that day, that night, was more demon than doll.

Jenny got Raelene settled sometime after ten, in the double bed. Jim would have to sleep in the kitchen.

They sat late then, Jenny balancing baby and bottle with one hand, drinking tea and eating toast with the other. There had been no time to cook a meal that night.

'Not much of her,' he said, watching her place the baby into her basket. 'Doesn't it scare the daylights out of you, handling her?'

'I've handled a few.'

'You look good together,' he said.

'It feels weird. She's not mine. She's a whole patchwork of genes accidentally come together. A smidgen of old black Wadi, a pinch of Harry, a sprinkle of Juliana Conti and Archie Foote — not too much Macdonald — and she feels like mine.'

'A blending of nations,' he said.

'What would you say if I said I wanted us to raise her?'

'That you were giving me a second chance to do something worthwhile,' he said.

Margot's bed was still there in the kitchen. Eighteen years ago, he'd picked Jenny up and carried her to his camp bed in Monk's cellar. Joint will drew them to Margot's. He'd grown accustomed to Jenny seeing him take that leg off, to sleeping with it beside the bed.

That was the night they made love, the night the butterflies flew again. That was the night Jenny's world tilted, then righted itself, the night she kissed the tears from his face while Trudy slept on in her basket, on the table.

Dear Florence,

I'm not having Raelene taken away from me by some judge who hasn't got a clue what he's talking about, so if you are willing for us to work out our own arrangements, I'm willing to talk about it . . .

Dear Elsie and Harry,

Jim and I are going to raise Trudy. We know you love her and want to be in her life, and the only way we'll manage that is if we move back there, which we are not going to do until Teddy and Margot sign the enclosed papers giving up all claims to her.

Jim and I are going to adopt her, through the courts. I suggest you don't tell Margot what it is she's signing.

Jim has written to his Willama solicitors about Vern's house. It's been vacant for a while. They say it needs a bit of work . . .

Scott and Wilson, the Willama solicitors, replied by return mail, with a manila envelope containing a bulk of papers. Jim had been six years old when his mother died on an operating table. Vern Hooper was her second husband, Jim her only issue. Her first husband's money had been placed into a trust fund for her son. Untouched for thirty-odd years, it had ballooned.

Scott and Wilson released money enough to buy a two-toned Ford Customline. Too big for Jenny, but it fitted Jim's long legs. A Frankston solicitor was given the job of fixing up the paperwork which would give Raelene into the Keatings' care.

Jenny took her driving test in August, in Vroni's car. Jim left his job at the timber yards on 29 August, the day Florence and Clarrie drove to the solicitor's office to sign the papers.

Happy Florence that day, bawling Florence as she hugged, kissed Jenny, hugged Jim who, not expecting it, almost lost his footing. Clarrie shook their hands.

Raelene, who didn't like that baby and called Jim 'Gimpy', didn't kiss or shake hands with anyone. Poked her tongue out at Gimpy, or Trudy, as the Keatings' car drove away.

The Frankston solicitor was responsible for Jenny's second registry-office wedding. He'd told them they were wasting their time thinking about adopting the baby unless they married.

Jenny's 'until death do us part' vow sounded different the second time. No new ring necessary. The gold band she'd worn for sixteen years, though well worn, had worn well. It came off for two minutes while the words were read, then *Jen and Jim, 1942* slid back to where it belonged.

WOODY CREEK GOSSIP

Charlie's new tenant had mowed Vern Hooper's lawns before vacating the big house on the corner. It took a while for a buffalo lawn to become a cow paddock. Vern's lawns were long enough to qualify. Weeds, ostracised for years, denied their right to breed, had got their roots down and shed their million seeds. Birds bred beneath the abandoned veranda – as did a few of the bored town youth. Beer bottles, cigarette packets, a condom told its own tale.

The rosebush hedge, denied its winter pruning, reached out to grasp the attention of walkers and bike riders. Windblown newspapers snagged on rose thorns, waved to passers-by, while brown paper bags danced merrily along the verandas, sidestepping the splatter of birds who found perches at night in the rafters.

'What a terrible waste of good living space,' people said. 'They've got six bedrooms in that house, two bathrooms, two sitting rooms.'

'They say it's sold. Marylyn was saying that there was a car parked in the drive for two hours on Wednesday. She didn't recognise the driver, but he had a key.'

'Another Melbourne retiree. The town is getting overrun by Melbourne retirees.'

'She said he looked too young to be one of them.'

The chap came again, left again. The rains came and left. The rosebush hedge had begun to shake off its spiny mood when they came in force, an army of small trucks, utes, sedans, to park in Vern's drive, on his cow-paddock lawns. One came with paint cans and ladder, one with rolls of carpet. One was Percival Scott, a Willama solicitor.

Maisy Macdonald heard about Percival Scott from Nelly Dobson, who had been employed by the Hooper family for years. Together they came up with a possible answer. Scott and Wilson had been Vern Hooper's solicitors, back before the war. They decided that one of the Hoopers was moving back to town.

Vern Hopper, dead since '52, had produced three offspring. All three were still living. Jim, the only son, had spent two years in a Jap prisoner-of-war camp. He'd lost half of one leg, some said his sight, and a few still believed he'd lost his mind over there. It was generally agreed that he wouldn't be the one moving back to town.

Lorna, unwed, heading for fifty, had made her views on Woody Creek society very clear during her years in the town She wouldn't come back. Which left Margaret.

'It will be Margaret. She was on the Red Cross committee for years,' Maisy said.

'She got married, you know. She brought her husband up here that time to their manager's funeral. What age would she be now?'

'Well into her forties. When my Rachel was nineteen, Margaret was twenty-six,' Maisy said, doing her sums on her fingers. She'd produced eight daughters before presenting her husband, George, with twin sons. 'She'd have to be forty-eight, or close to it,' Maisy said.

Vern's roses were sprouting leaves, even buds, when the furniture van arrived. Two chaps unloaded a large refrigerator, a washing machine, a bed, table and chairs – and a baby's cot.

It warranted a phone call from the nearest neighbour to her mother. 'Someone is moving in. They just unloaded a cot. One of those polished wooden ones.' The nearest neighbour had a fine view of Vern Hooper's driveway from her eastern window.

Dawn Macdonald worked at the telephone exchange. She passed the news on to her mother. Maisy passed it on to umpteen more, and before that day was done, the town had Margaret Hooper breeding up a change-of-life family.

'She was always a gentle dithery little thing. She'd probably make a good mother.'

*

They came on a Thursday in late September, in a showroom-new, two-toned green Ford Customline, and for minutes the telephone exchange ran hot.

'It's Jenny Morrison. She's standing on Vern Hooper's veranda, Mum, and she's had another one. It's in one of those baby baskets, and there's a tall grey-headed bloke with her who has to be Jim Hooper.'

'What are you talking about?'

'Jenny Morrison. She's got a baby and the bloke with her is unlocking Vern's front door.'

'No.'

'I'm telling you she is, and that bloke is definitely Jim Hooper. He just took his glasses off.'

'The last I heard, he was in an insane asylum.'

'She never was too fussy. Wasn't she on with him years ago?'

'She had a boy to him. Her husband is hardly cold in his grave! How old is the baby?'

'How can I see that from where I am? It doesn't look heavy. They've gone inside. He's limping badly.'

'That's how she ran him down.'

'I thought he was supposed to be half-blind?'

'He was wearing dark glasses at Vern's funeral and didn't seem to recognise me when I spoke to him.'

'They've got a car, a big classy-looking two-toned green thing.'

There were more walkers about that afternoon, a few stopping to look at Vern's overgrown roses. At midday, smoke was seen coming from Vern's kitchen chimney. At one-thirty Jenny Morrison was sighted hanging napkins on the clothes line, and again the telephone exchange ran hot.

Two o'clock and Elsie Hall, who never walked into town, walked in alone, or walked as far as Hooper's corner. She went inside and didn't come out. At four-thirty, Josie, Elsie's youngest, jumped off the school bus and made a beeline for Hooper's.

'Darkies wandering in and out of his house, Vern must be rolling over in his grave. She didn't bring that retarded boy back with her?'

'I heard that she put him in a home a few days after his father was killed.'

'What about that dark-headed girl who was supposed to be Ray King's?'

'She's not with them, or if she is, I haven't sighted her. When did Ray King die, Mum?'

'July of '58. During the floods. Why?'

'I was just working out if that baby could be his. I wonder how long she's been on with Jim Hooper.'

'She broke up her sister's wedding by getting pregnant to him, I can tell you that. He was engaged at one time to Sissy Morrison.'

'Hang on. She's just come out with the two Halls. They're walking towards the car. Jesus! She has come up in the world! She just got into the driver's seat. I'm hanging up, Mum. Jim's out, looking at the roses. I'm going to pop in and welcome him home while she's not around. Call me back in fifteen minutes.'

Jen and Jim's every move was reported that day. Robert Fulton, who had played cricket with Jim before the war, knocked on Vern's door at six, after he'd closed his shop. He didn't drive away until seven. The town would get nothing out of him. The Fultons were a close-mouthed lot, as was John McPherson and Amy, his schoolteacher wife, who were invited inside at seven-thirty and didn't leave until after ten.

For days Jenny Morrison and Jim Hooper were discussed beneath the butcher's veranda, in the newspaper shop, on telephones, over fences, though not in Charlie's shop. Women eyed Georgie when they popped in for a pound of sugar, a few working so hard on questions they could legitimately ask that they forgot what they'd come in to buy.

Thank God for Maisy Macdonald. She called on the couple with one of her lemon meringue pies and came away full of information.

Trudy Juliana Hooper had been born on 11 April. She'd arrived two months early, and spent her first two months of life in hospital, a lot of that time in an oxygen crib. Maisy told the town that Jenny and Jim Hooper had been together since the night of the Magpies and the Demons grand final, twelve months ago.

'Allowing for it to have been born two months early, she had her pants off that same night,' the people said.

*

Trudy could have been Jim's. She had Teddy's brown eyes, his long legs, no hair yet, or not enough to say if it would be dark or fair.

Margot wore the scar of her caesarean birth, though no one, other than the Hall family, Georgie, Jack Thompson, Jenny, Jim, Vroni Andrews, her doctor partner, the medical staff at the Frankston hospital and a Frankston solicitor knew it – more than enough without Maisy, great-grandmother to that baby, knowing. She hadn't been told, wouldn't be told. According to Elsie, Margot had suffered a nervous breakdown. On her return to town, Margot had explained her illness to Maisy as indigestion and constipation.

She never looked at that scar, never touched it, never stood naked when there was light enough to see it.

There was a second scar on her belly, to the side, smaller, shaped like an eye, where she'd pushed the three-inch blade of Jenny's vegetable knife in deep enough to let the air out of her belly. It had worked too. They'd put her to sleep at the hospital and when she'd woken up her indigestion had gone.

For a long time, Elsie convinced herself that Margot would come around, that she'd agree to marry Teddy and raise her own baby. A born mother, Elsie, a mother since Joey's birth when she was twelve or thirteen years old, a mother to her nephew and niece and to five more of her own and Harry's – and to Margot. Elsie never mentioned the scars, to Trudy or Margot. She'd wanted to raise her granddaughter, but for Margot's sake had delayed bringing the baby home. Jenny and Jim had saved her making the choice between Margot and Trudy.

At forty-eight, Elsie's hair was a salt and pepper grey. Her lighter hair colouring darkened her complexion, making her touch of colour more obvious. She still raised a few stares when she came into town, which she did, daily now.

It was assumed by most she'd been given the job of nurse-maid. Vern Hooper had always employed someone to do his dirty work. It was generally agreed that Jenny Morrison thought she was someone, living in Vern Hooper's house, driving her latest husband around in a brand-new car.

'Have you found out what happened to her dark-headed girl?'

'Her mother claimed her.'

'Mother? Jenny had her to that Vinnie dago bloke, didn't she?'

'I've told you before. Ray brought those two kids with him when he came back. It's turned out that he stole them from their mother while she was in hospital, or so Maisy says.'

'I never did like the look of that man. You remember how his mother died?'

Give a kid a new toy and in days the novelty will wear off and he'll swap it or leave it out in the weather. The novelty wore off

Jenny, Jim and their baby. Within two weeks Jenny could back that fancy car out and turn it towards Forest Road or Willama, and not a curtain would lift nor a phone ring.

CHARLIE'S ACCIDENT

*O*n the second Sunday in October an ambulance screamed its bad news through town. A hit-and-run driver had knocked Charlie White off his bike, out on Cemetery Road. With no house now where he might visit his Jeany, each Sunday he'd been riding his bike out to the cemetery to sit and talk with her a while.

A crowd gathered to watch the ambulance take him away. He looked dead. Joss Palmer, an army medic during the war, diagnosed a smashed leg and arm and a dented head.

'What a way to go,' the people said.

'At his age, he never should have been riding that bike.'

'Hilda tried to put him in the old folks' home a year ago. That redhead should have left him where he was put.'

Anyone who knew Charlie knew he didn't take chances on his bike. He'd been riding it for as long as Georgie could remember. She phoned his granddaughter. The cop who had replaced Jack Thompson, who would never replace him, came back from wherever he'd been all day. Georgie and Joss Palmer spoke to him. He barely knew old Charlie White. Didn't care about him.

He knew his age, and when they told him Charlie had always been a careful rider, he doubted their word. They told him about Charlie's trouble with the feral tenants, and of the robbery, how one of the blokes locked up for the robbery had been married to a Duffy, that the Duffy family owned land just out past the cemetery, and at any given time there were car loads of drunken fools speeding in and out of that place.

The new copper drove out there. The Duffy family had seen nothing and knew nothing – which most in town would agree was pretty close to right.

No one had seen the impact. Two kids had seen a dark blue car racing off, then turning right onto South Road.

Long gone, back to the city, or back to where it'd come from. And finding out who had hit him wouldn't do Charlie a lot of good anyway. He wasn't dead but close to it. The doctor Georgie spoke to didn't expect him to live through the night. He'd snapped his shin and thigh bones, broken his arm and maybe his collarbone. They didn't waste any plaster on him.

'We're keeping him comfortable,' he said.

They kept him comfortable through the night, through the next day, and still no plaster.

'We're keeping him pain-free,' a sister said. 'Has his family been told?'

They didn't know Charlie White's family. They didn't know old Charlie either. He regained consciousness on the third morning.

The young doctor didn't know Georgie, but she was beginning to know herself. She attacked him verbally, as Gertrude might have. He wasted a lot of plaster on Charlie that day, and that night Georgie sat with the old man, feeding him slices of preserved peach from a can. With one arm in plaster and the other shoulder out of action, he couldn't feed himself.

'Did I ever tell you that your blood is worth bottling, Rusty?' he said, slurping peach slices from a fork.

'A few times, Charlie.'

She told him she'd given Emma Fulton a job for a while. Charlie trusted the Fultons, and Emma was always available when they called. The shop wasn't much more than a one-man business. Georgie could have managed it alone, had there not been more than Charlie and that shop on her mind.

Too much more on her mind. Jenny and Jim, and Jack Thompson who wouldn't stop phoning, and Margot. She was in hospital too, with a miscarriage this time, thank God – and even Elsie saying thank God – and telling Georgie every second breath to marry Jack, or to move into town with Jenny and Jim.

There were four spare bedrooms in Vern Hooper's house, large rooms, with floors that didn't rock and a huge empty sitting room, a library too, with bookshelves on two walls and only a bare scattering of books on them. Verandas to sit on, lawns to walk on and all Georgie's for the taking – as was Jack Thompson's two-bedroom East Malvern flat.

They moved Charlie down to the old folks' annex when they realised he wasn't going to die. He wasn't happy.

'Half of 'em are gaga,' he said. And no doubt a damn sight easier on the staff than he. He demanded trousers. They clad him in a gown.

'They can't get trousers on you, Charlie. Start behaving yourself or they'll start putting you in pink gowns.'

Hated leaving him there in his nightgown. Hated going home too. Hated driving by Hooper's corner, scared stiff that Jenny had gone and made another mistake.

All of her life, Georgie had known about Jim Hooper. She'd imagined him to be something more than the lanky yard of pump water that he was, who limped like Vern Hooper had limped and at times resembled his father, or his hair and his jaw did. Different eyes, nose, probably a different personality, not that she'd seen enough of any personality yet to be sure on that point.

She hadn't seen a lot of Margot's baby either – and didn't want to. It had spent weeks in an oxygen crib. Kids who spent too much time in those cribs came out of them with problems. A reader, Georgie, a hoarder of useless information, and one who had lived too long with Donny to want to go through that again.

As had Jenny. And Georgie didn't understand her, and at times wondered if she'd ever known her. The Jenny she'd known wouldn't have lived in Vern Hooper's house. He'd kidnapped Jimmy, or his daughter had. Vern might have been dead, but to Georgie that house represented what he'd been. And she'd given up Raelene.

Twelve months ago Georgie had a little sister. Now she didn't. Like with Jimmy. She'd had a brother – then she hadn't. Twelve months ago, she'd had Jenny. Lost her too. And now she'd lost Charlie to the old fogies' home.

She had a chance to clean up the storeroom while he was away and was considering taking his overcoat down to him, to cover his gowns, when she lifted it from its hook behind the shop's back door. And found his share certificates, on a wire spike, hung over that same hook, a pile of them. She tossed the overcoat and stood, bug-eyed, leafing through flyspecked, yellowing paper. Valuable paper some of it.

Didn't know what to do with his spike. Knew he'd bought those shares with ill-gotten gains, that if she took them over to the bank manager, it might somehow get Charlie into strife with the taxman.

Didn't want the responsibility of knowing about them. Thought about ringing Jack. Considered hanging them back where she'd found them. Thought about Jim Hooper. Jenny had said that some of his money was in shares. He should know something about them.

He knew a lot. He told her they needed to be in the bank vault. She told him about Charlie's filching from the cash drawer, about the tax accountant going through him not too long ago.

'Your name is on a few of them,' Jenny said. 'He could get you into trouble.'

'Get a safety-deposit box,' Jim said. 'In your joint names.'
'Where?'

'At any bank.'

Not Woody Creek's. Everyone would know about it.

'We're going down to Willama on Friday,' Jenny said. 'Come with us and we'll do it there.'

She rode in the back seat, Margot's baby crowing in her car basket beside her, and growing too big to fit that basket. She didn't look like Donny, or sound like him.

Jim went with her to the bank. He knew what he was doing. She stood back, allowing him to do it. She signed papers, then got rid of the shares, now sorted by Jenny into *his* and *hers* and placed in separate envelopes. *His* were worth a fortune, according to Jim. *Hers* were worth big money.

They saw Charlie that afternoon and he'd got his trousers, washed-out and baggy pyjama trousers. He had four fingertips sticking out of his plaster cast, and with them shook Jim's hand. He wasn't interested in his safety-deposit box. He wanted to go home.

'We'll talk about it when your plaster is off and you can walk, Charlie,' Georgie said.

*

On Gertrude's land it was generally agreed that Teddy and Margot had the sex instincts of rabbits, and smaller brains. Small or not, Teddy's had been wired directly into motors. Georgie hadn't spoken to him since Margot's miscarriage. She had to when her old ute went 'Bang!' And stopped dead. Roy, the garage bloke, was in Melbourne visiting his kids.

'Rear axle,' Teddy said.

'Can you fix it?'

'We'll have one somewhere.' In the shed, or behind the shed, or maybe under Roy's house.

'How long.'

'Tomorrow or the day after – if I can find one. One side of the diff has to come out.'

'Ta,' she said.

*

By December, Charlie was escaping again from gaga land, with the aid of two walking sticks. A determined old coot; if they'd given him a pair of trousers and boots, he might have made it home. In pyjamas and slippers, he was an easy target. They kept picking him up, taking him back. His daughter wanted him assessed for mental incompetency. He assessed the assessors, asked them if they knew their thirteen times tables, then showed them that he did. That was the day Georgie decided to kidnap him again.

They made an appointment for ten o'clock on Sunday morning, around the corner from the old fogies' annex.

He needed help to get into the ute, and more help to get out, but there was no happier man in Woody Creek that day.

'Did I ever tell you your blood is worth bottling, Rusty?'

'You're repeating yourself, Charlie White. I'll tell the gaga assessors on you.'

He ate Christmas dinner with the Fulton family, always had since Jeany died. He gave the many Fulton grandkids ten bob each, always had.

Georgie ate with Jenny, Jim, John and Amy McPherson, and Trudy seated in a high chair, chewing on a chicken bone, her Father Christmas hat fallen over one eye. Eight months old now, old enough to enjoy being the centre of attention and playing for it.

It was a good Christmas, normal. It brought back memories of Georgie's last Christmas.

Wondered if Jack was eating dinner in Molliston.

*

Not a good Christmas at Elsie's table. Margot and Teddy ate there, though not side by side. They didn't speak, didn't look at each other.

'What the hell do you two think you're playing at?' Josie said. 'It's no secret that you sleep together.'

'Shut your trap,' Teddy said.

Josie, the last of Elsie and Harry's brood, was a freckle-faced redhead. Brian, the second youngest, was fair and not as tall as his brothers. Teddy and Maudy had inherited Elsie's darker than average hair and complexion, which had never worried Maudy. It worried Teddy. Since childhood, he'd resented Brian's fair skin and Ronnie and Josie's red hair. They'd spent their childhoods arguing, and the older they grew, the more they argued.

'Stop!' Harry demanded. 'You give a man indigestion.'

'As long as Margot doesn't end up with it again,' Josie said.

The table erupted into laughter, initially, but Margot hadn't inherited Jenny's fingernails. Unworn by labour, hers were long, strong. Josie, who sat on Margot's left, wore the proof of their strength in three long raking gouges down her cheek.

Josie had less weight than Margot but a lot more height. Raised amid brothers, she'd learnt early how to hit back. She hit back, her open palm connecting with Margot's jaw, the full weight of her arm behind it. The last they heard from Margot that Christmas Day was her *ahzeeing* wail across the goat paddock.

'She's been a sister to you,' Elsie said. 'To all of you.'

'Try explaining that to Ted, Mum,' Brian said.

'Keep your mouth shut, you whitey bastard, or I'll shut it for you,' Teddy said.

'Keep your fly shut and we might, you black bastard,' Brian said.

No more eating was done. Brian and Josie took off towards Flanagan's, the short cut to town.

Ronnie, who shared a room with Teddy and threatened regularly to leave home, started tossing his belongings into his car.

'Stop being silly, Ronnie,' Elsie said.

'I'm going this time, Mum. Move her in with him. What you can't change, you accept.'

He drove into town to phone up his girl in Mildura. Brian and Josie saw his car parked beside the phone box.

'We're going with you,' they said.

All three drove home to pack. Elsie's bawling may have worked on one, it didn't work on three. Harry, white-faced and chain-smoking, gave up and walked over to the creek. Margot spent the afternoon upending Georgie's room, looking for the key to her bedroom door confiscated by Georgie months ago.

She was still looking when Georgie came home. 'What do you think you're doing in here?'

'You've thtill got that thtupid photo.' Margot had the framed newspaper mug shot of Laurie Morgan in her hand.

'Put it back where you found it, Margot.'

'Ath if he careth about you.'

Georgie manually retrieved the photograph, and was manually removing Margot from her room when Jack Thompson drove in. She released Margot and walked out to his car.

He drove her out to a lane behind the old slaughteryards and they walked down to a bend in the creek where she sat on the bank, pitching twigs into the water, watching them float downstream, while he spoke of Melbourne, about Charlie, asked about the new cop. She had little to say.

'Mum said to invite you over for dinner.'

'No thanks.'

'I need you with me, Georgie. I love you. The flat has got two rooms. You can have your own room and I promise I won't pressure you into doing anything you're not ready to do.'

She sighed. 'I'm only six months older than I was in June, Jack, and Charlie is about ten years older.'

'You should have left him where he was.'

'You're starting to sound like his daughter.'

'Has she been to see him?'

'Ha.' She pitched a clod of earth, watched it plop, watched the ripples circling. 'She rang me and blasted a hole through from my left ear to my right, threatened to have the law onto me if I didn't take him back to where I'd got him.'

'He can't look after himself, love.'

'Joss Palmer helps out with him. Mrs Fulton brings him down a meal at night. A few of the old blokes wander around to talk to him. He's happy, and I'm not going to be the one to take what little he's got left away from him. And that is the end of the story.'

'Are you happy?'

'Happy enough.' She pitched another clod, watched the ripples fade, die.

'I wake up missing you. I go to bed missing you, love.'

She stood, brushed grass from the seat of her shorts. 'I'm too young to jump into something I don't understand and have never understood and, to tell the truth, don't want to understand.' She slipped off her rubber thongs and walked into the creek, stepping carefully through slimy mud, clinging waterweed, and over submerged and slippery timber.

'What are you doing?'

'I don't want to breed, Jack, not now, not ever. Don't call me any more. You mess up my head,' she said and walked deeper.

'Get out of there.'

Waist deep now in water, she tucked her thongs beneath her bra straps, then dived, not re-emerging until she was well downstream.

'Georgie!'

Swam faster, her arms cutting the water, swimming hard until she rounded the curve.

'Georgie!'

Heard him. The creek altered sound. Just a bird, calling to its lost mate. Couldn't get back to him if she'd wanted to. You can't swim far against the current, so she swam with it.

She knew that creek, knew it twisted and turned like a snake with a bellyache. She knew every inch of the forest on the far side of the creek. Had roamed there with Teddy, set rabbit traps there. Knew if she swam down to the next bend, she wouldn't be far from home, as the crow flew.

*

Brian, Josie and Ronnie Hall left home that night. Only Teddy now, and Lenny, a big blue-eyed blond-headed football hero, engaged to a Willama girl for eighteen months and planning to live at home for eighteen months more.

They'd bought a block of land out on Cemetery Road, and with both of them working and socking every penny away, they'd build a house before they wed. A steady man, Lenny Hall, steadied perhaps by seeing Ray King die at Davies's sawmill.

He sorted Teddy out. He tossed him a packet of condoms and told him if he didn't use them he'd end up in the creek with one of his motors chained to his ankles.

He got Margot's signature on Trudy's release papers too. 'You don't eat until you put your name on them,' he said.

'Pith off,' she said.

'Let her eat,' Elsie said.

'Stay out of it, Else,' Harry said.

Margot put her name on the papers. She liked her food.

SECRETS

*D*ino Collins was out there again, marking his turf with the stink of hot rubber. 'Don't think you can make a fool of me, you moll, and get off scot-free,' he'd said when she'd told them she wasn't going up to Sydney. 'Watch your back,' he'd said.

Myrtle was big on turning the other cheek. Robert told her to ignore him. He said he'd grow bored with his game.

They'd been so wrong about so many things. If they'd told her the truth the first time she'd asked them, in Sydney, they'd still be living in Sydney.

'No more secrets,' Robert had said the night they'd told her about Jenny.

She was full of secrets, overflowing with secrets and no one to tell them to.

She'd told Rosie about everything, where she'd been born, how she'd been born, Rosie her best friend, her only close friend – back then. If Cara had learnt one worthwhile lesson from these past months, it was just how fast a best friend can turn into a worst enemy – or second worst. Dino Collins was her worst enemy.

And she didn't understand why. Just by crooking his little finger he could get almost any girl he wanted. He was good-looking, he owned a motorbike, always had money to spend. He'd probably only gone after her to get back at Robert, who had been the main instigator in having him expelled from school – which, had Robert not been new to the town, he may not have done. People pitied Dino and she now knew why. His parents had run off the side of a bridge and drowned in their car and he'd spent an hour diving for them when he was only eleven years old. Then he'd ended up living with his mother's seventy-year-old aunty. Everyone pitied him, which was why he got away with the things he did.

Cara pitied his aunty. He'd taped her cat into a box while she was in hospital. It hadn't died, but it should have. His aunty was in hospital for two weeks.

He had Cara boxed in now. She never left the house unless she was with Robert or Myrtle, and he wasn't even scared of them.

Over Christmas she'd got out. They'd driven up to Sydney and it had been like being in heaven, or like life was supposed to be. Aunty Beth and Uncle John had a new television, which Gran spent all day watching, which Uncle John and Aunty Beth spent half the night watching. Robert had refused to look at it. He blamed television for everything. He said the mass viewing of mindless drivel was brainwashing the younger generation, that television was responsible for the fall in moral values. He said that the drivel on those boxes was aimed to be understood by the lowest common denominator, and that a society geared towards the lowest denominator would end up ruled by the lowest.

He could have been right too. Gran loved that box.

'Keep your noise down out there. I can't hear a word they're saying.'

They'd gone to Amberley to look over the manager's books, and Cara had felt like a sinner locked out of paradise. She loved that tall house, loved its front window that used to paint magic patterns on the parlour wall. And she hadn't even been allowed to go into the parlour, or into her own room.

She was back in her box now. She couldn't even go shopping with Myrtle and Robert. Dino tracked them when she did. And he phoned, phoned a dozen times some nights.

She never answered the phone. She was too scared to play tennis. The last time she'd played, he'd sat beside the court, not taking his eyes off her. She'd conceded the match and telephoned Robert to come and pick her up.

School was double, triple hell. She'd scraped through last year, or Robert had managed to get her a scrape-through. She was going to fail this year because she couldn't stand being there.

Rosie clucked like a hen, flapped her elbows every time Cara walked into the classroom. She flapped her elbows if they met in the corridor, or at the lockers, and she was probably the one who had broken into Cara's locker and smashed eggs over everything. Robert had to buy a heap of new books and she'd spent a week of nights copying work from one messed-up book into another.

She had no friends. Rosie had plenty. There were always kids eager to take sides in a school war. Hated going to school. Couldn't concentrate on anything the teachers said. She tried to study at home, but that bike-riding mongrel wouldn't let her. He spent his nights racing his bike up and down the street, doing screaming turns in front of the house.

'What's wrong with that boy?' Myrtle said.

'Ring the police, Mummy.'

'Ignore him, pet. He'll find someone else to annoy.'

Myrtle didn't know what she was talking about. The day of the eggs in her locker, she'd told her mother that Rosie had done it. 'There are more suitable girls in town for you to mix with, pet,' was all she'd said.

Such as Sarah Potter, a farmer's daughter, who had come around to the house one night, asking if Cara would like to go to the pictures with her. She was one of Rosie's new pack who had bailed her up in the school toilets a week after school had gone back and four of them had pushed her head into a bowl and flushed it. Had to wash her hair in cold water, with school soap, and was too scared now to go to the toilet even if she was busting.

Head up, Cara listened. Silence. She sighed and opened her Maths book to stare again at Robert's figures. He'd gone over her homework with her three times. All of his workings were there, and when he'd been explaining it, she'd thought she understood how he'd got from A to B. That screaming bike had washed it from her head.

And he hadn't gone. He'd never give up.

His aunty had kicked him out after the cat business, which was why the going to Sydney business had started, why all of the bad stuff had started.

Like the cat, Cara might not starve or die of thirst, but she couldn't get out of that box until Robert retired in 1964. When she was twenty. She'd pleaded with him to get a transfer back to home; he'd said that if he retired as a principal he'd get more pension money. She'd begged him again to be allowed to live with Uncle John and to repeat last year with Pete. Not on your life. He didn't trust her – probably never would.

She'd tried to delay coming home from Sydney by asking him to take her to Woody Creek.

'It's a good place to stay away from, poppet.'

As was the Traralgon high school, but he drove her there five days a week.

If she'd told Myrtle what Dino had done the day she'd got home late from the library, they might have allowed her to live with Uncle John. She should have. Though people like Myrtle didn't quite believe in the bad that existed outside their God-safe little world. 'Give your problems into God's hands, pet,' Myrtle said.

Her parents expected her to stay at that school and matriculate, then go on to university and become a high-school teacher. Robert was a great one to talk about television brainwashing the younger generation. He'd started brainwashing Cara about teaching when she was six or seven years old, and Myrtle had been as bad.

The way she was going this year, she'd end up working in a sewing factory like Jennifer Hooper/Morrison, except she couldn't sew on a button.

She'd only need a reasonable pass in form five to do primary teaching. Last year a girl in form five had got a scholarship to a Melbourne teachers' college. It was an option. Not much of an option, because if she happened to get in, and if she happened to finish the two-year course, she'd be bonded to the Education Department for three years, which might mean one less year in Traralgon but extra years before she could go home to Sydney.

The book before her, pencil in hand, nothing in her head bar escaping from him and his roaring bike, she jumped two feet from her chair when something hard landed on the roof.

Wished he'd broken a window. Robert might do something about that.

Before Christmas Dino had been in trouble for smashing windows in a vacant house. His aunty wrote a cheque for the damage.

Wished the police had put him in jail, and he was pacing backward and forward behind metal bars like tigers at the zoo. And Rosie too. Wished she was in a cage, flapping her elbows and clucking to get out.

Every good part of life in this town had been spent with Rosie. Now being in the same classroom made Cara want to vomit. Then yesterday the history teacher, Mrs Hunter, had asked them to stay back at lunchtime so they could sort out their problem. Cara had played noughts and crosses with herself while Rosie put on such an act of howling innocence, Mrs Hunter had started comforting her.

'Have you anything at all to say, Cara?' she'd asked.

'Only, why doesn't she get a job acting on television?' That was all she'd said. It had felt good too, because Mrs Hunter had looked as if she might have believed her.

Should have said more. Should have told her what she'd done, just opened her mouth and let it out. Should have climbed up onto the roof of the school and screamed it out. Hadn't. She'd looked down at her noughts and crosses game and tried to beat herself.

She was supposed to hand in her Maths homework and a fiction essay tomorrow. She was usually good at fiction. Not tonight. Life was too real to think up fiction.

Closed her Maths book and opened her English book, wrote her name. *Cara Norris.* It looked lonely – and wrong. She added *Hooper-Morrison-Billy-Bob Someone* to it and wondered what her English teacher might make of that.

Ripped the page out and the corresponding page at the rear of the book. The blank paper invited her pen back.

Jennifer Hooper or Morrison, twenty-year-old mother of two daughters and a son, fell in love with Billy-Bob Someone and had a baby to him. Jenny Hooper or Morrison must have had her first baby at fifteen or sixteen and liked it so much she kept on doing it. Fancy having four kids by the time you're twenty.

Jenny Hooper or Morrison was a slut like Rosie.

Cara Jeanette Hooper-Morrison-Billy-Bob Someone, Norris by default, was not born to be an only child. If she'd had a big brother, he'd go out there now and fix that bike-riding mongrel.

How does a woman who has already got three kids have another one, hand it over to a stranger, then get on a train and forget it was ever born? Wouldn't she want to know how it grew up, if it grew up? Was she such a slut, she couldn't get rid of it fast enough so she could go out and have another one?

Jenny Hooper-Morrison had me on the kitchen floor at Amberley, without a doctor or a nurse, then she got dressed and went upstairs to get Mrs Collins and Miss Robertson to witness the birth of her landlady's baby.

Cara could almost visualise that scene. What had Myrtle done with the round velvet cushion? Had she taken it out before

Mrs Collins and Miss Robertson came down? Maybe she'd been sitting on it.

She wrote again, filled one page and started on the other, writing the tale of her birth from an all-seeing, all-knowing point of view. She turned the full page over and wrote on the back, then around the edges when the back of those two pages were full. And when she stopped, the street was silent.

She stood, stiff with sitting, and walked out to the kitchen for a glass of milk – and found out why the street was silent. It was ten past one and she hadn't started her homework.

Crept into the lounge room and lifted the phone from the receiver, as she did every night once her parents were in bed. When Dino had no petrol for his bike, he phoned. He'd phoned one night at two o'clock and kept it up until four. And with Gran Norris threatening to die at all hours, Myrtle and Robert refused to leave the phone off the receiver.

Brushed her teeth, dressed for bed, then sat reading her night's work. It wasn't fiction but it sure sounded like it. If she changed the names and dates and places and cut out the personal bits, it would do for her fiction assignment. She had to hand something in tomorrow.

Altered Sydney to Melbourne, Woody Creek to Lakes Entrance, Myrtle to Martha, Jenny to Jessica, Robert to Captain John Amberley, fitted it into three pages and ended it at Spencer Street Station, where Jessica held her baby one last time, then handed it to Martha and boarded the train.

She knew that if she should turn her head, she would run back and snatch that tiny infant from the stranger's arms. Jessica didn't look back.

Child of Jessica, she'd named it. And her English teacher gave her a nine and a half out of ten.

Myrtle and Robert were delighted with her mark. They wouldn't have been so delighted if they'd known what she'd got that nine and a half for. She hid the essay in her diary, hid her diary behind the bottom drawer of her dressing table.

It didn't take much to delight Robert and Myrtle. An invitation to Sarah Potter's birthday party delighted them.

It was a set-up. If Sarah and Rosie got her away from school, they'd do worse than flush her head down a toilet.

'I'm not going, Mummy.'

'Of course you're going,' Myrtle said. 'You never go anywhere, pet.'

They bought her a new frock, a very nice pale green frock for a twelve year old. Cara didn't bother telling them she wouldn't be seen dead in it, just told them again she wasn't going.

She didn't tell them she'd started a novel about Jessica and Bobby-Lee. They wouldn't have approved.

She didn't tell them she wasn't going to the end-of-year social until half an hour before they were ready to go. One big argument with them was preferable to umpteen little ones. The school principal was expected to put in an appearance, and where he went, Myrtle went. They had to give up arguing and leave. Myrtle was never late for anything.

Cara locked the doors behind then, turned the inside lights off but left both outdoor lights burning. She knew the windows were locked but checked them again, pulling blinds and drapes, and ending up in the bathroom. No blind on that window. It was high, small, its glass bubbled so no one could see in. The back veranda light had been fitted beside that window, and if it was turned on, there was light enough in the bathroom to write, though not sufficient to see what she'd written, which offered her a freedom she never found during the day. She could write anything at all, and couldn't see to erase what she knew she shouldn't have put on paper.

Carolyn's father referred to Jessica's town as Pandora's box. 'Don't open it, my dear,' he said.

In her head, Carolyn knew he was probably right, which didn't stop her from wanting to meet Jessica, or at least to see her from a distance, or from behind one of those one-way mirrors maybe where you can see without being seen.

She'd seen a couple of photographs of her half-brother, taken when he was tiny. They were in Martha's old photograph album. There were no photographs of his sisters. Did they look like her? Were they married? There were so many questions for which she had no answer . . .

The phone rang. A phone jangling in a silent house when your mind is a thousand miles away makes your heart jump. She walked to it, stood over it, counting the rings until it rang out. It could have been Myrtle or Robert checking on her, but they knew she never answered the phone. It could have been Uncle John. Gran Norris might have decided to have a deathbed scene. She hadn't had one for six months. Cara waited, expecting the phone to ring again. And it did, and expected or not, each time it rang it sucked the marrow out of her bones. Three times she allowed it to ring out, then, when it gave up for the third time, she removed the receiver from its cradle and buried it.

She was in the bathroom, writing about the sound of telephones in the night, when a motorbike roared up the street. Her pencil stilled. Dozens of men rode motorbikes in this town. It wasn't him.

But it was. It slowed out front, putter-spluttered for a moment, then the putter-splutter died and her heart jumped up to her throat and stayed there. She should have let that phone keep ringing. He knew now that she was in the house, and alone. Robert's car wasn't parked in the drive.

'Stupid fool!' Stood frozen in the bathroom, listening.

Heard the crunch of footsteps on gravel, then the wire door opening.

She was a rat in a trap in that bathroom. Crept out to the

passage as he knocked again; then, her shoes off, she continued to the entrance hall where she armed herself with a crystal vase. Stood, her back to the wall. She'd be hidden by the door if he got it open. And with only a cheap wooden door between them, when he knocked again it vibrated her lungs. She couldn't breathe.

He gave up. His footsteps crunched away.

Heart beating too fast, thumping in her ears, attempting to listen for the gate over its thumping, listen for the bike's motor. Then she heard him at her bedroom window, tapping on glass. It was locked, all of the windows were locked.

He knew how to break glass.

She ran to the telephone, waiting for the sound of breaking glass. A car approached spraying its light across the front of the house. Too early to be Robert and Myrtle. The car went by.

Stood, phone in her hand, panting air through her mouth like a caged cat as the rear wire door squealed on its hinges. No car lights to expose him out there. Trees to hide behind out there. Shadows.

And what use was a telephone? What good would it do? If he broke in it would take too long for that phone to bring the police or anyone else. She had to open the front door and run. Or find something better than a vase.

She was in the kitchen, feeling for Myrtle's long carving knife, when the screen door slammed shut. No gravel at the rear of the house. No footsteps. Stood, listening, waiting, that long knife in her hand and heard the gate slam. Heard his bike cough. Cough-cough-cough, then roar its frustration to the night, then gone. Cara, her lungs screaming for air, her hand shaking, placed the knife on the table and sat down. Sat in the kitchen close to that knife until Myrtle and Robert drove in at eleven. She was in bed before their key turned in the lock.

She sat beside her parents in church on Sunday morning because she was afraid to stay alone in the house. Myrtle and Robert didn't know they had Dino Collins to thank for her company. She prayed too, not that she expected her prayers to be answered.

God wasn't into causing his children to crash motorbikes into brick walls, to have head-on smashes with semitrailers. That's what she prayed for.

*

God works in mysterious ways his wonders to perform, according to the Bible and Myrtle. He didn't manage the semitrailer or the brick wall, but he got Dino Collins. He and Tony Bell were seen climbing in through the back window of a shop and someone called the police. They got them as they were climbing out, and that night Cara wrote a chapter about Carolyn, who converted to the Catholic faith and became a nun . . . except, who had a clue how girls went about becoming nuns? She had to skip over that part, jump over a few years then send her off to work in an orphanage.

Tony's father put up money to get him out of jail. Dino's old aunty didn't. The local newspaper ran a full-page story about him, a rehash of the boy hero story, and an old photograph of him and his parents. The judge would likely let him off with a warning but maybe he'd get a taste of how that cat felt in that box before the judge let him off.

She flipped pages to the editorial, which was sometimes interesting. Glanced at the first paragraph, about murderers released back into the community after they'd served their sentences, and about one woman locked in a Melbourne asylum for the criminally insane, and the group of people working to have her released. She'd been abused by her brutal husband since her wedding day, then one night she'd murdered him with a carving knife, in his bed. Cara was thinking about murdering Dino Collins with a carving knife when *Woody Creek* jumped up from the page.

And *Morrison. Amber Morrison*.

How many Morrison families lived in that town? She was probably one of Cara's relatives.

She scanned the editorial for Jenny's name, found out that Amber, who was fifty years old, had given birth to four dead babies in about four years, and no wonder she'd murdered her husband.

An unusual name, Amber. Cara glanced at Myrtle, wondering if she dared ask her if Jenny had ever mentioned an Aunty Amber, or a cousin Amber. Glanced at Robert. He'd read that editorial, see *Woody Creek stationmaster* and that newspaper would disappear.

She knew the story of Pandora's box, how the lid once lifted could never be closed, and how the plagues of hell had come pouring out. Her father may well have been right about Woody Creek.

LETTING GO

Six times though 1960 the Keatings and the Hoopers met at Kilmore where Raelene and her luggage were moved from one car to the other. Her first visits with Jenny went well, Raelene pleased to see her and to go with Georgie to see what the men had done to Granny's house. She liked Jim's house, didn't like him sleeping in Jenny's bed, did her best to ignore Trudy but, all in all, she appeared to enjoy herself.

The fourth visit, in January of '61, didn't start well. Clarrie drove her alone to Kilmore. He looked stressed, and within minutes of making the transfer, Jenny knew why. Raelene didn't want to be there. She was going to miss her friend's birthday party.

'You could have come after the party, Raelie.'

'Clarrie said I couldn't because his mother got sick and he has to go down there, and Florence is sick too, and I'm sick of her always sick, and I'm sick of here too. It's too hot.'

It was. They'd had three days with temperatures in the high nineties.

'At home when it's hot I'm allowed to go to the swimming pool.'

'We've got a whole creek up here to swim in,' Jenny said.

'At home people swim in clean blue swimming pools.'

'You used to swim in the creek with Georgie when you were little.'

'It stinks of dead fish,' Raelene said.

John and Amy McPherson popped in at four and caught Raelene in a foul mood and Jenny attempting to bribe her out of it with an ice-cream from the café. Amy had been Raelene's teacher for two years. She'd known a happier child.

'Do you like your new school?' she asked.

'No, and you said we'd go up and get an ice-cream.'

'When the sun goes down.'

'Before you didn't say when the sun goes down. I want one now. Why haven't you got ice-cream in your fridge anyway? At home we've always got ice-cream.'

'Aren't you a lucky girl,' Amy said.

'How long is she staying here for?' the little bugger said.

'Mrs McPherson is visiting with me, and if you can't behave like a good girl, you can go to your room and there'll be no ice-cream.'

Amy and John went home, and Jenny went about the preparation of dinner.

She had served the meal before she noticed Raelene was missing. They searched the house and garden, unaware that Jenny's purse had also gone missing until they sighted Raelene returning with the purse, and a double-header ice-cream.

They met her at the gate where Jenny claimed both. She had a good lick of the ice-cream before tossing it into the gutter.

Raelene's scream of disbelief might have raised the dead. Her kick to Jenny's shin would raise a bruise. She didn't hang around to see the results, but took off towards Blunt's Road, bellowing like Flanagan's bull.

'Was that a bit harsh, Jen?' Jim asked.

'Not if it teaches her that there's no gain in stealing,' Jenny said.

A few years ago, she would have run her down. Tonight she tracked her, over Blunt's crossing and into South Road, through the little park between Maisy's house and the town hall. Raelene didn't stop to play on the swing.

Jenny tailed her to the sports oval, where she kicked off her shoes and chased her down. And Raelene threw herself down to kick. Jenny grabbed an ankle and got one shoe off, fought her for the other shoe, dodging blows.

'I can hit back, Raelene,' she warned.

'You hit me I'll tell Flo, and she won't ever make me come back to this rotten hot place again.'

Do I want you to come back? Jenny thought.

She carried her from the oval, Raelene screaming and fighting all the way. She carried her into the park where she put her down and held her arms, dodged her barefoot kicks. The town must have heard her screams. Jenny was damn near ready to give up the fight when Joss Palmer, one of Maisy's sons-in-law, came out to the veranda and asked her if she needed a bit of a hand.

He drove them home.

The papers signed in the Frankston solicitor's office had given Jenny a week with Raelene in June and September, and two weeks in January. That night, Raelene still screaming, still kicking, but at her locked bedroom door, Jenny walked up to the phone box to call the Keating number.

Clarrie picked it up. 'Flo is feeling a bit seedy,' he said. 'Everything all right?'

'Raelene is miserable. She wants to go to her friend's birthday party.'

'She can be a bit of a handful,' Clarrie admitted.

'We'll get her down to you tomorrow, Clarrie.'

'I can't take time off from work,' he said.

'We'll get her out to Box Hill.'

They left before daylight and took the back road into Melbourne, through Seymour, Yea and Lilydale, where they parked the car and hoped it would be there when they returned. They caught a train to the Box Hill station, a taxi out to the Keating house, unloaded Raelene and her luggage, and minutes later the taxi delivered them back to the station for the return trip.

The car was waiting where they'd left it, and hot. The seats hot enough to fry eggs on, the steering wheel untouchable. And Trudy worn out by her day.

'Never again, Jim.'

'You'll change your mind,' he said.

'It's over,' she said. 'She might not look like Ray, but she's his daughter!'

By three they were home, red-faced and sweating. Jim put Trudy into a cool bath; Jenny, stripped down to bare feet, shorts and a halter top, was tossing a salad together for a late lunch when someone knocked at the door.

Strangers, a balding male, a chubby female and two kids.

'Would Jim be in?' the male said.

'I'm his wife.'

'Ian and Lorris Hooper,' he said. 'Our girl, Belinda, and this is Owen.'

Jim heard them, he came with a towel-wrapped Trudy in his arms. 'Come in,' he said.

They were on a touring holiday. Thought they'd detour a bit and drop off a couple of photographs. They'd heard from Margaret that Jim was back in Woody Creek.

Jenny had spoken to Ian Hooper on the phone. She hadn't told him she'd been in touch with Jim, only that she'd come across his number in the phone book. She'd given him her married name, Jennifer King. Jim's cousin didn't know she was the Jennifer King, the mother of Jimmy he'd spoken to on the phone.

He handed two photographs to Jim, who handed one to Jenny. And there he was, her beautiful boy, ten candles on a birthday cake. A happy ten year old caught by the camera about to blow out his candles. Still Jimmy. Her eyes filled, her throat threatened to close.

Wanted him to be happy. Didn't want him to be so happy without her. Wiped a leaking tear, then, taking Trudy from Jim's arms, she escaped with her to the bedroom, to clothe her in a napkin and put her into her cot.

Had to go back. She didn't sit with them, but picked up the second photograph, this one of a lanky boy clad in his school uniform. His father's son.

'He would have been around fifteen when I took that one,' Ian said.

At first glance he looked like Jim, tall, lean, same hair, but not his face. Jenny was still in his face. She saw her own eyes looking back at her, her nose too, her cheekbones.

God. God, God, God.

'He's grown into a lovely looking boy. We saw him a month or two before they left. He's filled out a bit since that shot was taken,' Lorris said.

Jenny nodded, her heart breaking but determined not to let Vern Hooper's nephew see it breaking. But it wasn't fair. She'd given him life and those strangers had been allowed to watch him grow. It just wasn't fair. And she couldn't stand to be in that kitchen with Vern Hooper's nephew. Opened the back door and walked out to the heat of the garden, determined to control her tears and to not make a fool of herself in front of Jim's cousin. Hoped Jim wasn't telling them who she was. They'd know she'd signed her son away.

Shouldn't have signed anything. Should have fought Vern for him.

She wouldn't have won. She was Jenny Morrison. She never won.

Jim came out to the rear veranda. 'Jen.'

'Coming,' she said and she went back to the kitchen where she lit a rare cigarette. Today she needed to borrow guts from nicotine. Kept herself busy then, filling the jug, emptying the teapot.

'You're in contact with Margaret?' Jim asked his cousin.

'Through her accountant.'

'Lorna thinks we know where they are. She's on the phone every second week,' Lorris said.

'And still as mad as a nest of hornets that Margaret finally got the better of her,' Ian said. 'She's living in Kew. We're just across from her in North Balwyn.'

'Too close for comfort for my liking,' Lorris said. 'She's still paying your father's bloodhound to look for Margaret and James. He's been around to our place. Six or eight months ago, I caught him talking to Owen out front about his Aunty Maggie. I gave him short shrift,' Lorris said.

'I'll send you her address,' Ian said.

'Don't bother,' Jim said.

'She'd probably land on your doorstep,' Lorris said.

The three-way conversation continued at the table, Jenny no longer listening. Her mind had gone to Jimmy. Born on 3 December 1941, he'd turn twenty this year. Not a boy but a man now. He'd drive a car.

Would he remember Woody Creek, Granny's house – and her? Jim was six when his mother died. He'd never forgotten his mother.

Why hadn't Jimmy come back to look for her?

Because little boys believe what the grown-ups tell them, that's why. Because the Hoopers had brainwashed him before he was ten years old, that's why.

The three were discussing Ian's wife's relatives who lived on the land somewhere near Swan Hill; Jenny turned from the sink to pick up the earlier photograph of her beautiful boy. It changed the subject back to where she didn't want it. Wanted to absorb him, that was all, to possess him for a little while.

'Margaret threw him a party every year,' Ian said.

'She made him some fantastic cakes,' Lorris said.

'Remember when she made him a motorbike, Mum?' the boy, ten or twelve years old, piped in, and Jenny placed the photograph down, opened her cup cupboard and caught a tear as it trickled, tickled down the side of her nose.

'We've been down to the city and back. We didn't stop for lunch. You'll have a cup of tea with us?' Jim asked.

'A cool drink would go down well, then we should get a move on,' Ian said.

'We're booked in at a motel in Swan Hill tonight,' Lorris said.

Cold water in the fridge, lemon cordial; Jenny filled four glasses, delaying the pouring of tea, wanting them gone so she might look her fill at the photographs.

'I'll write to Maggie when we get back and let her know we've seen you and your family, Jim. She'll probably get in touch with you.'

'She'll be up at your door when she hears about your little girl. She used to visit us just so she could play with our kids – that's what we used to say – when the kids were babies,' Lorris said.

Besotted by Jimmy too, Jenny thought. Couldn't keep her hands off him when he was five months old. She'd got what she'd wanted.

Jim saw them to the door. He hadn't told them she was Jimmy's mother. Jenny knew why. He wanted Margaret to get in touch with him. Jenny's name would kill any little chance of that.

'Thanks for calling in,' Jim said.

Jenny didn't thank them.

NINETEEN SIXTY-ONE

*T*echnology rushing forward, satellites moving around the heavens, America and Russia in a race to dominate space, and Russia winning every time.

In January of that year, John F. Kennedy, a young go-getter, was sworn in as the thirty-fifth president of the United States. In February, Sydney withdrew its last tram from service. A big mistake, according to many. Yuri Gagarin, a Russian cosmonaut, rocketed into space that year; he orbited the earth and was brought safely home.

Home to what? That was the question in many minds. Eastern Berliners, under Soviet rule, didn't appreciate home: they were defecting to the West in droves. Nineteen sixty-one was the year the Russians started building a wall to keep their people in.

A few American states might have liked to build a wall to keep the blacks out. They were demanding their fair share of freedom and equality, protesting for it, fighting in the streets for it.

Charlie White's daughter wanted him walled in but her diagnosis of senile decay wasn't backed up by Doctor Frazer or his colleagues. Charlie White, sparking on at least three of his six cylinders, was back behind his counter, chiacking his customers and filching again from his cash drawer, on the phone to his city broker, buying an occasional batch of likely shares.

'Got to keep my hand in, Rusty,' he said.

He bought no more in his name, and when the new certificates arrived, instead of impaling them on his wire spike, he handed them to Georgie.

'Stick them in with your stash, Rusty. They'll be worth something to you one day.'

He'd never been the most popular man in town; he'd reached the age of 'couldn't give a damn', an age where he enjoyed his unpopularity. He knew every man, woman and child in town, knew him by his father's reputation and by his father's father's. He'd never trusted a Duffy as far as he could kick one. Since the accident, since he'd lost his kick, he terrorised Duffy babies in their prams. If he removed his dentures, he could contort his face into something so far removed from humanity that the little buggers screamed when they sighted his twin green front doors.

Jenny had known Charlie forever. She'd never feared him. In November of 1961, Raelene's tenth birthday, she'd walked around to Charlie's shop to phone her and wish her a happy day.

'The number has been disconnected,' a voice on the line informed.

Georgie rang the exchange and received the same reply.

Raelene hadn't been back in June, or September. Florence hadn't been in touch since July.

'Try Donny's home, Georgie,' Jenny said. The Keatings were listed now as Donny's next of kin. If their phone number had been changed, the home would have it.

They didn't, or if they did, they wouldn't give it up.

'Florence didn't look well in January when we took Raelene home,' Jenny said.

She wrote to her that night and asked her to call the shop, during business hours. She didn't call and three weeks later, the letter was returned.

'Something has happened to Raelene. I'm going down, Jim.'

He was licensed to drive. He drove in Woody Creek, could manage the trip to Willama but rarely did. Jenny did the distance driving. She didn't have the confidence to drive in the city, but as Christmas moved nearer, her need to find out what was going on with Raelene and the Keatings grew.

Georgie still considered Raelene a little sister. 'I'll go with you, Jen.'

They left on a Sunday morning, a week before Christmas, left at dawn, Jenny planning to go the back way into Melbourne, to leave the car at Lilydale again. Georgie had driven through town with Jack. She had a road map and no fear of city traffic, so Jenny drove to Kilmore where Georgie slid over to the driver's seat and Jenny opened up the road map.

They worked their way from west to east, Jenny calling the roads as they crossed over, and by nine they were parked out front of the children's home.

Georgie hadn't seen Donny since the night Bernie Macdonald had driven her, Jenny and the kids down to the Willama hospital, the night of Ray's funeral.

Not the fat boy-baby he'd been, but a giant boy-toddler, intrigued by Georgie's abundant hair, or its colour. He stared at it, as he had at the flame of Granny's table lamp.

'He remembers your hair,' Jenny said.

Maybe he did. Georgie took his hand, and with his palm smoothed her hair, and he sang his dirge.

'Poor little bloke.'

Not so little. He was eleven and the size of a fourteen year old. He looked clean; thick, but not fat.

'I should have bought him some chocolate,' Georgie said.

'He's still in napkins,' Jenny said, remembering his napkins when Ray had fed him chocolate.

'How do they pay people enough to do what they do, Jen?'

'They're the heroes of this world, not the footballers and champion swimmers. I used to dream once about nursing the sick. I couldn't have done it.'

They didn't stay long with Donny. The map unfolded again; too large for the confines of a car, they spread it on the bonnet and plotted their course to Box Hill.

For Jenny, it was a replay of the day Laurie had driven her to Surry Hills, to Mary Jolly, her childhood penfriend's house. A stranger opened the Keatings' door.

'We bought the house in August,' the woman said. And no, she hadn't met the previous owners. 'Try next door.'

Jenny tried next door, as she had in Surry Hills. The neighbour had known the Keatings well.

'Clarrie's mother died. He was an only child and the house was left to him – down near where they make the electricity – Moe. Yes, Moe. Flo said she'd write as soon as they got settled, but she had her hands full. Did you know her baby turned out to be twins?'

'Twins?' Jenny hadn't even known she'd been pregnant. Sick, Clarrie had said. A bit seedy – or getting ready to shed her seeds . . .

'They're identical, boys. The dearest little curly-headed mites. She was sick for the nine months she was carrying and spent the last months on her back.'

She offered tea; they thanked her but got away. Georgie wanted to see the house in Armadale, wanted to visit the school she'd attended when they'd lived with Ray.

They found the house as they'd left it. Years don't alter bricks and mortar. They alter gardens. Shrubs planted along the fence line. A square of lawn where they'd been no lawn.

They left the car to walk, to blatantly stare in. No sign of movement behind Flora's sitting-room curtains. No sign of their old vegetable garden. A new car parked in a cemented drive, a new tin shed down the back.

'I wonder what Lois is doing these days?' Georgie said. She and Jimmy had played for hours with her.

'She was a couple of months older than Jimmy,' Jenny said.

'Hard to believe we lived in here,' Georgie said. 'What would we have been doing now if we'd stayed here, Jen?'

'What do you wish you were doing?'

'Dunno.'

'Had enough of sightseeing.'

'Nope. The school now, then your sister-in-law?'

'Who?'

'Lorna?'

Sister-in-law? Lorna Hooper? It was almost funny. 'That's where I put my foot down,' Jenny said.

'What if she's found him, Jen?'

'He's old enough to find us, love.'

'That's a numbing device you've installed in your head,' Georgie said. 'I haven't got one. Where's Kew on your map?'

'I don't know, and I don't want to know – and Jim wants nothing to do with her.'

'If there was one chance in a million to find Jimmy, wouldn't he take it?'

'If Jimmy lived next door to Lorna, she wouldn't tell me. She resents the air I breathe. If we leave for home now, we'll be there by five.'

'There's not a memory I've got of Armadale that Jimmy isn't in. I can remember the day you brought him home from Sydney. He's my brother, Jen.'

She was in the car. Jenny got in and they drove around the corner to the deserted school. Not much to see. Same buildings, same fence, same gate – a new phone booth out front.

Georgie swung the car in beside it. No phone book there. She swung in beside two more phone booths before she found a tattered book. The H pages were intact. There was a bunch of Hoopers. Only one *L. D. Hooper Miss* with a Kew address, which Georgie copied to the rear of the map.

'We're not going there, Georgie.'

'Chicken.'

Georgie found Burke Road and followed it to Cotham, which turned out to be the continuation of White Horse Road. She drove in circles around the Kew area until she called out to a young chap mowing his nature strip.

In Charlie's shop, Georgie, dressed for comfort and her mane of copper hair tied back with a rubber band, was still a beauty; but well dressed for her day in the city, her hair hanging free, she was . . . beyond superlatives. The lawn-mowing chap couldn't do enough for her. He stopped his noisy machine and went inside, returning with a map book of Melbourne, every street marked on it, and Jenny wanted one for herself. Didn't want Lorna's street, but he put his finger on it, and five minutes later Georgie drove by Number Forty-Three, a red clinker-brick, hard-faced house with a matching clinker-brick fence, black wrought-iron gates and big old black Ford parked in the driveway that looked like Lorna Hooper's.

Clothe yourself, she'd said, and while Jenny had been clothing herself to take Jimmy down to the hospital, Lorna had picked him up and carried him out to the car.

Hated her. Feared her – and her own reaction should she come face to face with Lorna.

'Don't do this to me, Georgie.'

'Stay in the car and keep your head down,' Georgie said, pulling into shade beneath a tree opposite Number Forty-Three and two houses down from its gate.

And Jenny saw her, not in her yard but on the footpath and walking towards the car.

'That's her! Drive!'

'Where?'

'I want to go home!'

'Where is she?'

'That evil old hag in black. It's her!'

The dame in black was now crossing over the road, her back to them.

'She's as tall as Jim,' Georgie said.

Not unless she was wearing spike-heeled shoes, which she wasn't. Always wore black lace-ups and lisle stockings. Always clad her lamppost form in black garments, walked with a male's stride.

'Go, Georgie! Please.'

'Stay low,' Georgie said, and she got out of the car. Jenny ducked low and saw no more.

*

Georgie and Lorna's diagonal paths across the road intersected at the iron gates.

'Miss Hooper?' A hand offered. 'Gina Morgan,' she said, deleting the Morrison from her name.

'Who?' The gust of stale sardine breath issuing with that one word might have forced a step backward in a lesser mortal. Georgie was not one of the lesser.

'Gina Morgan.'

Lorna glared at the extended hand, didn't take it, didn't shake it.

Not a pretty sight, black hat, out of fashion since the twenties, spectacles balanced on a long eagle-beak nose, skirt near ankle length. She was the taller of the two, or would have been had Georgie not been wearing high heels.

'I believe you have been looking into the disappearance of your nephew.'

'You know where they are residing?'

'No.'

Lorna's sardine 'humph' released with maximum effort expressed her disinterest in continuing the conversation, but the gate latch was at her visitor's back, and to get to it would require her visitor to move.

'Who . . . employs you?'

'Charles White and company. We are representing Jim Hooper and his wife.'

A moment spent in consideration. A decision made.

'You might inform him that I have spent a veritable fortune in attempting to trace the whereabouts of his son. The boy attended Carey Grammar. My representative has spoken to the masters and students who knew the boy. They have had no contact with James since 1958.'

Narrow lips, fighting to release words and not her false teeth, spitting sardine saliva. Georgie stepped back, just a little.

'You might also inform him that since the thirteenth day of December 1958, when the family home was sold over my head – for the second time – I have neither seen nor heard from my sister or nephew. Nor do I expect to. Now remove yourself.'

Georgie removed herself, and Lorna opened the gate.

'However, should your company be successful, I would expect to be informed. You have a card?'

'We have your address, Miss Hooper,' Georgie said.

Lorna humphed, then strode into her yard and latched the gate. Georgie returned to the car where Jenny remained low until they were out of the street.

'I'll never forgive you for that.'

'Yeah, yeah, yeah. What did she look like when she was young, Jen?'

'The same.'

'The family home was sold over her head – twice,' Georgie said.

*

They bought petrol in Kilmore, ate a late lunch there, then Jenny took the wheel for the final leg home, and for the first time they spoke of Jim.

'You don't like him, do you?'

'I like his car. I'm reserving my opinion on him.'

'You've been reserving it for two years.'

'He was in a nuthouse, Jen. Don't take this personally, but your record for picking blokes hasn't been exemplary, so I'm reserving my judgement.'

'That evil bitch – and her father – is the reason he was in a nuthouse. What do you weigh, Georgie?'

'Around nine stone.'

'He was under six when the war ended, too sick to bring home. He was in hospital over there for months. He told me a while back that he survived that camp for me and Jimmy. I sent him a poem when I was waiting for him in Sydney. He said that every morning he was in that Jap camp, he'd hold the tatters of it in his hand and promise me and Jimmy he'd make it through that day. And he did. And he came home to us and I'd gone and married Ray. There was nothing left of him but determination to get home to us, and his bloody father and sister told him I hadn't waited for him.'

'You can't cry and drive at the same time, mate. Pull over.'

'I'm not crying. I hate that evil bitch and hate the Hooper name. And I wear it. Do you think I'd wear it if I didn't love him? Do you think anything else could make me live in that house?'

'I like his house.'

'I want you to like him.'

'You've got to admit the family doesn't have a lot going for it. What was the other sister like?'

'I used to think she was harmless. She looked like Beatrix Potter's mother mouse, wearing a bustle. She couldn't keep her hands off Jimmy. And she got him, and as far as I'm concerned, she's as bad as that hawk-faced lamppost.'

'She told me Jimmy went to Carey Grammar.'

'Ian Hooper told me that ages ago. I rang them. It's a dead end.'

A maniac in an old car was itching to pass, and on a curving road; Jenny wasn't driving fast enough for him. He stuck to her bumper bar and she stuck to fifty, and the fool pulled out and passed.

'If someone had been coming around that bend, they would have ended up dead.'

'Want me to drive?'

'I'm fine – just as mad as hell at you for dragging me around there.'

They drove on in silence and the speedo crept up to sixty.

'Is he enough for you, Jen?'

'I've already told you I love him.'

'What's love?'

'Something you know you've found when you find it. I knew I'd found it when I was eighteen.'

'Is it sex, or desire to breed?'

'I had no desire to breed when I had Jimmy.'

'Just sex then?'

'I explained the birds and bees to you when you were twelve years old,' Jenny said. 'And I'm not in the mood to do it again.' She slowed to make a left-hand turn, then drove slowly through a town. They were back on the open road before she spoke again.

'Animals have sex. Loving someone is what differentiates us from the rutting animal. Sex lecture over.'

'Define love?'

'Total trust, with fringe benefits. It's knowing that the world could end, but if you were holding his hand it wouldn't matter. It's wanting to remake him too, so a new generation will know him – which I can't seem to do these days.'

'You actually want another kid? Haven't you done enough of it?'

'I want to do it right this time.'

'That's all you want from life, Jen? Him and six kids?'

'One. A brother for Trudy,' Jenny said. 'When you reach the stage where there is nothing more that you want, it's probably time to curl up and die. What do you want?'

'You'll be the first to know when I work that out. I wouldn't mind this car for starters.'

'Do you still hear from Jack?'

'He got married two weeks ago.'

'Who told you that?'

'He wrote to me.'

'Why didn't you marry him?'

'I plan to find out who I am before I give up who I might have been, Jen.'

CONDITIONAL RELEASE

*F*ive-thirty, one of those days when spike-heeled shoes leave indentations in Melbourne's bitumen roads, when Swanston Street is thick with sweating humanity, all hurrying towards tram stop and station. They ignore the shop windows at five-thirty. A few will steal a glance at bulbous twenty-three-inch television sets playing cartoons in one window. Poor old Roadrunner, still attempting to outrun Wile E. Coyote.

Beep-beep.

By the end of 1962 a large percentage of the walkers owned their own television sets, and with luck, they'd be home in time to watch the six o'clock news, or to catch the tail end of it.

Cara wouldn't be home by six; she'd be lucky to make it by seven, and only the radio news when she got there. Robert had fought in two world wars, had lived through the Great Depression; he took English, History and Maths classes if one of the teachers was away – and he denied progress.

Not much good denying it. It was coming to get him – and proving him wrong too. Before the advent of television, ask most Australian schoolkids the name of the top man in America and they'd say Elvis Presley. Ask them today and they'd come back fast with John F. Kennedy, wife Jackie, two kids, John Junior and Carolyn. Five-year-old kids could tell you the names of Russian cosmonauts, of American astronauts. Three year olds could recognise their sports heroes. The percentage of the population buying newspapers might have diminished, but who needed to read all about it in the daily paper when television newsreaders read and condensed it for you, and fed it to you while you sprawled on the couch with a beer?

A fast year for Cara, this one, and a better year. Rosie had left school halfway through first term to marry Henry Cooper – and had a baby four months later – and lived with Rosie's parents and two brothers in a three-bedroom house.

Dino Collins had spent two months on a prison farm, and would spend another month there. It might teach him that his actions had a consequence. Probably should have started teaching him sooner.

*

Amber Morrison had been released back into society in late winter of '62, a conditional release, a supervised release. For sixteen years she'd been fed, clothed and medicated; she wasn't handling freedom, or not their supervised freedom.

They'd supplied her with a few items of clothing, a room, pills and a pension – the old-age pension. Forty-nine when they'd locked her in. Forty-nine plus sixteen made her old enough to get the pension. And she didn't believe it.

She hadn't believed how much pension they'd given her when she'd held those first banknotes in her hand. During the depression it would have been riches. In '46, she could have lived well on it. Now it paid the rent on a room in a crumbling rooming house she shared with eighteen more of Melbourne's rejects who dropped their filth for her to step over. She slept there. Had to sleep somewhere. She made a point of being there when *they* came to talk their bullshit at her – *they*, the all-powerful.

They knew she had two daughters, or they spoke of her two daughters. She didn't tell them she had one daughter and the stray. *They*'d found Sissy, living with the Duckworths, and she wanted nothing to do with her mother. The stray was in Woody Creek. Amber wanted nothing to do with her.

Five babies she'd carried, four of them were in the cemetery. Had they lived, Norman would have turned them into Duckworths as he'd turned Sissy into one. 'Nothing, no one,' Amber muttered. 'Nothing. No one.'

She had a hessian shopping bag, half a loaf of bread and a lump of cheese in it, a tin mug, a photograph of her and Maisy, pills, a few items of underwear. That's all she had, all she owned, all she was.

Prettiest girl in Woody Creek once. Could have had her pick of the boys. Hadn't wanted the dirt scratchers, the mill workers. Always wanted better.

Bitter better.

Walked along Swanston Street with the crowd, locked in by them, but separate. Businessmen in white shirts, ties off or loosened, women in light dresses, women with children holding tight to their hands, or held tight by their mother's hand, children who hadn't yet learnt not to stare at those who were different.

Amber was different. Haircuts cost money. Overcoats were easier to wear on the back than to carry.

'No sense, no feeling,' a passer-by said.

Anger prickled beneath her coat, but conditional release meant no anger. Conditional release meant controlling the desire to swipe at that female with her bag, it meant slowing her feet, allowing the female to become lost in the crowd.

She stood a while before a shop window, watching the cartoon bird kicking up dust as it raced towards a dark tunnel. And a truck came through it and ran it down.

Beep-beep.

A world she no longer understood was attempting to run her down. She'd taken her eye off it for sixteen years and now nothing was as it had been. Boxes that played cartoons in shop windows. Trucks spewing stinking fumes into the street. Cars, cars and more cars, and a world moving too fast for her to catch up.

Walked on.

The smell of oranges was still the same. A Mediterranean man locked inside a small street kiosk was eating his profits. She stood before his counter, eyeing three oranges, measuring them, wanting the best of them. She'd never had the best.

Pointed to it, then dug into her coat pocket for pennies she counted into his palm. Hers then. Held it like a jewel in her hand. Smelled the scent of home on it.

Home?

Memories have always been long in this town, Amb. It wouldn't do you any good coming up here. I get down to Melbourne two or three times a year to see Maureen and the kids. I'll let you know when I'll be down next and we can have lunch somewhere . . .

Maisy's letter was in the hessian shopping bag, with their photograph – two boot and pinafore clad kids. The man from the newspaper had given her that photograph.

The golden jewel held to her nose, she walked on with the crowd, smelling orange and remembering so clearly the girl in the pinafore, remembering the miles she'd walked when she'd grown too old – or too embarrassed – to sit behind her mother on the horse. Ten, maybe. Walked to and from school thereafter. Walked for miles as a bride, determined to stay out of Norman's bed.

A brutal husband, *they*'d said. An abused wife, four dead babies, three illegitimate grandchildren she'd never been allowed to hold, *they*'d said. She hadn't said a word, not this time. She'd learnt control. Kept her head down, her mouth shut this time.

Then no more barred doors.

How many miles had she walked in their rooms with their barred doors? How many miles down corridors that led to barred doors?

The city streets were endless. Turn a corner and there was another block to walk. Turn right. Turn left. The decision her own to make. Only the traffic lights dictated to her on the city streets. They forced her feet to still.

*

Amber Morrison and Cara Norris met at the lights on the corner of Flinders and Swanston streets. It was after five-thirty. A crowd waited for the green light to cross over, workers and shoppers packed tight together, all wanting to be first across the road, first onto the tram, onto the train.

Cara carried a canvas bag with little in it, other than pen, pad, purse and her return ticket to Traralgon. She'd come alone to the city, had gone alone to the Burwood teachers college – and had to argue for her right to travel alone. Until this morning, Robert and Myrtle had been determined to drive her to Melbourne. Next year she'd be free. Next year she'd wash the smell of Traralgon from her.

They weren't happy with her decision to do primary teaching. They wanted her to do one more year at school, to get her matriculation certificate then go on to university. She'd argued about that too, and when she couldn't win the argument, she'd dug her heels in and applied for the teaching scholarship anyway. They were beginning to realise she wasn't . . . wasn't who they were.

She glanced at the straggle-haired dame standing beside her, or noticed her worn overcoat, its astrakhan collar, her orange. Kept a space between them, or did until two boisterous boys bumped her, she bumped the dame's arm and her orange fell and rolled to the pavement.

'Sorry.' Cara stopped its roll with her foot, picked it up and offered it.

The old dame's hand was reaching, then her eyes looked higher. 'Stray slut,' she snarled and the orange was swiped from Cara's hand and bounced to the gutter.

Shocked by the response, Cara attempted to step back. The crowd held her captive, then the crazy old dame, still cursing, stepped forward, into the path of a truck.

You can't allow people to kill themselves, not right in front of your eyes, you can't. Your reflexes won't allow it. Cara grabbed a handful of the dame's black coat and yanked her back.

'Get your filthy hands off me, you hotpants slut.'

The truck rattled by, lights changed and the crowd jostled forward, that crazy dame gone with the initial rush. Not Cara. She wanted the black overcoat swallowed up by the crowd. That crazy old dame had made her sweat, made her hands sticky with sweat.

She felt for a handkerchief. Myrtle had asked if she had one before she'd left the house this morning. Yes, she'd said, as she'd said every day of her life when she'd left the house for school.

No more school. No handkerchief either. She wiped her palms on her hips as she crossed Flinders Street with the tailenders.

*

Amber walked on, cursing that stray slut to hell. She'd ruined her life, ruined Sissy's life. Cursed her for the lost orange too, and walked faster. Heads turning to stare at the muttering, straggle-haired one pushing her way between them. Kids still too young to know that fingers shouldn't be pointed at crazy old dames pointed, and their mothers grasped small wrists and urged them forward.

Jim Hooper and Jenny got married a few years ago. They've got a little girl they named for your mother. She doesn't take after Jenny.

You wouldn't recognise the inside of Vern's house, Amb. They've stripped off all of his dark wallpaper and lightened the whole place up. His sitting room looks like something out of one of those women's magazines. Jenny calls it their blue room.

'Wriggled her arse at him and he went sniffing after her like the scrawny mongrel he always was,' Amber muttered.

Sissy had been meant to live in that house, or in Monk's old mansion. For a time, Amber had believed she'd live out at Monk's with her girl.

'Stray slut.'

Another corner. Another decision. Turn left, turn right, continue forward or turn back. Her choice to make.

She looked back. She'd chosen that orange. She'd paid for it and she wanted it. She turned back.

And found it too, found it squashed, run over, as her life had been run over by Norman and his stray. Walked on, against the current, back to the shop window to watch the television cartoons.

They'd turned it off. Gone home. She had no home.

And Amber walked on to the next corner.

COLLEGE

*C*athy Bryant was from Ballarat, and secretly in love with Gerry Jasper, the local doctor's son who had lived all his life in a house diagonally opposite, who was six years older than her and looked on her as a kid. He'd finished university and gone to England to practise his doctoring skills on the Pommies before he started on the neighbours, or that's what he'd told her father before he'd left for London – on a boat, and he'd been sick for a week. He'd sent her a postcard from the boat and told her. He'd sent her a second postcard for her eighteenth birthday. She'd written to him a dozen times. Her mother told her to stop writing to him, that she was making an ass of herself, but he was fabulous and she was going to marry him when she was a few years older.

It went on and on. Five minutes after setting foot in the room she and Cara were supposed to share, Cathy Bryant had spilled her life story, not prepared to waste time in finding a new bosom buddy to replace the dozens left behind in Ballarat.

Cara had left no bosom buddy behind and wanted no bosom buddy replacement. Two minutes after meeting her roommate, she felt breathless. Two days of it and she went down to the office and asked to be moved. And the woman she spoke to didn't appreciate it – and didn't move her either.

She was at that college to escape Traralgon, to escape Myrtle's 'pet', Robert's 'poppet', and to write her novel without both of them looking over her shoulder and asking every five minutes what she was writing.

'I love the colour of your hair,' Cathy said. 'What do you use on it?'

'Shampoo,' Cara said.

'I mean its colour.'

'Still shampoo.' By the fourth week, Cara had given up on well-mannered silence. Her replies were brief. She spent a lot of time perched on the seat of a toilet, behind a locked cubicle door, escaping into her fictional life.

'I thought it must have been a rinse. You can't trust them, can you. Mum put mine in for me then spent the rest of the weekend trying to wash it out. What's it look like now?'

'Pink.'

'I almost put in a black. Black curly hair looks better than blonde. The Hill-Jones sisters are blondes but they've got straight hair. I love blonde straight hair – if it's long. They've got long hair they all wear in a pageboy style. You'd swear they were triplets if you saw them from the back. They're different in the face though. Leonie, the youngest, is the best looking. I wish mine was straight. Have you ever tried to straighten your hair?'

'How?'

'When mine was long, I could straighten it a bit with large rollers, except you can't sleep in them. Mum ironed it for me one day. It looked really good too, except it didn't last. A bit of wind, a bit of rain and I looked like a floor mop. I might get it cut short like yours, except, from past experience, I know that as soon as I hear that first snip of the scissors I'll wish I could take it back. It's almost long enough to put up in a French roll now.'

'Short is easy,' Cara said.

'It's boring though. You can't do anything with it except comb it. I promised myself I'd grow mine long this year then get it permed straight.'

'Permed straight?'

'They can do it. I read it somewhere. The Hill-Jones trio got their photos in the local paper last year with their hair up in French rolls – when they went to the Melbourne Cup. Their father has got shares in a horse that was running in it. I forget its name. It didn't win. Have you ever been to the Cup?'

'No.'

'Me either. I can't stand horseracing, car racing or any racing. Have you been anywhere?'

'Sydney.'

'What's it like?'

'Home,' Cara said.

'How come you're at a Melbourne college then?'

Five foot two, round-faced, round where the boys liked girls to be round. Every male at the college flirted with Cathy Bryant, and whether she was in love with Gerry Jasper or not, she flirted back.

'Why don't you wear makeup, Cara? Is it your religion or something?'

'Something.'

'Why did you freeze Paul off this afternoon? He's nice.'

Been there, done that and lived to regret it.

'Does your mother buy your clothes?'

'Why.'

'That skirt looks like a Fletcher Jones.'

And probably was. Robert wore Fletcher Jones trousers. Myrtle wore Fletcher Jones skirts. They'd brought down two new pleated skirts and a twin set, pink, three new blouses too, one blue, one pink, one white. She wore them. For the past few years she'd worn whatever Myrtle bought, saving her arguments for the battles she'd needed to win.

'Their stuff is so expensive,' Cathy said. 'My grandmother on Dad's side buys Fletcher Jones skirts and pays a fortune for them. When you're old you don't worry about stuff going out of fashion I suppose, so it doesn't seem like such a waste to spend a fortune on a skirt. Do you dance?'

'I'm not down here to dance.'

'It's just that I've got a cousin down here, a cop. Actually he's Dad's cousin, but he's a lot younger and not married yet. He said he'd take me and a friend down to St Kilda on Saturday night. Want to come with me?'

'I thought you were going home to put in a black rinse.' Cara lived for Cathy's weekends at home.

'Gran would kill me if I did. They're coming down on Sunday – Gran and Pa, not the other ones. Want to come out to lunch with us?'

'No thanks.'

'Does your family ever come down at weekends?'

'Not out here.' They came down on the train. She met them in the city.

'You never go home. Don't you get on with them or something?'

'Is that any of your business, Cathy?'

'Probably not. To get back to the dance, St Kilda's is supposed to be the best dance in Melbourne. Michelle said she'd come.'

'No thanks.'

She'd told Cathy she wasn't accustomed to sharing a room, that she was an only child. Just one more thing they had in common. Cathy, too, was an only child, an only grandchild for one set of grandparents.

College had been in for eight weeks before Myrtle and Robert came to see where she spent her life and who she spent it with. She had to introduce them to Cathy, who tagged along to get a look.

'Were they your parents or you grandparents?' she asked later.

'I was a change-of-life baby.'

'I was a change-of-lifestyle baby. Mum was seventeen, Dad was eighteen and my Nan was thirty-six. What's your father do?'

'He's a high-school principal.'

'He looks like one. I bet he pushed you into teaching.'

'Why?'

'Because you don't seem to want to be here.'

Didn't.

Had they pushed her? More or less, though not into primary-school teaching. She'd done that all by herself. For years this college had been a light dancing at the end of a dark tunnel. Not much of a light, and a shared room hadn't been a part of that light. She'd seen herself in a single room with a locked door, had imagined sitting at night, writing ten novels, making enough money to buy herself out of her bond before Robert retired. The only place she could get away from Cathy was locked into a toilet cubicle.

'Gerry reckons that's why he's a doctor, because his father pushed him into it. He reckons that a kid following in his parent's footsteps justifies a parent's own choice of profession. Mine are sort of exceptions to the rule. Dad sells cars. Actually he owns the garage that sells the cars – or Gramps does, except he's semi-retired now. I told him to give me a car for my birthday, but they all ganged up and said I wasn't driving in Melbourne yet.'

Cathy was ceaseless – even when she slept. She snored. One of Cara's first purchases had been a roll of cottonwool. Jam enough into the ear canals and it will muffle a snore.

During her fourth month at college Cara admitted to herself that there could be advantages to sharing a room with a girl who never shut up. She left few spaces to fill, and hanging around on the fringes of her growing group was preferable to hanging around alone.

Cathy was a born organiser. Couldn't play tennis to save her life but could organise the tennis matches, then elect herself Cara's partner. Cara played well enough to carry her. She'd had years of tennis lessons, had won kids' tournaments, junior, even one senior tournament. The Traralgon mantelpiece was full of trophies. She could dance too. During her last two years at Traralgon, just to get her out of the house, Myrtle and Robert had driven her miles out of town to ballroom dancing classes.

Child of Jessica was almost finished, or one exercise book of it was, in her locked toilet cubicle. She'd need to type it. These days publishers wouldn't accept handwritten submissions. She'd written to one in Sydney and received a reply – or a page they probably posted out to anyone who sent them a stamped self-addressed envelope. Cara treasured it. It had been touched by someone in a publisher's office.

Child of Jessica, by *Cara Norris*. One day she'd see it in a bookshop. She liked the title, though *Cara Norris* didn't sound like an author's name, more like an old maid schoolteacher's.

Wished Billy-Bob's family name had been Steinbeck. *C.J. Steinbeck* sounded good. *C.J. Morrison. C.J. Hooper*. Either one of them looked better on paper, sounded better then Norris.

Cathy Bryant didn't sound like an old maid schoolteacher. She should have stayed in Ballarat and sold cars.

*

Robert called the college on a bleak Wednesday in late winter. Gran Norris had been taken to hospital with a suspected bowel blockage. She was too old to withstand an operation, he said. They were leaving now to drive up to Sydney, and would pick Cara up on the way through.

'We should be at the college around one, poppet.'

Didn't want to join them in their death watch. Been there, done that – last winter. Gran usually decided to die in winter.

Cara didn't refuse, not immediately. She'd see Pete, her cousin, see Amberley. Didn't want to do the deathbed bit, the concerned granddaughter bit. She felt nothing for Gran, and less since she'd found out why she'd always been 'that girl' to her.

'She's got John and Beth's kids up there, Daddy. I'll come up on the bus if . . . if anything happens.'

'She's ninety-four, poppet.'

And had probably been a pain in the bum at twenty-four. She hadn't caught herself a husband until she was over thirty, and when she had, she'd only run him down because he'd been consumptive. Pete, the family detective, had dug that information up. Blood cousin or not, she loved Pete, the rebel of John and Beth's perfect family. He was working at a tyre place, fitting new tyres onto cars. The other boys had good jobs.

Robert must have checked on bus times and the availability of cabins on the overnight train. Myrtle rang back with the information.

'Thanks,' Cara said. She'd been on the phone to Ansett. If she had to go up there, she was going to fly. Her college fund would pay for it.

They phoned from Sydney the following day to let her know they'd arrived, then at eight-thirty on Sunday night when she was called again to the communal phone in the common room, she knew that this time Gran had gone and done it.

'Hello,' she said.

'Look out the window, moll,' he said.

She knew that voice. Dropped the phone and ran to look out the window, her hand burning with the touch of that phone. Green lawns outside that window. No bike, no sound of a bike.

She hadn't heard Dino Collins's voice in almost three years but her hand shook as she fumbled the phone back onto the receiver.

He called back.

After his third call, she stood beside the phone, disconnecting the instant she heard his voice. Everyone was watching her, amused or annoyed, until Marion, another of Cathy's collection, called her boyfriend. That stopped him, but only for fifteen minutes.

At nine-thirty, he was still at it.

'I've called the police,' Cara said. 'They're currently tracing your call and have asked me to keep you on the line for as long as possible.'

He hung up and didn't call again. She went to her room, Cathy and Marion behind her.

'When you play hard to get, babe, you play hard,' Marion, or Humphrey Bogart, said. The college comedian, Marion; long, lean, dark, wore glasses, and could do dozens of voices.

Cara picked up a pencil and exercise book and went to the bathroom to lock herself in, and that cubicle wasn't so private tonight. Cathy's head popped over the wall. She must have been standing on the toilet seat.

'No foreign matter will be placed into the toilets,' the head of the establishment said – or Marion, from a wall away. 'That applies to pencils, exercise books, pads and cigarette butts.'

Then the two of them were standing on the toilet seat, tossing wads of toilet paper at her.

'We made a rule about privacy,' Cara said.

'Which does not apply to the toilets,' the head of the establishment said.

'Who is he?' Cathy asked.

'Go and annoy someone else.'

'You're conveniently placed on a convenience, Norris.'

'And you said you didn't have a boyfriend. Who is he?'

Marion could do Queen Lizzie too, and was funny enough to make a cat laugh. Two minutes of Lizzie's annual address to the constipated and Cara closed her book and opened the door.

'Is he why you won't go home?' Cathy asked.

'Get lost, both of you.'

'What's his name?'

They were eighteen-year-old kids, and making the most of their first year away from home. Marion's parents lived down on the peninsula. She had four brothers who had made her childhood hell, so she said. The reverse may have applied.

There were days when Cara knew she couldn't survive another hour of either one of them. There were other days when she envied them. Cathy's mother looked like her big sister, and her grandparents looked younger and were more in tune with today than Robert and Myrtle. Marion's mother was like one of the kids, and her youngest brother looked and even sounded like Pete. Wished she'd grown up with them. Wished she'd had four brothers to make her childhood hell.

She was called to the phone again on Tuesday night. Knew it was Dino Collins, and it wasn't. Myrtle and Robert were home. They'd left Sydney at dawn and driven straight through. Myrtle sounded weary, or teary.

'Is she all right, Mummy?'

'She's fine, pet.'

'You have to stop running up there every time she decides to die.'

'I know, pet. I just wanted to let you know we're back.'

'Dino Collins has got the college number, Mummy. Who told him where I was?'

'Who?'

'James Collins. He's got this number.'

'Robert.' Myrtle's hand must have been covering the mouthpiece, though not quite covering it. 'The phone pad,' Cara heard, and she heard Robert curse. He never cursed.

'Don't take his calls, poppet.' Robert was on the line.

'What's going on down there, Daddy?' She could hear another male voice, hear Myrtle speaking to someone. 'Have you got visitors?'

'The police are here. We've had a break-in through one of the rear windows.'

'It was him. That's how he got this number. Tell them it was Dino Collins, Daddy.'

'You are probably right, poppet. Your mum had your name and number on her telephone pad. We can't see it around.'

'Tell them he phoned here on Sunday night and kept it up for an hour.'

'I'll tell them. We'll call you tomorrow night.'

*

Robert had been aware the attack on his house was personal. He'd smelt it when he'd opened Cara's bedroom door. A dog marks his territory with urine. He'd left his scent in her room. The phone calls to the college killed any doubt as to the culprit's identity.

Robert joined Myrtle and the two constables in the kitchen, where for the first time he spoke of Collins's ongoing harassment of his daughter. Making unwanted phone calls was not a capital offence. Myrtle's jewellery box was still in the drawer. Nothing of value appeared to have been taken.

Vandalism the police constable wrote on his report.

A departmental house, it was insured, as were the contents. For a month Robert and Myrtle became nomads, living out of the large case they'd taken with them to Sydney, spending their weekdays at a Traralgon motel, their weekends at a city hotel, where Cara joined them.

She'd had time to learn Melbourne, its markets, its trams, its beaches. They rode trams with her at weekends, playing tourists, Cara their guide. Away from their natural element, she had time to know them, and to accept that though she had little in common with either, she loved them. She had time to decide, too, that God had known best when he'd allowed no issue to come from their marriage. They had each other and needed no one else. Like two halves of the same bowl, each side was useless without its other half.

She watched them at dinner one evening, selecting their meal, the waiter waiting.

'The last time you ate asparagus you were covered in hives for three days, Robert,' Myrtle said.

'Are you sure it was asparagus?'

'Yes I am. I haven't bought it since, and you haven't had hives since.'

He couldn't make a cup of tea; had, to Cara's knowledge, never washed a dish; but at the hotel, he ordered the meals. He carried the cash or chequebook when they shopped, then carried the shopping bags.

The hotel had staff to make up the beds. Myrtle's bed was made up to hotel standards before she left the room, and if Cara walked away from her own unmade bed, Myrtle hurried in, just to tidy things up a little.

Robert paid the bill. He carried the heavy case to the car park.

He'd always driven a car but never considered teaching Myrtle to drive it, and she would have been aghast had he made the suggestion. The eternal passenger, Myrtle, and happy to be the passenger. Cara wasn't. She sat in the rear seat, her head between them, seeing street names before them, directing them where and when to turn. One day she'd drive a car. Cathy could, Marion too.

The lines between male and female may have been clearly defined back before the war. The sixties were erasing them, though not for Robert and Myrtle. For them the line between male and female had become a deep groove they couldn't step across.

COKE AND ASPIRIN

O ne of Myrtle's designated responsibilities was to remember family birthdays, to place early phone calls, and on the morning of 3 October 1963, Cara's nineteenth birthday, she wasn't disappointed. The call came at eight-fifteen, but it was Robert's voice on the line.

'I'm in Sydney, poppet. I flew up last night.' He wasn't calling to wish her happy birthday. 'Gran passed away three hours ago.'

'Mummy flew!'

Shouldn't have said that. Should have said, I'm so sorry to hear that, Daddy – or something. Couldn't take it back.

'Mummy is in Traralgon. I've booked a twin sleeper on tonight's train. You'll need to pick up and pay for the tickets at Spencer Street, poppet.'

Belatedly she asked what had happened, how, if he'd got up there in time to say goodbye.

'John and I were with her. We'll talk later, poppet.' Always that promise to talk later. It never happened. 'I'll ring Mummy now and let her know that you're on your way up there.'

'Not up there!'

'She needs you today.'

'Not up there, Daddy. Tell her I'll meet her down here at the station.'

'I need you to put your own feelings aside, Poppet, and to think of Mummy,' he said. And he hung up – and he hadn't wished her happy birthday – and it was no longer her birthday anyway, Gran had commandeered it for her death day.

Cathy said happy birthday. Cara told her she had to go up to Sydney, that her grandmother had died. Cathy's eyes filled, then she hugged her, and Cara felt like a fraud.

She considered asking Cathy to go with her to Traralgon, then decided against it and asked her to check train times to Traralgon, to double-check the departure time of the night train to Sydney. She made the calls while Cara showered, tamed her hair, packed a small case, and nothing she owned was suitable to wear to a funeral.

Marion owned a straight black skirt. She was a smidgen taller than Cara. Cathy, the organiser, found suitable clothing. Michelle owned a nice black sweater. Not much she could do about shoes. They packed Myrtle-supplied black court shoes with inch-and-a half heels – old ladies' shoes, Cathy named them.

Cathy went with her to the bank, and that day Cara appreciated her company. She and Marion saw her onto the Traralgon train.

*

Myrtle was waiting at the gate when the taxi pulled into the kerb. A kiss but no birthday greeting. Only Gran.

'She hadn't been well all day. John rang around noon, and I was convinced she was crying wolf again, pet. I'll never forgive myself.'

'Are you ready to go?'

'I should have driven up with your father yesterday when John rang.'

'If Daddy had driven, he wouldn't have got there in time to say goodbye. It's lucky you thought she was crying wolf, so stop the guilt bit, Mummy.'

'You sounded like Jenny then,' Myrtle said.

'Are you ready?'

Cara had no intention of paying the taxi driver until she was back at the station. He waited, meter running, while Myrtle checked the wireless, toaster, jug, bedlamps, the back door and windows. She'd probably been ready since ten o'clock, had probably checked everything a dozen times already, but for five minutes Cara waited at the open front door, sniffing the scent of new paint, looking at new carpet.

'Why the new carpet?'

'It was very worn when we moved in,' Myrtle said.

Had Cara gone further than the doorway, she would have noticed the new bed in her room, the brand-new easy chairs in the lounge room. She went no further. Two years ago she'd promised herself she'd never enter that house again.

Twenty minutes later they were on a train back to the city.

Cara wanted to book the luggage through then hop on a tram up to Myer's. She could fill hours in that store and they had four hours to kill. Myrtle wanted to keep her case with her. Her jewellery box was in it, her night attire. Left her guarding it while she picked up the tickets, and not even a queue at the ticket office to kill five minutes of those four hours.

An hour on, and their cases weights around their necks, Cara booked them through. Freed, then, they sat in the cafeteria drinking tea, eating flavourless cake, just to fill a little time.

A dragging day. By five, Myrtle was sitting, turning the pages of a magazine; Cara was walking, attempting to shake off a Traralgon headache. When exercise wouldn't move it, she bought a packet of aspros and a bottle of Coke.

Stood off at a distance, washing two pills down and watching Myrtle, wondering how she'd become who she'd become. She had no close women friends. She socialised with the wives of Robert's friends, spoke to her neighbours, had at one time babysat for one of them, but never visited their houses. She went to church every Sunday, had joined some women's money-raising church group – paid for her magazine with her emergency five-pound note she'd been carrying around so long the moths had probably been at it.

And she owned Amberley, which these days had to be worth big money. She and Robert had a joint bank account most of the lodgers' rent was paid into. Myrtle could have walked down to the bank this morning and withdrawn enough to pay for tickets to Sydney and a taxi all the way to Melbourne, but she'd waited for Cara to travel home, collect her and bring her down here.

How had she managed to run a boarding house during the war years? She must have written cheques, paid bills, made bank withdrawals, caught taxis. With the men away, women had kept the county running, and when the war was won and the men came home, many women had refused to give up their new-won independence. Not Myrtle.

Maybe dependency was healthy. She never had a headache. She was overweight, but as fit as a Mallee bull. Didn't drive, wouldn't fly, dressed as she might have twenty years ago. Her body looked its age, her unlined face didn't. No worries to make worry lines – maybe a few when Cara had been fourteen, fifteen. Round face, curling not quite grey hair, big brown innocent eyes – currently searching the crowd for her daughter.

Cara washed a third aspro down, and the bubbling Coke attempted to flush it out through her nose. Myrtle didn't approve of girls drinking from bottles. Maybe Coke trickling from her nose was why.

Wished they'd all flown up last night. If Robert had asked her to fly, Cara would have gone, not to sit by Gran but to be a bird, to see what the world looked like from the clouds. One day she would. One day she'd drive a car too.

Myrtle now on her feet looking for her, Cara waved the empty bottle before placing it into a rubbish bin.

Cathy swore that Coke plus aspros made you drunk. Theory disproved. She walked a straight line back to Myrtle.

Or maybe not disproved. She asked a question she'd been wanting to ask for years.

'How did you ever find the nerve to register me illegally, Mummy?'

Startled by her words, Myrtle looked over her shoulder. 'People are listening, pet.'

'They don't know us from a bar of soap. You're going to be stuck in a dog box with me all night, so you may as well tell me now.'

'That college is changing you.'

'A lot of things changed me. How did you do it?'

Again Myrtle glanced over her shoulder. 'God meant you to be mine. He worked it out, He and Jenny.'

'How?'

Myrtle frowned, and maybe wished she'd flown. She settled her hat on her curls and looked over her shoulder again.

'You arrived in a hurry in the kitchen. I . . . slipped and fell. Jenny placed you into my arms and told me not to move from the floor. She . . . she dressed, she put her high heels on and walked up those stairs to fetch Miss Robertson, barely half an hour after giving birth to you. They didn't doubt for one moment that you were mine, Miss Robertson and Mrs Collins.'

'She must have been . . . tough.'

'She was a strong girl, and quite wilful.'

'What was she like, Mummy?'

'Look in the mirror, pet.'

'You've told me that. Was she a slut?'

'What sort of girls are you mixing with down here?'

'If she had four kids before she was twenty-one, she must have been a slut.'

'She cared very deeply for her tall soldier. She was like a lost soul when he died.'

'When did he die?'

'In '43. I believe it was May.'

'And seven or eight months later, she was pregnant to Billy-Bob, which doesn't say much for her, does it.'

They spoke then of Gran, of the funeral, of the borrowed black skirt and sweater. Myrtle suggested they buy something more suitable in Sydney.

'What did you bring to wear?'

'My black frock and coat.'

She'd clad herself for the trip in a brown frock and matching lightweight coat, a brown hat. Everything she owned looked fit for a funeral. Most of what Cara owned was pink or beige.

'Did Jenny dress well?'

'She did in the evenings when the band had an engagement.'

'She sang with a band? What sort of a band?'

'Three elderly gentlemen.'

'Elderly?'

'In their sixties. They picked her up from Amberley and drove her home. Now that's enough about it, pet.'

'It's not, you know. Whatever I am, beneath my skin, is her and Billy-Bob Someone. I've got a brother somewhere, two sisters. How would you feel if you had sisters and a brother you didn't know?'

'I still think about Jimmy and wonder how he's grown. He used to call me "my Myrtie".'

'If you got on so well with her, she'd probably like to see you. When this is over, could we go up there?'

'She has no doubt made a new life for herself, pet. It would be wrong for us to disrupt it.'

'Don't I come into the equation? I'm going up to the funeral of an old lady who was no more to me than I was to her. John and Beth's kids were her blood. She was fond of them. I was never more than "that girl".'

'Be kind, pet. She was an old lady who had lived a very hard life.'

'So I heard – a few hundred times. Everyone at the college was saying, "I'm so sorry to hear about your grandmother's passing," and I felt like a fraud. All it means to me is movement forward for Daddy and Uncle John, like life is a big conveyer belt and Gran has been an immovable barrier keeping Daddy and John safe from old age. They've got no protection from it now, and that makes me scared.'

'You come out with the oddest things, pet.'

Cara turned away to watch a family group to her left. They looked like a family, looked more like her than her cousins looked like her. They could have been her cousins.

'Do you know if Jenny had brothers and sisters?'

'She had a sister, Cecelia.'

'How long did you know Jenny?'

'Two years.'

'How come you've got photographs of Jimmy but none of her?'

'One of the lodgers owned a camera. He was fond of Jimmy.'

Old Mr Fitzpatrick had been fond of Jenny too. Until Cara's fourth birthday, Myrtle had owned two photographs of her. She and Robert had decided it might save questions later if they destroyed them. They hadn't foreseen a future where they might speak openly about the girl who had altered their lives.

A voice was calling their train, and gratefully Myrtle rose. 'I've never known a day to go so slowly.'

'Next time we have to catch a train, you'll get here with five minutes to spare.'

A TRAIN THROUGH THE NIGHT

*T*ime out from life, that cramped dog-box compartment, travelling through dark lands. Nothing now to see from the window, only their own reflected faces. They stopped at the occasional station, took on or offloaded one or two, then on again into the dark.

The chap who would turn their couch into bunk beds had already knocked and asked if they wanted their beds made up. Myrtle had been ready for bed at eight. Cara delayed the inevitable, but he knocked again at nine and Myrtle invited him in.

Lights out then and the bunks narrow, hard, and how was anyone supposed to sleep on them?

'How could a woman give birth to a baby then get on this train and forget that baby had ever been born? She must have been a slut.'

'I was almost asleep, and that's a terrible word for a young lady to use.'

'Was she morally corrupt, Mummy?'

'I've already told you she wasn't.'

Myrtle wasn't wishing yet that she'd flown, but perhaps wishing Robert had booked individual cabins. Cara had her trapped below, had her railed in by the ladder and clad in a skin-tight petti-coat, her night attire, her dressing-gown and her jewellery box in the luggage compartment, and Myrtle convinced it wasn't in the luggage compartment.

Cara leaned overboard, her face almost in Myrtle's. 'It's dark. You can answer me honestly.'

'She sang at a serviceman's club for the two years I knew her, and after her soldier was killed, she worked at a clothing factory. The only friend she brought to the house was a girl she worked with at the factory, Lila.'

'Was she a good singer?'

'I only heard her once. I'd turned the radio volume up to silence her, and to annoy me, she sang over it. She had a beautiful voice.'

'Was she educated?'

'She told me once she'd won a scholarship but for some reason was unable to accept it.'

'You don't know why?'

'Family reasons, I believe,' Myrtle said.

Silence then, though a train racing through the night is never silent. There is a rhythm to the metal wheels on metal rail, the howl of warning as the night beast crosses over busy roads. A train will glide on smooth lines, lull its passenger to the very edge of sleep, then shake her awake with that rocking clack-clack, clack-clack.

'She worked at a factory and sang at night while you looked after Jimmy?'

'Yes.' Myrtle yawned. 'She sewed beautifully. She told me once that the only time her mother had sat still was when she was at her embroidery.'

'Did she ever mention her mother's name?'

'I don't recall her doing so. She told me her mother had once embroidered a rose that looked as if it must have had a perfume, that she'd tried her own hand at embroidery but hadn't been able to give a rose perfume, so had given it up. She made all of her own clothing while she was with me, and Jimmy's; she stitched pretty frocks for her girls. She made your first baby gowns, and all by hand.'

'She actually knew me?'

'She remained with us for three weeks.'

'Did she touch me?'

'I was inexperienced. She taught me how to bathe you, to pin on a napkin.'

'She would have been around my age when you first knew her.'

'She was two months away from her twenty-first birthday when you were born.'

'What did she do when she left me?'

'Boarded this train.'

'I mean, did she cry? Was she pleased to be rid of me?'

'We went with her to the station, you and I. She took your hand and said you were shaking hands with her, thanking her for Amberley and a fairytale life. She asked me to write and to send her a photograph.'

'Did you?'

'No.'

'Why didn't you?'

'I was afraid she'd return to claim you. For many years I was afraid.'

'You never heard from her?'

'Never, though on one occasion, when you were quite young, an unpleasant-looking fellow came to our door asking questions. Initially I was petrified she wanted to claim you, but our inquisitor's only interest was in learning how Jenny had supported herself and Jimmy while she was with me.'

'Was he or Sarah North responsible for us leaving Sydney?'

'Moving was a mistake – for all of us, pet, which we very quickly became aware of. At the time, we thought it was for the best. We can never know what the future will hold. I'd taken you illegally. At the time your father and I were determined to hide the truth of what I'd done from you.'

'Which brings us back to my first question. Where did you find the nerve to do something illegal?'

'I'd waited too long to hold my own baby, and there you were, hidden away from me but growing daily. I loved you long before I knew if you were to be my daughter or my son – and I did what I had to do to make you mine. Now go to sleep. We've got a big day tomorrow.'

*

Gran Norris died on a Wednesday. She was buried on a Friday. Robert couldn't get sleepers on the Saturday train so they rode the Sunday bus home, and with every seat filled, the trip was long. Myrtle and Robert sat side by side. Cara was jammed in against the window by a grossly overweight woman who should have paid for both seats. She wanted to use both. Then a hundred or so miles out of Sydney, she took her shoes off.

Hell is sharing a seat with a fat dame and her smelly feet. Cara opened the window wide. The woman complained, so Cara complained of her companion's feet. The dame put her shoes half on so Cara half-closed the window.

Pete had loaned her a book for the journey. It was one of those novels that promise much in the first chapter then fail to live up to expectation. She learned something from it – that a novel needed a good opening chapter. She didn't have a good opening chapter. That's what she'd do when she got home.

Home? Where was home? Sydney hadn't felt like home this time. Blame the funeral. Blame the crowd at Uncle John's, the screaming kids. Pete knew how to handle kids. He would have made a good teacher.

She screwed her neck around to look for Robert. He had the aisle seat, two rows behind her own, his leg stretched out. His bad knee had been playing up since the funeral. His chin was down. He was probably sleeping; the pills he took for his knee made him sleepy. She couldn't see Myrtle. Her chin had probably dropped as they'd driven down George Street.

They woke up when the bus stopped at Albury, and by then Cara was mentally cursing Myrtle for refusing to fly. They would have been home hours ago.

Home?

Myrtle and Robert wouldn't be going home tonight. They'd booked a room at a hotel, had wanted to book one for Cara. She wanted her own bed. Maybe that bed was home. Maybe the college – or Melbourne.

She knew the central city like she knew the back of her hand. She'd been a stranger in Sydney. Robert had given her money to buy a black suit she'd never wear again. She'd bought a pair of shoes Cathy would approve of. Wore them with Marion's skirt and Michelle's sweater and for the first time in her life, at her first funeral, felt smart. Natalie, a cousin-in-law, said she'd looked smart.

She'd met her twice, at Christmas dinners, the only time she saw her cousins now. Grown apart by distance and age and interests – though not from Pete.

He'd made the funeral bearable. She'd sat beside him at the church service and he'd whispered: 'I thought you would have worn your purple,' and she'd damn near cracked her face in her effort not to smile.

Then at the graveside he'd taken two sprigs of artificial purple flowers from his pocket and handed her one. 'Double dare you. On the count of three.' He'd counted three with his fingers, and they'd tossed their sprigs together. That time, Cara had to run.

He'd found her hiding behind a tombstone and they'd shared a smoke. They'd shared a few more in the shrubbery behind John and Beth's house.

He'd grown as tall as Uncle John but not as broad, not yet. Still the same cheeky-faced lovable ratbag kid he'd always been.

She sighed and stared out the window, the breeze in her face. An interminable journey, those five hundred miles between cities. She knew this road too well, had travelled it too many times.

And the fat dame's shoes were off again. Cara slammed the window wide, then lifted Pete's book to shelter her face from the wind. As a good read, it stunk; as a wind shield and air deodoriser, it worked to a degree.

THE RED DRESS

While Cara was in Sydney, Cathy and Marion had been sharing her phone calls, determined to find out who her lovesick swain was. Marion could do a serviceable Cara. All it took was a mild adjustment to her Queen Lizzie voice and a more major alteration to sentence structure. She tested it on the Friday night.

'Where are you calling from?'

'The street out front of your place. Have a look out the window,' he said.

'Did you remember my birthday?'

'Make the most of it, you cock-teasing moll, it could be your last,' the caller said.

Marion tried to hang up the phone. Cathy snatched it. 'Her grandmother just died and you should have more thought for people's feelings.'

She heard just how much thought he had for people's feelings until Marion gathered her wits sufficiently for Humphrey Bogart to snarl, 'Get off this line, slimeball, or you won't have the necessary parts to play with in phone boxes.'

That night they went over and over their conversation with the Cara's caller and were still at it the following day, wondering what they'd said to make him turn nasty.

'He knew I wasn't her,' Marion said. They settled for that.

He rang on Sunday night. Cathy told him Cara was in the shower, that she'd tell her he'd called.

'Tell her I'll call back,' he said.

'She shouldn't be too long. I'm Cathy, her roommate. She probably mentioned me to you – the one who talks too much,' she said.

He asked where they lived, and Marion, listening in, elbowed her and mouthed, 'Don't you tell him.'

'Brighton,' Cathy said. 'She changed her job. She's working with me at Myer's now. I know she's niggly with you about something, but if you wanted to see her, you could come into Myer's. We're on the second floor.'

He told her he might drop by tomorrow. She told him she was dying to meet him, that Cara talked about him all the time. 'I am talking to Robbie, aren't I?'

He wanted to know who Robbie was.

'I thought he was you. Which one are you?'

'Dino,' he said.

'Oh. She's mentioned you too – Dino, like Dean Martin,' she said. 'Can you sing like him?'

He said he could do a lot of things, then he hung up.

'He sounded pretty normal to me,' Cathy reported. 'Do Cara when he calls back and try being nice to him.'

'I'm not playing around with him, Cath.'

'He doesn't know where we are. Just say, "Stop calling me, Dino. We had a good time, but now it's over."'

She did. She said it nicely, too, and released the devil. Cathy called her cousin, Dave, the cop.

*

It had gone eleven before a taxi dropped Cara back to the college, desperate for a shower then her bed. Cathy and Marion were waiting to pounce. They followed her to the bathroom, speaking over the rush of water.

'I've been sitting on a bus for twelve hours. Go to bed.'

'But Dave knows him.'

'So do I. Butt out, Cathy!' Cara emerged, dressing-gown clad, a towel wrapping her hair. She walked to her private toilet cubicle.

'Shoving your head down the lav won't stop his phone calls, but Dave will. He's coming out to talk to you in the morning.'

She used the toilet, while they stood in the next cubicle, relaying their phone calls. She washed her hands, brushed her teeth, pitched the towel at Cathy then led the way to her room where she made a major production of plugging wet ears with cottonwool.

'Him and his friends did something so bad in Traralgon that his friends are in jail, Dave said. They've been looking for him,' Cathy said.

'Turn the light off when you leave.'

'Talk to her in the morning,' Marion said.

Cathy picked up a Myer bag and tossed it at Cara's head. 'Happy birthday, ostrich.'

Something red spilled to the bed. You can't ignore red, not when the head of the establishment where you spend your life frowns on anything red. Young college ladies did not clothe themselves as women of the night, though a few may have been as available. Cara rose up on her elbow to identify the red.

'You can't do that.' It was a frock she and Cathy had looked at weeks ago: straight skirt, empire line, pintucked bodice, small sleeves; absolutely gorgeous and expensive as hell. 'You can't do that, Cathy!'

'I've already done it.'

Tears in Cara's eyes, tears of weariness and something else she couldn't explain. She was home, this room, this bed, and those girls were home. They'd joked about buying that dress, of wearing it into class one morning.

'You can't spend that sort of money on me.'

'It's spent – and I didn't spend it for you anyway. I had a dream the night you left that they were having a huge ball here and I went with Gerry, who had come home for his father's funeral, so I had to wear black, then you turned up in that dress . . .'

'You're mad, Cathy Bryant.'

'. . . and you had long red bobble earrings and ultra-high-heeled black sandals. And anyway, it was marked down to thirty per cent off because someone had split the seam under the armpit.'

Cara was searching for the split under the armpit. Not a long split, but hand-stitched. She knew its original price, and even with thirty per cent off, Cathy had spent too much. 'You can't spend that sort of money on me, Cath.'

'I can't take it back with my sewing in it. Do you still like it?'

'You know I love it.'

'All right then, now shut up and listen. He told me his name was Dino so I told Dave, and you just should have heard him go off about Dino Collins. I don't know what he and his mates did, but Dave said he also broke into your parents' house and peed and pooped all over everything, which is how he got this phone number.'

'He didn't say what they did in Traralgon?'

'No, only that the other two with him were arrested for it.'

'Did he say their names?'

'No. It happened three weeks ago. They've been looking for Dino since. Now go to sleep.'

Go to sleep after that, after that bus trip. She could still see the road when the lights were out. Cathy went to sleep to dream of Gerry; Cara wandered into a place where Dino Collins and the bus became confused. She was going to Sydney with him, and she knew she had to get away, but he had her jammed in against the window.

Woke with a splitting headache and for an instant had no memory of the previous night – until she saw that splash of red and the Myer bag. Remembered then. Looked at her watch, at Cathy's empty bed, and already late for class, she sprang from her blankets to dress. Then saw her hair in the mirror. Wet when it hit the pillow last night, it had dried flat on one side and corkscrewed on the other.

Swallowed two aspros in the bathroom before running her head under the tap and doing what she could with her hair.

Cathy found her there. Dave had arrived with a female colleague.

Police cars and uniforms not being familiar sights on college grounds, the two constables raised more than their fair share of interest and supposition that morning. Cara spoke to them on campus. Cathy and Marion also missed the morning class. They learned that Tony Bell and Henry Cooper had been arrested for the carnal knowledge of a high-school girl, abducted by the trio then driven out of town.

'She was taken home after the attack, where she swallowed every pill in the house then got into the bath and locked the door. Her sisters got in through the bathroom window. The girl is in hospital.'

A Traralgon schoolgirl, Robert would have known. He and Myrtle would have recognised the girl's name – and Cara had spent four days with them and they hadn't said a word about it. 'Rape' wasn't in their prewar vocabulary.

'Cathy said he's been calling you at the college for some time,' Dave said.

'Since the break-in at Mum and Dad's place.'

'You knew him well?'

'We went to the same school when I first moved to Traralgon. He's three years older than me. I'd seen him, but didn't know him until the end of the year when my girlfriend started going out with Henry Cooper. I stopped seeing them and he's been doing what he can to drive me crazy ever since.'

Then Dave asked if she'd agree to meet with him somewhere. She shook her head adamantly, and the aspros hadn't shifted her headache. It pounded so hard, she thought she was having a stroke. As if she'd willingly go within a hundred miles of Dino Collins. As if he'd believe she'd go within a hundred miles of him.

'He'd know it was a set-up.'

'I got his name out of him,' Cathy said. 'I bet I could set it up.'

'No.'

'Do you want to be scared of him for the rest of your life?'

'The courts will let him off. They always do. I'm not getting involved.'

'You're already involved, Cara,' the policewoman said.

'He was the town hero when he was a kid. He gets out of everything. I'm not getting *further* involved.'

'For the rape of a minor, I can guarantee that he won't be let off,' Dave said.

'No.'

'How long could he get?' Cathy asked.

'Ten or fifteen years.'

That got Cara's attention. She looked at Cathy's cousin, seeking the truth in his eyes. She feared Dino Collins. Wanted him locked up, still flinched every time she heard a motorbike. Even in Sydney she'd flinched when Pete rode his bike into the yard. Hated the sound of the telephone ringing.

He'd lie. People would lie for him. 'How old was the girl?'

'Fifteen.'

'Cathy and Marion can set up a meeting. You don't need me.'

'He has the ability to blend into the surroundings,' Dave said. 'You'll recognise him, Cara.'

She'd recognise him anywhere. Known him first as a Jimmy Dean lookalike, then he'd become a bearded bikie, skull and crossbones painted in white on his black leather riding jacket. He could be the boy next door too. For months, he'd bleached his hair white, then, when his dark roots had started growing through, he'd had his hair clipped to the bone. He could cover his eyes with dark glasses, but couldn't change them or the *HATE* on his knuckles or his voice. She'd recognise his voice.

'If you meet him somewhere, in broad daylight, with cops all around you, he wouldn't be able to do anything,' Cathy said.

'He's probably parked out the front now.'

'Prowling the streets of Brighton, or in the dress department at Myer's. He's got your number but he hasn't got a clue where he's calling you,' Cathy said.

It may have been possible to keep on saying no to two police constables; it would never have been possible to keep on saying no to Cathy. Before Dave and the policewoman left, Cara agreed to go with Cathy to Flinders Street Station – if she and Marion could set it up; if Dave could guarantee that Dino would stay locked up if they got him.

*

Cathy haunted the common-room phone that week, but when he finally called and she told him Cara wasn't available but that *she* was, he hung up.

'You'll have to take the next one, Marion.'

He didn't call back.

Myrtle called on Tuesday night, and midway through their conversation Cara handed the telephone to Marion.

'Have you heard anything about Dino Collins?' she asked.

'Has he been calling you again?'

'No.'

'Call the police if he does.'

'What's he done?'

'He was involved in some dreadful thing with the youngest Hunter girl. Her mother is out of her mind with worry.'

'The youngest Hunter girl,' Marion reported when the phone was down. 'Do you know any Hunters?'

Mrs Hunter, the high-school History teacher, had four daughters. Dino Collins hadn't liked schoolteachers.

He didn't call again, not that week, or that month. They heard, via Dave, that Tony Bell had been refused bail, but Henry Cooper, father of one, had been granted bail because his wife was expecting a second baby in February.

Marion had her twentieth birthday in November. Her boyfriend couldn't come down and she wanted to dance, so they took her to St Kilda, Cathy, Michelle and Cara, Cara in red, though until the girls were well away from the college the frock was hidden beneath a skirt and blouse, which spent the evening rolled up and stuffed into Cathy's large handbag. It was a good night, a brilliant band, partners lined up four deep, drawn in by Cara's red frock – only to suffer freezer burn, according to Cathy.

'They're not all like him, you know,' she said.

'You wanted me to dance, I danced, Cath.'

And went home in crumpled skirt and blouse, in a taxi, happy, laughing. It was so good to be a part of a laughing group again. So good to dance again too, and to wear something Myrtle hadn't chosen.

Mid-November, Dino Collins almost forgotten, the Christmas holidays still a few weeks away but Cathy, Marion and Michelle already working out their holiday plans and including Cara in them. She told them she had to go home, to Sydney.

'Two's company, three's a crowd, four is just right. You're coming.'

'I can't.'

'Try finding "can't" in the dictionary,' Cathy said.

Then Myrtle called. There had been a change of plans. Uncle John and his family were driving down to spend Christmas in the Traralgon backyard again.

'I've been invited up to Ballarat, then we're going down to Marion's place near the beach,' Cara said.

'John's family is making such an effort for us to be together. We won't have Gran with us this year.'

'You knew what I'd say when you rang, Mummy. We'll be home in Sydney next year. I promise faithfully that I'll be there, but I'm not setting foot in Traralgon.'

She got away, Myrtle unhappy, Robert more so. Two minutes later she was called back to the phone. Expecting further argument from one or both, she sighed.

'I await my execution,' she said.

Not a sound on the line. Knew it wasn't them. The hairs on the back of her neck knew who it was. Instructed, under threat of death, by Cathy not to hang up on him, she didn't, but signalled wildly to Marion – and if she didn't hang up or say something, he'd smell a rat.

'I haven't seen you in Myer's,' she said.

And Marion came. She was wasting her talent at a teaching college. She was Cara, her tone, even her sigh.

'I'm already in strife with Mummy and Daddy. If they knew I was even speaking to you, they'd be down here so fast they'd leave a trail of smoke behind them.'

If nothing else came of that night, hearing herself as others heard her would stop her calling her parents Mummy and Daddy. Marion sounded like a two year old. And nothing else would come of it. Fifteen seconds later, the phone was down.

'I need a shower,' Marion said. 'He makes me sweat.'

Ten minutes later, Cathy hooked him. 'She's having a shower,' she said. 'You're so rotten to her, you make her sweat. Hasn't anyone ever told you that you catch more flies with honey than you do with vinegar, Dino?'

She may have been in love with Gerry, but she was a born flirt. Fifty per cent of the male students would have lain down and let her walk over them in her stiletto heels.

'Why waste your time on someone who won't even talk to you? There's plenty more fish in the ocean.'

One-sided conversations are difficult to decipher. Cara listened, from a distance.

'I bet I could,' Cathy said. 'Because she did once before. I had a blind date with someone's cousin or something and she came with me in case he was a creep.'

Silence, then, on Cathy's end. 'I won't tell her who, will I . . . I'll say you're some mate of someone's. Not on your life . . . No, it would have to be in the daytime . . . Some of us have to work, you know . . . At lunchtime, I could . . . Come off it . . . How about Friday?'

She organised it. That's what Cathy did – organised tennis matches, holidays, and dates with rapists – at twelve o'clock on Friday, at Flinders Street Station, under the clocks.

A DIFFERENT CITY

*T*hey crossed over at the lights at midday on Friday, Cara, Cathy and Marion. Dave and his colleagues would be there. The girls had been told not to look for them, to take up their position beneath the clocks and try to look as if they were pleased to be there.

Not easy to do. Cara got her back to the wall and looked at her shoes. Cathy opened a bag of Coles butterscotch, popped a lump into her mouth, then offered the bag. Marion took a piece and crunched. Cara's heart needed a slow-down pill, not more sugar. Every nerve in her body was screaming, 'Run!' Only determination to see Dino Collins caged had got her here, was keeping her here.

'Suck on a bit,' Cathy ordered. 'You look as if you swallowed a prune.'

'He won't come. He's smarter than that.'

'He'll come. Tell her your brother's joke, Marion.'

'There was this bloke with a bad lisp. He saved his money for years to buy . . .'

Cara missed the punchline. People everywhere, coming and going, and not him. A dero, sitting on the steps three feet from her, was forcing commuters to walk around him. He had a bottle, disguised in a brown paper bag. He didn't look old enough to be a dero, but he wasn't Dino Collins. Probably a cop.

'There's Dave,' Cathy whispered. She'd found him clad in a business suit, reading a newspaper.

'It's almost ten past –'

'Your watch is fast. Tell us another one, Marion.'

'Have you heard Fred's goodbye to his father as he was heading off to war?'

It was a long and detailed tale, and Cara determined not to miss the punchline. Missed it anyway – if it had one. She'd been watching the steps, the street, expecting a motorbike, certain he'd come that way. He came with a crowd from the rear, from the platforms, came well dressed for his date, in sports slacks and shirt, his hair blond, cut in an Elvis style, fashionable sunglasses to hide his eyes, four bandaids to hide the tattoo she'd watched him cut into his left knuckles with a razorblade when she was fourteen.

'Waiting for me, moll?' he said.

Marion was the actress, Cathy the organiser. Cara was a runner. She ran.

*

The lights must have been green at the Flinders and Elizabeth streets intersection. She didn't notice if they were or not but was on the far side when Cathy called her name. She waited, her hand on her heart, holding it in behind her ribs.

'They got him,' Cathy panted. 'They dived on him from every direction, and you should have seen his face. I was expecting a big bruiser in bikie gear. He's fabulous looking! I could go for him in a big way – if I didn't know.'

Cara walked on. Cathy kept up, panting as she told her story. 'I sort of stood in front of him when you took off. He shoved me out of the way. I could have fallen down those steps and broken my neck. I spilt all my lollies, then cops came at him from everywhere and you should have seen his face.'

She was a bored college student, playing at cops and robbers, but obligated to keep her eye on Cara, she'd missed out on the final scene.

'Slow down, will you. These shoes are killing me. You shouldn't have taken off like that. No one was going to let him hurt you.'

He'll find a way, Cara thought and crossed over Little Bourke, Cathy at her elbow.

'We have to go up to the police station now so they can do the official bit or something. I've always wanted to see the inside of Russell Street.'

'I've done my bit and I don't want to see the inside of Russell Street. I'm going home.'

'You can't yet.'

'I can. Leave me alone now, Cathy.'

'If you want them to lock him up, then we have to finish what we started.'

Cara swung around to face the girl who had got her into this mess, the girl who never shut up, who kept her awake half the night with her snoring, who forced her to write in the lavatory – who had killed her writing stone dead these last months.

'I'm crawling with him, Cathy. He's crawling through my head.'

'It's crawling because you're an ostrich who has got her head in sand thinking that the dingo pack can't see you, then you wonder why you get bitten on the backside – and your parents are as bad as you are. If he'd been scaring the tripe out of me since I was fifteen, Gramps would have belted him up and Gran would have been beside him, putting the boot in.'

'They didn't know! And you know nothing about me or my parents, so don't start making your uninformed judgements –'

'Me make judgements? Me? You're the one who spends her life making judgements, and none of us come up to scratch, do we?'

'Go to hell, Cathy! I'm sick of you trying to run my life. I'm sick of your snoring too.'

'Me snore? You're the one who snores. You tick. Every morning when I wake up, you sound like a ticking time bomb.'

'You snore every bloody night –'

'Yeah, well you tick every bloody morning! I stood over you watching for an hour the morning after you came back from your gran's funeral, trying to work out how you did it – and I never said one word to you about it, did I? And I still haven't got a clue what makes you tick – and if you think you can pick a fight with me, then you haven't got a clue what makes me tick either, so stop trying.'

Cara gave up and walked faster. Cathy kept pace, taking three steps to Cara's two.

'Have you ever trusted anyone in your life?'

She'd trusted Rosie, and look where that had got her. She'd trusted her parents and found out they weren't her parents.

'He raped you too, didn't he?'

'He didn't rape me, now shut up about him.'

'It's plain obvious that he did something pretty horrible to you.'

Cara crossed over Bourke Street, turned towards Swanston and walked fast towards Myer, Cathy now limping at her side, limping until they were directly out the front of Myer's entrance, when she gave up keeping up and flopped down to the step to take her shoes off.

Black stiletto sandals, though very smart, were not great to walk in. Cara wore flatties, chosen by Myrtle, paid for by Robert, probably expensive, and very comfortable. She walked on in them, merging with the crowd, walked six or eight yards with the crowd, then stopped, forcing the crowd to fork around her. Easier to keep on moving with them, to be swallowed up by them, a separate part of nothing, one grain of sand on a lonely beach, a solitary bean in a bean bag.

Cathy was a part of the whole, sitting unconcerned, attempting to unclip her stocking suspenders without lifting her skirt.

Cara walked back. 'What do you think you're doing?'

'They're brand-new stockings and I'm not walking in them, that's what.'

Cara shielded her from the disinterested crowd until the stockings were off, rolled in a bunch and stuffed into her handbag. Cathy, the organiser, the fixer, the problem solver, Cathy sitting there, wriggling her toes and purring with ecstasy – and she looked like a twelve-year-old kid wearing her mother's lipstick, too small to run her own life, let alone the world.

'I'm sorry.' Cara sat at her side. 'My insides are shaking. I've had a headache for six months and I want to vomit.'

'Me too – or while we were waiting for him I wanted to vomit – except I wanted Dave to get him more. Marion would have seen them handcuff him, and I had to chase you, you twit.' She wriggled her toes. 'My little ones feel dead. The bottom straps cut off their blood supply. What if they turn black and drop off?'

'Then your strap won't cut into them,' Cara said. Plump little feet, stubby little Cathy toes, a kid's hands but nice fingernails, painted an unacceptable red for her city date. 'Buy yourself a pair of flat shoes.'

'I look like a midget in flatties.'

'Feet were given that we may walk,' Cara said, studying her nondecorative shoes and at the step below them. Saw the shape of a telephone in the wear pattern. No telephones in jail cells. No more phone calls. Lots of metal bars. He'd be locked in by now, a prowling tiger in the zoo. They'd give him prison clothes, cut off his hair, and when the roots grew through dark, he'd look piebald – and forever more he'd blame her for it. And be more vicious when they let him out. And they would. His aunty would pay for the best solicitor and he'd pull out the old sob story.

Dave had said ten to fifteen years. Michelle Hunter was fifteen. He might get ten years.

Even if he only got five years. She had one more year of college then three years working wherever the Education Department sent her. Then after that, she'd go to England with Pete.

'Girls never broke up with him,' she said. 'He was the one who broke it off. The girl he raped must have broken up with him.'

'Do you know her?'

'Her mother taught History at high school. She's got four daughters. Cynthia is my age. The youngest is Michelle.'

'Michelle?' Cathy's appetite whetted, she wanted more, so on the steps out front of Myer's, Cara gave her more.

'He started coming after me when I was fourteen. Having him after me made me popular for a while. We'd just moved to Traralgon. I didn't know anyone.'

'You went out with him?'

'Not really. He was a part of the group. I let him give me a ride home a couple of times, danced with him, smoked his cigarettes. Then his aunty kicked him out and he and Rosie, my girlfriend, and her boyfriend, Henry Cooper, decided that we were all going up to Sydney. I backed out, and a week later was walking home from the library and they pulled up beside me, Tony Bell, Henry Cooper, Rosie, Leanne and Dino. They asked me if I wanted a lift home. I said no thanks, then Rosie and Leanne got out of the car to walk with me and the boys drove along beside us. It was normal for them, just a normal Saturday afternoon.

'We were about a block from my place when Dino and Tony Bell got out and Leanne and Rosie got into the front seat. I was standing beside the car, telling Rosie I'd see her at school on Monday, and Dino and Tony Bell pushed me into the back seat, got in and the car took off.'

She was reliving it, seeing that afternoon as she'd seen it a thousand times, but today Cathy was at her side. And not a word out of her either.

'I'd borrowed two books from the library, two of Jane Austen's. I dropped one when they pushed me in. I had one in my hand, *Mansfield Park*. I wasn't concerned. I'd been in Henry Cooper's car a dozen times. I told them I'd dropped my library book and they drove around the block and Leanne got out and picked it up.

'Rosie said they were still going to Sydney and were having a going-away party. They drove out to the bush at the back of town and they got out. I tried to, but Dino held on to me until they closed the door. Once the rear doors of Coop's car were shut, you couldn't get them open from the inside. He'd taken the handles off. It had been a joke. Coop's bird coop, they'd called it. Catch them and they can't fly away.

'I thought Dino wanted to talk me into going up to Sydney.' Cara shook her head and closed her mouth.

'We got him,' Cathy said. 'Keep telling yourself that.'

'We got him, Cath, and if you think he'll forget that, in ten years, in twenty years, then you're wrong. There's something missing in his head.'

'Tell me the rest.'

'*Mansfield Park*,' Cara said. 'I don't know how it happened. He was all over me, trying to get my . . . my clothes off. I was yelling out to Rosie, my best friend, and fighting him. Then the book was in my hand and somehow I must have smashed it into his face.

'I could have stabbed him in the heart and he wouldn't have stopped, but he was in love with his face. I didn't wait to see why he stopped. I was over the front seat and out and running for my life. There was a farmer on the road, driving his cows home. He and his wife took me back to my house.'

'Did you go to the police?'

'The farmer wanted me to. You only had to say Dino Collins's name and everyone knew him. They told me he had to be stopped. I said I'd tell Mum.'

'What did she say?'

'I'd been giving her and Dad the run-around for months, and Rosie had already been there to drop off my library books – and tell her I'd left them in Henry's car. "You promised Daddy and me that you'd have nothing more to do with those boys," Mum said. I didn't tell her what they'd done.'

'You twit.'

'If I'd known what I'd done to his face, I would have. I snapped off one of his front teeth, broke his nose.'

'Didn't look so fabulous, eh?'

'Not until the plaster was off his face and his aunty bought him a false tooth.'

'Good for you.'

'It wasn't. Rosie took his side. She turned going to school into hell. And every time I left the house, he was there. Mum and Dad used to take me to Sale, to ballroom dancing classes. He must have followed us one night. I stopped going. He stopped everything.'

'That's why you never go home. You have to put all of that in your statement,' Cathy said.

'I'm not repeating it, and you're going to swear not to tell anyone.'

'I'm too trustworthy to swear to something like that! That Michelle kid will be too young to do much good at the trial, if she even goes to it. What happened to you is proof that she's not lying. And it can all be backed up too. Dentists and doctors keep records, and the farmer and his wife will remember. What were their names?'

'Stop, Cath.'

'I won't. We're going down to Russell Street now and you're going to tell Dave exactly what you told me – and if you won't, I will,' Cathy said, forcing her foot back into the stiletto sandal.

'Stop crippling yourself with those things!'

'I'm not going to a cop station barefoot!'

'Stay there and I'll buy you something.'

'No. We'll get a tram.'

'Do as you're told for once in your life!' Left her, sitting, one sandal on, the other one in Cara's hand.

And something had changed. Melbourne's streets looked cleaner, wider, the shop windows brighter, the crowd in Myer's basement happier – just something different.

Something different about Cathy too. So she talked too much, so she snored, so she thought she was the axis that moved the world, but she was too trustworthy to swear she'd keep a secret she didn't plan to keep, which for some weird reason meant more to Cara than the keeping of that secret.

And when all was said and done, would it matter if Myrtle and Robert and the whole of Australia learned what had almost happened to her when she was fifteen? Kids of fifteen are brainless. They need to live a few more years before they learn to judge who they can and can't trust.

She bought a pair of size-four cushioned flatties, then the girls continued on with the crowd, Cathy keeping her eye out for Marion, wanting from her a blow-by-blow account of the taking of Dino Collins.

Cara didn't search for Marion. She looked at the street, at the sky, smelling the scents of Melbourne, seeing it for the first time as *her* city. She'd just spilled her worst secret to it, on the steps out front of Myer, and the city walls hadn't crumbled, hadn't come tumbling down on her.

The sun burned down from a too-blue sky, trams trundling by, cars and trucks jamming the street, newspaper men squatting on pavements, their wares spread. Nothing had changed since the last time she'd been into town, yet everything had. The vampire feeding on her since a month after her fifteenth birthday had been turned to dust, not with a silver bullet, or a wooden stake driven through the heart, but by a curly-headed kid who barely came up to her shoulder, and who couldn't stand Jane Austen. Along with the size-four soft-soled flatties, Cara had bought a cheap paperback copy of *Mansfield Park*. She'd never read it.

'We did one of her books in form four and I vowed never to read another one,' Cathy said. 'How much were my shoes?'

'How much was my red dress?'

'It's not red, it's claret, and it was a birthday present. How much?'

'Merry Christmas,' Cara said.

'It's not Christmas yet, and I like opening surprises. Are your parents going to let you come up to Ballarat with us?'

'Yep,' Cara said.

A Shrinking World

*T*hat same evening, Jenny and Jim were seated at the McPhersons' dining-room table, sorting through dusty boxes of photographs, flipping through old school albums, pointing to near-forgotten faces, when someone knocked at the door.

John rose from the table and returned with the local constable at his side. He was looking for Jenny.

Police don't go door-knocking the neighbourhood for you to let you know you've won the lottery. Jen and Jim stood up when he walked into the room.

'I took a call earlier tonight from Melbourne. They've picked up a lass claiming to be your daughter, Mrs Hooper.'

And a ghost walked over Jenny's grave. Jim didn't know about the baby she'd left with Myrtle in Sydney. No one knew about it. A shock of adrenalin hit her bloodstream, every pint of it racing to her eardrums. Barely heard Raelene's name.

She heard Jim's reply. 'She's Jen's first husband's daughter.'

'She was taken into custody three days ago. Until this evening she's refused to give her name.'

'Into custody? She's twelve years old!' Jenny said.

'Eighteen, I was told, Mrs Hooper.'

'She's not even twelve until next week!'

'All I know is what I've been told,' the constable said. 'She was picked up for shoplifting in the city.'

'She's a little kid. She's with her mother, in Moe.' Jenny turned from the constable to Jim, then back to the constable. 'Her mother's name is Florence Keating. She and her husband moved down to Moe a few years ago.'

He took down the names of the Keatings, then questioned Raelene's age.

'She was born on 27 November 1951. Raelene Florence King. I married her father. He died in July '58. Where have they got her?'

The constable couldn't, or wouldn't say. 'I'll make a few calls and get back to you, Mrs Hooper,' he said.

'We'll be at home,' Jim said.

The constable knocked on their door at ten-thirty. Florence and Clarrie Keating had not yet been located. Raelene had been moved to a juvenile detention centre.

'We'll go down there in the morning,' Jenny said.

*

She didn't sleep that night and at six drove down to the old place and woke Georgie. They left at seven and were at a Kilmore road-house by nine, placing their breakfast orders, a radio playing in the background.

'Toasted raisin bread and coffee,' Georgie ordered, and the radio announcer interrupted the song.

'*President John Kennedy, aged forty-six, was assassinated in Dallas Texas . . .*'

For Georgie, John F. Kennedy's assassination would forever more be associated with coffee, toasted raisin bread and the Beatles singing 'Yesterday'.

'*His wife Jacqueline cradled his head in her arms as secret service agents raced towards the car . . .*'

The woman behind the counter was still waiting for Jenny's order. 'Tea and a cheese and bacon toasted sandwich,' she said.

If she lived to be a hundred, Jenny wouldn't forgive America. Every time she heard that country mentioned, or read of it, she thought of waking naked on the Sydney beach, and the baby one of those drunken raping sailors had made.

While Georgie listened for more news on the assassination, Jenny stared out the window, seeing thick-necked Hank, baby-faced Billy-Bob.

Crazy names. Crazy country with a penchant for murdering their leaders.

The waitress brought their order; they ate fast, paid for their meal, and Georgie behind the wheel, they drove on.

The country roads had been all but deserted. Not so down here. Saturday or not, traffic sandwiched them in, traffic lights held them fast in jams of exhaust-spewing vehicles while Jenny played navigator, tracking main roads on her Melbourne road map, and Georgie amused herself by multiplying the capacity of petrol tanks in the stretch of vehicles hemming her in.

'How can they keep sucking enough oil out of the ground, Jen? What's filling up the spaces they leave behind? Do you reckon we'll implode one day?'

Australia was pumping her own oil now; America had been pumping it out for years. Cavities had to fill with something, though Jen had enough cavities closer to home to worry about: Margot's teeth were falling to bits.

Maisy swore she'd lost two teeth with each of her ten babies. Margot may not have acknowledged giving birth to Trudy, but if something wasn't done soon about her teeth, she'd lose the lot. Doing anything with that girl was a problem.

It's strange how the mind works, how, while it's pondering one imponderable, an unrelated brain cell sparks.

'Lincoln,' she said.

'What?'

'Abraham Lincoln. They assassinated him when Granny was a girl,' Jenny said, realising the root of one crazy Yankee name. Link would have been short for Lincoln, Hank would have been a Henry, Billy-Bob would have been William Robert. She'd never given a thought to the roots of their crazy names, tried not to think about them. Put them away in a dark cave and posted one of Granny's signs in front of it – *Wrong way, go back*. Hadn't thought about them in years. Had told Jim everything, except about them. Told herself the Japs had sunk their boat and that sea snakes were playing in and out the windows through their eye sockets.

Could have told Jim. He was the gentlest of men – as he'd been the gentlest of boys. She'd never known his mother. Jim must have taken after her. Vern Hooper had been a hard old coot.

Jim hated the Japs. Jenny hadn't known any to hate. She'd read about them throwing themselves off cliff tops to avoid surrender. She'd surrendered. At fourteen she'd surrendered on old Cecelia Morrison's tombstone. She'd surrendered again on that Sydney beach. Surrendered to Vern Hooper's blackmail.

You've got the recoil of a rubber band, Granny used to say.

How many times can a rubber band recoil before it perishes? This morning it felt worn out. Didn't want what was waiting for her in Melbourne. They had a beautiful life, she, Jim and Trudy.

She hadn't wanted to move back to Woody Creek. She'd done it for Jim – and Elsie, Trudy's grandmother.

During their first weeks of living in Vern Hooper's house she'd felt the old coot and his daughters in every room, felt them in bed with her too. Loved Frankston, loved the anonymity of Melbourne. Had loved Sydney – for a time.

Very different cities. Melbourne sprawled; it had a ditch instead of a harbour. Both had miles of suburbs, miles of streets.

Back in '39 when she'd spent four months in Melbourne with Laurie Morgan, the buildings hadn't been as tall, there'd been few cars on the roads. In '46 and '47, when she'd lived down here with

Ray, horses had still commanded their fair share of the roads. No horses now. All died of exhaust fumes.

Wondered at times what Laurie was doing, if he was still taking what he'd considered his due, if he'd married, had other kids, if they looked like Georgie.

She was all Laurie – or seventy-five per cent of her was. A good, kind-hearted, beautiful kid, and capable with it. There was much Jenny regretted in her life. Marrying Ray came high on the list, though no higher than not signing Margot away at birth. Never, never had she regretted keeping Georgie.

Glanced at her, sitting behind the wheel, as patient as a judge. Jenny would have been cursing the cars hemming her in, cursing every traffic light.

They found the address given to them by the constable, found a parking space and Georgie backed that big car into it on her first attempt.

Jenny regretted giving Raelene into Florence's care when she saw her. She barely recognised her. That kid was twelve years old and had the build of a woman – and was dressed like one: makeup, dangling earrings, high-heeled shoes.

'What the hell have they done to you?'

'I'm not going back to her,' Raelene replied.

A long, long day that one. Florence and Clarrie turned up after midday, with small identical boys.

Jenny, out front, having a smoko, saw them approaching and walked down to meet and accuse them.

'We can't control her, Jenny,' Florence said. And after their long drive to get there, Raelene refused to speak to her mother.

'If I can't live with you, I'll stay here,' she said to Jenny.

'Six years is a long time, Raelene. You'll be locked up until you're eighteen.'

They left her with Georgie and walked out to a corridor, Jenny and Clarrie to light cigarettes, Florence to weep while tiny boys explored.

'She won't go to school, Jenny.'

'She's twelve years old!'

'She's very cruel to her little brothers.'

'Slap her backside. She's twelve years old!'

'She's got too much of her father in her,' Clarrie said.

'She's half his size. Sit on her if you have to.'

'Flo is having another one,' Clarrie said. 'She's been as sick as a dog.'

The day ended with Jenny agreeing to take responsibility for Raelene until school went back next year. It ended with Clarrie Keating looking relieved, a twin on each arm, with Florence bawling, with Raelene refusing to say goodbye to her. But it ended, or the city part of it did, and too late to visit Donny, had they known where to find him. He'd been moved from the children's home. He was thirteen, and according to Florence, almost as big as Ray.

It took an hour to get out of the city, and by six, when they pulled in to buy ice-creams, the news of John F. Kennedy's death was on a small wall-mounted television, a crowd standing around watching it.

Technology, not empty oil wells, would shrink the planet. Across the world that day in November of 1963, newspaper, telephone, radio and television told the sorry tale of John F. Kennedy's assassination.

Robert Norris's radio was tuned in to the news. His attitude towards America differed from Jenny's. The Americans had saved Australia; they'd ended the war. Little else on the news that night, until the tail end.

A twenty-two-year-old Traralgon man was arrested in Melbourne yesterday and last night charged with the carnal knowledge of a minor.

'They've got him!' Robert said.

'Those poor people,' Myrtle said.

Not until the following day did they learn of Cara's role in the arrest of James Collins, and not from her did they learn it. Two city police came early to the house and caught Myrtle in her dressing-gown.

For a week strange policemen wandered around Traralgon. For that week televisions replayed the assassination of John F. Kennedy. Viewers saw the bullet's impact, saw Jackie throw her body across her husband's. Lee Harvey Oswald became a house-hold name. His subsequent murder was played and replayed.

For a time, the world pitied Jackie and her two fatherless children, but the world moves on. Christmas was coming and viewers had their own problems to deal with.

There came a day when the constant replays no longer raised that initial response of stunned abhorrence. Too familiar with the tale of how Lee Harvey Oswald shot the president, then Jack Ruby shot Oswald, viewers began to see those replays as they might a commercial for a third-rate crime show, one in which the writers had failed dismally to suspend their audience's disbelief. As if one bullet could pass through the president then get his bodyguard. As if the police would march the American president's murderer through a corridor crowded with newsmen, past a crazed club owner toting a gun. It was all a bit too convenient, a bit too Shake-spearian – he'd had a bad habit of reaching for the 'kill 'em all off' endings.

And what happened to Jack Ruby anyway? Did someone shoot him? Did he hang himself? Something happened to him, but by Christmas, who really cared? He was only a bit player in an uncon-vincing tale.

'Change that bloody channel, Roy. There'll be something better on than that.'

PARENTHOOD

If couples, young and starry-eyed,
Read contracts, signed by groom and bride,
  They'd never don parental halter
  But leave each other at the altar.
  'You take what kids which God might send,
  Though they will drive you round the bend.
  You'll love, obey and vow to feed
  Those monsters sprung from your own seed.
  And you shall seek no escape clause
  And in your labour never pause
  Until you're sixty, sixty-five —
  If you should happen to survive.'
  Oh parenthood
  Cruel guarantee,
  Of life-long sweat and drudgery.

Jenny read the poem again. It had won the Country Women's poetry competition and they'd published it in one of their recipe books – her name beneath it. Jim's fault, he'd typed it up, posted it to them.

Vern Hooper's library was Jenny's escape room, her reading, writing, sewing room, and since she'd brought Raelene home, Jim's typewriter and paraphernalia had joined her own. A busy room that one, but not a hint of Vern Hooper in it. No room for him. Fabrics were piled on her large cutting table, with Jim's typewritten pages. He was currently compiling a history of the town and surrounding district.

In Armadale Jenny had taken in sewing to survive. Miss Blunt, town draper and dressmaker for fifty years, had sent Jenny a list of her prices back in '47. Two weeks after Jenny had moved back to town, Miss Blunt came to her door to ask if she'd be interested in taking on some of the finer work her own eyes couldn't handle. It had led to a lot more than that.

As a girl Jenny had dreamed grand dreams of fame and fortune. For a few brief months of her life, her voice had fed her offspring. She'd achieved fame in Woody Creek, not for her voice, but for a big Italian wedding. She'd made the bridal gown, six bridesmaid and three flower-girl frocks – and charged Miss Blunt's prices.

Not that she needed the money. Jim had money and what was his was hers, but she'd never learnt to be dependent on a man. It was more than that though. She delighted in inviting her customers into Vern Hooper's library for fittings, and liked it even more if those customers were women who had once looked down their noses when Jenny Morrison had brought her illegitimate trio into town.

Loved offering them her accounts, every item, every zipper, button, reel of thread added to the bill, with her name, address and new telephone number professionally printed at the top. Miss Blunt had ordered the docket books for her.

Until she'd brought Raelene home, they'd managed without the telephone, but Raelene now had a city welfare dame allocated to her by the children's court, a fifty-odd-year-old Miss Lewis, who was very good at rubbing in the guilt. According to her, Jenny and

Florence were the ones at fault, not Raelene. Maybe they were, or maybe Florence and Clarrie were right about Raelene having too much of her father in her.

Living with that brat of a girl reminded Jenny of living with Sissy. She'd rarely thought about her sister in years. Thought of her daily now. Thought of Norman too. He'd possessed the patience of a judge. A week of Raelene and Jenny had run out of patience.

She had patience with her sewing, with her bookwork. Norman would have been proud of her bookwork. He'd kept itemised household account books, station books, books for the town committees. As a kid she'd loved watching him turn those big pages with his chubby fingers, then place a ruler beneath the day he'd last had a haircut. She could flip back through her carbon copies to the day she'd charged Joe Flanagan's wife twelve pound for a new suit – or charged him. He'd delivered his wife for her fittings, had probably chosen the gruesome fabric. For years that mean old coot had refused to allow electricity wires to be taken across his land to Granny's. She could flip through the pages to the day she'd charged Hooper's farm manager's snobby wife fifteen pound for a green flyaway outfit she'd worn to her daughter's wedding – and her bill for the Italian wedding blew her mind. She'd charged him one hundred and twenty-three pound twelve and six, then spent a pile of it on Margot's teeth – and would spend more on Tuesday.

Margot was twenty-four. She should have been well out of her parental guarantee, but she had no income and was never likely to have an income. Someone had to pay for her teeth.

Someone had to clothe her too. Jenny's Christmas gifts, birthday gifts were clothing. Elsie fed her. Maisy took her with her to Willama every month or two. Teddy slept with her. She still denied Trudy, which was to the good.

Initially Jenny had planned to tell that little girl how she'd come into being, but the older she grew, the older Margot grew, the less Jenny thought about telling her. Trudy was a Hooper, and in town, only Georgie and the Halls knew that she wasn't. Maybe they'd tell her she was adopted when she was older, and maybe they wouldn't.

Every Friday, Maisy drove down to Willama. She had two married daughters down there and umpteen grandkids. Last Friday she'd taken Margot with her and had her hair and Margot's permed.

Perms frizzed. Everyone knew it. Margot's hair was too fine and Maisy should have known it. It had frizzed more than most, but did draw the eye away from her jaw and her rotting teeth. Then Elsie told her she looked like Jenny, and Raelene laughed and said, 'More like Harpo Marx.'

Jenny should have known better than to take that brat down there. When Raelene was six years old, she and Margot had damn near burnt Granny's house down with their arguing.

'You're a nasty-mouthed little bugger. That was cruel,' Jenny said when Margot went *ahzeeing* across the paddock. 'You won't be going to Willama with us on Tuesday.'

Later, at home, Raelene, fighting angry, shoved Trudy, who slammed into a cupboard door, and Jim, who didn't have a violent bone in his body, looked as if he wished he had a few. Jenny manhandled that brat of a girl into her bedroom and locked her in. That had been Norman's way. It was the only way Jenny knew. Raelene would learn what they considered to be acceptable behaviour, or she'd go back to Florence.

Margot had never learnt. Jenny drove down to the old place at nine on Tuesday morning and found her wearing Gertrude's old black felt hat, with what appeared to be a nursing uniform, and brown sandals with white ankle socks.

'You're not going like that, Margot. Get those socks and hat off,' Jenny said.

'I've tried, lovey,' Elsie said.

Fifteen minutes Jenny wasted in trying, then had to give up. And Elsie wasn't going with them. Maybe she'd had enough. And Margot wouldn't sit with her. She got into the back seat.

Gertrude's hat ended its life eight miles from Willama, when Jenny reached back, snatched and tossed it through an open window. The rear-vision mirror explained why Margot had refused to take it off. She'd attempted to cut off the frizz.

'Jesus Christ, Margot!'

Diverted to Maisy's daughter's house. It was all she could do. Borrowed a pair of scissors and did what she could with what was left, then wet it and hoped there was enough left to frizz. They sat on her then and got her socks off.

Neurotic, obnoxious, obsessive to the extreme, and to Jenny as a solid block of kryptonite is to Superman – Margot stripped Jenny of her powers, had given her a kryptonite headache before she got rid of her into the dentist's surgery.

'Do what you have to,' she told him.

He'd anaesthetised her the last time, and she'd gone home with six fillings and three missing molars. On that Tuesday in January '64, Jenny returned her to Elsie with more fillings, one less molar and only space and bloody cottonwool gripped between her eyeteeth.

'He'll make her a partial plate when her gums heal,' Jenny said, and headed for home and a handful of aspros.

To find Lila Jones/Roberts and a young bloke sitting with Jim in the kitchen, Trudy on Jim's lap and no sign of Raelene.

'Steve Freeman, my new bloke,' Lila introduced.

'Pleased to meet you,' Jenny said, unpleased to meet him, reaching for aspros before screaming out the back door, 'Raelene!'

Didn't expect her to reply. She didn't. Swallowed pills and turned to her visitors.

Lila was two years her junior, her new bloke looked twenty-five, and the last thing she needed today was visitors, and the last visitor in the world she ever needed was Lila Jones/Roberts, soon to be Freeman.

'We're getting hitched when the divorce is final,' Lila said.

As girls they'd worked together at the clothing factory in Sydney. Lila knew Jenny had been pregnant when she'd left work. Way back, when Lila was married to Billy Roberts, Jenny had told her she'd aborted that baby, but abortion or not, she didn't want Jim to know about it. She was scared stiff of Lila's flapping mouth.

And they wouldn't leave. At four, Raelene still not home, Lila had the gall to ask how she and Steve might be fixed for a bed for a night or two.

'We're full up. Try the hotel,' Jenny said. 'And I have to go and look for Raelene.'

They left – and Jenny left to look for Raelene.

She wasn't with Georgie, wasn't at the Dobsons'. Young Neil told her he'd seen her with Sharon Duffy.

Found her out there.

'Get in the car, Raelene.'

'Get mad at me again, why don't you.'

'Get in that bloody car, Raelene.'

She got in.

GOOD BEHAVIOUR

*C*ara spent Christmas and New Year in Ballarat, then the first three weeks of January at Portsea. She bought a bikini, and one of Marion's brothers told her he was in love with her. Like their sister, they were merciless tormentors. There was only one way to treat them, like she treated Pete, which turned those weeks at Portsea into the best weeks of Cara's life. Freed of Myrtle chasing her with a hat and protective clothing, she perfected a tan for the first time in her life.

And thank God for that unforgettable January, because the February that followed it was the worst month of Cara's life. She had to give evidence in court, had to sit in a courtroom with Dino Collins and the other two Traralgon mongrels.

The trial had been going for a day before she had to give her evidence, which was worse than her worst imaginings.

Someone had supplied the trio with suits, white shirts, quiet ties; they looked like three up-and-coming young businessmen, off to work in the city. Collins's left hand was bandaged, his tattooed *HATE* hidden. No sunglasses in court. He couldn't disguise the hatred in his eyes when he looked at her.

And Rosie was there, wearing a maternity frock. Cara hadn't expected her to be in court – and sitting beside Henry Cooper's deadbeat mother and two of his deadbeat sisters. No sign of Dino Collins's aunty.

Mr and Mrs Hunter were there. No Cathy, no Marion, who had to wait their turn in the witness box. With no one she dared look at, Cara looked at her hands.

She wasn't a good witness. Replied easily enough to the prosecutor's questions. Knew what he was going to ask her, that's why, and she'd practised her answers. He'd told her to look at the jury when she replied, or at the judge. Couldn't. If she looked up, she saw the three deadbeat Cooper women murdering her, saw Rosie's eyes doing likewise.

Tony Bell's father owned half-a-dozen electrical shops. He had money. Dino Collins would have inherited his parents' money by now. Between them they'd hired three white-wigged, black-gowned barristers. One would have been fifty, two might have been thirty. It was one of the younger men who attacked Cara.

'I put it to you that you got into the car of your own free will,' he said.

'I've already said that Tony Bell and James Collins pushed me into the back seat.'

'You had been in the car previously, as part of a group,' he accused. She had, and couldn't deny it. 'Were you raped that day, Miss Norris, harmed in any way?'

'No.'

'Is it not true that it was James Collins who came away from that particular encounter with the injuries?'

'Yes.'

He kept her in the witness box for an hour, going over and over the same ground. He knew she'd agreed to go up to Sydney with Rosie, Cooper and Collins. She couldn't deny that either. Couldn't deny she'd kissed Collins a couple of times, that she'd ridden on the back of his motorbike a couple of times. There was too much she couldn't deny, and by two-thirty she was shaking and having difficulty forcing her mouth into more than monosyllabic replies, and mentally cursing herself for not sticking to her guns and staying clear of the whole putrid mess. And cursing Cathy and Marion, too, for dragging her into it, because the truth didn't matter in this place, because the truth in the hands of clever men was malleable, because Collins would get off again and this time he'd rape and murder her. He knew now that she was a student. He'd work out where pretty quickly.

She glanced at the jury. Their faces told her that they didn't like her. She turned to find Mrs Hunter, and saw Rosie, smiling, triumph written all over her face.

For two years they'd been inseparable friends. She knew about Jenny, about Woody Creek. Knew everything. Cara wanted to vomit. Closed her eyes, wiped sweating hands on her skirt. And the judge told her to answer the question. What question? She hadn't heard it. As she turned to look at him, Collins showed her his closed fist, his concealed hate, like a promise, like, You wait, moll. I'll get you.

Wanted him hanged. Wanted him hanged, drawn and quartered, and his bits dragged to the four, eight, ten corners of Australia.

The question was asked again, or a different question, about the car's missing door handles.

Again she wiped her hands on her skirt. 'They called the back seat of Henry Cooper's car the bird coop. Once they got a bird – a girl – into the back seat she couldn't get out.'

'You had been in the rear seat on previous occasions?'

'Yes.'

'How had you managed to open the back doors on previous occasions, Miss Norris?'

'I opened a window and reached out.'

'I suggest the reason why you didn't open the window and reach out that day was because you wanted to be there, because you had chosen to be there.'

'I didn't open the window that day because he was on top of me trying to get my . . . my underclothes off. And Henry Cooper's wife didn't open it because she and the others were having a smoke and laughing, as if it was the best joke in the world, and if I hadn't smashed him in the face with my library book, they would have stood there smoking and laughing while he raped me, like those other two had when he raped Mi– another fifteen-year-old schoolgirl.'

She wasn't allowed to mention Michelle Hunter's name. She was in hospital. Two days before Christmas she had tried to stab herself with her mother's hairdressing scissors because that bastard had got her pregnant. Dave knew, so Cathy knew. Robert and Myrtle probably knew – not that they'd tell Cara.

An hour later she walked head down from that place, and collided with one of Henry Cooper's sisters, who was standing out front, smoking.

'Lying, stuck-up bitch,' she snarled and spat in Cara's face.

Ran then, ran wiping spittle with her handkerchief, threw the handkerchief into the gutter and ran to the tram stop, holding her tears at bay until she was back at the college and in the shower where she could bawl if she wanted to.

Cathy and Marion had to go back to court the following day. They didn't mind. They expected Cara to go with them. Like hell she'd go back to that place. If the judge wanted her again, he could come and get her.

She spent the day in her room, writing out that court scene. She wrote until the girls came home, full up with their big day in court and eager to relay it. Robert and the Traralgon farmer had given evidence.

'Your father was good,' Cathy said. 'He backed us up about Collins's phone harassment, and said how Collins had been expelled from school at sixteen for sexually molesting one of the young female teachers.'

He'd spoken of the defilement of Cara's room while the family was in Sydney, of the missing telephone pad and the college phone number. A returned soldier, a school principal, he would have looked at the jury, looked the judge in the eye.

The farmer said that he and his wife hadn't known the identity of the girl who had run to them weeping one Saturday afternoon. He couldn't remember the exact Saturday the incident had occurred, but he had learnt later that the girl was the daughter of one of the high-school teachers. He said that he had not seen the girl's attackers, that he and his wife had suggested she report the attack to the police. She'd asked to be driven home, and no, at no time had he or his wife doubted the girl's story. The three accused were known troublemakers in the area.

A middle-aged doctor stated that he had known the victim's family for twenty years, that he had seen the girl after her first suicide attempt, and yes, he had done a genital examination, and yes, the victim had been a virgin before the vicious rape. He spoke of the second suicide attempt in December, when, the girl's mental health being of paramount importance, a pregnancy had been terminated, and yes, blood tests had been carried out on the foetus and it was possible that the accused had been the perpetrator.

Statements given by the two schoolboys who had seen their classmate bundled into the back seat of the car were read to the jury. The statement named all three of the accused and identified the car. Everyone in town knew Henry Cooper's hotted-up Holden.

The newspapers followed the case. Collins didn't take the witness stand, which to many was an admission of guilt. Henry Cooper took the stand. He had a cute two-year-old son, a pretty wife almost ready to pop their second child. Cooper admitted to driving the car but said the girl had been sneaking out to meet Collins for two months, that she'd asked Collins to pick her up after school. He hadn't seen what had taken place in the car. He and Bell had gone for a walk to give Dino and his girl a chance to work things out. Bell told the same story, word for word. The Hunters' second daughter was forced by the defence to take the stand to answer one question. Yes, her youngest sister had sneaked out at night to meet the accused. Under cross-examination she was able to say more, but the damage had been done.

Expensive lawyers, multiple character witnesses, a jury wanting to get back to their jobs or home to their kids – all three were sentenced, but on a variety of charges. Henry Cooper received a twelve-month, fully suspended sentence; Tony Bell would serve a minimum of six months, and James Collins was given a lousy five years.

Twenty years wouldn't have been enough for Cara, but Robert was retiring in December, and by the time Collins was released, she'd be free of her commitment to the Education Department, and home at Amberley.

PART TWO

A ROAST DINNER

*L*orna Hooper still drove Vern's '49 black Ford, which she might with near honesty claim to have only driven to church on Sundays, wet Sundays at that. On fine days, she walked to church. She didn't lunch with friends, was a member of no women's guild, had no contact with her sister, nephew, brother or neighbour.

She could claim one long-term, ongoing relationship. During the late forties Lorna had first written *Jenison* on a cheque. Vern had signed that cheque; she'd been signing her own since '52, when the Balwyn house had been sold and the cretins had absconded with her nephew.

Jenison, a retired sergeant of police, had celebrated his seventy-sixth birthday in July '64 – and been given an ultimatum by his arthritic wife. She'd had enough of Melbourne's winters and was retiring to Queensland. He could go with her or move in with Miss Hooper for all she cared. He chose the former, and when Lorna received his resignation along with his final monthly report and bill, she was not pleased.

In a good mood, Lorna had the appearance of a termite-riddled totem pole. In a bad mood, the termites turned into African fire ants.

Jenison's report stated that two more of her father's properties were on the market.

'Thieves, cretins.'

'As you say, Miss Hooper.'

She wrote a final cheque, no bonus for long service. She didn't see him out. He closed the door behind him while she stalked the rooms, angered by his desertion, and by the female Jenison's. She'd written her a monthly cheque for two mornings of cleaning, two afternoons of baking.

A three-bedroom house, one resident, mounds of books and newspapers accumulated since she'd moved to Kew in December '58 left little space in which to stalk. No veranda on that hard-faced, clinker-brick house. She missed Woody Creek's verandas, its garden. She missed Margaret, younger sister and family maid, who since she'd wed, Lorna had referred to as *the cretin*.

For weeks prior to her sister's escape, Lorna had smelt infamy on the wind, but her nephew in his final year at school, she'd not expected them to jump the gun. They had. They'd taken off in the night, ten days before the school term ended.

She'd risen that morning, as usual, at six-thirty. The cretins and Muir, their skivvy, had rarely moved from their beds before eight. Lorna had taken her morning constitutional, done a little bookwork then at eight, and still no call to break her fast, she'd rung her bell for the skivvy, and later pounded on, before opening, her bedroom door. Her bed and the cretins' double bed had been empty. Their car was in the garage, blocked in by her own vehicle. Each evening she'd made a point of blocking them in. At nine she'd placed a phone call to her nephew's school and been told he'd left the grounds on the previous evening, in a taxi, which Jenison had traced to a city theatre, where he'd lost the scent.

Few, if any, items had been missing. Until the Saturday after-noon, she had not been overly concerned – until a male and his son knocked on the door and stated that they were there to take possession of the cretins' vehicle. She'd told them quite succinctly where they might go. They'd gone, but returned with two constables and a receipt.

On the fourth day, she'd received a phone call from Vern's accountant, who had informed her that the house and contents had been sold and that she had ten days in which to vacate the property.

Jenison spent those days attempting to pick up the cretins' trail. Lorna had spent the tenth day defending her family home from a second-hand dealer, his offsiders, the accountant and the same two constables who had forced her to release the cretins' sedan. The house was emptied around her, the floor rugs ripped from beneath her feet.

And thus she had vacated another family home, the two constables seeing her to her car.

The Kew house was her own, for her lifetime. Her father's estate paid the rates, insurance, electricity and gas, and paid her a quarterly stipend, which, since the eviction, she'd been forced to draw on.

In the years since, she'd hired a constant stream of cleaning women and cooks. Few had remained for any length of time. By the time Jenison offered his wife's services, there had been little for her to do, or little space in which to do it. Fortnightly she'd cooked a roast, filled the biscuit and cake tins, swept the passageways, washed the dishes, and for a day or two Lorna had been able to find a kitchen bench and table – and little else.

Windows were never opened in Lorna's house. They were, for the most part, inaccessible. A clutter of heavy furniture, a muddle of dust-collecting ornaments, Margaret's idea of decoration. The female Jenison packed them away, cleared what she could, stepped over what she couldn't.

As with many of those who survived in chaos, there was method to Lorna's. Jenison's reports lived on Vern's long dining-room table. A solitary eater only requires a small area in which to eat.

Two weeks after receiving the final report, she cleared her eating area with her forearm, forcing back salt and pepper, sugar basin, an empty tin which had once contained red salmon. The new space, wiped clean of crumbs with her palm, she selected Jenison's final report, plus a copy of Vern's will — she had several. A fountain pen located, she sat, underlining a paragraph of the will pertaining to the Woody Creek property.

Will not be sold.

It was not to be tolerated, and would not be tolerated.

Again she returned to the pile of reports, delving until she located the one she sought. The three items folded together, she took her elderly handbag from its convenient doorknob and placed the papers into it.

She'd require her driving spectacles, which for a moment eluded her, until she retraced her movements of yesterday to the kitchen where she lifted a saucepan lid. Washed the spectacles at the sink tap, shook them dry enough, donned them then left the house.

God help any child running or riding along the footpath. God helped them, kept them indoors, in yards, until the big black '49 Ford was out on the street and the iron gates closed, the padlock clicked.

In a good mood, Lorna was an atrocious driver. In a bad mood, she flung that old car around corners, stopped unwillingly at traffic lights, refused to give way to fools on her right where there were no lights to force the issue. She knew her way to the city, drove straight through it, drivers blasting, mouths screaming abuse, trams parting her hair, her eyes never leaving the road ahead.

She hadn't seen her brother since the day of their father's funeral. He'd been little more than a limping vegetable. He had not been mentioned in the will, other than as a drain on the estate, which for years had paid out hard cash on his so-called treatments. His son, her nephew, was to inherit his grandfather's estate on his thirtieth birthday, or on his wedding day. Until then, the cretins, guided by

Vern's accountant, had total control – total control, given into the hands of two mindless fools, who had moved Jim from the secure sanatorium of her choice to a rest home in the hills, from which the fool had absconded. His disappearance had, however, alleviated one drain on the estate.

Since the redhead from White and Company had approached her that day with her claim that Jim had wed, she'd spoken to the halfwit cousin. He'd met Jim's wife, and sighted an infant daughter.

Lorna had no desire to repair rents in her relationship with her brother. She was not expecting to be made welcome by him. Her interest was in his offspring, legitimate issue of Vern and therefore more entitled to inherit than the illegitimate get of the Morrison slut. One way or another, Lorna was determined to prevent the sale of her father's properties.

The trip was long and wearying, the last of it done with the sun in her eyes. Five-ten when she drove into Woody Creek. Dogs have an ancestral memory. They cleared the road. A bike rider cleared the footpath as Lorna drove into Vern's yard. A green car parked amid greenery gives too little warning of its presence to weary eyes. Before Lorna's brakes got a grip, her Ford's bumper bar communicated with the bumper bar of a younger relative.

*

Raelene watched the collision. Saw Jenny's car shudder. She'd been looking at it, wishing she knew how to drive it.

Hated school, hated the baggy, daggy uniforms, hated the teachers, hated Woody Creek and hated Jenny, watch-dogging her all day long.

They must have heard that clang of metal on metal inside. Jenny came to the front door to see what was going on. She saw the old dame getting out of the black car. 'No,' she said, as she slammed the door and ran back to the kitchen.

'It's Lorna,' she said. 'She's not coming in here, Jim.'

Raelene smiled. Payback time. She opened the door before the visitor knocked.

'Jim Hooper,' the dame said.

'Someone wants you, Jim,' Raelene called.

*

Lorna's eyesight was good enough to recognise the Morrison tramp at fifty paces. There were only six or eight good paces between them in the entrance hall. Lorna spun on her heel to vacate the premises, and collided with an infant coming at a run from the opposite direction.

Children have good reflexes. The infant stumbled, then continued her run. Lorna's reflexes, slowed by weariness, by speechless disgust, didn't save her. She spun into the wall, one narrow ankle connecting with the leg of a Queen Anne table. Grasped for the table. It was too low. Grabbed at the wall. Photograph in the way, and unstable. Then her feet went from beneath her and she hit the floor, hard, and for the first time since her sixth birthday, exposed her knobbly knees.

The shock of a fall to those of average height is . . . shocking. Lorna had more height than most and no flesh to cushion scrawny hips. She stayed down.

*

Jim approached to within three feet of that length of wrinkled-lisle-stockinged leg. He didn't offer his hand. Jenny had backed off to the kitchen doorway, Trudy now hiding behind her. Raelene leaned against the open front door, eyeing an aged black handbag. It had flown, landed at her feet like an offering from God. Wondered how much might be in it. Wondered if she dared. With her foot, she moved the bag behind her.

'Can you get up?' Jim asked.

Lorna's driving spectacles, jarred from her hawk's beak of a nose, had retained their grip on one ear. She had large ears.

A talon-tipped hand felt for the spectacles, slid them back into place, then seeing her disarray, she drew her skirt down.

Raelene picked up the handbag.

Watch-dog Jenny saw her. 'Jim.'

Jim stepped around his sister's feet to claim the bag. He placed it on the hall table.

'Can you give me a hand to get her up, Jen?'

'She can rot where she is,' Jenny said and disappeared from the scene, Trudy gripping her hand.

The rear door slammed. Raelene left via the front door.

*

Having satisfactorily cleared her father's house of the unmentionable, Lorna got down to the business of why she'd come.

'Your father's properties are on the market,' she accused, gathering her limbs, reaching for the Queen Anne table and gaining her feet.

On one leg or two, Jim was the taller. She rarely looked up to men, preferred to look down on them.

'You need to leave, Lorna.'

'Are you in touch with our cretin sister?'

He had not previously heard Margaret referred to as *the cretin*, but was familiar with earlier similar references. He offered her handbag. 'You need to leave now, Lorna.'

'Were you informed before our father's land was placed on the market?'

Monk's land had been on the market for months. They were asking a ridiculous price for it and, according to Paul Jenner, wouldn't budge an inch. Jim answered her question with a question.

'Are you in a fit condition to drive?'

'I have driven,' she said. 'The will states that the land will not be sold. I ask again, are you in touch with the cretin?'

Raelene opened the front door. 'Her car is blocking Jenny's in.'

'She's leaving,' Jim said.

*

Not soon enough for Jenny. She drove forward, ran over a rhododendron, over two azaleas, spun the wheel and backed up, nudged a large elm. Forward again, back, twice, three times before she had space enough to drive across the lawn, between two trees, around Lorna's car and out to the road.

'Wait,' Jim called.

He had fifty years of John McPherson's photographs and negatives on the dining-room table which he wasn't prepared to leave at risk. Jenny waited, the motor running, until he emerged with a large carton. Carton in the boot, Raelene forced from the front passenger seat to the rear, they drove towards town, their meal left in the oven to burn. Roast chops and vegetables. Raelene liked chops.

*

As did Lorna. The smell of a roast drew her out to the kitchen, to the oven. She hadn't eaten since leaving the city and hadn't eaten a roast since Jenison, the female, had deserted her. She found a plate, helped herself from the roasting pan, found a teapot, a cup and saucer, found tea and brewed a pot. She found bread in the bread tin, cut two slices, buttered them liberally, then sat down and ate.

When they didn't return, she walked the house. No heavy furniture, no Hooper photograph on the walls. Pale blue curtains in the sitting room, a lounge suite, tapestry upholstered in blues. She scoffed and walked on by to the rear of the house, to the bedroom she'd named her own for forty years.

The furnishings were new. They'd provided the occupier with a comfortable chair. She sat on it, perusing a large river scene hung over the fireplace, artist unknown. Never fond of gum trees, Lorna rose to test the bedsprings.

*

Jenny bought fish and chips for dinner. Mrs Crone now retired, a Greek couple had moved into the café and turned it upside down. They did a roaring trade with their fish and chips and hamburgers.

Six o'clock was not a good time to go looking for sanctuary. Margot would throw a screamer if they took Trudy and Raelene down to the old place. They couldn't take a mess of fish and chips to the McPhersons'. Jenny drove by the park, considering a picnic, but Maisy lived over the park fence. She'd want to know what was going on. Jenny turned left at Charlie's corner, considering his storeroom. He didn't trust Raelene as far as he could kick her, which wasn't far these days. Drove on over his railway crossing and back to Three Pines Road, which she followed over the bridge.

'What does she want?'

'She heard Monk's land was up for sale,' Jim said. 'I told her to leave.'

'Our fish and chips is getting cold,' Raelene said.

'It's well wrapped.'

'Where are we going?'

'We'll have a picnic,' Jenny said.

'Where?'

Anywhere but that house.

They'd painted Vern out of it, where they could. You can't paint bathroom tiles and their condition was too good to justify ripping them out. They'd ripped out the kitchen and modernised it. It was her own now. They'd altered the back garden, dug up the lawn for a vegie patch, but Vern's big trees were still standing, and his rosebush hedge. As a kid she'd loved his roses. She'd never rip them out.

Eight miles is not far in a modern car. They were driving by the old Hooper land when Jim asked her to slow down. Back in the thirties, the early forties, he'd spent a lot of time out at the farm – most of it on the Monk section. He'd planned once to live in Monk's old mansion. Until a few months ago, the property manager and his wife had lived in it. They'd moved into a new brick house, built on the original Hooper land. Monk's old house was crumbling, or so they said in town.

It appeared solid enough from the road.

Always a classy-looking property, Monk's, with its section of curved brick fence supporting fancy iron gates. Jenny parked the nose of the car a few bare feet from the gates and turned off the motor.

Granny had known this property when those fancy gates had been new. A proud man, old Maximilian Monk. He'd immortalised his property's name, *Three Pines*, in the ironwork, then on top of each gate, held high with swirls of iron, were a pair of large and ornate M's, so no one might forget his name.

The bank had sold up his grandson during the depression. Vern Hooper, who had shared a fence with Monk, put in a bid at the auction and walked away owning the property. Got it for a song, he'd always said. He'd got a lot more properties for a song during the first years of the depression. To Jim's knowledge, he'd owned fifteen houses and over a thousand acres of good river land.

Rick Thompson, Vern's first farm manager, had cared about that land. Tonight it looked lonely, neglected, a fading *For Sale* sign wired to one proud gate; a few sheep wandering up to look at the green car – maybe hoping for a taste of green or of grain.

Jim's eye turned to the house, set well back from the gate, his mind wandering to Sissy Morrison, to a cancelled wedding, to the old root cellar, to Jenny – and to Jimmy who had been conceived in that cellar.

Back before the war, he'd loved this place, loved the way dusk crept in from the forest, how the land had fought against it. How many times had he stood on Monk's veranda, watching the sun sink down between the trees?

'If I had the sort of money they're asking, I'd buy it,' he said.

'They say the house is being eaten by mould. Eat your fish before that pair of locusts get it,' Jenny said.

'We had a crop of mushrooms growing in the corner of the dining hall back before we did the renovations,' he said, but he ate his slab of fish. Most are partial to fish and chips out of paper.

The last chip eaten, Raelene prowled, rattling gates, lifting the lid of a makeshift mailbox. Every farm along the road had one of sorts. Monk's was a twelve-gallon drum, fixed to a pole, large enough to accept mail, newspapers, bread and sundry, though unused since the farm manager had moved.

Raelene found something of interest. She returned to the car jangling two keys on a ring.

'You're a Hooper,' she said, presenting them to Jenny.

Jenny didn't feel like a Hooper and never would. Jim was, and he wanted one last look at that house he'd once watched brought back from the near dead.

The smaller of the two keys fitted the gate's padlock. He and Raelene pushed the gates wide.

'Drive through, Jen.'

She drove down a long track, tree-lined once. Dead trees interspersed now with the living, the track to the house overgrown and potholed. Three tall conifers sheltered the western walls of the house. Jenny didn't remember them being there.

'I planted them,' Jim said. 'They were a foot tall the last time I was out here.'

'Three pines,' Jenny said.

'That was the idea. They've done well.' Before the war he'd planned to turn this place into an oasis of green. For a time he'd convinced himself he could live with Sissy Morrison on this piece of land.

They walked the verandas, peered in through windows. Not much to see by twilight, only an old, old house, defeated by time. Not much to say, Jim's mind away with that crop of mushrooms, with hand-painted tiles, that big old fireplace – and the cellar.

Raelene, set free to roam, came at a run from the far side of the veranda. 'There's an old-fashioned door around that side with a new lock in it. I bet that other key fits it.'

'We're trespassing already,' Jenny said, but Jim followed Raelene to the west side where he unlocked the door, the old servants' door once leading to an outside kitchen. He'd known the history of this old house before he was sixteen years old.

Raelene was first in, Jenny last, Trudy clinging to her hand.

'It's scary, Mummy.'

'It's just an old empty house, darlin'. Daddy and Mummy used to come out here a long time ago.'

Wallpaper peeling from passage walls, looking ghostly in the half-light, might be scary to a little kid. Jenny tried the light switches. The electricity had been disconnected.

'It smells like ghosts,' Trudy said.

It smelled of mould. 'There are no such things as ghosts,' Jenny said. 'It smells stale because all of the doors and windows are closed.'

'There's a torch in the glove box. Could you fetch it for me, Raelene,' Jim said, and for once she ran to do his bidding. She was enjoying herself, and when Raelene was having a good time, she was compliant.

They toured then by torchlight, studying ceilings, floors, flashing the torch beam over fallen tiles in the bathroom, across ornate ceilings, over the huge fireplace, and later in the room with the trapdoor.

Still there. Its rusty hinges groaning their complaint as it lifted. They propped it back against the wall, hooked it back. New ropes had been attached to it and to hooks beneath the floor which offered something to hang on to until searching feet found the top step, and hands, the handrail.

'The steps could be rotten, Raelene,' Jim warned. Raelene, who heeded few warnings, went down anyway, and hearing no crunch of falling timber, Jim followed her.

'They're solid as a rock,' he called up, the earthen walls swallowing his voice – as they had way back when . . .

Jenny got her feet onto the first step, then helped Trudy down, holding her hand until Jim reach up to take her. It wasn't a staircase. Always too steep to be named stairs, always too wide to be named a ladder. She was halfway down when an overwhelming scent from the past rose up to engulf her, as if the air she'd breathed out twenty years ago had remained unmoved. Scent of earthy love in that cellar. Memory of the flight of butterflies in that scent.

And for him, and she knew it.

'I used to think my way back here when I was away,' he said.

Away, in the army, in the Jap camp. He rarely mentioned the war – had told John McPherson once that he'd seen the worst of mankind and the best of it in that Jap camp. Whatever he'd been through had stolen enough of his life. He was back now, and looking more like the suntanned soldier she'd waved away at Sydney's Central Station.

'She's aged,' he said, and for an instant Jenny thought he was referring to the house, for an instant she'd forgotten why they were out here.

He meant Lorna. 'I'm not going back while she's there, Jim.'

'I told her to go.'

'Your cousin said Margaret and her husband told her to go a hundred times.'

'Who is she, Mummy?' Trudy asked. She hadn't liked that black-clad, wicked-witch lady at their house and didn't like this house. She hadn't left the steps, nor had Jenny. Raelene, who had claimed the torch, was investigating the depths of that hole in the ground.

'She's Daddy's big sister,' Jim said.

'Is she sleeping at our house?'

'Yes, and she'll creep into your bedroom tonight and kidnap you,' Raelene said.

'That's enough out of you. And no, she's not sleeping in our house, darlin'.'

'It's too late for her to start back tonight,' Jim said.

'There's a hotel on the corner,' Jenny said.

Raelene's concentration span brief, having found nothing of interest in the cellar, she was going back up. Trudy raced ahead to the top, afraid she'd close the trapdoor and lock them in like she'd locked her in a wardrobe one day.

Jenny was on the second step when Jim took her arm and, just for old times' sake, kissed her in the dark. She shared his bed each night, passed him his leg some mornings, watched him strap it on. She was forty, he was forty-five, and kissing him in the dark still made her want more than his kiss.

The torch beam found them. 'It looks ridiculous when old people kiss like that,' Raelene said.

'It looks more ridiculous when twelve-year-old kids do it,' Jenny said. They went up, Jim first, his missing leg making the climb up more difficult than the down. They closed the trapdoor, left the way they'd come, via the servants' door. They locked it, and the gates, and returned the keys to the drum mailbox.

'Did you live in this house when you were a little boy, Daddy?' Trudy asked.

'I lived in our house, but I slept in that cellar on a few hot nights, and even on the hottest nights it was never hot down there.'

'If she's still at the house, we'll bring our mattresses out here,' Jenny said.

'I'll second that motion,' he said.

They expected Lorna's car to be gone. It was still blocking their drive. Jenny parked on the street where they sat for minutes. Not Raelene. She wasn't into sitting still. They watched her walk to the door.

'Would it kill us to give her a bed for the night?' Jim said.

'It would kill me.'

Trudy needed her bed, and curtains were being lifted at the

house next door. They had to go in. Jenny took Trudy to the bathroom. Jim went down to the kitchen.

Used plates and cup still on the table, with the teapot; their visitor had helped herself but was no longer in there. Raelene was, and gnawing on a still-warm chop. Like her father, she ate too much meat and not enough vegetables.

Jim found Lorna seated in the lounge room, and in that pretty room they'd created she stuck out like a black bandaged sore toe.

'The hotel has rooms,' he said.

She turned, offered him a copy of their father's will. 'Your illegitimate son inherits all on his thirtieth birthday. As he now appears to have a legitimate sibling . . .'

Her voice carried down the passage to where Jenny was tucking Trudy in. She kissed her, then crept out to listen.

'I intend to prevent the sale of the land and expect you to join me in the suit against those cretins.'

'I thought I'd made it pretty obvious that I want nothing to do with you, or Pop's estate.'

'You have an obligation to see that there is something left of the estate for your daughter . . . or your son to inherit.'

'You stole our right to have any say in the life of our son the day you kidnapped him. Get out of my house now, or I'll have you put out,' Jenny said.

Lorna's hearing was selective. She didn't turn to the passage. 'My own funds are somewhat limited –'

'There are motels in Willama,' Jim said.

'My sight is inadequate for night driving.'

'The constable has bunk beds in his cell,' Jenny said, and she went out to the kitchen. Jim followed her as far as the wall-mounted telephone. The telephone books lived in a small cupboard beneath it. He retrieved the local book, but requiring a better light, took it out to the kitchen's fluorescent glare where Jenny had begun clearing away the remains of Lorna's meal.

A noisy occupation, the scraping and stacking of dishes, the splashing of water, amplified tonight by her anger. Baked-on chop juice gone black in the roasting pan. That brainless old battleaxe hadn't possessed sense enough to leave the pan out once she'd helped herself. Jenny filled the pan with water while at the table, Jim flipped pages, searching for motels.

And she came, into Jenny's new kitchen, brandishing her papers.

'Get out of my kitchen,' Jenny said.

A scoff, a toss of her head, and Lorna pulled out a chair, sat, her back to the skivvy at the sink.

That was when Jenny knew why Margaret had taken Jimmy and disappeared off the face of the planet, and at that moment, for the briefest second, she was grateful to that dithering Beatrice Potter rat for saving Jimmy from a life with this evil hag.

A shake of detergent added to the roasting pan, and she stood, noisily scraping the pan while staring at Lorna's narrow back, reflected in the window, at Jim writing on a sheet of paper.

'It's a thirty-minute drive. There'll be little traffic on the road.' He was too soft. She loved him because he was, but tonight wished he wasn't. Watched him take a five-pound note from his wallet and placed it with the notepaper.

Lorna ignored both.

'Leave under your own steam or I'll call the constable,' Jenny said.

Not even a scoff in reply, not the turn of that grey wiry head. Jenny picked up the baking pan, which would need to spend the night in the oven to soften up what that scoffing witch of a woman had baked onto it.

A sixteen-by-twelve-inch metal roasting pan half-filled with water is heavy. She stood between stove and table, the pan between her hands. Difficult to balance a full pan. Easy to spill.

'The will states clearly, *The Woody Creek properties will not be sold . . .*'

Spilt it. Spilt the lot, and every skerrick of it in Lorna's direction, most of it down her back, on her hair. A pleasurable experience, perhaps one of the most pleasurable of Jenny's lifetime, as was watching that dripping totem pole head turn, watching a pinched-nostril sneer alter to one of mute shock as talon claws reached for hair and came away with a segment of soggy potato.

Later, it was a loud experience, and slippery. Lorna dripping, screeching, stepping high and carefully to the rear door, to avoid a little of the flood.

'That's the servants' entrance,' Jenny yelled after her, then turned again to the sink to refill the baking pan.

COLLISION COURSE

*A*mber Morrison's night vision was good enough. She didn't need to look far ahead. Nothing there she wanted to see.

The boarding house had been a hotel in some long-forgotten era. Its rooms once boasted locks, keys. The keys long lost, a few latches failed to latch. Amber's door failed.

An inquisitive lodger peering into her room would have seen an old bed made up hospital tight; a battered chest of drawers, bare; no item of clothing hanging in the doorless wardrobe. What little Amber owned she wore on her back or carried in her hessian shopping bag. In recent months she'd procured a string bag, her weapon, once loaded with a water-filled lemonade bottle. She swung it at tormenting youths, used it to slash at overhanging shrubbery, to swipe drunks from her pathway when she entered or left her lodgings.

She slept there, slept badly, slept little. Didn't eat there. Couldn't stomach the company in the kitchen, the filth and confusion of it, the odours of boiled cabbage, cheap wine, rancid fat and the stink of unwashed humanity. Left her bed in the early morning, splashed bleach around the bathroom before she washed or bathed, then left the house. Bought a yeast bun from the bakery for breakfast. Bought a piece of fruit for lunch, a pie, or a few slices of cooked meat for her dinner. Carried bread and cheese, lived on bread and cheese when her purse was empty.

An angry woman, Amber Morrison. Insane? In 1946 she'd been judged insane by the courts. In the early sixties, a variety of doctors had decreed her sane enough. She was sane enough when necessary. Sanity was unnecessary at a lodging house she shared with sluts and drunks and a few who had a lesser claim on sanity than she.

In some future year there might be a syndrome to explain her lack of feeling for humanity, her need for constant movement. In the sixties, by those who shared her residence, she was labelled *that crazy old walking bitch*. Had they been aware of how close they were to being right, aware she'd spent sixteen years in an asylum for the criminally insane, they may not have slept so soundly in their own beds. The raving wino in the room beside her own shouldn't have –

While Jenny giggled and mopped greasy water from the kitchen floor, while Jim boiled the jug for a cup of tea, while Raelene stood on the hotel corner with three gangling youths and Lorna drove dark roads, smelling of mutton fat, Amber Morrison walked the inner suburban streets of Melbourne.

A full moon had always drawn the youth of Woody Creek from their homes. It drew them from high-rise commission flats, the older of them to huddle in the shadows, the younger to run, laughing, screaming beneath that orange ball in the sky. Everything had changed while Amber was away, but not the sound of children at play. Like a vibration from the past, that running, that screaming, that laughter of moon-mad children.

She'd been a part of it once. Once, long, long ago, she, Maisy, Julia and Sylvia. She was a part of nothing now.

Swiped with her loaded string bag at shrubbery and walked on by, lost in the past where she lived her life.

Always loved moonlit nights. As a child, as a girl, a woman, she'd walked. The girl was close tonight, washed in on waves of the past, with the scents of the past. It was the perfumes and stinks of life that sustained. The stink of urine and unwashed humanity was the place where they'd left her to rot for sixteen years. The smell of an orange was home, when home had been Nan and Pa and happy days, and her pretty-boy Daddy only a photograph on the wall.

Almost thirteen when his doctor hands had shown her how a man could raise that aching need in her. She'd let him take her in the dirt for his promise of a life with her handsome doctor father, and pretty gowns and maids to keep them clean, and pretty shoes and a fine house and a carriage to ride in. He'd promised he'd come back. She'd spent ten years waiting for him to keep his promise.

Smelt his scent on that stray bitch. Right from day one when she'd placed the newborn to her breast, she'd smelt him. Hadn't put a name to the odour, not then. Had allowed that stray to suck the life from her. The knowing had come later. The knowing had come with her crown of golden hair – his hair. Smelt him in it.

He'd come back for his stray, not for Amber. She'd seen him, hiding his face behind a beard, disguising the doctor beneath a long black coat. Saw him standing beneath Charlie White's veranda, watching half-a-dozen ten year olds at play. He'd walked by Sissy, hadn't known her, or Amber. She'd known him – smelt him. Stood at his side one day at Charlie's counter and he hadn't turned his head to look at her.

'Evil bastard.'

Two walkers on that same moonlit path walked faster. Amber didn't see them. She wasn't there. She was young and wandering the streets of Woody Creek.

She'd approached him one afternoon in the park. 'I know who you are,' she'd said.

'I believe you are mistaken, madam.'

He'd taken her in the dirt beneath the bridge and now he denied her? She'd wanted to kill him for that denial. He was her pretty-boy Daddy, and all he'd ever given to her was a heat in her loins no man could cool. He'd deserved to die. She'd taken hours of pleasure in honing her carving knife.

Found him one evening, down by the creek, watching two dozen laughing, screaming kids at the swimming bend. He'd been standing out in the open. She'd stood amid the trees, waiting for him to walk her way.

Things happen when blood is pounding red in the head, when the aching heat is in the loins and only fat, grunting Norman in your bed. Golden curls lose their colour at night, lose their curl when wet. Watched her run in behind a clump of blackberry bushes, pull her bathers down, squat.

Like a dream, the stillness of the bush at twilight. Things happen in dreams and there's no guilt until you wake up – and only for an instant, then dreams dissipate, float away like thistle-down on the wind.

Norman had missed the carving knife. He'd bought another she'd later used to silence his snore.

Used a pillow tonight. Less mess. She'd probably done him a favour – but she couldn't go back to the boarding house, so she walked on.

By eleven-thirty, Amber was in the central city, heading for the GPO. Pension day tomorrow. She'd go . . . go somewhere.

*

Eleven-thirty, Lorna again negotiating the city, following land-marks unfamiliar by moonlight, sitting forward on her seat, squinting left, squinting right. She'd spoken the truth when she'd claimed her eyesight was not good for night driving, nor were her tinted outdoor spectacles.

Lorna saw the dark shape as it was upon her. Neither her reflexes nor the brakes of her old Ford at their best, and little she could have done had they been. She felt the impact.

I have killed, she thought. Then nothing.

*

An ambulance transported two unconscious women to St Vincent's Hospital. In the main, Lorna's injuries were to her face. It had had a head-on with the steering wheel. The windscreen had shattered; her spectacles had shattered into her eyes; her eagle-beak nose was pulp. The heavy bumper bar had broken Amber's leg. She'd flown thirty feet and landed on her head, on concrete. Her injuries were life-threatening.

Through the night two teams of doctors worked on the accident victims. They did their best.

The Melbourne *Sun* reported the accident, a bare line or two beneath a report on a three-fatality head-on with a transport on the Hume Highway.

Lorna regained consciousness thirty-six hours after the impact and she was blind – bandaged blind, but unaware of the bandage. Lorna, never known to panic, panicked. They sedated her and when she next awoke, she'd gained sufficient of her senses to listen. And to remember that dark shape on the road.

'Have I killed?'

She hadn't, or not yet, though the pedestrian had not regained consciousness.

'My vehicle?'

They couldn't say what had become of her vehicle. 'We need to let your family know where you are, Miss Hooper.'

'I have no family to inform,' she said.

*

On the third day, Amber opened her eyes to a white-clad sister with gentle hands.

'You're in hospital, dear. You had an accident but you're going to be fine.'

Dear? For too many years she'd been dear to no one. Too many years of stink and filth and no touch of kindness. Smell of clean on that hand, on the air.

'Can you tell me your name, dear?'

Knew her name. Didn't want that clean-smelling sister to know it.

Knew why she'd been out on the roads. Wondered what day it was. If they'd found him. If she'd been asleep for long enough for them to smell him.

Closed her eyes again, safe a while in sterile heaven.

They moved her to a different bed, surrounded her with curtain screens, spoonfed her broth, wiped her chin when she dribbled. And they asked their questions.

'We need to know your name, sweetie. Your family will be worrying about you. Can you remember your name? Do you have a husband, children?'

Only Sissy. He'd turned her into a Duckworth.

'Where is home, sweetie?'

Memories are long in Woody Creek, Amb.

'Where do you live, dear?'

'Here.'

'This is a hospital. No one lives here, sweetie.'

Norman's mother had called her *dear*, served her tea in a fine china cup, shown her a vase presented to a Duckworth by Queen Victoria – had until she'd been in town long enough to learn that *dear*'s mother lived in a two-room hut and was on with Vern Hooper. No more *dear* then, but too late. Norman had wanted *dear*, and she'd wanted his mother's bone-china tea set, her Queen Victoria vase and superior furniture – superior to anything Amber had known in her mother's hut.

They kept asking her name – the tall sister and the pretty little nurse. They called her *dear* and *sweetie* and washed her face, cared for her, 'We need to know your name, dear,' so she gave them a name. 'Duckworth.'

'Mrs Duckworth?'

No ring on her finger. Had never wanted it there, so removed the scar of it.

'Miss. Elizabeth,' she said. Elizabeth was the Queen of England.

Her right leg and foot were encased in plaster. She learned why her head hurt. No hair on it, long rows of spiky stitches and raw flesh. Sighed, happy with the pain of it, and safe, and at peace, she slept.

*

'Miss Duckworth. Sweetie. You can't sleep all day.'

Lorna recognised the name but was unable to see its owner. She'd spoken to the eye specialist. He'd assured her that she'd have some sight. The plastic surgeon, brought in to reattach her nose, told her she'd require a second operation once the swelling subsided.

He'd packed her nostrils with gauze. She'd never been a mouth breather and panicked when she awoke and could not draw breath. She'd panicked when the eye surgeon removed her bandage and she'd seen little more than light. He'd replaced them, and she'd calmed.

Each morning she was assisted from bed, led by an arm to the bathroom where her backside was guided to the toilet seat. She suffered the stripping off of some form of nightgown, suffered the showering, the chatter of a garrulous staff member, and her laughter when Lorna informed her that the great Roman Empire had fallen due to too frequent bathing.

'I think you're a bit of a wag, Miss Hooper.'

Lorna was no wag. For the past fifty years, she'd bathed once a week, which was more than adequate for one who never raised a sweat. Trapped within the hospital system, dependent on others for her every need, her lack of sight, her fear of its permanent loss, led to a modicum of humility, a smidgen of civility.

Bruises become less painful, wounds heal. Two elderly women, bedded side by side in a two-bed ward, one denied sight, the other denied movement, listened in to the other's conversations.

Miss Duckworth, of Launceston, had recently buried her father. She had come across to the mainland to take care of dear old Aunt Lizzie, who incidentally she'd been named for, but Aunt Lizzie had not long outlived her brother. Miss Duckworth had found accommodation at a house in . . . and for the life of her she couldn't recall the name of the suburb.

Existing without sight sharpened the other senses. Lorna's ears pricked up at the mention of Tasmania, and for an hour she lay sifting memories. She'd written the invitations to her brother's aborted marriage to Sissy Morrison. A dozen or more envelopes had been addressed to Duckworths and surely one to Tasmania. Had it been to Launceston?

It was not until the morning Miss Duckworth was moved from her bed to a cane chair where she might take a little sun that the two communicated. Lorna heard the turning of newspaper pages and sighed at a future with insufficient sight to read the morning papers.

Amber wasn't reading, but studying her bandaged neighbour. She'd known two Miss Hoopers in another lifetime. Her ward mate resembled neither of them. Had Lorna's hair been the black of her youth, worn in a tight coiled bun on the nape of her neck, she might have recognised her, but her ward mate's hair was grey wire, each strand standing on end. She'd known Lorna Hooper's acidic tone. Gauze-packed nostrils neutralise acid. Her ward mate's eyes were bandaged, her nose held together with lengths of plaster, false teeth smashed, gums cut by her dentures – had she not been toothless, Amber would have recognised those biting teeth, or her clothing, had she been clad in her permanent uniform of black. She wasn't. Amber saw a tall, thin woman, her bare sparrow ankles jutting from hospital-loaned male slippers; she saw a hospital-issue washed-out dressing-gown. Lorna Hooper had as little resemblance to herself as did a featherless cockatoo.

Then the featherless cockatoo spoke. 'My bandages will be removed in the morning. I was an avid reader.'

Amber nodded, realised a nod was insufficient. 'Oh,' she said.

Conversation needs to be practised. Amber, never good at it, had done none of it in recent years. The newspaper was open. One of the sisters had offered her a selection of reading glasses when she had initially refused the offered paper. She'd tried on two pairs before settling for a pair of blue-rimmed bifocals.

'*Dawn Fraser made history in the most desperate swim of her career when she won the women's one hundred metres for the third time,*' she read.

'I saw her swim in '56,' Lorna offered. 'A fine sportswoman.'

A forcing ground, a hospital ward. When Lorna's bandages were removed and replaced with a single patch and darkened spectacles, she regained a little independence but not her ability to read. Prior to the accident she'd required reading spectacles.

Amber learned to move around on wooden crutches and to make her own way to those chairs in the sun where Lorna waited for her to read aloud of the great human horde, and for the first time since 1946 Amber began to again count herself amongst them.

The women were of similar age, Lorna younger by ten years than Amber Morrison, though barely three years junior to Miss Elizabeth Duckworth. When one is weaving fiction, then why not allow fiction to deduct a few of those lost years? Strong women both, strong hearts and lungs, good healers who would have been released into the care of their families had they possessed families who cared. Instead, they were found beds at a convalescent home, in a four-bed ward, two of the beds occupied by a pair of the lower order.

Lorna had never doubted her rightful position in society. In her youth, Amber had possessed aspirations to rise above dirt scratcher. She'd lived with Cecelia Morrison for five years, a dame who had considered herself to be one of the upper, upper class. Miss Hooper and Miss Duckworth were given the beds on the eastern side, and the east and the west sides did not mix or converse until one of the lower order learned that Miss Duckworth's dear departed father had been a parson.

'Me and my hubby got hitched by a Reverend Duckworth,' she offered. Amber nodded, but made no reply. 'We lived at Richmond at the time. Was your father ever there?'

'No,' Amber said, and Lorna scoffed and tapped the newspaper.

It was that scoff that went a long way towards Amber's late identification of her ward mate, and her street garb, brought to the convalescent home by Lorna's minister and his wife. Her conversation with them removed any doubt.

'I had business with my brother in Woody Creek and intended staying overnight, but having learnt he'd wed the local trollop, I decided to drive home,' Lorna said.

Amber took up her crutch and hobbled from the ward. And nowhere to hobble to but the bathroom. She locked herself in and stood staring at her reflection in the mirror.

A bald head alters a male's appearance. It alters a woman's more. Amber Morrison had never worn spectacles. Miss Elizabeth Duckworth wore blue-framed bifocals which she lifted now to study her scarred scalp. Like a road map, red scars crisscrossed there, but hair was sprouting, growing through white.

In Woody Creek, her hair had been a beige blonde, worn shoulder-length. In Woody Creek, she'd been younger. She barely recognised herself; a woman with poor eyesight had little hope.

The parson and his wife had gone when she returned to the ward with a copy of the *Age*. Lorna preferred the *Age*.

'*Prime Minister Menzies announced the resumption of national service training, with conscripts liable for overseas service. Service will be for two years, and the intakes determined by a birthday lottery . . .*'

*

Beds in convalescent hospitals are provided for deserving cases. Lorna, no longer deserving, clung longer than necessary to her three meals a day, cups of tea and cake, domestics to make her bed each morning. She clung overly long to her damaged eyesight, or perhaps to her reader-companion. Admit it she would not, not even to herself, but she and Margaret had spent most of their years side by side, and who amongst us does not crave companionship?

'You have an income, Miss Duckworth?' she asked one evening.

'Father's income died with him. The house belonged to the Church.'

Norman's income would have died with him. His house had belonged to the railways. The easiest and safest way to play a role was to retain fact where she could and alter what she couldn't, but not outrageously. She and Sissy had spent months with Norman's Uncle Charles, a parson, and his wife and their son Reginald, after the death of Leonora April. Amber had known the life they'd led, had lived it for a time.

'The Church would not have seen you put out on the street,' Lorna argued.

'I have been more accustomed to giving than to receiving charity,' Amber said, then continued her reading.

But Lorna was not done. 'You receive a pension, I assume?'

Amber Morrison received the old-age pension. Her cheques would be piling up at the Melbourne GPO. She'd been on her way there, had planned to wait for the doors to open, get her money and catch a train as far as her pension would take her.

Miss Duckworth shook her head. 'Father believed that pensions were for the unfortunates, not for those of strong mind and limb.' Or Amber's mother had.

'Pride may nourish the soul, Miss Duckworth, but it supplies a very limited meal,' Lorna said, studying her reader-companion as she returned to her paper. She enjoyed the reports on horrendous accidents.

'*The thirty-seven-year-old mother of five was pronounced dead at the scene, a five-year-old boy died on his way to –*'

Lorna interrupted again. 'For your assistance in the house, once you are on two feet of course, I would be prepared to make my guest room available. If you so desire.'

Amber desired. She looked at her benefactor, breathless with desire, wordless, as her benefactor laid down the regulations of communal occupation.

'My funds are limited. I am therefore unable to offer a wage. It would be necessary for you to swallow your pride and apply for a pension.'

'I am . . . overwhelmed by your generosity, Miss Hooper.'

*

Lorna Hooper was all but evicted from the convalescent bed. Miss Elizabeth Duckworth would retain hers until the plaster was removed from her leg. On two occasions, Lorna returned, as a visitor. On the first, she brought papers required to be completed in order to obtain a pension. She supervised their completion. On the second occasion, she brought two oranges, her address and cash enough to pay the taxi fare to Kew.

Amber was released on a Tuesday morning. She didn't go immediately to Kew but took a taxi to the Melbourne GPO where she collected her batch of pension cheques from an elderly chap who eyed her suspiciously. Perhaps he recalled the draggle-haired hag in her black overcoat, or her name – or her bulk of cheques.

Her leg was not strong yet. She had much to do, but where to begin the doing of it?

She walked to a bank where she opened an account with two pension cheques. She cashed two more. She'd feared collecting her money, but there it was, in her hand, with a small blue book. She could collect no more – or had no intention of collecting more when she took a tram to Richmond, where at an opportunity shop she accrued a past. A handbag, black, a little worn. A walking stick. She required it today – and surely it had belonged to her dear departed father. Someone's discarded wedding photograph in a fake silver frame became her dead parents. She purchased a large case, two pairs of shoes, and a pretty china teapot, obviously long-departed mother's favourite teapot – and expensive enough at two shillings.

She was selective with her clothing. 'I lost everything in a house fire,' she lied. The charitable woman manning the store was both sympathetic and helpful.

A black suit looked made to measure for Elizabeth Duckworth. Two blouses, one blue, one blue striped. Three frocks, undergarments too, and nightwear, and such a pretty embroidered maroon dressing-gown.

Private mailbox! Amber thought while her purchases were totalled and packed into the case, other than the walking stick and the handbag. Too much weight in the case, she left it with the sympathetic woman and caught a tram back to the post office, where she bought an envelope and spoke to a middle-aged male.

'How do I go about obtaining a private mailbox?'

It had been a long time since Amber Morrison had gone shopping with money in her handbag. She liked the feeling. And unless she contacted the pension office, they'd keep sending Amber's cheques. Why not fix up a safe harbour for them, and for her bankbook, which Miss Duckworth couldn't take with her to Kew.

It took time, but she got it done, then her bankbook sealed into the envelope she posted it to Amber Morrison's private mailbox at the GPO, the key to which was safe, pinned into a zipper compartment in her black handbag.

Hailed a taxi out front of the GPO, collected her case from the sympathetic woman, then Miss Elizabeth Duckworth continued on to Kew, to a solid house, situated in a quiet street, externally much as she'd expected.

Chaos within. But chaos had once bowed to Amber Morrison's hands.

*

Lorna's elderly Ford was written off by her insurance company, for too little. She purchased a new vehicle, a Morris. Amber spent a portion of Miss Duckworth's first pension cheque on beeswax and turpentine. She'd always mixed her own furniture polish.

She spent hours at the sink, washing fine china she'd found hidden deep in a cabinet she recognised as the one from Vern

Hooper's dining-room. She washed an expensive vase that had once held pride of place on his sitting-room mantelpiece, always a delight to Amber's eyes – as were six dainty figures.

Within a few days, chaos began to back away. Within a week, the rooms had undergone a dramatic improvement; within two weeks, they were transformed.

As was Amber. When her hair grew sufficiently, she clad herself in her black suit and blue blouse and drove with her benefactor to church, where Lorna introduced her as 'Miss Duckworth, my live-in companion'.

A few eyebrows were raised, a few elbows jabbed a neighbour's ribs. 'Companion, my foot.'

There were more who stared at Lorna's blob of nose. The surgeon hadn't had a lot left to work with.

A symbiosis of misfits, an interdependent, mutually beneficial relationship, theirs. Lorna had saved Amber's life the night she'd all but taken it. For Lorna, she'd had the good fortune to bowl over a skivvy-companion who cleaned, baked, polished, did the laundry, knew which drawer, which shelf or cupboard would reveal what Lorna sought.

Relieved of the stresses of living, Lorna returned to her bookwork and, in time, to her reading. She had one good eye and blurred sight in the other. Given time, the brain makes its own adjustments.

'Duckworth, could you fetch my driving spectacles.'

In time the request would become a demand, but not yet.

AMBERLEY

*R*obert's retirement in 1964 had been an eternity away for Cara, the fifteen year old. She was twenty now and going home to spend Christmas at Amberley, and Myrtle couldn't remember what she'd done with her jewellery box. The string of pearls Myrtle's mother had worn on her wedding day was in it.

They were at Spencer Street Station with still an hour to wait before boarding the train.

'Did you see me pack it, Robert?'

She'd been packing for months. Robert shook his head.

The train had been Myrtle's choice. They could have flown north. Robert's old car might have made one last trip up the Hume Highway, or he could have bought a new car and driven it home.

Be a brain, go by train. There was no luggage limit on trains – and Myrtle had a ton.

'I remember putting your box of war medals in the grey case. I meant to put the jewellery box in with them, but I can't remember doing it.'

Six large cases had been booked through to Sydney and Myrtle wanted to have a quick look in the grey. If the jewellery box was in one of them it would be the grey, or perhaps the smaller of the brown cases.

'What are you going to do if it's not in either of them, Mummy?'

'I'll feel better if I know it is.'

'And you'll feel worse if you know it isn't,' Cara said.

'Those pearls will be yours when I'm gone.'

'You're not going anywhere and I'm not a pearl person.'

Myrtle had inherited few of her mother's possessions. Anything with value had been sold in their fight to save Amberley. Cara glanced at her only jewellery, a gold watch. Its hands had barely moved since the last time she'd looked. She wanted to board the train and get the trip started, to go to sleep on a narrow bunk and wake tomorrow in Sydney, then, until she began teaching, God alone knew where, to sleep in her own room, in her own bed.

'My grandparents gave those pearls to Mother on her wedding day,' Myrtle said.

'You've told me, Mummy.' Cathy had bought a similar string of pearls for two and six at Coles. They may have been made by a machine instead of an oyster, but when the string snapped at a dance, she hadn't spent a week crawling around the floor looking for pearls. Cara turned away to watch the people, almost able to pick those going home and those heading off on a holiday. Myrtle looked as if she was going to a funeral and Cara wondered if she'd make it through to New Year when Cathy was coming up to spend a week in Sydney. She'd never been out of Victoria.

Two women caught her eye, so obviously mother and daughter in shape, feature and colouring, and the tiny girl in the stroller looked like both of them. If I stood beside Jenny, would a stranger pick me as her daughter? Cara wondered. Is Jenny's mother still alive? Do I look like her? Cathy was the image of her mother and grandmother. Marion was like her father – tall, thin, dark; fast-talking comedians, both.

The mother, daughter and grandchild left the counter and Cara took their place to study a map of train lines until an elderly man in a grey suit asked if she required his help.

'Would you know if there is a daily service to Woody Creek?'

A knowledgeable man, the man in grey, with no need for book or chart; he told her of train times, platform numbers, but couldn't offer her a daily return service. She wasn't planning to go there anyway.

Myrtle watched her approach. Cara had dressed comfortably for the trip. At fourteen she'd wanted a pair of boys' black jeans and one of Robert's white shirts with tails. Myrtle hadn't approved. She didn't approve of bottom-hugging jeans and breast-hugging tops either, but since the trial, or since Dino Collins had been locked up, Cara had come to terms with her early stupidity and become more comfortable with who she was, or who she wanted to believe she was – which wasn't pleated skirts and twin sets and pearls.

'A train passes through Woody Creek every weekday,' Cara said.

'She's no doubt moved a long time ago, and gotten on with her life, poppet.'

'Probably,' Cara said.

*

Strange to return home in two taxis, to unload cases from the boot, the back seat of Cara's taxi, then to haul them one at a time to that familiar front door. Then wait impatiently while Robert found the right key that would swing the door wide. It was stranger to see Miss Robertson hurrying towards them down their private section of passage.

'I've been keeping my eye out for you,' she said. Had she changed her clothing since they'd left? Same skirt, or similar, same long cardigan, same spectacles and hairstyle, a little more grey.

'Mr O'Conner not about?' Robert asked.

'Things aren't as they should be, I'm afraid, Mr Norris.'

Difficult to see much before the eyes adjusted from full sun to indoor light. 'We haven't sighted either of the O'Conners since Saturday, and they took the washing machine.'

Cara heaved heavy cases into the entrance hall, which wasn't as it should be. Boxes, rags, an old shoe, sheets of newspaper on the floor.

'Someone packed in a hurry,' she said.

'On Saturday night, we believe, Cara. And haven't you grown into a modern girl.'

Myrtle was looking up, her expression one of disbelief. Cara followed her gaze to a naked globe swinging dolefully from where a crystal chandelier had hung when they'd left – also Myrtle's mother's.

'What happened to our chandelier?'

Miss Robertson looked up. 'The light fitting too?' she tut-tutted before continuing. 'The smaller of the two refrigerators from the lodgers' kitchen is also missing. They left our goods on the table to spoil – my steak left to bleed into Mrs Collins's cheese.'

'This is not happening, Robert. He said –'

Cara stepped away from the group to the parlour which, at first glance, appeared to be intact. The old table was where they'd left it. It weighed a ton, and to Cara's knowledge had never been moved. She counted six dining-room chairs, hoped the other six were about. Along with the chandelier and the pearls, those chairs had belonged to the halcyon days of Myrtle's childhood when servants, not lodgers, had occupied the excess rooms.

'We became concerned on Sunday morning when Mrs Collins took her washing down to the laundry, though we believed it may have been undergoing repairs. We knocked on the rent hatch, but by midafternoon, and not a sign of either of them, we began knocking on both doors. Mr Waters forced the rent hatch on Sunday evening and climbed through. He was convinced they'd been murdered in their bed.'

The tour group had moved to the doorway of the main bedroom. Bed still there, unmade, wardrobe doors hanging open.

Cara went through to the kitchen. It was bare.

'In here, Daddy.'

The small kitchen setting, cutlery, crockery, pots and pans left for the O'Conners' use had gone. They hadn't bothered to close the cupboard doors, and it was too much for Myrtle. She returned to the parlour to sit weeping into her handkerchief.

Two beds in Cara's room where there should have been one, both unmade and reeking of stale smoke and sweating stranger. Closed the door and turned back to Miss Robertson, waiting in the passage to continue the tour.

Robert was in the kitchen attempting to close a cupboard door which refused to close. Bang. Bang. Bang. It was as close as he came to expressing anger. Or maybe not. The strength of those bangs increased.

'Leave it, Robert!' Myrtle wailed.

Bang! Bang! Bang!

'How dare he do this to us!'

Bang!

'Will you please leave it be, Robert!'

'I spoke to him on Friday,' Robert said. 'He told me everything was in order.'

'He was in the grip of the drink, I'm afraid, and the female shared his vice,' Miss Robertson said, and her entourage again in tow, she led the way to the side door and down to the rear of the house where empty bottles stacked against the laundry wall offered evidence of the manager's vice.

A small truck was parked in the backyard, a stranger, his head beneath its lifted bonnet tinkering, two half-grown boys passing him tools.

'The Bertrams,' Miss Robertson said behind a hand.

'Children?' Myrtle said. 'They're not living here?'

'I'm afraid so.'

'How many?'

'The two boys. In Number Five – and they are up and down the passage, up and down the stairs all day long.'

'How many . . . lodgers?'

'Nineteen, Mrs Norris –'

'No.'

'Nineteen, including the Bertram children –'

'Where?' Robert asked.

'We are, to use young Mr Waters's expression, packed in like rats in a cage, Mr Norris. Until Friday, O'Conner had a couple in Cara's room. They were moved to the storeroom before he left.'

'The storeroom!' A chorus of three.

'The storeroom,' their tour guide said. 'And the female half of that duo is particularly objectionable – and more so since their move.'

This wasn't the way coming home was meant to be. Robert had given the manager and his wife three months' notice in which to find alternative accommodation. On Friday O'Conner had agreed to meet with them at Amberley to hand over the keys.

'Ten lodgers. He told me there were ten. When you lost Mrs . . . the woman from Number Six . . . back in July.'

'We've had nineteen for the past month – since the Smiths arrived,' Mrs Collins said, joining the tour. 'And no washing machine since Sunday, Mr Norris. What a homecoming for you.'

Cara left the four lamenting in the laundry and walked out to stand and stare at the street, or at the traffic on it. Since the day they'd left, she'd protected her image of life at Amberley, of that road, of the shops up the hill and around the corner. Shook her head and walked up the hill.

Not the same. No Mr Hodge at the café. A new Australian woman sold her a bottle of milk, a loaf of bread, butter, ham, a small jar of coffee. The greengrocer hadn't moved. The girl working with him might have been one of his daughters, infants when Cara had been thirteen. She sold her three tomatoes, three bananas.

She walked downhill on the far side of the road, stood in front of Sarah North's house for minutes, waiting for a break in the traffic so she might cross over. There'd always been cars, but insufficient to prevent her running across the road to Sarah's house.

A constant stream of traffic on it this morning and no more Sarah North. They'd moved on. Wondered if they'd taken their chain-crazy barking dog with them.

From the far side of the street, Amberley looked as it always had, a mite superior to its neighbours. Not so superior inside.

Robert was struggling to open a window when she entered; Myrtle was walking in circles. Their tour guide had gone.

'Have you called the police?' Cara asked, dumping her load on the kitchen bench.

'Don't put it down there. Take it into the lodgers' kitchen where it's clean.'

'By the look of a pair I ran into out there, it won't last ten seconds,' Robert said.

Cara stood, her shopping in her arms. 'Ring the police or I will, Daddy.'

'If we bring them out here, we'll get nothing done today, poppet.'

'We've been robbed!'

'What we need to do is to get these rooms habitable before the removalists get here. See if you can find a broom somewhere,' he said.

'And a mop,' Myrtle added. 'And a bucket.'

'It's not just what's missing, Daddy. He's been getting rent from nineteen lodgers and paying us for ten.'

'Find a broom.'

'He's a thief and you are both ostriches,' Cara said, then, her shopping given into Myrtle's arms, she went off to look for mop and broom.

*

The manager, who for years had been Mr O'Conner, became the unmentionable *he, him*, as they swept, as Cara pitched rubbish out the front door and Myrtle complained about her pitching it out there for the neighbours to see.

'Concentrate on your kitchen!' Robert said.

The ragged mop from the laundry might have housed the cockroach, two cockroaches, who appeared to be halfway through making baby cockroaches, which slowed their getaway sufficiently for Myrtle to scream and for Cara to stomp on them.

There is always a final straw. The third cockroach running into her cupboard was Myrtle's.

'Call the police, Robert.'

'They don't arrest cockroaches, Mummy.'

Robert called a taxi. He and Myrtle rode it to a hardware store where they paid the driver to wait while they shopped for new mops, plastic buckets, brooms, washing powder, detergents, bleach and two varieties of bug sprays. By three-thirty the removalists hadn't arrived, but no self-respecting cockroach would consider those rooms a healthy home.

The beds had been stripped, their wire mattresses doused with bug killer, Myrtle convinced that if *he* could live with cockroaches *he* would have slept with bedbugs, would have shed fleas to the floor rugs too. The rugs had been sprayed then hauled down to the clothes line. Mr Bertram moved his truck to give them space, then helped hang the rugs and offered his boys to beat them with the old brooms.

The room Cara had named her own since infancy had fared worse than the main bedroom. The paintwork was scuffed, the floor scorched by cigarette butts, the windowsill, convenient ashtray, seared. She'd ripped the curtains from their rod, adding them to the pile of junk out front. The mattresses had been dragged outside to where the sun might fry any flea or bedbugs eluding Myrtle's spray.

Four-thirty and still no furniture van. Five, and every truck that drove by had to be it – and wasn't. At five-thirty Robert dragged the mattresses indoors.

'I'm not sleeping on them,' Cara said.

'If the removalists don't arrive, we'll need to sleep on something,' Robert said.

The sheets stripped from the beds had been boiled clean. They'd dried. You can't boil blankets.

'I'm not sleeping here,' Cara repeated at seven while they ate sandwiches, drank more coffee in a now clean parlour, and listened for the furniture van, all three weary, Myrtle yawning, worn out, worn silent by labour, staring out through coloured glass as night came down on Sydney.

They'd been living, breathing, dreaming of Christmas dinner eaten around that table. Not enough chairs. They'd found two, one in the lodgers' kitchen, stained, one in Miss Robertson's room, cleaner than the ones in the parlour. Six still missing. According to Myrtle, there had been fourteen chairs, not twelve.

'Father ordered them from America when the house was being built. We should have put them into storage, Robert.'

'We've got bigger problems than a few missing chairs,' Robert said. He was in pain. He'd been limping for the past three hours, and Myrtle couldn't remember in which bag she'd packed his pills. Cases everywhere. Cara hadn't opened her own but she found Robert's pills, and her mother's jewellery box, in the grey case. The pills eased Robert's pain, the pearls didn't ease Myrtle's.

Nine o'clock when they gave up on the removalists and took a taxi out to Beth and John, where Myrtle bathed then fell into the guest's bed and died for eight hours, where Robert and John sat late and Cara smoked cigarettes with Pete behind the shrubbery in the backyard; they washed the stink of bug spray from her nostrils, and a little of the disappointment.

A warm night, a different warmth from Melbourne's. The sounds were different.

'Still going to England?'

'When I save a bit,' Pete said.

'What does it cost?'

'Depends on how you go.'

'If I owned a bike I'd give you a dink over there tonight,' she said. 'I've been looking forward to coming home since the day I left. Now I'm here and I'd rather be just about anywhere else.'

*

John owned a trailer. They hooked it up to his car the following morning and he, Beth and Pete drove them back to Amberley. Still no sign of the removalists. They'd expected to see the van waiting out the front. The men took two loads of junk to the tip; the women washed walls, cleaned windows; the lodgers complained about the missing washing machine; and ten- and twelve-year-old boys ran up and down the overhead passage, had races up the stairs.

'Something will have to be done about the Bertrams,' Myrtle said.

That day was lost, along with their Traralgon furniture, which Cara had never appreciated, which now grew more precious every hour they waited for it.

'I just ran into that female from the storeroom,' Myrtle said. 'She is . . .' There was no fitting way to describe her other than as an unclean, foul-mouthed middle-aged slut.

Was Jenny an unclean, foul-mouthed middle-aged slut?

There was no fitting way to describe the middle-aged creep in Number Nine, other than as a bug-eyed cockroach looking for spoil. Cara felt soiled when she carried another of the dining-room chairs from his room. Five to go. Locating those chairs had become her focus. She found one in the laundry, a rag of towel hung over its ornate back, a carton of clothing on its mutilated upholstered seat. She claimed it.

Four to go – and probably gone with *them*.

Nightfall, Beth, John and Pete gone home to sanity, Myrtle and Robert, too weary to do more, sat at the dining-room table, attempting to sort out the rent book. Mr Bertram and his two boys had been renting Number Five since early October, and could show no record of having ever paid rent, though the father swore he'd paid a fortnight in advance last Friday. Miss Robertson had already informed them that *he*, the unmentionable, had demanded rent to be paid two weeks in advance.

The couple in Number Ten, a single downstairs room, who also had no rent book, told the same story, and Miss Robertson backed them up. She'd queued at the rent hatch behind them and seen them pay.

'The Bertrams will need to be given notice, Robert.'

Robert yawned. 'There's little harm in his boys other than youthful exuberance.'

Slept that night at Amberley, between twice-boiled sheets. The old copper in the laundry, unused in years, had got them back to white, or Myrtle's bleach had. No blankets necessary that night. Had they been necessary, Cara would have chosen to shiver.

Sunday, and Myrtle so looking forward to returning to her old church.

'Next week,' Robert said and got down on his bad knee, not to pray, but to fix the kitchen cupboard's snib. Uncombed, clad in singlet and trousers, his thinning grey hair in need of a wash, he didn't look like a high-school principal. He closed the cupboard door, but when he attempted to rise, his war-damaged knee decided otherwise. He paled and sat on the kitchen floor, the leg stretched out before him.

They brought his pills. They helped him into the parlour, where he couldn't bend his knee to sit. They walked him to the bedroom.

And someone knocked at the rent hatch.

'See what *they* want, pet.' The lodgers had now been parcelled into a convenient *they*, *them*, *those people*.

Only Mrs Collins. She still had a name. 'I'm sorry to add to your problems, dear, but the upstairs toilet isn't flushing.'

Robert tried to rise, but his knee screamed and he stayed down. He had half-a-dozen pieces of shrapnel floating around in it. Myrtle looked as if she'd been run over by a truck.

In five weeks' time Cara would be Miss Norris, schoolteacher. Miss Norris took charge. She locked the upstairs toilet door and stuck an *Out of Order* sign on it. There was a toilet downstairs and one outside behind the laundry.

For thirty years, with barely a shudder, Amberley had absorbed selectively chosen lodgers. O'Conner hadn't chosen selectively. The floors rocked with nineteen, and when Cara went upstairs to demand the Bertram boys turn their noise down, she found another dining-room chair. The Bertrams were using it as a stand for a small portable television set. She won the chair, and before she left with it, the volume had been turned down a notch. Not enough. The parlour was directly beneath Number Five, and they could still hear every whiz, bang, screech.

'It's intolerable, Robert.'

'We're not putting children out on the street at Christmas time. Now that's enough about it.'

He was swallowing more pills, and he looked like Gran Norris – looked as old as her too.

The phone rang at seven-thirty. Cara answered it, expecting it to be the removalist. Cathy's gabble greeted her, and tonight it was the warble of a messiah magpie.

'So, how are the bright lights of Sydney?'

'I'm considering jumping off the Bridge.'

'That good, eh? I was hoping so – not really, but it will make my proposition that much more attractive. I just got a brand-new Mini Minor for Christmas. It's powder blue and it needs a good long drive to run its motor in, so I thought –'

'It's chaos up here, Cathy. We'll need to change our plans.'

'That's what I'm trying to do if you'll listen. Guess who I've just been talking to for the last half-hour?' She didn't wait for Cara's guess. 'Gerry is home and he's brought a Pommy mate back with him, and I asked them if they'd be here for the New Year dance, and Gerry said he wouldn't miss it for quids, and to save him the first dance. So you have to come down here and keep his mate occupied.'

'I can't.'

'Can. Then after New Year, I'll drive you back up there and stay until we find out where they've posted us.'

'You can't come here. Will you listen for a minute –'

'You listen first. Remember that dream I had about me and the black dress and you wearing that red dress, and Gerry being home for a funeral. Well, there's no funeral, but his father has been in hospital with something wrong with his heart, which is what brought Gerry home. He's not going to die or anything – or not yet. So it's all sort of preordained. I'm buying a black dress and you're going to wear your red.'

'I'm not going anywhere – and you said it was claret, not red.'

'Yeah, but we're out of the convent now, so it's allowed to be red. You'd only be away for maybe four days. As soon as I get him interested, I'll drive you back and he'll realise how much he misses me . . .'

'The house is stuffed to the rafters with lodgers. Dad is crippled, Mum is ripping her hair out, and on top of that our furniture has gone missing.'

'Leaving them for a couple of days will give them less grief than jumping off the Harbour Bridge,' Cathy said.

'You could save a lot of depressed people with your kind of logic.'

'I know. Dad reckons I should hire myself out to the government – like a secret weapon. Anyway, you have to come. Two blokes and one girl never works, and Marion and Michelle have got blokes, and Gerry's mate is fabulous-looking.'

'If I leave Mum and Dad, they'll jump off the Bridge.'

'They're old enough to make their own decisions –'

Sound of a truck out front, barely worth a glance. She glanced, the phone cord at full stretch.

'It's them, Daddy!' she yelled, then spoke into the phone. 'I've got to go, Cath. Our furniture just turned up.'

'I'll call you back in ten minutes.'

'Make it ten hours.'

If someone had told Cara that one day she'd be pleased to see that green laminated kitchen table from Traralgon, she would have laughed in their face. She smoothed the door of the big clean refrigerator as two burly men hauled it indoors, explaining in bursts how they'd done a clutch outside of Wangaratta, how they'd been stuck there waiting for a new clutch to arrive from Melbourne, then waiting longer for it to be fitted, how the dame in the office had tried to call them but every time she called she got someone telling them it was the wrong number.

The kitchen suite settled happily into Myrtle's kitchen; the old couch gave way to the Traralgon easy chairs; the old refrigerator was moved by the men into the lodgers' kitchen and Traralgon's twin-tub washing machine installed in the laundry. Old beds were carried out to the front porch and Traralgon's near-new beds carried in and made up with Traralgon bedding. Suddenly, home began to look possible, to smell possible.

Robert tested an easy chair before the men were out the door, leather chairs with built-in footrests. He leaned back and, his knee at peace, or drugged to the eyeballs with painkillers, he nodded off.

*

John taxied Robert to the doctor's office, to the hospital for X-rays, to a car showroom where Robert ordered a cream Holden station wagon. They bought paint for the bathroom. John climbed the ladder. He painted the ceiling and the high sections of wall, Robert below copped the drips, and Cara wanted a brother like Uncle John, and she had one and hadn't been allowed to know him.

John picked them up on Christmas morning and taxied them to dinner. His two daughters and four sons were there, five had partners. There were enough little kids and babies to start a new civilisation, and Cara felt like excess baggage, which by midafternoon was delivered back to Amberley by Pete while Robert nodded off in the back seat and Myrtle clung to what she could. Pete drove like a maniac.

Six o'clock, Robert nodding off in his easy chair and an explosion shook the house. It was followed by an explosion of invective, the likes of which Amberley walls had never been subjected to. It got him to his feet. Cara beat him to the lodgers' kitchen, as did a handful of lodgers. The objectionable Mrs Smith from the storeroom, a somewhat singed Mrs Smith, had blown up the gas oven. The kitchen smelled of singed hair and brimstone – the objectionable one's hair was still smoking.

Her husband was there, attempting to shut her mouth. She turned her abuse from the gas oven to him, then the war became physical. It was his fault that she'd turned that (language deleted) oven on. He wanted that (language deleted) bloody chicken.

Had Amberley's walls previously been subjected to gutter language? Had they witnessed physical violence? Myrtle hadn't. She stood back with the gathering crowd while the singed dame got in a knee that almost floored her male.

The Bertrams returned from where they'd been; the boys stood on the outskirts of the crowd, watching real-life whiz, bang, whack action while their father entered the fray. He dragged the male outside, but the dame wasn't letting him off that easily. She followed them out the side door.

'It's got to be a nightmare,' Robert said.

'I wanted to sell up when you came home from the war, Robert,' Myrtle said.

'I was twenty years younger when I came home from the war.'

Audience still grouped there. Waiting for the next bout?

Miss Norris took charge. 'The show appears to be over. The kitchen will be off limits until further notice.'

'It's only the oven –' Myrtle began.

'The kitchen will be off limits until we can get someone out here to check it.' Cara's voice rose, her hand held up, demanding stop, silence.

It didn't silence Myrtle. 'We can't do that to *them*. Get our electric frying pan –'

Like hell she'd get the frying pan. She picked up the toaster, the electric jug and looked for hands to take them. 'There are two power points in the laundry.'

'Turn the gas off,' someone suggested.

Her husband encouraged to leave the premises, the singed female was back for her chicken. 'You've got a bloody oven in there,' she said to Cara.

'As did the lodgers until you blew it up,' Miss Norris said. She had been trained to raise her voice to obstreperous children. 'This door will be locked until we find the problem.'

'Our food is in the fridges,' someone said.

'Then I suggest you take what you require before the door is locked.'

'It will be a gas build-up in the oven,' Myrtle said. She had her head in the oven, sniffing for a leak. Robert was leaning against a table, watching her, perhaps waiting his turn to put his own head into a gas oven.

'Find me the right key, Daddy,' Cara ordered. He looked at the cluster of lodgers, at his daughter, then he did as she instructed.

Bill Bertram and Mr Waters carried the smaller of the two tables out to the laundry. Mrs Collins took her milk and butter upstairs. Miss Robertson asked if she might make a phone call. She made several before locating a hotel with an available twin room. Fifteen minutes later, she and Mrs Collins left in a taxi.

For an hour Cara guarded the kitchen door, informing late arrivals of the gas problem, and offering any resident who chose to permanently vacate the premises a refund of a week's rent. There were no takers. The position was good, close to train, bus and shops. At nine she increased her offer to a refund of the last fortnight's rent.

And she got a taker. The male member of the objectionable duo wanted his. Myrtle found the chequebook. They woke Robert to sign one. He didn't ask why. He signed half-a-dozen then went to bed to sleep while one cheque was exchanged for the key to the storeroom door. Cara saw the duo off the premises. She locked their door and, at ten, locked the private door to Myrtle and Robert's private quarters then went to her room to sort through the smaller of her two cases, tossing items out, tossing items in. The black high-heeled sandals she'd bought to wear to Gran's funeral were packed, then her claret dress. She was going to Ballarat.

She'd need to get to a bank as soon as a bank opened. Her signature had been registered up here, at Robert's old bank. She couldn't remember how to get there, if she'd ever been there. Knew where the banks were in Melbourne. Robert had paid for her return ticket on the train. Tomorrow, if the railway office was open, she'd see if she could change the return date on the ticket.

A second cheque changed hands at nine the following morning. She got rid of two women from upstairs. Four from nineteen equals fifteen, take away Miss Robertson and Mrs Collins, if temporarily, and that made a near-manageable thirteen.

Myrtle caught her on the telephone at ten, attempting to change the date on her ticket. Couldn't get a sleeper south.

'What are you doing, pet?'

'Going down to spend New Year's Eve with Cathy.'

'You just got home!'

Home? She dared call this home? They'd returned to a madhouse. 'Just for a couple of days, then Cathy will drive me back.'

'We can't have her here!'

'We'll put one of the old beds back into my –' And their eyes turned to their private door. Someone out there knocking. 'Was it always like this, Mummy?'

Myrtle shook her head and walked back to the parlour, to Robert, glued again to his easy chair.

Cara unlocked the door. Only the two-legged cockroach. Hoped he'd come for his refund. He hadn't. He apologised for disturbing her, but could someone please show him how to work the new washing machine.

Cara walked with him to the laundry where a young married couple were attempting to make breakfast. They gave up and asked if they might please make a long-distance call home. They'd pay for it. Cara led them back to the house, to the telephone, and didn't make them pay, and at midday, the wife's parents arrived. The young couple took their refund and went home – the parents didn't look old enough to have a married daughter, and Cara envied their daughter. Robert had retired from teaching to read a thousand books, to do all of the things he'd never had time to do. Instead he'd become the new Gran Norris, sitting, swallowing pills.

Bill Bertram fixed the upstairs toilet. He unscrewed an external pipe, shoved a long wire up it, down it, and whatever had been causing the blockage decided to move on. He tested the gas oven and pronounced it as safe as a bank. The lodgers' kitchen door was unlocked and a form of peace settled over Amberley.

Until Cara phoned the bus depot.

'You're not still thinking about going, pet?'

'If I can get a seat I'm going.'

'Try the airport,' Robert said. 'We didn't buy you a present this year.'

She got an early flight on the morning of 31 December and rode alone to the airport in a taxi.

BALLARAT

*T*wo hours after leaving Sydney, Cara was queuing at her own bank in Melbourne, and twenty minutes later she was on the train to Ballarat.

An old town, rich in its heyday, its station still whispering tales of gold for the taking. Traralgon had been built on brown coal, by brown coal, in a hurry, and therein lay the difference.

Cathy and her little blue box on wheels was waiting for her, Cathy full of Gerry, Cara full of her first flight, of Amberley's manager and the nineteen lodgers.

'That red MG is Gerry's . . .'

'One crazy dame blew up the gas oven on Christmas Day . . .'

'He's had it since '56 . . .'

'Someone blocked up the upstairs loo . . .'

'He took me for a couple of rides in it when I was a kid . . .'

They had the house to themselves until Gwen and Len Bryant came home from work. A different life, Cathy's, a different world. She had a home, had a modern bathroom, a separate shower room next door. Amberley bathrooms had been built before showers were thought of, the showers later installed over aged bathtubs.

Cathy's bath was a shiny white, her shower room was white-tiled. So much light in her house, so much noise, good noise – a television set, a classy radiogram, hundreds of records and a telephone that rang every five minutes.

'Grab it, will you.'

Cara grabbed it. Only Gwen Bryant reminding Cathy to put a casserole into the oven or there'd be no dinner tonight.

It rang twice more, one call from a Meg, a girl Cathy had started school with, one from her grandmother, who lived less than a block away, who was making her a black dress to wear to the dance tonight and she still had to put up the hem.

No sign of Gerry, or not until a little red sports car pulled out of the drive across the road.

'That's him,' Cathy said. Cara sighted the backs of two heads, one blond, one dark.

They put the casserole in then drove half a block to her gran's house where a hem was pinned while Cathy stood on the kitchen table, then they peeled potatoes and got the washing off the line while Gran stitched the hem.

*

Eight-thirty when they left for the dance, a pair of claret baubles pinching Cara's lobes. She hadn't argued about wearing them, hadn't argued about the eye shadow, the eyeliner, guaranteed not to run.

'They'll swarm you,' Cathy said. 'Just keep your eyes off Gerry.'

'Obsessions are dangerous, Cath.'

'Love isn't,' Cathy said, expertly slipped her blue box into a narrow parking space, not much of it to slip but Cara envied her skill anyway, envied her gran, her house, her parents – and her trust in mankind when she placed her car keys into her purse then left the purse on the cloakroom bench.

'Someone will steal it!'

'I always leave it there – anyway, Jeff, the mechanic from Dad's place, fitted a switch under the dash that cuts off the power to the ignition or something,' Cathy said, leading the way into the hall.

'Who died, Cath?' a male greeted her.

'My love for you,' Cathy said, smoothing the narrow black skirt a fraction lower. 'Cara, meet Frank. One of my exes.'

He wanted to dance with Cathy. She told him she'd promised the first dance to Gerry. Cara danced with him and he asked her why Cathy was wearing black. He worked at a bank, seemed nice enough. She'd danced with a less memorable partner before Cathy gave up waiting for Gerry, who must have had a better offer for New Year's Eve. He wasn't in the hall.

Eleven o'clock and he still hadn't arrived, they were dancing – Cara with a long lean bloke who had a style midway between marionette and whirling dervish. If she expected him to step back, he stepped forward; if she expected him to whirl to the right, he went left; if she took evasive action, he took the same action. She dodged left, he kicked her exposed toe; she took evasive action, one of her too-high heels slid, and when she attempted to dance on, the heel wobbled.

'The classic country dance,' he said. 'Five-piece band up one end, the males at the other, cliques sitting in their reserved corners as if their cultural rankings were engraved there.'

And he had a Pommy accent. Was he the fabulous-looking friend of fabulous Gerry, the one she was supposed to keep occupied while Cathy set her trip wires? He couldn't be. He had a huge pus-topped pimple on his jaw.

'Have you booked the last dance?' he said.

'Yes,' she lied. In Ballarat, booking the last dance meant you were agreeing to allow the dance partner to walk or drive you home.

She glanced at his face, attempting to see some reason why Cathy might think he was good-looking. He was as pale as washed suet, except for his pimple, a red and yellow blot on washed suet.

Not enough sun in Pommy-land? He was well dressed, had hands as soft as a baby's backside. Had no sense of rhythm.

No sign of Cathy's black. She'd pinned her hopes on tonight. Wondered if fabulous Gerry was amongst the dancers, if he looked like washed-out suet after two years in Pommy-land. Her mind far away, her partner swung her into an uncoordinated series of back steps, and the wobbly heel wobbled – which might teach her not to buy shoes from bargain tables but probably wouldn't. The earrings pinching her lobes had come from Coles.

'An aging flock of ewes waiting in the stockyards for a purchaser,' her pale partner said as they gyrated by a row of wall-flowers. Amused by his description, his cheeks stretched in a smile, and Cara dodged, expecting pus to fly, then she left him stranded in front of his wallflowers and escaped to the cloakroom where she hitched her stockings up and her skirt down.

Loved that dress, had at first sight, but could have done with a size larger. It clung to her hips and was too short, according to Myrtle, and like the college head, she believed that only scarlet women wore red. Cara was combing her hair when the dance ended and a horde of girls came in to queue for the toilets. Cathy wasn't with them. Probably out in her car having a breakdown, Cara thought.

Outside the hall two dozen males congregated, leaning against walls, on cars, in groups or alone. Four dozen eyes turned to stare at the red dress or what was beneath it. Cara changed her mind about finding Cathy and returned to the hall where an aging Elvis claimed her. She'd danced with him earlier. He knew how to dance.

Then midway through the bracket the music stopped and one of the band members called a progressive barn dance. If there was a dance Cara loathed, it was the progressive barn dance, where the females were passed from hand to hand like the collection plate in church.

Dancers were forming a circle when Cara caught a flash of black. Cathy was dancing. She kept her eye on her until the first partner change, then made a beeline across the dance floor, creating confusion, but the little bloke Cathy had been dancing with claimed her and she danced on.

Danced with a dozen pairs of hands. Interesting things, hands. They told the age of their owners, and sometimes their occupations. She began picking her partner's occupations by his hands, sorting the farmers' sons from the bank clerks, the mechanics from the shop boys. Ian, a sandy-headed kid she knew from college, greeted her like an old friend.

He was midway through a story when she swung away from him and into a pair of chubby hands attached to an overweight fifty year old who stunk of nicotine. His hands went for the bare flesh of her back, then held her against him in a gorilla embrace. She danced with a pair of lily whites she pegged as belonging to an undertaker's son, who passed her to a pair clean enough to belong to a bank clerk, large enough to be a farmer's – and he knew her name.

'You look bored out of your brain, Norris,' he said.

She looked him in the eye, aware she was supposed to know him. Cathy had introduced her to a dozen groups tonight, and two dozen more last Christmas. She couldn't place him, and at the partner change he danced her out to the centre of the floor instead of on to the next pair of hands, then tried to do the same at the next swap. She sidestepped him, her heel wobbled, and for the second time she almost lost her footing.

'Born with two left feet?' he said.

'My heel is loose. I need to sit down.'

'It's socially unacceptable to leave your partner stranded in the middle of the dance floor.'

'It's also socially unacceptable not to change partners in the progressive barn dance,' she said and left him stranded.

Cathy joined her in the cloakroom. 'Did Morrie introduce himself? You danced with him.'

'I just danced with every sweaty coot in the hall, and how dare you bring me all the way down here to entertain that pus-faced Pom?' Cara said, pulling the earring clips from her lobes and reaching for Cathy's purse to drop them into.

'They're all pus-faced to you,' Cathy said. 'What did you think of Gerry? You danced with him too.'

'I need some fresh air,' she said and walked outside again.

Cooler air out there, air laced with the scent of tobacco smoke, and she wished she had a smoke. The one thing her parents and Cathy's had in common was their aversion to cigarettes. She was looking across the road to Cathy's little blue box, dreaming of owning her own, when a kid who might have been sixteen approached her, his packet of smokes open.

'They'll ruin your lungs,' the schoolmistress said, accepting one anyway, and a light. And Cathy came out and caught her.

'I'll dob to your mother, Stevie.'

'I'm old enough,' he said, but whether he was or not, Cara lost her companion. She didn't waste her smoke, smoked it down to the butt, then pitched it into a trough-sized ashtray.

'What did you think of him?' Cathy asked.

'Give him a year or two –'

'Gerry. I was dancing with him when they called the barn dance. He danced with you after me.'

Cara couldn't remember who she'd danced with. 'My heel is wobbling, my middle toe is broken and I'm ready to go home.'

'I would have gone ten minutes ago, but he had to put in an appearance at the Hill-Jones party – and he's going back there after the dance. So are we.'

'You weren't invited.'

'Was so, except Mum and Dad were going out there so I came here.'

The band was playing; Cathy went back to the hall and Cara returned to the cloakroom to remove her stockings. Her toenail had cut its way through one and she could feel a ladder crawling up her shin. They were throwaway items now, bought in packets of three from Coles. She tossed them into a bin then went back to the hall, wanting to be there when they welcomed in 1965. She'd be employed, and the first thing she'd buy with her own money was driving lessons.

Found a seat amid the wallflowers. Pus-face eyed her as he danced by. The wet behind the ears kid raised the nerve to come inside and find her.

'How about it?' he said.

'My heel is loose.' She demonstrated its wobble. He ogled the bare leg it was attached to, then asked the next wallflower. She danced with him.

The drum roll, the deafening communal countdown to midnight, the bunches of balloons festooning the hall, popping, whistles blowing as the sweating men on stage put everything they had into the last dance. The saxophonist, a master of his tool, had it weeping for the wallflowers who waited or quietly wandered out to the cloakroom. The trombone came in, deriding the youths who had stood outside for most of the evening. She was tapping her foot to the rhythm when the last bloke from the progressive barn dance approached her. She beat him to the punch, lifted her foot and wobbled her heel.

'Good dancers dance on their toes,' he said, and not too unwillingly she got to her feet. It was a quickstep. She loved the quickstep.

'You can dance, Norris.'

'I had lessons in Sale,' she said.

'On a boat.'

'Sale, the town,' she said. And the band started playing 'Goodnight Sweetheart'.

The cloakroom was packed solid, but Cathy had found an edge of mirror where she freshened her lipstick for the party.

'Drop me back at the house, Cath.'

'Stop being a party pooper. It will be fun. The last time they threw a party we came home at dawn.'

'I was up early.'

'I told Gerry we were going.'

'I'm not going. You go.'

'I'm not walking in by myself. Come for half an hour and if you're not enjoying yourself I'll drive you home.'

They left the hall with a crowd and were crossing the road when Cathy deviated and walked across to her neighbour's red sports car. Up close, its hood folded down, it looked like a toy. A blond-headed bloke was behind the wheel, Cara's last partner was stepping over the passenger door.

'Cara is being a party pooper,' Cathy told them.

'My heel is hanging on by a thread!'

They worked it out, or Cathy did. Morrie didn't know anyone and he'd done enough celebrating. Cathy would drive Gerry out to the party and Morrie could drive Cara home.

'I learned early not to argue with her,' Gerry said to his mate, and he got out of the car and handed his keys to Morrie. Cara shrugged and got into the passenger seat, to do what she'd been brought here to do, to keep Gerry's mate occupied.

Glanced at Cathy and Gerry, standing side by side. They could have been brother and sister with their blond curls. Gerry, barely of average height, in Cara's view, was a long way from fabulous. The two stood together until the motor roared, until Morrie backed out to the road, found a forward gear and roared away.

*

'A beautiful model,' Morrie said. 'Have you ridden in one before?'

'No. Have you driven one before?'

'A few times,' he said.

Wind in her face, tangling her hair. She'd never ridden in an open car, had twice clung onto the back of a motorbike. Similar.

He turned left at an intersection, then a hundred yards on, turned right. She believed he was taking her home via the scenic route until she saw the sign pointing to Melbourne, where he put his foot down.

'Where do you think you're going?'

'I've never driven it on an open road.'

She wasn't afraid of him. He was Gerry's friend, driving Gerry's car – and there wasn't enough room in the car to rip her clothes off and no back seat, and the doors were low enough to climb over anyway. She was more scared of having nothing beneath her, nothing over her, and of his speed.

'Have you got a death wish?'

'You don't like speed?'

'I have this crazy desire to begin my teaching career.'

'They're made for speed,' he said, but he slowed, then swung the car in a wide circle and headed back to town.

She'd lost any bearings she may have thought she had. Minutes later, when he swung the car into a driveway then drove deep down the side of a house, she didn't have a clue where she was. Apprehensive now and angry at Cathy's desertion, she sat, her arms folded.

And the swine tried to kiss her.

'You offered to drive me home,' she said, taking a handkerchief from beneath her bra strap and making a point of wiping where he'd connected.

'I thought you were waiting for the obligatory kiss. You're home – or walk over the road and you will be.' He'd pulled into Gerry's drive, which, in Cara's mind, had managed to transpose itself from one side of the street to the other.

Embarrassed, blood rushing her face, feeling like an idiot, she fumbled for the door handle, and when he reached across her to open it, believing he was making another move on her, she whacked him across the ear.

'Out,' he said, the door pushed wide.

'You drive like a maniac, drive me in circles, pull into a strange yard – you could have told me where we were.'

'You could have asked where we were.'

'You had no right to touch me.'

'Wave a red rag at a bull and he'll chase it. Wear a neck-to-knees fur next time. We can rub noses, Eskimo fashion – exchange frosty nasal drips.' She was out. Her heel forgotten, she ran across the road, but not done yet, he followed her to Cathy's gate. 'More acceptable to chip icicles from the nostrils and less insulting to the other participant.'

'Participant suggests I was participating.' She flung the words over her shoulder as she swung the gate hard at him, then ran to the dark semi-enclosed porch.

No lights on at Cathy's house. No key in the door either. She tried it, and of course it was locked, Cathy's parents were out at the Hill-Jones party and, like their daughter, would probably stay out until dawn. Should have thought about the house key. Cathy should have thought about it. She was too busy trying to get off with Gerry.

Cara turned around and, in the dark of the porch, bumped into him.

'Locked out?'

Hadn't known he'd followed her onto the porch. She pushed by him and headed down a path leading to the back door. Darker down there. Had to feel her way. He, less familiar with this house than she, tracked her every step.

'I'll drive you out there – if you know where to go.'

'I don't.' And as if she'd get back into that car with him. She found the back door. Didn't expect it to open. It didn't.

Barked her shin on an outdoor stool as she turned too fast to the east side – the bathroom was on the east side. Its window had been open earlier, a high window and small.

He tailed her, two paces behind. 'Got a hidden key?'

'A drainpipe, and with luck, an open window, and I don't need an audience.'

'As if I'd miss seeing you scale a drainpipe in that skirt.'

She swung around to murder him, and a garden hose left where it had been trickling water onto rosebushes lay across the path.

She trod on it. The hose rolled beneath her shoe, and her reflexes screaming snake, she threw her weight onto her left foot; with no reliable heel to drive deep and regain her equilibrium, she was going down.

We'll save ourselves on anything. Rosebushes are prickly. The wall was too far away. Flailing arms reaching for what they could, found him.

'Show a little self-restraint, woman,' he said. And he kissed her, held her up and kissed her until she saw stars, or until her blush went internal and the backs of her eyelids turned red. She would have whacked him again, had she had a hand free to whack with, but her feet were spread, one shoe sinking deeper into a garden bed, one heel useless, and if she released her hold to whack him, she'd go down properly.

He took his time, and when he was done, he took a handkerchief from his breast pocket, brushed it across her lips, spat on it theatrically, then wiped his own mouth thoroughly.

Nothing she could say. Nothing she could do but remove her sandals. Sure-footed then, she found the drainpipe Cathy had spoken of utilising once when she'd lost her key and come home too late to wake her parents. She found a foothold, a new handhold, heard something split as she got a knee onto the windowsill, but the upper sash was open and the lower slid up easily. Everything slid easy in Cathy's house. It wouldn't be easy to slide in through the narrow opening, and he wasn't seeing what she'd have to do to get in.

'Goodnight,' she said.

'It was until half an hour ago.'

'Go.'

'Never let it be said that I slept soundly in my bed knowing there was a Sydney cat burglar on the loose.'

And to hell with him. She hitched her skirt up to her thighs, got her backside onto the sill and slid one leg through. So he'd get a good view, but a dim view. Starlight tonight, but no moon.

Blessing the lack of moon, clinging to the drainpipe, she flattened and wriggled her other leg in through the gap, then slowly, hands clinging, she went in backward, lowering herself until one muddy foot found the washbasin. Her head and shoulders still on the far side, she reached down. 'Could you pass up my sandals, please.'

'*What light through yonder window breaks? It is the east, and Juliet the sun,*' he quoted.

'My shoes, you halfwit.'

'*The brightness of her cheek would shame those stars, as daylight doth a lamp.*'

'Will you please pass me my shoes!'

'Pull your head in,' he said, and he was gone, a sandal in each hand.

THE MASTER PLAN

Cara had been raised in the knowledge that God had a master plan for each of his children. She'd been raised in the certain knowledge that for each girl child born there was a boy child, and that one day they'd meet, fall in love and live happily ever after. She'd been raised to believe that if she placed her life into God's safe hands, he'd guide her in the direction she was destined to go.

Maybe it worked for some of his children. Gerry had come home to his old street after two years of London, Dublin, Madrid, and there was pretty kid Cathy, all grown up and overeager to welcome him home. He treated her like his kid sister but didn't appear to find her hero worship unwelcome.

God was wearing a blindfold when he glanced Cara's way. She'd spent years imagining her return to Amberley and been greeted by cockroaches. Cast adrift at birth, Cara not-quite-Norris was destined to float between half-worlds forever, her blueprint mislaid when two women pulled a swiftie.

The girl child she'd been born to be may have liked Morrie. He'd fixed her sandal's wobbly heel and brought them across the road the morning after New Year, the mud all cleaned away. She should have gushed, told him how brilliant he was. Cathy had. Cara had asked him if he'd booby-trapped the heel.

'Stop freezing him off,' Cathy ordered when he walked back across the road. 'He's interested in you.'

For two years she'd been accusing Cara of freezing boys off. She didn't freeze them, just let them know early that she wasn't interested – and maybe had been doing it for so long, she'd forgotten, or never learnt to treat them any other way.

Cathy's original plan had been to leave for Sydney on 3 January, but on the third, she delayed their departure date until the fifth, then invited Gerry and Morrie and two dozen more around for a barbecue. Her parents had a built-in barbecue in their backyard, and according to Cathy's gran, the way to a man's heart was through his stomach.

They bought four pound of sausages, half-a-dozen loaves of bread and two dozen eggs. Gerry loved pavlova and Cathy's gran had an infallible recipe for it, which in the girls' hands proved almost infallible. Fruit and cream covered their failings. Gerry praised their effort and came back with his paper plate for more.

'When are they going back?' Cara asked that night.

'Gerry's not, or not for a while. He said tonight that his father is supposed to take things easy and that he's going to take over the practice for three months while his parents have a holiday. Did you see him kiss me?'

She'd seen him peck her on the cheek. Could girls fall in love at twelve? Maybe he'd looked better when she was twelve. He had a pleasant enough face, was six years Cathy's senior – and his curly hair appeared to be receding. His father's dome was billiard-ball smooth.

After the barbecue, Cathy delayed their trip until the eighth. Gerry and Morrie were going on a yacht to Tasmania on the eighth, and until they were safe in the middle of the ocean she was not about to leave Gerry unguarded.

'If we leave before they leave, he'll think I'm not interested.'

'I can't say you leave a lot of room for doubt, Cath.'

'You're just copying what Mum says.'

'No. I'm saying that you're hurling yourself at his head.'

'I don't care if I am. See that posh car parked out front of his place? It's Roger's, one of his university mates from Melbourne. Gerry went out with his sister for about six months and I think the girl Roger brought with him is her.'

'Keep looking through the curtains and he'll see you spying on him.'

'I'm trying to get a good look at the girl.'

It was a side to Cathy Cara hadn't realised was there. She'd flirted her way through college, had half of the boys in love with her. Up here she was like a wife with a philandering husband. While the maroon Rover was parked in front of Gerry's house, she sat at the window, peering through filmy white terylene curtains.

'So we leave on the eighth, definitely.'

'Whatever.' Cara was in no hurry to return to bedlam, which was wrong but didn't feel wrong. There was freedom in this house.

She'd grown up with lodgers, elderly lodgers who said good morning or good afternoon, who had occasionally knocked at the rent hatch to hand over money, but Amberley hadn't seemed like a boarding house, not back then.

It was now. And it wasn't home. But if it wasn't, then where was home? Her room at the college had been, though not any more. Another student would sleep in her bed, hang her clothing in Cara's wardrobe.

The boys left for Melbourne on the evening of the seventh, and that night Cara printed in huge block letters, *GERRY KISSED CATHY*, on page seven of her new diary, a gift from Gwen and Len Bryant's car yard. Gwen had caught her writing in an exercise book.

'Diary,' Cara had said.

In the early morning of the eighth, the little blue car crept out of a sleeping street, then from Ballarat to Bendigo, Cara suffering a blow-by-blow replay of Cathy's previous night. It didn't end in Bendigo, or in Albury where they found the motel, booked for them by Len Bryant who had ordered that they break their trip halfway, and to give him a call from the motel.

He'd supplied them with a strip map and a large map of eastern Australia. They opened it that night in their twin room, discussing towns.

And maybe God hadn't lost Cara's master plan, just mislaid it.

'My great-grandparents on Dad's side were farmers up that way,' Cathy said, prodding a finger at Willama.

'Cow farmers?'

'Crops – or I seem to remember paddocks full of crops.'

'You've been up there?'

'Once.' Cathy searched the map with her finger until she found what she was looking for and prodded an insignificant dot. 'There it is,' she said. 'Their farm was a few miles out of Woody Creek. Pa was raised up there. He used to ride a horse to school with two of his sisters clinging on behind him.'

'Woody Creek,' Cara read, and the ghost of Jenny trailed its fingers down her spine. 'What's it like, Cath?'

'I was about ten at the time. I remember Pa telling me not to blink as we drove through the town or I'd miss it. Why?'

'I'll probably end up teaching there,' Cara said.

'You won't. We're both going to get placements in Melbourne. I dreamed we did. Did I tell you Gerry is going to stay in Ballarat for at least three months?'

'Only a few dozen times, but go ahead.'

'You have to admit now, though, don't you – it pays to listen to your dreams.'

*

Robert and Myrtle drove the new station wagon out to meet them and to guide Cathy in through the chaos of Sydney. They looked better. Myrtle looked as if she'd just come from the hairdresser.

Amberley looked better than when Cara had left it. Mr Waters and Bill Bertram had been giving Robert a hand with a paintbrush. They'd painted the storeroom and bought bunk beds which they'd set up in the small room for the Bertram boys. The storeroom gave the boys direct access to the backyard. Bill Bertram had moved into a small room across the passage from the storeroom and Number Five was again locked. No more herd of boot-clad elephants over the parlour. No more wild horses galloping down the upper floor passage, or having races up and down the stairs; no more whiz, bang, screech of kids' television shows.

The lodgers' sitting room had lost its bed and was furnished now with Myrtle's leather couch and two of the original easy chairs, found somewhere. The television sat on a small coffee table.

Robert and Myrtle had met Mrs Bertram and the three Bertram daughters. They lived with her parents in a two-bedroom unit fifteen minutes away.

'Separated?' Cara asked.

'No. They're building. The wife's mother is crippled. They sold up in Melbourne and came up here to look after her,' Myrtle said.

'He's a carpenter,' Robert said. 'His company is working on the conversion of one of these old places into self-contained flats. Given the price of inner-city properties these days, what the owners receive for one flat pays for the conversion,' Robert said.

'You're not thinking about it?'

'It's a thought, poppet. We've become accustomed to having our own lives.'

The new *Private Residence* sign on the locked passage door gave mute evidence of that, and the new sign on the rent hatch: *Business hours. 5 to 8 Fridays. 10 to 12 Saturdays.*

The cigarette burns on Cara's windowsill had been smoothed and painted away; her scuffed walls had disappeared beneath the two coats. Smell of fresh paint in the room, and a second bed, set up, made up for Cathy, who didn't plan to spend a lot of time in that bed. She'd never been to Sydney and wanted to see what she could of it, preferably without elderly guides.

They partied with Pete and his mob on Saturday night, and didn't get home until two, and found Robert and Myrtle pacing the floor when they came in.

Cathy giggled for half an hour.

'Shut up, Cathy.'

'I know now why you freeze blokes off. Your parents would have a fit if you ever brought one home.'

She wanted to drive into the city. Cara said she wasn't going unless they went on the train. They spent the day sightseeing, on bus and train, and came home before dark, Cathy with sore feet.

'That's why I wanted to drive,' she said.

'Wear shoes you can walk in, nitwit.'

She took delight in flirting with the middle-aged cockroach, then had the audacity to mention, at Myrtle's dinner table, that he was 'one of those', translating her words with a flopping wrist. Even Myrtle understood the meaning of that sign; she damn near choked on a mouthful.

Twelve hours after Cathy arrived, it had become obvious to Cara that her mother didn't approve of her. Robert formed his own opinion when Cara's guest began sitting with the Bertram boys, watching *The Flintstones* each evening. Cara sat with them one evening and wondered if Dino Collins watched that show in jail. Fred Flintstone's pet dinosaur's name was Dino.

Mrs Collins enjoyed the boys' television set. She knew what was showing and when it was showing. Cara and Cathy watched a war movie with her one night. It raised the subject of a Japanese submarine in the harbour and of the earlier war that had left her a widow.

'A young lodger we had here during the war was widowed in '43. She was left to raise her little boy alone – as was I. I hadn't considered teaching until I lost William. It was an easier profession to get into in those days and my mother was alive then. We lived with her until her death. Jenny had no family, or none up here. Your mother and I kept an eye on little Jimmy at night. She entertained at a servicemen's club,' Mrs Collins said.

'A stripper?' Cathy asked.

'In our era, such goings-on did not go on, dear – or not openly. She sang, with a band of elderly gentlemen.'

'Did she have boyfriends – after her husband was killed?' Cara asked.

'Goodness me, no. She wasn't that sort of girl, though there were a few around who were. She lived for her little boy.'

The ever-changing Jenny – not that sort of girl.

Then how did she have me?

*

A busy week, that first week in Sydney, an uncomfortable week for Cara who spent it balancing, not quite her parents' daughter, nor quite Cathy's sharp-tongued mate, but someone walking a tightrope midway between the two. It was a filling-in of time sort of week, Cathy counting off the days until Gerry came home from the sea, Cara watching for the postman and for the letter that would dictate where she'd spend the next twelve months of her life.

Night-time for Cathy meant one more day over. For Cara it was writing time in a stilled house. She'd started a new exercise book with a chapter she named 'The Telegram'. It began with the arrival of the telegram informing Jessica that her soldier, William, was dead, and when she read it later, it brought tears to her eyes.

One day, one glorious day, a book with her name on its cover would draw a tear from a reader's eye. One fine day.

*

'How come you only had the one baby, Mrs Norris?' Cathy asked.

'We weren't blessed with more, dear.'

'Mum either. I always envied kids who had heaps of brothers and sisters. I want six kids. Three boys and three girls.' They were shelling peas, Cathy eating as many as she dropped into the basin. 'Our street was full of kids when I was growing up.' One tooth wore a green pea skin. Myrtle pointed. Cara laughed.

'What's wrong?'

Myrtle told her. Cathy cleaned the tooth with a fingernail and continued. 'I walked to school with the same mob through primary and high school. One family had nine kids.'

'I used to envy my six cousins until Gran moved in with them,' Cara said, and Myrtle walked to the sink, not pleased by the turn of conversation.

'What do you really think of Gerry?'

'I've told you fifty times, he seems nice enough.'

'What's nice enough?'

'Nothing spectacular,' Cara said.

'Why not spectacular?'

'He'll be bald by the time he's thirty.'

'I don't care if he is. Do you expect her to ever get married, Mrs Norris?' Cathy asked.

'She's a beautiful girl,' Myrtle said.

'Morrie, a Pom, is very interested in her.'

'Shut up, Cathy.'

'Well he is. You should have seen the way he was looking at her the night he and Gerry left – as if he wouldn't have minded kissing her goodbye.'

'When did they say you'd hear where you'll be teaching?' Myrtle asked.

'They didn't,' Cara said. She shelled three more peas. 'They'll probably send me to Traralgon, then you and Daddy will have to mortgage this place to buy me out of my bond.' Which might put an end to talk of splitting it into flats. Myrtle was even thinking about it now, though not to sell off in bits, but to borrow the money and let the rent from the units pay off the loan – which sounded better, in theory.

'The last time I heard, they were going to send you to Woody Creek,' Cathy said, and Myrtle's hands stilled.

'We found it on the map on the way up,' Cara explained quickly. 'It's a tiny dot out the back of Willama. Cathy's great-grandparents had a farm there.'

Cathy left off shelling peas to watch *The Flintstones*. Cara could live without Fred and Dino. She holed up in her bedroom to rewrite two pages, which meant ripping out the original and sticky-taping in the new. Her hands occupied with tape, she couldn't close the book when Cathy came in. She snatched it.

'Why aren't you using Mum and Dad's diary?'

'Give it to me, Cathy.'

'Have you been recording my habits for the TV cop?' Cathy said, dancing back with the book. Robert's attitude to television was quite clear. Since her second night in Sydney Cathy had referred to him as *the TV cop*.

'It's private. Give it back, Cathy!'

They fought over it. Cara ended up with the front cover, which she spun at Cathy's head before walking out and slamming the door. She had a shower, washed her hair, vowing not to speak one word to her at dinner. She was still in the bathroom when Myrtle called them to the table.

Cathy exited the room with the book. 'You secretive bugger. Where's the rest of it?'

'I'm not talking to you.'

'What's that I hear? Was it your ears flapping?'

'I wouldn't consider looking at your private things.'

'I haven't got any. Who is Jessica?'

'No one.'

'She's someone you know. Come clean.'

'It's a novel, and you keep your hands off it!'

'Are you going to yell that at the people who buy it? It's brilliant, you secretive bugger. Where's the rest of it?'

'There's no rest.' There was. She'd filled three exercise books with the rest of it.

'I didn't know you wrote stuff like that. You told Mum and Dad it was your diary. I tell you everything and you tell me nothing.'

'You tell everyone everything.'

She did. Cara knew Cathy's mother had to get married straight out of school, that she'd tried to have more kids once Cathy was at school but hadn't been able to get pregnant. She knew Cathy had kissed a boy named Mike when she was twelve, that she'd lost count of how many she'd kissed since, that Frank was the only one she'd gone any further with than kissing, though not much further. The night Gerry kissed her, she'd woken her parents to relay the news.

Amberley was full of secrets. Cara would never have known that Myrtle's father had committed suicide if Pete hadn't told her. She'd never met Myrtle's brother, Richard. And it cut both ways. Myrtle and Robert wouldn't have known what Dino Collins had done if Robert hadn't been forced to give evidence at the trial.

It's brilliant. Where's the rest of it? Praise to a writer is food for the soul. Those words played through dinner, and continued to play long after Cathy's mouth was closed by sleep. *It's brilliant. Where's the rest of it?*

Cara wanted the rest of it. That chapter would lead into Jessica having her fourth baby, Carolyn. The early chapters, written when she was fifteen, had never been believable. She knew more about the world now. She'd had Jessica producing twins at sixteen, then falling in love with her soldier, and how, with twins, would she find time to fall in love with her soldier and have Jimmy, who had been almost three years older than Cara, which meant he'd been born before Jenny was eighteen?

If Jessica had been a stripper instead of a singer, it might have been easier to get her pregnant four times by the age of twenty. But if she'd been so in love with her soldier that she'd left her two girls at home to follow him to Sydney, how was a reader supposed to believe she'd fallen in love so fast with Billy-Bob . . . *Bobby-Lee.*

She'd trapped a real Jessica in that 'Telegram' chapter and knew it. Hadn't ever been able to make her a real person before; depending on her mood when she'd picked up her pencil, Jessica was slut on one page and victim on the next.

Contrary to what Mrs Collins had said, there would have been heaps of strippers and prostitutes in Sydney during the war, though they wouldn't have lodged at Amberley. If she turned Jessica into a stripper, she'd need to find her another rooming house.

It came to her, near midnight. Michelle Hunter would have had a baby at sixteen if they hadn't terminated the pregnancy.

Jessica had been raped at fifteen and her rapist's name jumped out of the dark, with the opening sentence to her novel.

Dean James was a purebred cur who ran with a pack of mixed breeds. Smarter than the average cur, he was more vicious –

Oh, yes! Yes! And she had to write it down or she'd lose it before morning.

She rose, found her dressing-gown and crept out to the kitchen with her exercise book and pencil.

It came so fast, her pencil couldn't keep up with it. Jessica was walking home from the library. They came in a car . . . what sort of a car? Dodge. Uncle John's first car had been a Dodge . . .

She wrote of a bush track, of a cow farmer and his wife. Had to alter a few details – the library book, her escape from Henry Cooper's car. She allowed the farmer to find Jessica cowering naked in his milking shed.

And it worked. It really worked. And the mixture of Cara and Michelle Hunter worked too, and making Jessica a Catholic. In those days, even if doctors had done abortions, a Catholic family would never have agreed to their daughter having one.

Dean James was a pure unadulterated Dino Collins, evil. Readers loved to hate evil characters. She'd used Lakes Entrance as the town, which was restricting. Where was the library? Where was the lane where the rapist and his friends had pushed Jessica into the car?

'Woodsville,' she whispered. 'Riverwood,' she decided, then flipped through the pages, erasing Lakes Entrance and replacing it with Riverwood.

She filled fifteen pages with the new Jessica, and when her pencil required sharpening and her hand could barely grip it to sharpen it, she sat reading, dreaming.

It's brilliant. Where's the rest of it?

She'd give her the rest, once it was typed. As soon as she started making her own money, she'd buy a typewriter. And as soon as she sold her first novel, she'd pay off the Education Department's bond and do nothing but write.

Didn't want to teach. Wouldn't admit it, even to Cathy. The thought of standing in front of a classroom full of kids, pretending she knew what she was doing, scared her stiff.

Cathy wasn't scared. She wasn't scared of anything.

How do people grow up unafraid?

They grow up in Ballarat.

She was standing before the fridge when the kitchen door squeaked open and Robert, pyjama-clad, entered, his eyes squinting against the light.

'Can't sleep, poppet?'

'I'm trying to see Amberley as flats,' Cara lied, not quite a lie. She tried to imagine it often.

'It's not for you to worry your pretty head about.'

She removed a bottle of milk and reached for two glasses, poured milk into each and offered one.

'How long have you been up?'

'Not long.'

'Every room needs money spent on it, and to be honest, both your mother and I have reached the stage where we don't want to share what's left of our lives with lodgers. Your mum doesn't want to sell. Having our own separate unit here is looking like the answer.'

'How many units are they talking about?'

'We'd need to bring in an architect, but Bill believes we'd get four good-sized units.'

'Architects cost big money.'

'We've got our retirement fund behind us and a good pension, and it wouldn't be the first time we've paid off a loan.' He squinted at his watch, and without his glasses he couldn't see the hands.

'It's a bit after three,' Cara said.

'Pop back into bed,' he said and returned to his own.

Cara picked up her book, pencil and eraser and returned to her room to bury her new work with its older and battered mates in the bottom of her small case.

'Put them in the cupboard,' Cathy muttered.

'Your wedding gifts, Cath?' Cara asked. Occasionally Cathy replied from her dreams. Not tonight.

She'd end up married to Gerry. She'd have her six kids. It was all about knowing what you wanted, and going after it. Maybe knowing who you were allowed you to set your sights on an objective early and follow it. Cathy could look at her mother and know what she'd look like at thirty-nine, look at her gran and see herself at fifty-seven.

I'll be twenty-one this year. Who will I look like when I'm fifty-seven?

No one. I'm a space child. I hitched a ride on a rocket ship, and landed at Amberley. I'm a shape, a shadow, not quite here. That's why I freeze boys off, because I'm scared there's nothing to find behind the shape of me.

The night Morrie kissed her, she could have asked him to give her a boost up to the windowsill. He would have. She could have thanked him for fixing her heel. At the barbecue she could have asked him where he'd met Gerry, what he did for a living, where he lived in England.

He was flying home in February.

Her mind wandering, wandered to Dino Collins, who could be back on the street by the time she'd worked off her bond – if he behaved himself.

When had he ever behaved himself?

She rose up on her pillow then, suddenly knowing that if Jessica had been raped at fifteen by Dean James she'd be scared off men for life. There was no way Cara could force her to produce Jimmy before Carolyn.

So give her triplets.

It's brilliant. Where's the rest of it?

Was Cathy any judge of brilliant literature? She loathed Jane Austen.

And the title was weak. The story was no longer about the child of Jessica, but about Jessica. *Fallen Angel*, she whispered, and it sounded too familiar. *She's No Angel*, she tried on her tongue. Discarded it too. *Angel At My Door*. That was a possible. Myrtle had once said God had sent an angel to her door. It sounded like a title, and she had the Martha character saying it . . . somewhere.

'*Angel At My Door* by C.J. Norris,' she whispered.

Sea Sick

'*G*et up,' Cathy said. 'We're going home.' She'd taken an early call from her mother. Gerry had flown home from Tasmania.

Cara pulled the blanket over her head and told her to go home if she wanted to go home.

'I'm not driving all that way by myself. Get up. I've already told your mother we're going and she looked relieved to be getting rid of me.'

'It's too late to start today.'

'It will be if you don't get out of that bed. Come on, on your feet.'

'That's not the way we work up here. We plan trips for a month, Cath.'

'You won't have a month to live unless you're in that car in ten minutes.'

They left at nine, Myrtle and Robert waving, and not appearing too unhappy about their daughter's sudden departure.

Two brief stops for eats and petrol, and twelve hours later they drove into Ballarat, the passenger more weary than the driver, who was halfway across the road before Cara's feet were on the ground.

'Nice to see you, Cathy,' Gwen Bryant yelled after her.

'Two minutes, Mum.'

Cara received Gwen's welcoming kiss. Together they unloaded the car and hauled the luggage inside. Cathy, true to her word, was back in five minutes, Gerry in tow. He told them of a rough crossing, of his days spent, head over the side, seasick. He told them they'd refused to put up with him on the way back so he'd flown home from Hobart.

Absence makes the heart grow fonder, or perhaps separation from his mate had him seeking company. Cathy and her family were available.

He was nothing spectacular, but nice – and nicer still when he crossed the street one night toting an elderly typewriter. He'd been cleaning out a room behind his father's surgery, and Cathy had told him Cara was writing a novel and that her handwriting stank.

Space was cleared on Cathy's desk. Len donated a ream of typing paper, plus a dozen sheets of carbon. Cathy tested it, typed, *Jessica, Chapter One, by Cara Norris.*

'You'll need to marry someone with an interesting name before it's published, though. Norris sounds like a book about growing brussels sprouts.'

Days disappeared thereafter as Cara's best chapters were transferred from tattered exercise books to loose pages. She typed at night while the television played, her fingers growing faster at belting words out of the rattling keyboard. No one to look over her shoulder, Cathy had been warned not to, and she had better things to do. She was helping Gerry paint the back room he'd cleared. They were turning it into a second surgery.

'He won't go back,' Cathy said. 'He hasn't said it, but he won't.'

*

Morrie came home looking tanned and healthy, and he played tennis, and looked spectacular in his tennis gear. Cathy, in her rush to get away from Sydney, had given Cara no time to consider what she might require. She hadn't packed her racquet or her tennis frock, but Cathy prised her away from her typewriter to play, with a borrowed racquet, in a too-short flyaway skirt, a pair of too-short shorts beneath it. She loved the competition of the game and knew she was good at it.

The early matches were played at night, under lights. Cathy spent more time shooing flying moths with her racquet than hitting balls. They were thrashed in the women's doubles. Gerry lost his first singles match. Morrie and Cara got through, then walked in their mixed doubles match.

They got through their Saturday matches. The finals were played on Sunday. Gerry had a woman in labour at the hospital, so Cathy claimed sunburn.

'Morrie will drive you,' she said.

He did, in Gerry's car. He told her to give her socks a party and invite her skirt down. She told him that one had been old when she'd been in second grade.

She told herself she wouldn't need to see him, apart from in their mixed doubles final, but he stuck to her like glue, and if he hadn't been watching her skirt fly, she might have won her singles final, but he was and she didn't.

He was waiting with an icy bottle of Coke when she came off the courts. She accepted it gladly.

'You know how to handle a racquet,' he said.

'My father's fault. He played – before his knee was damaged in the war. I must have been about three when he decided I'd play for Australia.'

She watched Morrie's singles match, a killer match, both winners, determined not to lose, and played in the worst heat of the day. He came off the court dripping sweat, but the winner – and he had to go back on in an hour or so for their mixed doubles match.

'I'm out of running condition,' he said.

'Yachting around Tasmania will do that every time,' she said.

'As will sitting over a typewriter day and night. Cathy said you're writing a novel.'

'Cathy talks too much,' she said – which was probably what Cathy meant by freezing blokes off. 'I'm trying to write a novel,' she added.

'About what?'

'A girl.'

'Is she a killer on the tennis court?'

'She has a lot of kids.'

They won their doubles match, which assuaged a little of Cara's disappointment at her singles loss. She held the trophies on the drive home, and he didn't drive straight home, but the wind on her face felt good and today she didn't tell him to slow down.

'I need a partner for Roger's engagement party,' he said.

She knew Gerry had been invited to a university mate's party, hadn't been aware that the mate was the son of the yacht owner, or that Gerry planned to ask Cathy to go with him.

'We left in a hurry. I brought next to nothing with me.'

'What happened to the red?'

'It's in Sydney – with a split in its seam.'

'Most cat burglars dress for the job,' he said.

'I've got a leather catsuit on layby.'

He was easy to talk to. Maybe because of today, because of the trophies on her lap.

'Have you got a licence to drive over here?'

'I'm going home soon,' he said.

'What part of England is home?'

'What parts do you know?'

'Dickens's London.'

'We've got a property forty miles from London.'

'When are you leaving?'

'After the engagement party. You won't change your mind about it?'

'I could be anywhere by then.'

'You still haven't heard where they're sending you?'

'Cathy has. She's got a new school out this side of Melbourne. My letter is probably in Sydney and Mum and Dad are too scared to tell me I got Traralgon.'

'What's wrong with Traralgon?'

'If they try to send me there, I'll stow away on the first flight out of Melbourne.'

'Choose a flight going to England and I'll give you a bed,' he said, and he turned the car around and drove her home.

*

In late January, she moved to a boarding house in Windsor, only a couple of tram stops from Armadale Primary School where her teaching career would begin. It was no Amberley, but the room was her own and comfortable enough.

A nightmare day, her first day in the classroom – flung to the lions with no whip to keep them off her throat, disapproving strangers eyeing her in the staffroom, knowing she had no right to be there. And no relief when she got out of the place. Strange women at the boarding house, sixteen-year-old kids, still close enough to the schoolroom to snigger when she said, 'I'm a teacher.'

Cathy had been given a position out the other side of Melbourne, at a brand-new school, in a brand-new suburb Cara had never heard of. She drove across town on the second Wednesday night and Cara almost howled with relief, might have hugged her if Cathy's hands hadn't been full.

'I told Morrie you changed your mind about Roger and Anne's engagement party, on Saturday. Gran fixed up my black dress for you.'

'It would just about do for a tennis skirt.'

'Not any more.'

The black frock had undergone a radical change. A three-inch strip of white fabric had been attached to its hem, a white silk rose stitched to its shoulder.

'It's gorgeous.'

'Yeah, I'm jealous actually – except it comes halfway to my ankles now.'

Gwen had sent down a pair of black and white daisy earrings with black centres, perfect for that dress, and Cara wanted to wear them, and that dress. For the remainder of the week every time she felt like howling and running from the lions, she thought of Saturday.

'Nothing to wear,' Morrie greeted her on the Saturday. His eyes said more.

*

She'd expected the party to be at a private house. It was at a reception centre, with tables and dance floor and a hundred or more guests. She and Morrie were directed to a rear table, Gerry and Cathy to Roger's; Morrie and partner, late inclusions, were seated with a young couple, two middle-aged aunts, three juveniles and an elderly uncle.

It was painful. Cara's nine-year-old brats started looking good. She answered questions, couldn't think of any of her own, and the entree smoked salmon she felt obligated to taste. Had she been at home, she would have spat it. Had she known where to find the ladies' room, she would have spat it. Swallowed it, and wanted a glass of the juvenile's lemonade to wash the taste from her mouth but the waiter had poured wine into her glass so she washed away the taste with wine.

The band was playing. Morrie asked her to dance. No one else was on the dance floor.

'No thanks,' she said, and emptied her glass, which tasted like grown-up lemonade.

The waiter came again, so she emptied her glass again, and the night changed. She spoke to the young couple, walked with the girl to the ladies' room, and when she returned and Morrie asked her to dance, she wanted to dance. It was a tango. She danced it as she'd been taught to at her dancing classes, and didn't care who was watching.

He held her hand when he walked her back to their table and she clung to it, uncertain she'd find the right table without him.

'How do you know Roger?'

'Through Gerry,' he said.

'How do you know Gerry?'

'He took on the job as locum when our local doctor broke his leg. My aunt called him in to do a caesarean on her dog.'

'He's a doctor, not a vet.'

'Same only different,' he said, then told her he'd played midwife while Gerry operated on the kitchen table. 'We dragged out nine pups of unknown parentage.'

'Did they live?'

'Eight of them did.'

'And the mother?'

'She survived.'

'Did she name the father?'

And he laughed, tossed back his head and laughed. Marion was the comedian. She could make people laugh, not Cara. Poor Marion, banished to Seymour. Poor Penny somewhere up in the whoop-whoops, and Michelle, who had wanted the whoop-whoops, had landed Doncaster.

Sometime between the main meal and sweets, he told her he'd done a couple of years of medicine before he'd realised he had an aversion to dead bodies.

'Weren't you supposed to keep them alive?' she said.

His laugh was infectious, and as she had with Pete, she got the giggles, and the aunts at the table probably thought they were laughing at the old uncle, who was nodding off on his chair, so they had to dance again, and when they returned to the table, their wine glasses had been filled. There's only one thing to do with a full glass.

'How are you enjoying your nine year olds?' he asked.

'They say that if you get caught smoking pot on school premises they'll sack you. Know where I can get some?' Someone at the college had suggested pot or getting pregnant as the only ways to get out of the bond. She almost told him that Marion had threatened to get pregnant, but managed to guide her tongue in a different direction.

'How much is the fare to England?'

'Boat or plane?'

'Chinese junk will do,' she said.

She wasn't Cara Norris, daughter of a retired high-school principal, not that night. She wasn't Miss Norris, schoolmarm, either; maybe she was Jenny's daughter.

It was late, she was miming her backhand when she knocked her glass and spilt the last of her wine. The waiter had run out of bottles, and Gerry and Cathy were ready to go.

'You're drunk,' Cathy accused.

'Party pooper,' Cara said.

She talked too much on the walk across the car park, and clung tight to Morrie's hand. Didn't have a clue where the car was, and the bitumen beneath her feet was moving anyway.

'How many drinks did she have?' Cathy asked.

'Half a one less than I would have,' Cara said. Morrie knew what she meant.

They drove her back to the boarding house and parked opposite. Morrie walked her across the road.

The boarding house door was locked at night, but she had two keys in her purse. Morrie dug them out, he found the keyhole, opened the door.

'Damn,' he said. 'I was hoping to get you into the shrubbery again.'

'There's plenty around.'

She should have thanked him for the evening, wished him a safe flight home, said goodnight and tried to find her room. Didn't want that night to end, to take off Cathy's dress and Gwen's earrings and wake up as Miss Norris-by-default, so she leaned against the doorjamb, waiting for the obligatory goodnight kiss.

'Cathy's right, you know. You're drunk,' he said.

'Party pooper,' she repeated.

He offered the obligatory kiss, and when he was done, she asked him if he please had a hanky. But his mouth came back for more and it didn't feel obligatory, and because she had to do something with her arms, they did their share of holding. He eased her away but her arms still needed to hold on.

'I'm too young for this,' he said.

'You'll be thousands of miles away next Tuesday.'

'True,' he said.

They broke apart when they heard a gentle beep-beep from the street.

'Sleep tight,' he said.

'Have a good flight,' she said.

Couldn't be bothered finding the bathroom to brush her teeth. Crawled into bed in her petticoat and Gwen's earrings, only realising she was still wearing them when one fell off and stuck into her face. A sleepy hand retrieved it, removed the other one, slid them beneath her pillow, then something happened to her head. It died.

GENETICALLY PROGRAMMED

*M*onk's old mansion was gutted by fire in February. With two or three local farmers wanting the land but not interested in restoring the house, there were whispers in town, which grew into rumour. Paul Jenner, now in his late sixties, needed more land. He had two sons still living at home and three grandsons. Any one of them could have put a match to Monk's house. Their own land was three miles east of Monk's.

There was rumour enough to encourage the constable to take a drive out to Jenner's land, where the eldest son, the one with the crippled leg who painted river scenes, told him he'd been down at the creek with his easel the afternoon of the fire, and that he'd seen a bunch of kids out there on bikes. He identified two.

'That pretty dark-headed girl with the Hoopers was one of them, and the youngest Lewis boy. There was another girl. She could have been a Duffy.'

In the late afternoon, the constable knocked on Jenny's door. 'I wonder if I could have a quick word with your girl, Mrs Hooper,' he said.

'I've never been out there,' Raelene said. 'Except with Mum and Dad.'

She sounded innocent, but to Jenny, that *Dad* was a giveaway. Her dad had been Ray, which she made very clear every time Jim opened his mouth.

Watch-dog Jenny these days: stop barking and Raelene was gone. She barked when the constable left.

'How many times have I told you to stay away from those Lewis boys?'

'You tell me to stay away from everyone.'

'I tell you to stay away from the ones who'll get you into trouble.'

'You should have stayed away from the Macdonald twins then.'

There were no secrets from Raelene in this town. And no controlling her. Jenny stopped barking to wash dishes, and she turned around and Raelene was out on the street with two of the Lewis boys.

The watch-dog barked.

'Lay off, will you? I'm not going anywhere.'

She'd been with Florence and Clarrie for a month. They exchanged control of her in the city, Raelene's welfare dame present. Florence had no hope of controlling her. Three weeks ago, Jim at her side, Jenny had driven that kid down to a juvenile court hearing, and in a month's time she'd drive her down there again – and she'd had it.

She had to persevere. Granny had – in a different era though, with different problems.

Barking from the doorway not achieving the desired results, watch-dog Jenny walked out to the gate to nip at Raelene's heels. The Lewis boys got on their bikes and rode.

'Did they light the fire?'

'How would I know what they do?'

'You knew where the key to the house was.'

'Anyone with half a brain could work that out.'

A week later, Raelene went missing from school, along with one of the teachers' cars and her chequebook, which she'd left in its glove box.

She didn't get far. The car ran out of petrol and Raelene was returned to her mother's care.

And thus Woody Creek wandered into autumn, and to new rumours about Monk's place.

'They say a city bloke bought it,' blokes on street corners said.

'He's probably the bugger who struck the match.'

'Did you hear how much he paid for it?'

'No, but I can tell you straight that Paul Jenner is as mad as a hornet with hives. He made a damn good offer for that land.'

A 'must see' sight, Monk's blackened, burnt-out hulk, a piece of Woody Creek history reduced to leaning stone walls and free-standing chimneys.

Jen and Jim drove out to sightsee. Trudy between them, holding their hands, they walked around the old mansion, at a distance, then past it to the creek, still flowing on by, undisturbed by man's minor catastrophes. Wood ducks diving there; a blue heron perched on a stump, nature's patient fisherman.

Life goes on. Always had, always would.

*

Typing near impossible with the typewriter on her dressing table, Cara's first purchase, with her own money, was a second- or fifth-hand writing desk with a ton of drawers. She moved her bed, her dressing table before the delivery men carried it in. Why does a piece of furniture look small in the showroom? It was huge, and near immovable. It left barely space enough to walk between it and the foot of her bed, but she could sit on the foot of her bed and type, and she did for hours on end.

Her second purchase was a driving lesson, which might be enough for her to find out if she had a chance of getting a licence.

The instructor seemed to think he could teach her, and he had his own clutch and brake. She booked him for Sunday mornings, which cancelled weekends in Ballarat, but with her typewriter in Melbourne and Cathy and Gerry a pair, Ballarat had lost its charm.

Teaching was a temporary state, she told herself when she sat late, drinking coffee she made now on her desk, smoking cigarettes, an ashtray also on her desk, her room smelling of smoke dreams while fingers raced over the keys, her day with the rabble nine year olds all gone away – until tomorrow.

Cathy and Michelle had drawn five year olds in the Education Department's lottery. Still babies, they had no preconceived ideas of what a teacher should be. Nine year olds had expectations.

Cara's bunch had her bluffed and they knew it. Bribery didn't work on them, or not for long. She raised her voice, stamped her foot, slapped books down hard on her table, sent two boys to the headmaster and prayed that he'd call her to his office and give her the sack. Not that she could go home if he did. The builders would start ripping Amberley apart soon.

Marion's father bought her a car in June. She spent her weekends driving home to her fiancé and family. Cathy headed for Ballarat and Gerry on Friday nights, and didn't drive back until Monday morning. Michelle's family owned a farm near Wangaratta. She rode a train home. Cara took driving lessons and typed, ate at night with strangers, breakfasted with strangers.

Eighteen weeks with her driving instructor gained her a licence to drive. No car, no money to buy one, nowhere to park a car if she'd had the money to buy one, and too far to drive home.

She finished typing up her novel in the June holidays, then settled down to read what she'd written, a pencil in hand. And fifty-four pages in, she started using her pencil on every line. The story had no structure. And how could it? It had evolved in disjointed chapters, and its time line was all over the place.

She bought a pair of scissors and a dispenser of sticky tape, and at night she attacked those pristine pages with scissors, then stuck previously unrelated pages together. She crumpled entire chapters and pitched them. Not the opening chapter. She still liked that one. She liked a few of them, but disliked more. School went back but became a secondary consideration as she attempted to give her novel structure.

September came. The builders had started on the splitting-up of Amberley, but assured by Myrtle that their private rooms would remain untouched until one of the other units was habitable, Cara flew home, her mutilated manuscript in her case, with her sticky tape and scissors.

Found Miss Robertson and Mrs Collins living as Myrtle's guests in Cara's bedroom. Found a narrow bed set up for her beside her parents' double bed.

They had to be kidding.

They saw her expression before she turned her back. She didn't say a word. Couldn't. Considered getting on the next plane south. Would have, if not for those two old ladies, more elderly aunts now then lodgers. Couldn't hurt their feelings. And couldn't stand ten days of tripping over them either, and would not sleep in her parents' bedroom.

'Can we move that bed into the parlour, Daddy?'

She rang the airport from a phone box and changed her departure date. She could stand three nights of tripping over old ladies, of waiting for them to get out of the bathroom, of eating with them, listening to advice on how to control obstreperous children, which may have applied in the era of the cane and strap. Corporal punishment was out of vogue.

Hammering, thump of boots, crash of timber on the upper floor, young males giving her the eye every time she stepped outside. The Windsor boarding house didn't look utopian, but a damn sight better on her return than it had when she'd left it. And ten minutes after setting foot inside her locked room, she was at her typewriter, bashing those taped-together pages into something more than disjointed words and sticky tape.

Had she been able to keep it up, she might have broken its back before school started again, but by her fifth night home, residents were hammering on her door, demanding she stop the infernal racket. Next year, when she knew where she'd be teaching, she'd find a flat with soundproofed walls.

October came after September. She was twenty-one. Myrtle and Robert sent her a card and a watch, dainty, expensive, more decorative than functional. She received half-a-dozen cards, then the night of her birthday, Cathy and Michelle arrived with a bottle of champagne, caviar and dry biscuits, and caviar tasted worse than smoked salmon. They ate the biscuits, drank the champagne.

And the next day a card came from England, a pen-and-ink sketch of a Chinese junk, and inside: *Happy twenty-first. Cathy told me. Got anything to wear to a wedding on the first Saturday in November? M.*

His address was on it. She wrote back.

I paid off my catsuit. Will it be suitable?

And he wrote back.

It's a black-tie affair. Can you afford a tie?

He picked Cara up at her boarding house in Gerry's MG at five on that Saturday in November and he told her he was buying the car.

'It's not the right look for a doctor,' he said.

It wasn't the right look for a couple dressed up for a black-tie affair either. Weddings are a bore, the reception wasn't, and seated with Cathy and Gerry, Cara barely sipped her wine.

Morrie didn't drive her directly home after the reception, but down to the St Kilda pier, where he parked so they might watch the moonlight playing on beach and ocean.

He spoke of plane flights, of London. He told her of his aunt's five-hundred-year-old house and she told him the sorry tale of Amberley's renovations. He asked if she'd finished her novel. She told him it was still a mess, and asked how he planned to take his new toy home.

'Gerry will garage it for me until I decide what I want to do.'

'What's the use of owning a toy when you can't play with it?' she said.

'I'll have two reasons to come back,' he said.

Did some growth hormone kick in when you turned twenty-one? Was there such a disease as falling in love? Did a switch flick on a light in your head? She hadn't seen him for eight months, might not see him in another eight, but for the month he was here, she allowed herself to be in love.

He spent a long weekend at a city hotel and she saw him every day, every evening. They went to a movie, drove out to the hills, had dinner at a hotel. Then he went back to Ballarat and she missed him. But he returned the following weekend, and the one after that.

She saw him off at the airport and her chest ached with missing him before his plane was in the air.

He wrote the day he arrived home, on an aerogram, blue paper as fine as tissue folded into an envelope, and when she ripped two of his words in the opening of it, she mourned their loss.

Marion had been in love at sixteen. Banished to Seymour, she'd sworn she'd be pregnant in a month and married in two. She made it through the year, and was the first to learn where she'd be teaching in '66.

'Burwood,' she said. 'We ought to get a flat together, or a house if Michelle is being kept on at Doncaster.'

Cara didn't want to move in with them. She wanted a single-bedroom unit with soundproofed walls and floor. She wanted freedom to write, and privacy – and somewhere to take Morrie when he came back in April.

PRECIPICE

*A*ustralia, the lucky country, the safe country, virtually untouched by war, had in the late forties thrown her doors open to the displaced, the dispossessed. They'd worked hard to make new lives, intermarried with locals and raised their kids to vote for Robert Menzies. An entire generation had grown to maturity believing Big Bob was next door to royalty and, like the Queen, a permanent fixture.

In January '66 the rot set in. After eighteen years at the helm, Menzies retired from Australia's top job.

A generation had grown to maturity knowing the six o'clock closing of hotels was the way it ought to be, that twelve pennies would always equal one shilling, that twenty shillings would always equal one pound – until Harold Holt, Menzies' deputy, stepped into the top job, when a new generation of kids began to learn that nothing was permanent.

In February of '66 a law was passed allowing hotels to remain open until ten, which ended the great Australian six o'clock swill. Sawdust got in the eyes, up the nose, it stuck in the throat. For generations, Woody Creek's mill workers had hit the bar after work and swilled down pots until Freddy Bowen called, 'Time, boys.' Then they'd gone home to their wives and kids for dinner. Now, with no call of time, the diehards stayed on at the bar. There was more money in the publican's pockets, more tax for the government, less pounds, shilling and pence for the wives and kids – or less dollars.

Harold Holt gave the country two years in which to accept that ten cents now equalled a shilling, to accept the fact that a two-bob coin would now be called twenty cents, that a pound note, the familiar green quid, would become a two-dollar note, and its blue mate, ten dollars.

Antique cash registers bit the dust in their thousands. Prewar permanent fixtures on shop counters all over Australia made way for the new. The makers of dollar and cent registers did a roaring trade.

There was a shift in the sixties, a movement that shook Australia's foundations, only an earth tremor but to some it gave warning of the massive earthquake to come – or it warned Charlie White.

Not a thing he could do to stop it coming other than ignore it. Back when he and Jeany had opened up that shop, after the first war, they'd managed with a cash drawer and handwritten dockets. That cash drawer and his docket books would see him out.

Bloody fool things, he named the new cent coins. His arthritic fingers couldn't handle them, his eyes could barely distinguish a two-cent coin from a one-cent, and both of the damn fool things jammed beneath the wooden partitions of his cash drawer.

Fulton's hardware invested in a new cash register. It totalled up a customer's order then spat out small printed dockets, though two dollars spent there didn't buy as much as the old quid had once bought.

*

Teddy Hall, a fixture in Margot's life – bed – for seven years, had his twenty-eighth birthday in 1966. His mother's son in colouring, his father's in height, he was himself in appearance, though rarely seen out of his grease-stained navy-blue combination overalls, his head beneath the bonnet of a car.

Teddy's boss, Roy, the garage chap, twenty years Charlie's junior, allowed dollars and cents to push him faster towards retirement, or maybe it was his wife who pushed him. She had half-a-dozen grandkids in Melbourne and was lucky to see them twice a year. And it wasn't enough.

'I'm putting the house and business on the market, Ted. We'll be moving down to the kids,' he said.

He was going the wrong way. By '66, two dozen or so Melbourne retirees had moved to Woody Creek – maybe to put space between them and their kids.

If there was one man in town who knew Teddy Hall, it was his boss. If there was a man in town Teddy respected, it was his boss.

'You'll get a job anywhere, Ted. I'll have a yarn to that big Holden place in Willama for you if you like. They're always on the lookout for good mechanics.'

Teddy knew more about cars than he did about people, though he had no papers to prove it. He was a darkie with a knack, that was all, the darkest of Elsie and Harry's brood and resentful since childhood of his nonwhite complexion. His brothers were white.

He'd never considered his future, never believed he had one. He went to work, went home. When he felt like it, he walked across the goat paddock. When he didn't he watched television. Every year or so, he realised that he had nothing and he went on a bender, but never in town. He took off somewhere in his ute, drank until he ran out of money, fought if he felt like it, then came back. His boss always took him back.

A loner, Teddy Hall, an outsider amongst the seven Elsie and Harry had raised, and little hope of ever being more – until Harold Holt's dollars and cents, until Teddy's boss's wife started having a go at would-be buyers who ran down her house and sneered at the figure she'd put on it. Roy got rid of her to the city, then came back to deal personally with prospective buyers. No one wanted his house. Very few considered his tin shed garage.

There was competition now in town. A new service station, with clean petrol pumps and uniformed lads to check tyres and clean windscreens, had sprung up out on the corner of Stock Route and Blunt's Street. They sold a lot of petrol, though most in town would tell you their mechanic didn't know his arse from his elbow.

'What price have you got on the place, boss?'

'Half of what I had.'

Teddy's brain, hotwired early into motors, had been trained since the age of fifteen by a man who had grown up with cars. They never pitched a used part away, could walk into the chaos of that tin shed and unearth a greasy axle off an old Ford, then name the owner of the Ford it had come from. They could crawl beneath Roy's house and pull out a 1939 Chevy truck motor and a wheel rim from the same truck. If you wanted your car fixed, you took it to that tin shed. They kept Charlie White's old ute on the road.

Teddy lived at home. Elsie removed his wages from the pocket of his combination overalls before she boiled them semi-clean. She handed the money to Harry, who banked it. Teddy had never drawn on the account, or not since he'd bought his ute in '58.

'Have you still got my bankbook, Dad?'

'What do you want with it?'

'To see how much I've got in it.'

'What do you want to buy?'

'The garage,' Teddy said.

One gear moves another. Somewhere a wheel turns. Those turning gears dragged Teddy in a direction he'd never considered going. Blame Harold Holt and his Yankee dollars. In a roundabout way, he was responsible for turning Teddy Hall into a business owner.

Blame the piles of mechanical junk stored beneath Roy's house for turning him into a house owner.

'How much have you got on your house, Boss?'

An old house, child-abused, grandchild-abused, it hadn't sighted a lick of paint since before the war. Most prospective buyers went no nearer than the front gate – or where the front gate had once been. One sod had made him an offer for the land. He'd intended ripping the place down and rebuilding on the site. Roy took a leaf from his wife's book and told him where he could put his puny offer.

'Match what the last bastard offered me and it's yours, Ted. Save me clearing out what's under the bloody thing.'

And thus Teddy was impelled forward again. Two weeks later Roy followed his wife, and Teddy gave young Michael Boyle a job.

Wheels within wheels within wheels.

Michael had a sister, Vonnie, not a lot older than her brother, a plump and pretty blonde who had a slow leak in her bike tyre. Every morning she wheeled her bike around the garage to pump up her tyre. She hung around one morning to give her brother a hand taking the radiator out of an FX Holden, then stayed on to have a cup of tea with them. Didn't turn up her nose at the grease-stained enamel mug either and, while emptying it, reeled off every Holden model to come off the assembly line since the FX in '48. Teddy had never met a girl like Vonnie Boyle.

Come May and Teddy, damn near desperate enough to ask his father for help, was standing, sealing greasy cheques into greasy envelopes, and when he got to the last of the greasy buggers, he ended up with a bill for twenty-two dollars and a cheque for twelve dollars fifty, and Christ only knew which of his five envelopes he'd sealed the wrong bloody cheque into, and he'd already wasted an hour in writing the bastards. The air was blue when Vonnie came to pump up her tyre.

'Give them here, Ted,' she said.

He gave them, then stood back, rolling a skinny smoke, watching her wipe his greasy biro on the rounded seat of her jeans, then to do in two minutes what he'd been sweating over for an hour.

'Still looking for a job?' he said.

'Yeah?'

He started off paying her for Friday afternoons and Saturday mornings, selling petrol, inflating tyres, checking oil and washing windscreens, and looking after his bookwork.

She came in on her days off too, and by June had cleaned up an area around his telephone, scrubbed down a filthy table and moved it to form a barrier between telephone and hoist. She brought a chair from home to sit on when she did his bookwork and answered his telephone.

'Good morning. Hall's garage. What can we do for you?'

He liked her being there, liked listening to the way she said, 'Hall's garage.'

'How old is your sister, Mick?'

'Eighteen in July.'

Before June ended, Teddy had moved into his house, or he'd transferred his mattress and bedding from Elsie's sleep-out up there.

*

Giving up sex is much like giving up cigarettes. Those who decide to quit cold turkey can be hard to live with. Margot, always hard to live with, suffered severe withdrawal symptoms. She was twenty-seven. Harry had lost patience with her in '59, and by '66 he'd had enough.

Most smokers who quit the habit notice a weight increase. The same goes for those who quit sex, which is one of the more enjoyable forms of exercise – and for some years, Margot's only exercise. Her girth increased in pace with her anger.

Then another molar started aching every time she ate. That was when hell broke loose on Gertrude's land.

Jenny made another dental appointment. She arrived to pick up her firstborn, told her to take her socks off, and Margot attacked her with Elsie's broom.

Jenny drove home and cancelled the appointment.

'If I didn't know better, I'd say she was going the same way your mother went,' Maisy said. She'd known how to handle Amber when she'd gone off her head, or Doctor Frazer had known how. Jenny called Frazer's office, but like everyone else he'd grown old, and was no longer making out-of-town house calls. A Polish chap with an unspellable, unpronounceable name arrived. By '66 many such names were creeping into telephone books.

He saw Margot, not a pretty sight in her white uniform gaping wide between the buttonholes. Since Teddy had moved into town, she'd refused to wear her partial denture.

'She says that's what's making her teeth ache, doctor,' Elsie said.

He looked at Margot's teeth. 'They all need to come out,' he said. 'They're poisoning her system.' He checked her blood pressure, told Elsie to cut her meals in half, asked if she received the invalid pension, told them he'd sign the necessary papers, then he left.

Margot wasn't going to the dentist again. They fed her pain-killers. Maisy got her onto the invalid pension, and thus labelled, Margot became an invalid.

'The doctor said your teeth are poisoning your system, lovey,' Elsie said.

'Your breath smells like a dead cow,' Maisy said.

'Thut up and leave me alone!'

They left her alone until late July when Harry and Elsie drove to Mildura for Ronnie's wedding, where Elsie, dressed like the Queen Mother in one of Jenny's creations, met Ronnie's in-laws. They left Margot again in October, drove down to Molliston to help Maudy with her first baby. They drove out to Joany's place on Sundays, five grandchildren out there, dark-headed dark-eyed little dagoes. Brian and Josie were working in Melbourne. They never saw them.

Harry knew why. He started spending his weekends slapping paint on Teddy's house, planning to move in with him, to place distance between Elsie and Margot.

And the grass grew long in Gertrude Foote's paddocks and gum saplings hidden in the grass grew tall. The old apricot tree, dying by degrees for years, split and fell that winter, but neglect had allowed a few dozen of its offspring to grow. One might produce comparable fruit.

The climbing rose, cut back to the earth when the working bee had constructed the abomination, determined to hide what had been done to Gertrude's little hut, had done what it could. The old climber again covered the west wall and was attempting to creep across the roof of Georgie's bedroom.

Jenny's tin plaque still hung on its nail over the front door – *Ejected 2.8.69* – as did Georgie's painted wooden board – *The Abortion.*

Owls still flew at night, their soft wings whispering secrets.

Not the same though. By 1966 nothing was or would be again.

HAUNTING THE LETTERBOX

*M*ichelle had been transferred to a country school – not
home, but closer to home. Marion was now teaching at
Doncaster. Engaged to her childhood boyfriend for three years,
attempting to get pregnant to him for twelve months, she was
planning a big, white Christmas wedding, Cathy, Michelle and
Cara her bridesmaids. They'd chosen the fabric for their gowns, the
reception rooms were booked.

She came to Cara's dog-box flat late one night, her eyes swollen
by tears. Like Margot, she'd been dumped for a younger model.

'I should have known when he wanted me to go on the pill.
Why didn't I smell a rat?'

There were multiple contraceptive pills on pharmacy shelves,
multiple opinions on their likely side effects too. The major
effect was, eighteen-year-old kids with no more fear of unwanted
pregnancies were out there test-driving the available merchandise.
Men had never had it so good.

Cathy was on the pill, and everyone who knew her knew it.

No pills for Cara. Her romance with Morrie was all on paper.
He knew she'd posted her three hundred and forty-nine page

manuscript to a Sydney publisher, posted it registered mail, with a money order to pay for its return post, just in case they didn't accept it. Cathy, who had now read the novel in its entirety, said it was brilliant, that they'd come beating down her door to get it.

They hadn't yet. She'd posted it weeks ago. She'd found a flat she could afford, a tiny, beige dog-box but almost new. She had her own mailbox. Rarely anything in Number Ten, but she checked it each morning when she left for work, just in case the postie had come late, and hurried home from work to check it again, and every day kicked herself for not including the school's phone number in her letter to the publisher.

Morrie had said he'd be back in April. He wrote to tell her he'd be delaying his trip. His mother had a serious operation. He'd said he'd try to get over in June. Like Marion's fiancé, he'd probably found a younger model – or one not half a world away.

August now, a blustery month, and cold, and Cara's second- or fifth-hand fridge empty. Marion had spent the weekend with her, on a narrow fold-up bed. Two can't live as cheaply as one.

There was little space in her flat; she owned little furniture, would have owned less if not for Myrtle and Robert. They'd driven down the weekend she'd moved in, the station wagon loaded to the hilt with ex-boarding-house items, from linen to crockery; the fold-up bed was ex-Amberley and the old easy chair had once lived in the lodgers' sitting room.

Cara had bought a miniature kitchen table and a double bed, secondhand – and Myrtle had almost had a fit when she'd seen the double bed, and had checked the bathroom for evidence of a man.

On the Monday after the weekend with Marion, she was walking with her shopping towards her block of flats when she saw red. There were hundreds of red cars in Melbourne. It wouldn't be him.

It was an MG. And there were probably hundreds of them in Melbourne too. She walked by it, and down the drive tonight, ignoring the letterbox.

And found him sitting out of the wind on the concrete stairs, and maybe her smile was too pleased but she didn't care if it was.

'We don't allow immigrants to camp here. Move on, mate,' she said.

His smiled was as wide. 'You're late.' No kiss. They sent their kisses airmail. Willed him to kiss her, but he reached for one of her bags and she led the way upstairs.

'Why didn't you let me know you were coming?'

'I wasn't sure I was until I got a cancellation. My folks are booked on a tour.'

She filled the jug, plugged it in and unpacked her shopping. She told him to sit down, that he made her flat look small.

'It is small,' he said. 'Mum is in hospital.'

'Over here?'

'She found another lump the day before we left.'

'Lump?'

He patted his left breast. 'They said they'd got the lot in April. It's probably nothing, but with her history it has to be checked out.'

'Where's your dad?'

'At the hotel, with the tour group. They're supposed to get on the train to Perth tomorrow night.'

'And you?'

'They'll be touring for a month. You're stuck with me.'

'What terrible sin did I commit to deserve that?' she said.

She showered, washed her ultra-short hair. He wanted to buy her dinner, and when she emerged, he kissed her and asked what shampoo she used.

'Sunsilk. Why?'

'It smells like Australia,' he said.

He bought her a glass of bubbly wine, bought himself a pot of beer, emptied his glass too fast and ordered another.

'You've got a car out there,' she warned, and he took his car keys from his pocket and passed them across the table. 'I can only drive real cars, not toys,' she said.

'It drives itself,' he said.

She wouldn't take his keys, so he took her hand and slipped the key ring onto her finger. 'Consider yourself engaged.'

'It's too big –'

'I'll have it adjusted,' he said.

For three hours they sat. She ate her meal, he, full up with words, allowed his meal to grow cold. He didn't allow his beer to get hot. She didn't comment, aware that if it was her mother in hospital with a lump in her breast, she might have been attempting to dull the pain too. Listened to him, sympathised, and felt very old, very responsible when she drove his silly little car to his city hotel at ten. Got it there without incident, parked it without mishap. And he refused to take the keys.

'I'm not driving it home, Morrie.'

'How will you get home?'

'Tram.'

'I've got a double bed,' he said.

'I don't sleep with drunk Poms I find on my doorstep. Take your keys.'

The lift doors opened and he stepped in. 'If I can't sleep, I'll drive.' And the doors closed.

She considered leaving his keys at the reception desk. People waiting there for service, she stood a moment, then turned and walked back to the car.

It looked like a forgotten toy left on the street by a kid called in to bed. She'd never left her toys in the yard. Didn't want the responsibility of that car. Didn't want him to lie alone in the dark, worrying about his mother either.

I should have got into the lift with him. Would it matter if I slept with him?

Yes. When I sleep with him, I want him to remember it. And if his mother needs another operation, he'll be on the first flight home.

She looked back at the hotel while checking the car doors. They were locked, though with that canvas hood it would be the easiest car in the world to break into. Cars were stolen every night in Melbourne, and this one would be a temptation to joy-riders.

She drove it home. There was little traffic about, and after manipulating her father's station wagon into her parking space at the rear of the flats, getting Morrie's toy into it was easy.

She'd eaten prawns for dinner, drunk one glass of wine. Maybe it was the combination that brought on her night of dreams. Or him, or his car keys on her bench, his car in her bay.

She was driving it, his mother beside her, or a woman who was probably his mother. She had to get her to the hospital and it was on the far side of Sydney Harbour, and she was driving the car across it, across glassy water.

She must have got her there because the dream changed, and she was in a huge hospital ward, and couldn't remember where she'd left his mother. There was barely enough light to see. Thousands of beds in a ward that was miles long and she'd done the wrong thing in bringing her to this place. Should have taken her to Gran Norris's hospital.

And how was she supposed to recognise her if she found her. She didn't know her face.

Then it wasn't his mother she was searching for, but Jenny. And suddenly Myrtle was there, and she didn't want her to find Jenny. She was walking ahead, covering the beds with ex-boarding-house sheets, and she had piles of them, covering the patients' heads too, and they only covered the heads if the patient was dead.

On leaden legs, Cara tracked Myrtle, lifting sheets to look at faces. All the same blurred, featureless face, and she didn't know Jenny's face, only her hands. And Myrtle knew it. She'd placed pink rubber gloves on their hands and Cara couldn't pull them off.

She was fighting to pull off a pair when she woke, her heart racing.

Only five-thirty, the ghostly hands of her alarm clock told her. Too early, too cold to rise. Her electricity bill had been mammoth last quarter. For half an hour she willed herself back to sleep.

Couldn't get Morrie and his mother off her mind – or Jenny. At six she gave in, got up, turned on the heater and made a mug of coffee.

Was Jenny Morrison/Hooper still alive? People died every day, in car crashes, from cancer, from a million different diseases. What if I go up to Woody Creek in ten years' time and find out she died a week before I got there?

What if I go this weekend and find out she died when I was fifteen?

At least she'd be out of my head.

I need to know who is behind me. It's not Myrtle and Robert and Gran Norris. Her son might still be up there, or one of her girls, or someone who knew them.

It took two cups of coffee to shake that dream, but by seven-forty she was driving in heavy morning traffic, planning to park Morrie's car and leave his keys at the reception desk. No place to park out front of the hotel, and on her second turn around the block, she saw him standing at the kerb.

'Where are we going?' he asked.

'I'm going to work,' she said. 'And I'll be late.'

He drove her to work and was waiting for her when the school day ended. He told her the lump was small, that the surgeon had removed it. Tests would prove it cancer or not. He told her his father had left Melbourne with the tour group after his mother promised to join him when she could, which, to Cara, said more about his parents than he may have meant to say. If Robert or Myrtle had been in hospital, the other one would have stuck to them like glue.

Morrie spent two nights on Cara's fold-up bed. She didn't expect him to remain in that narrow bed, but he did. On the second night, she all but offered him half of her own. Good sense stopped her. She'd need to find a lady doctor and get a script for the pill before she slept with him.

He flew with his mother to Perth on the Thursday, his toy car parked behind the flats, and the afternoon of his flight, when she came in from school, she damn near tripped over her manuscript, propped by the postie against the bottom step.

Snatched it, her dream of publication not ending, not on those concrete steps. It didn't end until she was inside, until she slid the bulk of pages from the oversized envelope, until she searched the envelope, shook it for a letter, for some proof that her words had been read.

Only an impersonal printed card, paper-clipped to her well-worked synopsis. Not a handwritten word on it, no signature.

That card made up her mind. Her years of labour tossed by the postie onto an unclean stairway like so much rubbish made up her mind. She could relate to that envelope, to being left behind like rubbish, and while the hurt was still sharp, she walked down to the phone box on the corner, called the Pioneer bus depot and booked a seat to Woody Creek on tomorrow's bus.

LOST AND FOUND

A brutal day in Melbourne, worse in Woody Creek, one of those evil country days when howling winds blow straight in from the South Pole, attempting to sweep walkers from their feet, when small electric radiators heat an inch at a time.

Five twenty-five, Charlie warming his scrawny shins before such a radiator, Georgie eager to lock up and go home to warmth, watched the Melbourne bus pull in, watched two passengers step down to the wind. One was Gracie Dobson, the other was a stranger clad in a blue overcoat and tartan scarf, which she removed from her neck and used to tie her hair down while waiting for her luggage. She looked remotely familiar, probably one of the Dobson girls who had got away.

Not a Dobson. Gracie took her case and walked to her son's car. The one in the blue overcoat and tartan scarf disappeared into the post office.

Charlie, hunched in his overcoat of unrecorded vintage, in a tweed cap of similar ilk, wanted to know who she was looking at.

'Grace Dobson is back. The other one is a stranger,' Georgie said.

'Granger? She died two years ago?'

'Sssss for snake, Charlie. Stranger.'

*

Cara closed the post-office door, shutting the worst of the gale outside while the youth behind the counter eyed her.

'The *Closed* sign's up,' he said.

'I was wondering if you could direct me to a motel, please. I came in on the bus.'

'Should have got off thirty miles back if you're after a motel – or gone on another fifty.'

'A hotel then?'

'Over the lines.' His ink-stained thumb pointing vaguely north-east as he came from behind the counter and walked to the door. She followed, believing he intended offering more concise directions. He turned off the light.

'We're closed,' he said. 'I'm going home.'

'Would you know if there is a family here by the name of Hooper?'

'Down the same way as the pub,' the youth said. 'There's a few more in the cemetery.' There is nothing worse than a joke that doesn't come off. The youth shrugged, eyed her again, then reached for the door to close it.

Cara clung to shelter. 'Do you know of a Morrison family?'

'Are you doing a survey or something?' He jiggled the keys.

'Something,' she said.

'Georgie Morrison works for Charlie.'

'More information please?'

His thumb pointed again. 'On the corner, the grocer.'

She stepped outside. He locked up and walked to his bike, parked against a leaning veranda post. Her case in hand, she watched him mount and ride east into the growing gloom, then she turned west, or in the direction he'd pointed, the wind attempting to blow the small case from her hand.

Fought that wind past a bare-faced brick building to the suggested shelter of a crumbling corner veranda, its posts painted green in another lifetime, to match twin front doors. They were closed, but light showed through what had obviously been a grocer's window in another lifetime. She tried the door. The wind did the rest. It flung one wide, and while she fought to close it, a cow bell fixed overhead jangled.

Not a lot of light within, bare boards, boxes, a long battered counter running the length of a deep and narrow store. She placed her case beside a crate of tomato-sauce bottles, sighted an ancient old bloke clad for outdoors but seated over a tiny heater.

'I was told George Morrison worked here.'

'Speak up,' he said.

'George Morrison,' Cara repeated, a tone louder.

'Who's looking?' a voice from the deep asked. Cara searched for the owner and sighted red hair at the far end of the counter.

'Good afternoon,' Cara said and walked deeper into the barn of a store. Should have said evening, shouldn't have said *good* anything. This was bad. This was as bad as it got and she was stark raving mad. She cleared her throat and walked to the counter. 'I'm attempting to locate a Jennifer Hooper. I believe her maiden name was Morrison.'

'You're here about Donny?'

Cara tried her schoolmarm voice, which these days worked with nine year olds. 'I was told I might find a George Morrison here. Would he be about, please?'

The redhead rose up from behind a large cardboard carton, an absolute stunner of a redhead, tall, clad in a zip-up navy windcheater, her long hair pulled back hard from her face in a long and bushy ponytail. 'Could be,' she said.

The bus had travelled north, or north-west. Logic suggested the weather would be warmer here than in Melbourne. This place was hell without the heat, but that stunner of a girl standing there, taking her measure, made Cara remove her headscarf and shake her curls free.

'You're from Raelene's welfare place?'

'The matter is personal,' Miss Norris said.

The redhead nodded and took a packet of cigarettes from her windcheater pocket, flipped one into her mouth and struck a match, all the while eyeing her visitor.

Cara turned back to the door, wanting out of this place. If she'd learn one thing from this, it would be not to make rash decisions.

The decrepit old coot had left his heater. He was blocking her way out, polishing his glasses. And he smelled of mould and mothballs.

'She's here to see Jenny,' the redhead yelled.

The glasses back where they belonged, he had a good look. 'I'll bet you a Yankee dime to a dollar that you're one of Gertrude's quack's mob,' he said.

'Archie Foote,' the redhead translated.

They were speaking in code. Cara looked from one to the other, then capitulated. 'My mother knew Jenny during the war.'

'She's got your mother's hair,' Charlie said.

The redhead blew three perfect smoke rings towards the ceiling, perfect until they contacted the polar air currents up there and dissipated.

'I'm Georgie Morrison,' she said. 'Jenny is my mother.'

And Cara's heart rose up from her breast like a dying frog then flopped down dead to the swamp of her stomach.

She was looking at her half-sister. She was standing across the counter from a half-sister, and her half-sister was offering her a cigarette.

Struck dumb. Staring at the redhead, then aware she was staring, she reached for the packet of cigarettes.

And the redhead caught her wrist.

This was *Psycho* country. She'd seen the movie. She swung around to face the old bloke, expecting that music, the long-bladed knife. He was staring at her, but three foot away.

Wrenched her wrist free and stepped back from the counter.

Had she been in her right mind she would have run out to the street, thrown herself in front of a truck, if there'd been a truck. She hadn't been in her right mind since Monday. She was in love, and he was in Perth with his mother. If she'd been in her right mind she would have been in a city doctor's office, getting a script for the pill, but the pill took a month to screw the female system into its unnatural cycle anyway, and by that time he'd be back in England.

And Cathy had said her novel was brilliant. And it was trash, and treated like trash by the postie. Anyone could have picked it up. And who cared if they had.

'How did she know Jenny?' the redhead asked.

'Sydney.' *And I want to go back there, be thirteen again and know nothing about this place. I want to do it again, and do it the right way – and put Amberley back the way it was.*

'How did she know her?'

'Jenny was one of my mother's lodgers –'

'Not the Myrtle who used to look after Jimmy?'

Cara nodded.

*

'Righto.' Georgie nodded and continued nodding.

What looks like a fish, smells like a fish and feels fishy is usually related to a fish. Jenny's hand had reached for that packet of cigarettes, and Charlie was dead right about her hair, so Georgie nodded, having a fair idea of why this stranger was here.

Years ago, back when Lila Roberts had moved to town, Margot had become obsessed about a fourth baby Jenny had produced while she'd been in Sydney. It had never taken much to get Margot started on one of her obsessions and most of them Georgie ignored. She may have got that one right.

I knew you when you were a bulge in your mother's belly, Lila Roberts had said to her when Jenny had introduced Margot as her daughter.

And Georgie knew she was looking at that bulge in Jenny's belly. She was dead certain of it.

When you're fishing, first bait your hook. Georgie was searching for that bait when a gale blew in the door with Maisy Macdonald.

'I thought you might have closed up early. I forgot to get tea when I was in Willama.'

'Shut that door or I'll start flying before they give me wings,' Charlie yelled.

She closed it, speaking as she approached the counter. 'Bushells, thanks love. It's got less dust in it.'

She saw Georgie's visitor – and saw the resemblance. A blind man would have seen the resemblance, and the longer Georgie looked at her visitor, the more resemblance she saw.

'That the lot?'

'Give me a couple of pound of sugar while I'm here, love.' Then never backward in coming forward, her next comment was to the visitor. 'You picked a bad day for your trip. The news just said there'll be gale-force winds tonight – which reminds me, love, I'd better have a bottle of kero just in case the wires go down again.'

'No bottle, no kero,' Charlie said.

'I'll bring you up a dozen tomorrow, you mean old coot.'

The visitor had stepped away from the counter, turned her back to the three-way conversation. Maisy took her tea and sugar, and her beer bottle full of kero and, with nothing more to learn, left, Georgie walking her to the door, opening it, closing it behind her, glancing at her visitor's case and deciding that fishing time was over.

'You'd be the one she had when she was up in Sydney,' she said. And she hooked her.

'You know about me?' the visitor said.

'I do now,' Georgie said.

*

Bloody fool, Cara's mind screamed. *You know about me?* Bloody fool.

Get out. Now.

Nowhere to get out to until eight-thirty tomorrow morning.

'What's your moniker?' the moth-eaten one asked.

'Foote,' Georgie yelled. 'She's Granny's niece – on her quack's side. Do you reckon we could have a bit of privacy, Charlie.'

'Knew it,' he said, then unplugged his heater and wandered with it swinging by its cord to the dark end of the store, where he disappeared behind a curtain.

Georgie returned to the counter and her cigarettes. She removed one, then again offered the packet. This time Cara took it and, with shaking hands, removed a cigarette and waited for a light.

'Where are you staying?'

'There's a hotel –'

'If the weather was better it would be packed out on a Friday night. You might get lucky. If not, the bloke out at the caravan park will have an on-site van.' Georgie struck a match and shared the flame, her eyes never leaving Cara's face. 'You're the dead spit of her.' And she showed her hand. 'Jenny's only legacy to me. You're taller than her. You've got the same haircut, or damn near. Decided to claim your heritage, eh?'

'I . . . I've always wanted to meet her, and Jimmy.'

'She's here. Jimmy's grandfather took him when he was six.'

'She's still in town?'

'A decent stone's throw away. If you stay at the pub she'll be your nearest neighbour. How long are you here for?'

'Tonight,' Cara said.

'What do I call you?'

'Cara. Cara Norris.'

And the old man was back, but behind the counter, gathering notes from a drawer.

'I'll drop you off at the pub on my way if you like – after I fix Charlie a bit of dinner.'

They disappeared with their money, and Cara walked back to her case to stare out the window, rain blowing in clouds now before a howling wind.

This place wasn't the place she'd packed for. She'd seen a different town, with motels in the main street. Every tiny town between Melbourne and Sydney had a motel. She'd seen herself unpacking that case in a comfortable room, with a telephone, had seen herself making anonymous phone calls to Hoopers, to Morrisons.

Her half-sister? A redhead? She'd thought her half-sisters might look like her. How could that redhead be her half-sister? What was a girl who looked like her doing behind the counter of a derelict grocery shop?

And she was back. 'Were you planning to knock on Jenny's door?'

'No! No. I'm not up here to upset anyone.'

'You've made my day – not that it would have taken a lot. Do you want me to give her a call for you?'

'No.'

'Then what are you here for?'

Cara shook her head. 'I didn't expect to find . . . anyone.'

'You have, so what's next?'

'I thought there'd be a motel, a telephone.'

'There's a telephone on the wall. Go for your life.' Cara shook her head. 'She's pretty shockproof,' Georgie added.

Wished the sun was out. Wished she'd driven Morrie's car up here. Wished she hadn't come up here.

'Is she married?'

'Yep. And I doubt he knows that she had you.'

'I shouldn't have come.'

'But you did, and I reckon that if I'd found the guts to come this far, I'd take the next step. Do you want to see her?'

She wanted to see her through a one-way mirror. No one-way mirrors in Woody Creek. But she was here where she'd been planning to be ever since she'd found out about her. Maybe she had to stop attempting to control what was beyond her control and allow this night to find its own ending, disaster or not.

'Got any idea why she gave you up?' the redhead asked.

Cara shook her head. 'Mum told me she had three children, that she was young.'

'She's sixteen years older than me. I'll give her a call and sound her out for you.'

Cara turned to the telephone, an ancient box fixed to a post behind the counter. 'Would she see me?'

'One way to find out.'

And Georgie made the call. Seconds later the ghost haunting the edge of Cara's vision for years was on the other end of the line, and Cara's heart hammering a hole through her lungs, pounding so hard in her ears it outdid the howl of wind in the wires, and Georgie's conversation.

Not a long conversation.

'She wants to see you. I suggested she doesn't go to the pub. Half the town will be there tonight and it's bad enough you going there. I told her I'd take you down to the old place for dinner. I hope you eat fish and chips?'

DINNER FOR THREE

*D*riven in an ancient ute through a wind-whipped forest. Led across a muddy yard, down a rattling wind tunnel, through a washhouse, a bedroom, then hit in the eye by an all-white kitchen, where she was introduced to Margot, the second half-sister, and whatever she'd been expecting, Margot wasn't it. Saw a rotund white-headed woman clad in a white uniform and grey cardigan, white ankle socks and fluffy boot-style slippers; she was seated on a kitchen chair, near on top of an old wood stove. Cara offered her hand. Margot ignored it.

'What'th th'e doing here?'

She had no teeth, or few. She spat when she spoke.

Sister?

And Georgie lying to her? 'She's one of Itchy-foot's relatives.'

An ancient black kettle lifted over the central hotplate, the firebox opened, then Georgie disappeared out the way they'd come in as Margot rose from her chair to unwrap the parcel of fish and chips while wind buffeted the house, threatening to blow it from its foundations – if it had any.

Georgie came back with an armload of wood she dropped with a clatter to the hearth tray. She jammed a lump into the firebox, closed it with her boot, brushed woodchips from her windcheater, then removed it.

The kitchen was warm. Cara unbuttoned her overcoat, hung it with her scarf over the back of a chair, with Georgie's jacket.

'That's Donny,' Georgie said. Cara had been staring at a photograph of an oversized baby-faced youth, hung at an angle on the wall. 'He's in a home for the retarded – in Melbourne.'

'Your brother.'

'Step. Jenny's first husband's son. He's got a sister, Raelene. She's with Jenny – or she is at the moment. Their father was killed in a mill accident and their mother is doing what she can to populate Australia. Sit down.'

Chairs surrounding a big old wooden table, but Margot had ripped off a section of the wrapping paper, placed a slab of battered fish on it, with a handful of chips, and taken it back to her chair beside the stove.

Georgie gathered salt, pepper, cut a lemon, took one plate, one knife and fork from cupboard and drawer.

'Path me the thalt,' Margot spat.

Georgie passed the salt, waited while it was shaken. 'Jenny's coming down later.'

'Th'e knowth better than to come near me.'

She had not addressed a word to Cara, and since her initial evil-eyed stare, hadn't looked at her.

'Tea or coffee?' Georgie asked.

'Coffee would be good.'

'Sit down and eat while it's hot.'

Cara sat, her hands on her lap, until the coffee was made, one mug placed on the stove hob for Margot, one on either side of the table, then Georgie sat down to a slab of fish, squeezed lemon, shook salt and pepper over. Cara mimicked her actions.

'Feel free to use the plate. I'm into labour-saving devices,' Georgie said.

She broke the slab into two. Cara broke off what appeared to be the tail end. Uncertain if her stomach would accept or reject it, she bit. It was a nice piece of fish. She ate a chip, which killed her need to find something to say.

Knew she should say something. Stunned by this place, concussed by her half-sisters, by her too-easy finding of Jenny Hooper/Morrison – and by fear of meeting her.

For years and more years she'd been writing their meeting, in this town, though this town wasn't the one she'd written. No one could have imagined Woody Creek, or those sisters. It was ridiculous. Margot was half as wide as she was tall. Georgie had to be five foot ten, and slim.

And Margot back at the table for more chips, clawing up a handful, Georgie eyeing her, eyeing her guest.

'You're a nurse, Margot?' Cara tried.

Margot gave her another dose of the evil eye and returned to her chair.

'She's on an invalid pension,' Georgie said.

Cara ate the last of her fish; then, like her hostess, wiped her greasy fingers on the wrapping paper. Margot clawed up the last of the chips, then the paper was wrapped, a hotplate lifted and the parcel poked into the flames.

'Go over to Elsie's. Jenny will be here in half an hour,' Georgie said.

'It'th raining. Take her over there.'

Windows rattling, a door banging, Cara looked up, expecting the roof to go.

'We get a bit of protection from the worst of the wind from Joe Flanagan's wood paddock. Elsie's place will be rocking. They built it three feet off the ground and the wind gets in beneath it. The land down here is flood-prone.'

Cara had seen lights from a second house when they'd driven

in. Elsie? Another relative? She didn't want any more. She wanted Morrie. She wanted Myrtle and Robert. Tomorrow she'd be back in Melbourne. All she had to do was get through the night to tomorrow.

'You've always lived down here?' she asked.

'Except for two years when Jenny was married to Ray – Ray King.'

'What are you telling her everything for?' Margot whined.

'She's a relative.'

'How?'

'Itchy-foot's sister was her grandmother,' Georgie improvised.

Pandora's box, Robert had named this place. A good place to stay away from, he'd said when at fifteen she'd asked him to drive her there. And she'd opened it. If she lived through to morning, if she ever got out of this town, she'd close that lid. She'd bury it beneath a ton of bricks.

Georgie lit a cigarette then slid the pack across the table. 'More coffee?'

'Thank you, no.' She accepted a cigarette and her fingers smelled fishy. Glanced at the sink, wanting to wash her hands. Looked at her watch, at Georgie, who was occupied in untangling a rubber band from her ponytail.

Like flame that hair, the darks, the lights of it when she scratched and shook it free of its bonds. She'd been gorgeous with her hair pulled back from her face. With it free, she was so far beyond gorgeous, words were superfluous. She had magnificent eyes and a complexion to kill for. Regal was the word that came to mind. In this place? She should have been on the cover of some glossy magazine.

Cara rose and went to the sink. Soap in a saucer. She used it, washed her hands and shook them dry enough, Margot staring at her back, and not fast enough to look away when Cara turned.

God help her, growing to adulthood in Georgie's shadow. *The Three Sisters . . . The Half-Sisters* by C.J. Norris or maybe Norris J. Cara.

And pseudonym or not, she wasn't writing it. She'd retired from the literary world, defeated by a postman. If she got out of this place alive she'd buy herself a television set and spend the rest of her days staring at it.

'Car's coming,' Georgie said. 'If you don't want to see her, go over to Elsie's, Margot.'

'It'th too cold, I thaid.'

Too cold, too windy and too dark, or Cara may have led the way over to Elsie's, whoever she was. Twin eyes were bumping down the track, the wind gusting the sound of a motor against the window.

The motor died. A car door slammed.

Then voices.

'Th'e'th brought thoth kidth down here,' Margot wailed.

'Go over to Elsie's.'

'Harry hateth me.'

'Then go bed – and if you turn your heater on, make sure there's nothing near it to burn.'

How did she stand it? Why did she stand it? Watched Margot waddle out the way Cara had come in. Georgie followed her to the door, watched her go, then turned and walked back to the table.

'Raelene doesn't need any more ammunition. Your grand-mother was Itchy-foot's sister, Archie Foote's – Granny's husband. I don't know if his sister had grandkids or not, but nor does Raelene. Sit down.'

Footsteps approaching, preceded by a blast of cold wind. Doors slamming, then a petite, dark-headed, dark-eyed gypsy of a girl burst in to commandeer the stove, a smaller girl behind her.

And Jenny, faceless no more.

'You're very much like Jenny. Look in a mirror, pet,' Myrtle had once said. Cara was looking in that mirror – at hair, shorter at the sides than her own, but the same. As slim, not so tall; apprehensive eyes, perhaps they were as blue.

There stands the ghost who for years has haunted the edge of my vision, Cara thought as she stood unmoving, staring, mouth parted but nothing to say. An hour passed, or an instant, and for that hour, that instant, the wind died, the windows stopped rattling, the door stopped banging and Cara's heart stopped beating. Perhaps the world stopped turning while that instant stretched.

'As they entered,' Georgie said, 'Raelene, Trudy and Jenny – meet Cara, our thirty-second cousin.'

Her introduction forced time to begin again, forced the hands of the old marble mantelpiece clock to jerk forward. It donged once for the half-hour and Jenny closed the door and stepped forward to offer her hand.

Cara took it, shook it. Since she'd turned fifteen, she'd tried to kid herself that she was a woman of words. Couldn't find one. Only the hands communicated, identical hands. Where did one end and the other begin?

'How come she looks like you?' the gypsy asked.

'Itchy-foot's sister looked like him,' Georgie said, and the hands released their grip and identical eyes, guilty eyes, turned to Raelene.

I wanted this, Cara thought. I dreamed and wrote this. Say something. Heart, mouth, mind shaking, she returned to her chair, and sat. And Jenny sat beside her on the long side of the table, Georgie opposite.

'Is Myrtle well?'

Myrtle, their only common link; Cara grasped at that link; 'Yes.' More was required. She nodded, cleared her throat. 'They're still living at Amberley.'

'I loved that place,' Jenny said.

'They've . . . they renovated recently.' Again she cleared her throat. 'They've turned it into units . . . four two-bedroom units.'

'You sound like her.'

'She speaks of you . . . fondly. And of Jimmy.'

Jenny's turn to nod, and Cara glanced by her at the smaller girl, wide brown eyes, long plaits, quiet as a mouse. A third half-sister. She hadn't written her in. Georgie hadn't mentioned her.

'Is your father well?'

'He retired at the end of '64.'

Cara knew Jenny's age. She'd been almost twenty-one when she'd given birth to her. She looked to be in her thirties. Long blue sweater, black stretch slacks, pierced ears, small gold baubles swinging from her lobes. A few crinkles around her eyes, a crease in her brow.

Is there a crease in mine tonight? Cara's hand rose to smooth that crease.

Look in the mirror, pet.

Identical noses, brows, the spacing between their eyes, and their hairline, eyebrows. Different mouths, different teeth, different chins. I'm Billy-Bob from the nose down. I have his height.

Can't ask her his height, where he came from, his family name. Tonight I'm Archie Foote's relative. Can't ask her why she kept the other three and gave me away. Nothing I can ask her, so nothing to say.

Georgie left the kitchen, and Cara's reflexes lifted her from the chair, needing to stay close to the one who had brought her to this place. Forced her feet to remain where they were, and Georgie returned with a bottle.

'I don't know much about this stuff, but it seems like the right time to open it.'

She had trouble opening it. It was somewhere to look while she struggled, while she forced the last of the cork into the bottle, while she found three unmatched glasses, ex-Vegemite, one honey, a portion of the label still attached to the honey glass. She filled them with something red and Cara's throat, desperate for lubrication, welcomed the wine – until her tongue picked up the taste of a vicious hard brew. But it matched this night, this house, this town, so she drank an inch while Georgie poured cordial for the girls.

Jenny took one sip then pushed her glass back. 'I'm not much of a wine drinker,' she said.

Cara drank another inch, desperate for alcohol to take the edge off near panic. Hard rain out there now, or hail belting against the window.

'You could have chosen a better day,' Jenny said.

'Yes.' Like never.

'You're still living at Amberley?'

'I work in Melbourne.'

'Amberley?' Raelene asked.

'It was a boarding house when I knew Cara's mother.'

'Are you still at school, Raelene?' Cara asked.

'Like hell,' Raelene said.

She turned to Trudy. 'How old are you, Trudy?'

'Seven.'

Dead end. Again she sipped the wine, if wine it was. I've seen her, she thought. I didn't come up here to find a mother. I've got one. I'm pleased she left me at Amberley. I wouldn't have survived in this place.

Georgie had. Georgie, sitting quietly, reading the wine label before topping up Cara's glass.

'I worked at a factory during the war. Myrt looked after Jimmy for me.'

'I've seen photographs of him,' Cara said. An inch of wine went down. Morrie had drunk five glasses of beer the night he'd told her about his mother's lump. He'd said he missed Aussie beer. She'd tasted it. It was no worse than this stuff. Burgundy, according to the label. She'd add that to her list of things never to buy, along with smoked salmon, caviar, brussels sprouts – and typing paper.

Glanced again at Trudy, attempting to see something of herself in her. Nothing. She must have taken after the new husband. Georgie must have taken after her father – and Margot couldn't have had the same father. Raelene was about Jenny's size, pretty, she had curly hair, and she wasn't Jenny's. She looked seventeen, eighteen, had a unique face and a large bust for her small frame.

'What is your teacher's name, Trudy?'

'Mrs McPherson.' A shy kid, she stood close to her mother.

More wine went down.

'There were two teachers living at Amberley when I lived there,' Jenny said. 'A Mrs Collins and a Miss Robertson.'

'They're still there. They share the rear ground-floor unit.'

'Give them my regards next time you see them – and Myrtle.'

Cara nodded. She wouldn't be giving her regards to anyone, wouldn't be telling anyone she'd been up here. She'd get on that bus tomorrow and never pass this way again.

'The first day I saw Amberley, I didn't believe it was a rooming house. Jimmy used to love Myrtie's leadlight window. One of the first words he said was "pretty".'

'The window survived the transition, and the staircase. It leads from a small entrance foyer up to a landing now. The upper floor units open off the landing.' Cara hadn't seen it finished, not quite finished. She'd see it in the September holidays, maybe with Morrie.

'It would have taken some doing, turning it into flats.'

'The builders worked on it for almost twelve months.' A safe subject, Amberley.

'What do you do for a living?'

'I followed Dad into teaching.'

'You sound like a schoolmarm,' Raelene said.

'Do you work, Raelene?'

'There's no jobs up here.'

'Where would you like to work?' Cara asked.

'Television.'

'One of my friends got a small part in a television show. She's a teacher too.'

Raelene's eyes almost met her own. 'Did she get piles of money for doing it?'

'No, but she had fun.'

The mantel clock struck a long aching eight, four sets of eyes watching it.

'It's slow,' Jenny said, checking her watch. Cara glanced at her own. Ten past eight. She looked at Georgie, hoping she might suggest they leave.

'I told Jim I'd pick him up at nine. He's at a meeting at McPherson's. I'll drop you off at the hotel. Have you booked?'

'She got one of the veranda rooms,' Georgie said. 'More wine anyone?'

'It tastes like bad vinegar,' Jenny said. 'Where did you get it?'

'A few of the salesmen give Charlie bottles for Christmas.'

'They're trying to poison him.'

'He deserves putting down,' Raelene said.

Jenny took cigarettes from her purse and offered the packet. Cara accepted one, accepted a light from Jenny's match and looked again at the hand holding the match, at the hand holding the cigarette. Same atrocious fingernails, same slightly curving pointer. Long fingers, square-topped. Looked at her own hands. Since January of 1964 they'd spent their lives typing. All for naught.

She'd burn *Angel At My Door* when she got home, burn it one page at a time, in her sink if necessary. Everything about it was wrong, the town, the people, the house they lived in, and Jessica. Every single thing. She'd started it with no plan and ended it the same way. It had served a purpose, that was all.

Morrie would be back in Melbourne on Sunday, and the way she felt right now, she'd sleep with him and hope he got her pregnant.

Margot knocked at the door. Georgie opened it. Margot didn't come in. Georgie returned to the kitchen with a hot-water bottle she emptied down the sink then refilled from the kettle.

'Fill your own bottle, you albino vampire,' Raelene yelled.

'Hold your tongue, Raelene!' Jenny said.

'That's what she looks like.'

My Sister, the Vampire. Another good title.

A pill-swallowing vampire too. Georgie offered pills at the door along with a glass of water and the hot-water bottle. Four sets of eyes watching Georgie's back – *Feeding Time for the Vampires.*

The door closed and Georgie returned to the table to drink her wine.

'Are they doing her any good?' Jenny asked.

'They're just sleeping pills,' Georgie said. 'She sleeps.'

'She needs exercise, not sleep,' Jenny said, and Cara turned to the clock, willing its hands forward while Georgie spoke of the Polish doctor, Raelene punctuating the conversation with comments, Georgie or Jenny translating for the interloper from time to time. Maisy was Margot's grandmother. Elsie was married to Harry. Granny had raised Elsie.

'Teddy is on with Vonnie Boyle and her parents are having kittens,' Raelene said.

'She's not much older than you.'

'Micky is older than me. She's eighteen,' Raelene said, and Cara sipped atrocious wine and wondered how old Micky was. She sipped wine and smoked their cigarettes until that old mantel clock struck an arthritic nine, and Jenny rose and Cara rose.

Nothing to say on the trip back to town. She found four words. 'It's a nice car.'

'It was the only one Jim's legs would fold into,' Jenny said.

Then the hotel where she'd left her case in a bleak louvre-windowed veranda room. Cheap. That was about all Cara could say for it, and breakfast thrown in.

'Thank you, Jenny. I'm pleased to have met you,' she lied as she slid from the car.

'I'm pleased you came, Cara.'

Then goodbye.

STALE CIGARETTES

*F*or five years Jenny had taken on a variety of shapes and personalities. She entered into Cara's dreams that night. A tossing, turning night, the howling wind and rattling door pushed in on a nightmare of being pursued by vampires through dark streets. And when she woke gasping for breath, she tasted vampire in aged bedding, and heard them scraping at the louvre windows. Only the limb of a tree, battling gale-force winds.

Grey daylight was filtering into the room when next she opened her eyes, and with the dawn came a calm. Too early to leave her bed, still hours until the bus arrived to deliver her out of this place, she clung to the limited warmth of musty blankets.

At seven she found her way to the bathroom, her overcoat now her dressing-gown. Intent on a long hot shower to wash the night away, she changed her mind when she saw the shower. Washed her face, brushed her teeth and returned to her room to dress in the clothing she'd shed last night, the smell of stale cigarettes, of fish and chips still clinging. Combed her hair at a mottled dressing-table mirror, and in the grim light of Woody Creek's morning, the mirror reflected Jenny. Turned her back fast, forgoing creams and lipstick, tied her scarf to cover Jenny's hair.

A good place to stay away from, Robert had said. Parents know nothing when their kids are fifteen. She was older now.

Breakfast was served in the dining room between seven and eight-thirty, according to a sign taped behind the door. She found the dining room, a room behind a bar, six tables with red and white checked cloths, four metal chairs at each table. It had to be the dining room. Chose a table and a chair which allowed her to get her back into a corner, and there she sat until a middle-aged man came in, his arms loaded with small logs.

'I didn't know you were in here, love. A wild old night, eh,' he said.

'It certainly was,' she said, watching him drop his load before adding a log to a meagre open fire.

'You might be a bit warmer over this side,' he said.

'I'm fine, thanks.' Watching him brush woodchips from his sweater, add smaller fuel to a dying flame.

'Tea or coffee,' he said, fire-stoker and waiter both.

'Coffee please. Strong, with milk, and two slices of toast.'

Watched the fire grow and, the width of a room away, could feel its heat before a woman brought her breakfast. Two eggs, bacon, fried tomato, four slices of toast, a slab of butter and two bowls of jam, one marmalade, one red jam.

'A wild old night,' she said, emptying her tray to the table.

'It certainly was. I only ordered coffee and toast.'

'Coffee's coming, love. There'll be a few trees down today, I'll bet.'

'I don't eat a cooked breakfast.'

'You paid for it with your room last night, love. Leave what you don't want. The cook won't be insulted.' She walked to the fire to warm her back as the male came in with a large pot and a jug of milk.

'Visiting relatives, are you?' he asked.

'Business,' Cara said. They took the hint and left her to eat.

She ate the tomato with a slice of toast, ate the bacon, crisped the way she liked it, poured strong coffee, buttered more toast and added raspberry jam. Eating filled time.

'A wild old night,' a second eater greeted her. Maybe he lived at the hotel. No one came to take his order, but he received his two eggs, bacon, his fried tomato, toast, jam and slab of butter.

'Where are you from?' he asked.

'Melbourne.'

'What are you doing in this neck of the woods?'

'Business,' she said, draining the coffee pot into her cup and wishing she had a cigarette so she might dawdle longer in that warm room where a roaring fire now burned.

Her breakfast companion ate fast. Perhaps he had a place to go. Cara had no place to go, but with no more coffee, at ten past eight she returned to her room for her case; then, following directions given by Georgie the previous night, crossed over the road to follow a well-marked path through a railway yard and over train lines. No crossing gates to protect walkers from passing trains. No trains passing.

She didn't know she was walking where Jenny's feet had trod a thousand times, that Norman Morrison, the stationmaster, had been her grandfather. She glanced at the small station, then at the railway house, at the collapsing paling fence beside the track. Then no more fence. She was back at the road where the bus had dropped her off.

In Melbourne at this time of morning, there'd be a constant buzz of traffic. No traffic in this town and little movement. She walked down to the post office's recessed doorway and stood a while in its shelter, willing the bus to be on time.

So much land, each house well separated from its neighbour, old houses, big and small; the police station opposite the post office was just another house with a sign. The town hall looked like a brick barn.

Heard the roar of a motorbike and, still startled by that sound, she stepped back against the door. Loathed the sound of motorbikes. Not his. He was in jail, and if it was a bike, it wasn't going anywhere.

Half-a-dozen dogs started barking. They woke the town. A truck went by, its driver hawking, spitting to the road. Then a ute, a red dog in the tray barking at a black and white dog, who gave chase — until it smelled stranger and walked across the road to check out Cara's credentials.

She picked up her case and held it protectively before her exposed legs, but the dog sat down to scratch, and maybe in dog language to mention the wild old night.

'It certainly was, and in more ways than one, Bowser,' she said. 'I'm up here on business,' she added.

He nodded, satisfied, had another scratch, approached to sniff her case, then went on his way towards Charlie's shop, where he watered a couple of veranda posts before turning the corner, to no doubt water more posts, or to find out who was burning rubber on that motorbike.

Cara placed her case on the culvert, where the bus had dropped her, where the driver had said he'd pick her up, then she followed the dog past Charlie's twin green padlocked doors, past his *Bushells Tea* sign.

And saw what was making the noise — a bloke with a chainsaw cutting wood in the middle of the road. Stood until the saw was placed down to quietly splutter while its driver pitched half a tree onto the back of a small truck, until he looked around and caught her watching.

She beat him to the punch. 'A wild old night,' she said.

He nodded, stepped over a larger section of the tree, picked up his chainsaw and allowed it to do what it had been made for.

Not a tree but the giant branch of a tree. She could see the scar where the branch had twisted free to crash through a picket fence, bits of tree and fence strewn. She walked on, sidestepping a small branch, walked as far as the train lines, looked west down the lines, looked east. Nothing to see other than twin metal rails disappearing into the distance. No hills in this town, no bends in those ruled lines.

Turned and walked back to the corner to watch sawdust fly and to keep her eye on the main street, uncertain of which direction the bus would come from. *The Chainsaw Man*, by Norris Caraj, she thought. What a perfect setting for a dark murder mystery Jenny Hooper/Morrison's town would be. Shrugged and walked back to her case. She was no longer a novelist.

Is there anything worse than standing waiting for a bus that won't come? It hadn't come by quarter to nine, and she needed a smoke to kill the taste and scent of stale smoke.

Georgie's old ute came from the east, passed her and pulled in, its nose to a deep and open gutter. She waved and Cara left her case and walked again to Charlie's veranda.

'No bus,' she said.

'He'll turn up. Did you get any sleep?' Keys in her hand, Georgie was breaking into the shop.

'It was a wild old night,' Cara said.

'There's a big tree down across our road. I had to bush-bash to get around it. It came out by the roots.'

'There's one down around the corner, or half of one.'

'Could be what's keeping the bus. A few months back we had one come down out near Three Pines. It took them four hours to clear the road.'

Cara followed her indoors. 'Could I trouble you for a small packet of Marlboro and a box of matches, Georgie?'

'That's what I'm here for – I think.' A packet slid across the counter. Cara opened it while Georgie unlocked the money drawer and made change of a pound note.

'Do you ever get away?'

'Daytrips to Melbourne. Not for a while though.'

'Shops are a tie,' Cara said.

'Yep.'

Her eyes were green by daylight, appraising eyes this morning, then she turned them away to flick on a light switch, to find an old cloth from beneath the counter and with it wipe accumulated dust, insects and what may have been a mouse's leavings to the floor.

Cara returned to the door to watch for the bus.

'You came, you saw, you conquered, now you want to get out, eh?' Georgie said, following her.

'It's been incredible –'

'Mind-boggling incredible, or the other type?'

Those eyes watched her face for the reply and Cara, unable to meet them, looked both ways for the bus.

'I didn't expect to find Jenny – or you. I don't exactly know what I expected to find, Georgie.'

Georgie found a broom. She swept the floor on the customers' side of the counter, swept what she'd collected to the door. Cara gave way while the accumulation was flicked outside to the street.

'What were you hoping you'd find?'

'Jimmy, I think. I've seen photographs of him as a tiny boy. I've always thought of him as my big brother.' She shook her head. 'It was a stupid spur of the moment decision to come.'

'Jim doesn't know about you – Jenny's husband. She was cleaning up the garden as I drove past. She said she would have liked to have spoken to you without the kids around. Have you got the phone on?'

'No.'

'Where do you work?'

And the bus was coming. 'Armadale Primary,' Cara said, relief flooding her limbs as she walked back to her case. And salvation only yards away, she realised what she'd done. Until that moment she'd given away no personal information.

'It's a small world,' Georgie said. 'Back when Jenny was married to Ray, we went to the Armadale primary. We lived around the corner from it. Life is crazy, isn't it, the way that sooner or later everything seems to connect up.'

'It does seem that way at times.'

Bus pulling in, door slapping open, the driver, who would have preferred not to leave his seat, saw her case. He left the motor running and stepped down. Cara stood with Georgie and her broom until the luggage bay was opened, the case tossed in, then for the second time their hands melded.

'It's been seriously interesting,' Georgie said. No makeup, hair pulled back from her face, old broom in hand, and still regal.

'It's certainly been that,' Cara said.

'Call me sometime if you feel like it – or Jenny. They're the only Hoopers in town. Charlie is the only grocer. The exchange will give you our numbers.'

Cara didn't say she would or she wouldn't. Wanted to say something. 'Do you have any idea how incredibly beautiful you are, Georgie?'

'Watch it!' Georgie warned. 'Half the town has already got me pegged as a lesbo.'

No time to say more, but more she might say, now that she was leaving. Bus driver, already running late, itching to be on his way.

'I'm glad I met you, Georgie.' She stepped on board then and the door slapped shut behind her.

Plenty of empty seats; she chose one on the left side so she might wave goodbye. Knew Georgie would stand there to wave.

And she did.

Then gone, and Jenny's town disappearing behind her, all of the old houses, the few new ones looking foolish beside their ramshackle neighbours. A scattering of shops on either side of another railway crossing; a scratching dog forced to give way to the bus's bleat; another ute, another hawking driver and his dog.

Watched the houses give way to paddocks and trees. Watched the land outside that window until her eyes stung with their staring. Then she closed them, closed the lid on Pandora's box, sealed it.

Sealed Georgie in.

I've done what I said I'd do one day. Now it's over.

Bus driving into fog, and it seemed so right that Jenny's town should disappear back into the mist like some godforsaken Brigadoon.

Let them sleep, she thought. I won't be disturbing them again.

THE CONNECTION

*T*oo late. She'd already disturbed Jenny. She walked her garden that morning, righting pots, collecting scattered garden furniture, staking leaning plants, knowing she had to tell Jim the truth about the relative she'd seen last night. He wouldn't blame her. She'd told him how she'd met Georgie's father, how she'd watched the police arrest him in Geelong. He knew about the babies she'd aborted in Armadale, about Vroni's health farm.

They ate a porridge breakfast and she couldn't tell him, not with Trudy and Raelene at the table. Instead she added to her lie when Raelene mentioned Amberley. Jim remembered that boarding house.

'Her mother lived there,' Jenny said. 'Cara was born a few weeks before I came home.'

Not a true lie, but sickened to the stomach by it anyway. Told Raelene to wash the dishes, told Jim to watch-dog Raelene for half an hour, then she walked across the railway line to Georgie, her protector of last night, her confessor that day – between customers.

'I have to tell Jim, but I can't stand for him to have the image of those raping mongrels in his head. It's bad enough having it in my own head.'

'She won't be back,' Georgie said.

'What did she say?'

'That she had no intention of disrupting your life – and you told her last night that you didn't want it disrupted.'

'I didn't say anything like that.'

'You took those kids down there so you wouldn't have to speak to her alone,' Georgie said.

'That wasn't the reason. Jim had to go around to McPherson's and I wasn't going to leave Trudy alone with Raelene.'

'That's your justification. If you'd asked him, he would have stayed home.'

Jenny couldn't deny it. 'She looks like me. I couldn't believe it when I saw her. I've tried to build up a mental image of her for half of my life and I could never see her other than as a tiny baby. I never for one second considered that she might look like me.'

'Charlie saw the resemblance before me – and Maisy saw it. She had a scarf over her hair when we booked the hotel room, but they would have seen her at breakfast.'

A customer opened the door. Georgie walked up to serve her and Jenny stayed on, stacking packets of biscuits onto battered shelves and watching her girl at work.

Some give birth to daughters who will ever be strangers. Georgie was a chip off Jenny's soul – and Granny's. In so many ways she was Granny. Couldn't tell a lie to save her life, but when she'd known a lie was necessary to save Jenny skin, she'd come up with a beauty. And it was no real lie. Cara was a relative of Itchy-foot.

The customer left with her basket, and Georgie returned to unpack and stack, only one topic on her mind.

'She teaches at the Armadale primary,' she said. 'She told me this morning.'

They spoke of Armadale, of Ray. Jenny spoke of Robert Norris, a teacher before the war.

'Were they snobs?' Georgie asked.

'I thought Myrtle was when I met her. Her family would have

been, but they lost everything in the depression – except Amberley. She spoke with a plum in her mouth but was a nice woman – shy, and very churchy.'

If she closed her eyes, she could raise an image of Myrtle, clad in her old-lady outfits, her whispering rubber-soled shoes. She could see her big wet eyes the day she'd offered Granny's telegram.

'The house must have been a palace in its heyday. Myrt told me once they'd had half-a-dozen live-in servants when she was a girl.'

'How old was Cara when you gave her up, Jen?'

'Minutes. I'd already given her to Myrtle before she was born, and as soon as she was, I . . . I gave her. I wanted to forget I'd ever had her, and thought I'd be able to. You can't,' she said. 'She was born on 3 October 1944, exactly two months before Jimmy's third birthday. How do you forget something like that?'

'Margot can.'

'And Elsie needs her head read. Harry wants to move in with Teddy. And you need yours read too. You've got to stop pandering to her, Georgie. Let her get her own sleeping pills, fill her own hot-water bottle.'

'She'd scald herself.'

'What did she say about Cara?'

'She ignored her. Cara thought she was a nurse. She told me this morning that she'd seen photographs of Jimmy. I think he was the only one of us who was real to her.'

'I gave Myrtle a couple of photographs.'

'He'll turn up one day. Everyone does sooner or later. It's uncanny about her teaching at Armadale.'

'Did she say what brought her to Victoria?'

'She didn't say much.'

'I knew they'd educate her, that she'd be something, do something with her life. I used to tell myself that if she ever found out what I'd done, she'd thank me for giving her away. We tell ourselves what we want to believe.'

'She's got guts. A spur of the moment trip, she said. Just caught a bus and came up here to see what she could see. I haven't got that sort of guts.'

'Do you still think about your father?'

'Not until something starts me thinking. I dreamed about him last night. He was trying to find your brooch,' Georgie said. 'You know you ought to keep it in Charlie's safety-deposit box.'

'Then I couldn't wear it when I felt like wearing it.'

'When did you last wear it, Jen?'

'I know what you're saying,' Jenny said. 'What did you think when she told you who she was?'

'She didn't.' Georgie tapped Jenny's hand. 'I offered her a smoke and saw your hand reach for the packet. It was one of those mind-bending moments, when your eyes are seeing one thing and your head separates from your eyes and sees something else. One and one still makes two, Jen.'

Cow bell ringing as three generations of Duffy entered, two women with three kids and a battered pram – and if she didn't watch them, that pram would exit with more than a small Duffy in it.

Georgie stopped stacking biscuits. 'I don't know if Margot ever said anything to you, but the day she was with you and you ran into Lila Roberts at Blunts, she mentioned a bulge in your belly in Sydney. Margot didn't let go of it for twelve months.'

Charlie didn't hear much but he heard the cow bell. He'd been keeping his eye on the Duffy family for sixty years. He toddled up to keep an eye on them and the Duffy pram left with only a small screaming Duffy in it.

*

The phone rang early on Monday morning. Only old Mrs Davies wanting to know if Ernie had been in yet, and could Georgie add baking powder and washing soda to her order when he finally got there.

'He'll be talking to someone in the street,' she said. 'I send him out to get butter for my breakfast and I'll be lucky to have it for my lunch.' Like her husband, Mrs Davies was partial to a chat.

Charlie's phone didn't ring often, but each time it did during the following days, Georgie picked it up, hoping for those STD beeps. She told herself Cara wouldn't call, told herself she hadn't been able to get on the bus fast enough, told herself her previously unknown half-sister had been expecting something very different from what she'd found. But you can't kill hope, or it refuses to die easily. All week Georgie hoped. All week she felt . . . felt the loss of some intangible something she couldn't quite grasp or name, maybe the loss of a connection never made.

WILLS AND THINGS

*I*n October, Raelene was transferred to Florence's care for two months. Jenny and Jim were flying to England with the McPhersons. They'd considered taking Trudy with them, but when Elsie and Harry offered to move into town to look after her and the garden while they were away and they accepted their offer. Trudy loved her Nana and Poppy and, because of Margot, saw too little of them.

Elsie was concerned about Margot. Jenny worried about Raelene. Georgie was more worried about ineffectual Florence and her four little kids.

Jenny and Jim had Raelene under semi-control, or they and their support team in the city had her under semi-control. Every six weeks they drove her down to an appointment.

According to the experts, Raelene's desire for proof of her parents' unconditional love was why she kept pushing the boundaries. Georgie had once driven Raelene down to Moe and heard that kid's verbal attack on her mother; she'd since made her own diagnosis, which was diametrically opposed to that of the court-appointed expert.

Raelene was the image of Florence but all Ray inside her head. One minute a pretty, compliant kid, then within an instant, a snarling, fighting wild thing.

On the morning the two couples were to leave on their grand tour, Georgie drove them and their cases to the bus stop, where Jenny offered her two sealed envelopes, one addressed to Cara Norris, care of Armadale Primary School, *To be delivered in the event of my death* printed over the seal. The second was a copy of their wills.

'Scott and Wilson have got the originals,' she said.

'Pilots want to get to where they're going as much as you, Jen.'

'I know. I just need to know that everything I can do is done.'

The bus arrived, the cases were loaded. They watched Jim mount the high step. He'd been fitted with a more modern and better balanced leg. He said it was better. They had a long trip ahead of them, a lot of steps to climb. For twenty years the McPhersons had been promising themselves a trip home. Amy had relatives over there, offers of free beds.

'Promise me you'll move into the house with Trudy if anything does go wrong, Georgie, that you'll keep her away from Margot.'

'It goes without saying, Jen.'

'I know. I just needed to hear you say it.'

Bus horn beep-beeping. Granny had known how to hug. Jenny had never been good at making the first move. She made it that morning.

'Love you, kiddo,' she said.

'Ditto, kiddo, now go or they'll see the sights without you.'

The bus may have been in Willama when the phone rang – still early enough to be Cara, calling on her way to school.

It wasn't. 'I can't stand it here! They're driving me crazy!'

Georgie stood, picking at a ripped fingernail, allowing Raelene to get it out of her system – five minutes of brainless Florence, moron Clarrie, shithouse Moe.

Raelene had good fingernails, as did Margot, both runts. Had their unused growth gone in fingernails? Cara had been tall enough to look Georgie in the eye – and had stubs of fingernails.

'I'll work in the shop, Georgie. You don't have to pay me.'

Charlie trusted her about as far as he trusted the Duffy mob. Georgie bit the nail. 'Two months will be gone before you know it.'

'I can't stand another bloody day of it!'

'I've got a customer, Raelene.'

A phantom customer, but he saved her.

*

At five-thirty Georgie fed Charlie, locked up, then went home to feed Margot. Fed her eggs on toast. The fridge was riddled with eggs.

'You know I can't eat toatht.'

'Put your teeth in.'

'They hurt!'

Heard it all umpteen times before. Tuned out tonight and ate her eggs on toast, made coffee, then took her mug out to the old kitchen to sit in the doorway and look over Granny's land. Summer letting the world know it was on its way tonight.

Had Granny been alive, her tomatoes would have been flowering, or getting ready to. No Granny. Mint growing wild where her garden had been, a few self-sown silverbeet plants, a clump of self-sown pumpkins. One of them might win the battle for survival and bear fruit. Gum saplings were winning the war for Granny's land. Should dig them out before she had a forest to cut down. Didn't have the time, or maybe the incentive to keep fighting the forest.

Granny had. Jenny had.

She could remember Jenny taking to a clump of saplings with the axe a few weeks after she'd brought Jimmy home from Sydney. Could remember Jimmy rolling his fleet of wooden cars along the floorboard roads of this room. No more floorboard roads. A slab of cracked and uneven concrete floored the old kitchen now.

She could remember Jimmy the day Jenny brought them home

from Armadale, Granny sick in bed, Jimmy finding eggs in the hens' nests.

He'd loved eggs. They'd been starved of them in Armadale. *There's millions, Jenny.* To Jimmy everything had come in millions. A million dandelions growing on the sides of the road in spring. A million stars in the sky.

She'd missed his millions. He'd been close enough in age to be a companion. Could still conjure up the feeling of his hand when they'd walked to school.

Hold his hand, Georgie.

Not the oldest one, but always the one made responsible for the other two.

Never wanted that responsibility. Didn't want it now.

No responsibilities for Cara. My half-sister, the schoolteacher. Wondered if she taught in her old classroom, or Margot's, or Jimmy's.

Meeting her, shaking her hand had been . . . been like shaking Laurie Morgan's hand, or like shaking an adult Jimmy's hand, unreal, but soul-bending.

'What are you thitting out there for?'

'Thinking.'

'Why did they have to go over there anyway?'

'To see something they haven't seen. Put your teeth in and I'll have a game of cards with you.'

'They hurt!'

'Suit yourself.'

*

A telegram arrived the day the travellers landed. FEET ON THE GROUND STOP WILL MAKE WAY TO DORSET STOP LOVE JEN STOP.

Amy McPherson had an elderly aunt in Dorset. They intended making their base with her. Georgie considered sending a telegram back, not that there was anything to write in it.

Two weeks into their trip, had she felt the incentive, she could have told her that Josie and Brian Hall, who hadn't been home since the Christmas Day war of '59, came up for the weekend; could have told her that Charlie was driving her mad with his denial of dollars and cents, that spending her days with him and her nights with Margot had diminished her tolerance levels to a point tolerance levels shouldn't reach.

Couldn't be bothered. Couldn't be bothered arguing with Charlie either.

'Signs have to be in dollars and cents, Charlie. It's the law.'

'Not in my shop it's not, Rusty.'

The concept had been simple enough for her generation to grasp, and the transition made easy. Twenty shillings had always equalled one pound, now twenty of the new ten-cent coins equalled a two-dollar note, designed to look much like the old pound note, as the dollar note had been designed to look much the same as the old ten bob. It was Charlie's lack of say in that transition that got up his nose.

He did a lot of sneezing, maybe an allergic reaction to the new plastic notes, or to dust. She'd pretty much given up her battle with dust. The shop's ceilings rained dust.

'What happens to the two pennies they've got left over? Tell me that, Rusty. Who gets them?'

As with many who lose their hearing, Charlie talked more, and louder. He had no trouble understanding what he said, only what others said.

'The cent is worth more than the penny, Charlie.'

'That useless bloody little thing. A kid won't bother to pick one up if he sees it on the ground. Look after the pennies and the pounds will look after themselves, my old man used to say. The government is looking after them. That's what's happening to them. Every time we spend a shilling, they end up with two extra pennies.'

'Every time we spend ten cents, Charlie, and there's only ten cents in ten cents. There's no extra pennies.'

Then she went home.

'Elthie maketh thoups and cuthtards.'

'Make your bloody own, Margot. You're here all day, sitting on your backside.'

Three weeks into Jenny's trip of a lifetime and Margot's sleeping pills lived on the table with a selection of Heinz's baby food and a tin opener. There was a good range of baby foods, egg custard, pureed peaches, chicken broth, pureed brains.

Two weeks before the travellers came home, she was frying a thick slab of rump steak when Margot went into her bedroom and returned with her teeth in and her eyes threatening murder, but she sat at the table and ate half of the steak and chips and eggs. She'd developed a taste for Ray's steak in Armadale.

A postcard arrived that week, a view of Paris by night. Not much space for words. *Not what I imagined. By the time you get this, we'll be back in London. Love London. Jenny XXX*

Two days later, another arrived, this one of the Bloody Tower. *I could spend six months here and not run out of places to see. Love Jenny XXX*

Charlie's phone rang on a Monday in early December. Georgie recognised Florence Keating's 'Georgina'. Most had learned that she didn't reply to it. Not Florence.

'What's your problem, Florence?'

'Raelene went to the shops on Saturday and she hasn't come home. I thought she might be up there with you.'

'She's not.'

'When is Jenny due back?'

'The sixteenth. Have you reported her missing?'

'No, and I'm worried sick about her.'

'Call that court-appointed mob in Melbourne.'

'She's on her last chance with them. I don't want to get her into more trouble.'

There are times when there's not enough air in the world to fill the lungs, when you keep sucking it in but it won't get to the places where it's needed. Georgie was panting it in that morning.

'I can't control her, Georgina.'

'I have to go, Florence. I've got a customer.' Another phantom, but the phone was down. Now all she needed was for Raelene to walk through that door.

*

The tourists returned as they'd left, on the bus. Elsie went home to mince steak and make custards. Margot took pleasure in displaying her vampire fangs. Harry spent his weekends at Teddy's house. Then three days before Christmas, Raelene turned up, her black hair bleached a brassy orange blonde.

Jenny didn't recognise her at first glance, and when she did, she didn't want to, didn't want the hangover glow from their trip erased, not yet. Didn't want the fight, the futility of the fight. But she fought her around to Maisy, the local backyard hairdresser. Maisy cut that orange hair near to the bone, then dyed what was left of it black, a dead flat black.

Always pixie-faced, the new hairstyle suited her, made her mouth wider, her teeth whiter, her black eyes darker.

'You've got it all, Raelie. You're a beautiful-looking kid. Don't waste what you've got.'

Along with her bleached hair, she'd brought a zip-up bag stuffed full of clothing Jenny hadn't supplied, that Florence certainly hadn't supplied – with four little kids and Clarrie on the basic wage, they had trouble making ends meet.

The contents of that bag brought back memories of Jenny's own return from Melbourne, Georgie in her belly.

'Who have you been with, Raelene?'

'I was working.'

'Where?'

'In a shop.'

Like a replay. Is that what life was? The same game, played over and over again?

'We have to persevere with her, Jim. We have to try to get her through to eighteen. It's all we can do.'

That was all Christmas was that year, the tree, the tinsel, the pretty baubles, the presents – a getting through it.

*

Georgie was in the newsagents, picking up Charlie's newspaper, when a Christmas card caught her eye, a photograph of a jolly Father Christmas with two little girls on his lap, a pigtailed redhead, and a curly-headed blonde.

It hit one of her nerve endings, the one attached to the *what might have been* nerve. She'd posted no cards, bought none, but she bought that one, and when she got back to the shop and Charlie started on his Yankee dollar lecture, she picked up a biro and addressed the envelope to Cara Norris, care of Armadale Primary School. Sealed it, used one of the shop's stamps on it, then walked away from Charlie's ongoing monologue, walked up to the post office and dropped the envelope into the postbox.

And what harm was there in sending a Christmas card? Every year Sissy Morrison sent a Christmas card to Maisy.

It was too late though. School had broken up for the holidays.

ENGAGEMENT RINGS

*T*hey hanged Ronald Ryan on 3 February 1967. He'd killed a
warder in a failed jailbreak, but no one had believed they'd
actually hang him. This was Australia, and how could a man be
paid enough to murder another in cold blood? How could he sleep
at night knowing that he'd taken a life?

'They fry them with electricity in America,' Raelene said. 'Their
eyes pop out.'

'Raelene!' Jim said.

Christmas was over. Watch-dog Jenny was back on guard duty,
Jim's rules were new. Raelene had never liked Jim and didn't tolerate
his rules well.

'Who are you to dictate to me?'

'This is my house, Raelene. I supply the food on the table.'

'Yeah, and you got her pregnant when she wasn't much older
than me too.'

She'd left school midway through form two, had learnt
a lot of history on the school bus. Wily as a fox, street smart, not
well equipped for life but full up to the ears with useful
information.

It was Raelene who came home with the news that Teddy Hall had bought Vonnie Boyle an engagement ring. Not a surprise to many. They might have been married by now, had Mick Boyle and his wife approved of their daughter's choice. They hadn't, but by January '67 they'd learnt to live with it.

> *Mick and Val Boyle invite you to celebrate with them the engagement of their only daughter, Yvonne, to Edward, son of Elsie and Harry Hall.*

Maisy didn't receive an invitation. She offered to sit with Margot, who had burnt the invitation with her name and Georgie's written on it.

Jen and Jim were going. Harry and Elsie's mob were coming home for the party, even Joey, who hadn't been home in five years.

They'd booked the town hall, and it was like one of the old-time parties. Few left the hall before midnight and the diehards didn't leave until two. Georgie and Jenny stayed until the end, then continued the reunion at Elsie's, where the kids were carried to any available bed, two or three to each, and adults sat where they could, on chair, floor or doorstep.

Georgie didn't walk back across the goat paddock until dawn, didn't notice Margot was missing until she reached for the sugar basin at eleven on the Sunday morning.

Maisy had left her a note.

> *Georgie. Bernie is driving me and Margot down to the hospital. She's gone right out of her mind. I've got a lump on my head the size of an egg. Maisy*

*

Margot spent the night in Willama, but by the time Jenny called the hospital, she'd been transferred to the city.

They were all at Jenny's that morning, Elsie, Harry, Georgie, Maisy and Joey, who lived in Bundaberg, Queensland. He had a wife and three kids up there on a cane farm. He'd flown down alone and would fly north tomorrow.

No one realised it was Georgie's twenty-seventh birthday. She didn't realise it until midafternoon, until she went home.

Harry and Elsie were arguing. 'I raised her from a newborn baby,' Elsie said. 'She's like one of my own.'

'She's not one of your own, and I miss my own,' Harry said. 'And the only reason I miss them is because every time they come home here you've got that lump of a girl stuck to your neck like a limpet.'

'She doesn't deserve to be down there in a house full of crazy people.'

'It's exactly what she deserves. She's turning this place into a madhouse. And I've had enough of it, Else, and if you'd admit it, you have too. Young Georgie has had enough of it.'

'Someone has to care about her.'

'Who did she last care about, Else?'

'She was in love with Teddy.'

'She's in love with herself. All she's ever cared about is herself. If you dropped dead tomorrow, she'd miss your cooking but somebody else would pick up the slack. Our kids would miss you.'

Georgie listened. She couldn't do much else. The house was only a small paddock away. They weren't family but something a whole lot like family, and they never argued, and she wasn't listening to any more of it.

Elsie saw her coming and went to her kitchen, Harry rolled a smoke. 'I'm with Harry on this, Elsie. Margot is staying exactly where she is until they decide to let her out.'

'She doesn't need to be with crazy people, lovey.'

'She doesn't need you to treat her like a five-year-old retard either. Now, say "Happy birthday, Georgie," and stop your arguing.'

She might have been Gertrude laying down the law on her land. She had her voice. She had her command.

They said happy birthday. Harry told her he hadn't realised how much he missed his kids until last night.

'Me too, Harry. It was the best night I've had in years.'

She didn't miss Margot. Wrapped her partial denture that night, slid it into an empty cigarette packet, and addressed it. Some city head-shrinker might get it into her mouth. Fried herself an egg, and left Charlie to feed himself. He could open a can of peaches, which was about all he'd eaten for days.

*

Found his opened peaches, found him in his storeroom at nine on Monday morning, sprawled on his stomach beside the rear door. She thought he was gone. She knelt beside him, rolled him over. He was breathing, shallow breathing, there was a weak pulse in his throat, fluttery. She ran to the phone to call the ambulance, then changed her mind and ran for the post-office kid.

'Charlie's down. I need a lift with him.'

Never a big man, Charlie, shrunken now by his ninety-four years of life; Georgie and the kid carried him out to the ute then she locked the door behind her, gave the kid Margot's denture and fifty cents for stamps, then drove Charlie away from his town, not wanting it to be for the last time but knowing in her heart that it was.

A male orderly took him away. She filled in the admittance papers. His date of birth, his next of kin. *Hilda Timms, daughter.* She added the shop's telephone number and his granddaughter's number. Hilda lived with her daughter and son-in-law, and in the years Georgie had been working for Charlie, she'd never set eye on any one of them. She'd spoken to all three on the phone, back when Charlie had broken his arm, back when he'd been knocked off his bike by a hit-and-run driver, but they hadn't been near him.

She'd been his carer these last years. He'd been her grandfather, tutor and her last link to Granny. Only last Friday she'd promised him a wild party at the town hall for his hundredth birthday. It wasn't so far away.

Hadn't been able to tell the doctor how long he'd been unconscious. Hadn't seen him since Saturday. Should have checked on him yesterday. Could have.

She hung around the hospital until the doctor and nurses finished with him. Aware they may not allow an employee into the ward at that time of day, she told them she was his adopted granddaughter.

Sat with him, smoothed his white hair back from his brow, found his knobbly old arthritic hand and kissed it, and wanted to do more, so she did. Like a granddaughter, she reached low and kissed his brow – and if she didn't have a right to, then no one had the right to. He offered no response. Should have kissed him on Saturday.

Left him then and drove back to the shop, three customers accusing her as she unlocked the door.

'Charlie is in hospital,' she said.

'What's wrong with him this time?'

'Old age.'

One, a stranger, stood back until she switched on the lights, unlocked the cash drawer.

'Who's first?'

Whether he was or not, he went first, a stranger, a male who might have been fifty. And he didn't want a packet of fags. He was the health inspector for the area.

'Do your worst,' she said and turned to deal with Grace Dobson.

And the coot headed straight for Charlie's storeroom.

Two customers at the counter when the kid from the post office came in to give her the change from Margot's denture, and a brown-paper-wrapped parcel.

'How's the old boy?'

'They didn't say,' Georgie said, tossing the parcel to the counter, wishing the health inspector had chosen another day.

She walked down to the storeroom once the shop cleared, saw

him standing over Charlie's unmade bed, saw him pick up the opened can of preserved peaches, look at a bottle of rum, and at the table, sticky with spilt peach syrup and more. She'd wiped it down on Friday. Would have wiped it down today. Sighed and walked back to her place behind the counter.

The inspector poked around for an hour or more, then presented her with a pink copy of his findings, which he proceeded to go through, item by item.

Fire danger. Mouse faeces.

'One of the conditions of my employment was an ability to read bad handwriting,' Georgie said and filed his pink report in the cash drawer.

'I'll be back today week,' he said.

Saluted him, Hitler fashion. Followed him out. Liked the car he drove. Didn't like him. Lit a smoke and watched him disappear to the west.

Should phone Charlie's family. The hospital might.

Do it later.

At five she rang the hospital. No change. At ten past, she decided it was probably late enough for Charlie's grandson-in-law to be home. On the phone, he sounded more human than his women.

No such luck. Hilda took the call.

'Charlie is in hospital,' she said. Stood, then, allowing his daughter to hammer holes through her eardrum while she lit a cigarette and looked around a shop little altered in the years she'd been standing behind the counter. She gave that screechy-voiced battleaxe one cigarette of her time, and when it burned away, she thought about dropping the butt into the cash drawer. Not enough paper money in it to burn. Plastic melted.

Dropped it on the floor, ground it out with the heel of her shoe, then reached for the forgotten parcel the post-office kid had delivered.

She hadn't looked at it, and when she did, she saw her own name on it.

Surprise parcels in the post may have been commonplace to some. Georgie had never opened one. Granny used to send food parcels when they lived in Armadale. She'd enjoyed watching them opened. She swapped the telephone to her left hand, allowing her left ear to take its share of the screech, and with her right hand eased off the string, picked off sticky tape, thought about telling Hilda about the health inspector's pink list. No space to say it in.

There was something soft beneath the brown paper, something as light as a feather . . . like the presents of dresses and pants Jenny used to send from Sydney, way, way back during the war.

'God Almighty,' she breathed, exposing a slit of emerald green. 'I've got a customer,' she lied, and the phone back on the receiver, she lifted a top free of its paper.

It was a superfine knit, silky, a rich emerald green with a silver lurex pattern woven around the low-cut neckline. As she held it high, a card fell to the floor and slid beneath the counter. She dived to retrieve it.

A birthday card, a woman in profile, head down, with hair as red as Georgie's.

Dear Georgie,
Thanks so much for your Christmas card. I hope you have a
wonderful birthday. Cara

*

Georgie never cried. She could sit through a tear-jerker movie and not shed a tear. Okay, so the world had ended the day Granny died. That was different, and she'd been a kid anyway, but there she was, standing behind the counter, blubbering over a birthday card and a gorgeous green top, just standing there, struck dumb by her tears or by that top, or by that *have a wonderful birthday*.

How had she known?

Her mother must have known.

Loved that green, absolutely adored it, and more than adoring the top, the colour and the knowing that her half-sister had known her well enough to choose a top she loved. It broke her up, or released floodgates she'd been controlling since she'd found Charlie on the floor.

And Bernie Macdonald came in for two packets of Marlboro and he caught her.

She turned her back, wiping her eyes with fingers, and taking her time in finding his brand of smokes. Slid them down the counter towards him, then hid her face behind her hair while writing his docket.

'The old bloke gone?' Bernie asked. News travelled like wildfire through this town.

'Unconscious,' Georgie said, allowing him to blame Charlie for her tears.

'He had a good innings.' Bernie pocketed his smokes, his docket, but didn't leave. 'Heard anything new about your sister?'

Georgie shook her head, shook some sense into it. Jenny had said she'd ring Melbourne today. She hadn't seen Jenny.

'Mum couldn't do anything with her. We didn't know they'd send her down to their nuthouse.'

Nuthouse. As a kid she'd known that Amber was in a madhouse, or at a funny farm. These days they were psychiatric hospitals.

What's in a name?

'Mum is going down next week with Macka,' he said. 'I suppose you know that your grandmother has disappeared off the planet.'

Georgie didn't have a grandmother, didn't know if Amber was missing or not and didn't care. Wanted him to go and he wouldn't. She ripped a length from a toilet roll she kept beneath the counter, blew her nose while he gave her the details of Margot's attack on Maisy.

Margot liked brooms and broomsticks. Jenny had been on the wrong end of one. Georgie had wrestled a few brooms from Margot's hands.

She removed the notes from the cash drawer, didn't count them, just stuffed them into a calico bag she pushed deep beneath the counter, then reached for the light switch. And Bernie took the hint. She followed him out. He lit a smoke while she padlocked the door.

'Take it easy then,' he said and he got into his brand-new ute, and Georgie wanted his ute. She got into Charlie's and drove to Jenny's house.

Found her at the sink preparing vegetables. Trudy at the table, drawing fairies with colourful wings. As Jenny took the green top into her hands, Raelene took it from her.

'How did she know it was your birthday?' she asked.

'Her mother?' Georgie said.

'Myrtle didn't know,' Jenny said.

'She might be your fairy godmother,' Trudy said.

'More like a lesbo girlfriend she's pretending is some long-lost cousin,' Raelene said.

'Watch your mouth or I'll wash it out for you,' Jenny said and turned back to the sink, to place a lid on a pot, add salt to another.

Georgie reclaimed her top. She wrapped it and picked up her bunch of keys.

'Stay for dinner,' Jenny said.

'Have you got enough?'

'Stew stretches, and I always do too many potatoes.'

*

A leftover from her years with Ray. He'd demanded mountains of mashed potato, and if she hadn't piled enough onto his plate, his eyes would become wide, greedy. Raelene's eyes were his tonight. They wanted that top.

She looked more like Florence than Ray. She had her colouring, her build, but none of her gentle simplicity. If anything other than thoughts of immediate self-gratification went on in that girl's head, Jenny hadn't seen it.

She hadn't wanted to take her back either, or to step back so soon into her role of watch-dog, not after England. Like a dream now, that freedom to wake in the morning beside Jim in a strange bed in a strange land and to know the day belonged only to them. No meals to prepare, no clothes line to fill.

Trudy was so easy to manage, too easy. She'd follow Jim around the garden, pulling weeds with him, would amuse herself in the kitchen while Jenny cooked, spend hours playing with her stable of dolls, or sit on the veranda with Jim, reading. Raelene was wound up and ready to go when she rose from her bed, and she didn't wind down until she was back in that bed. Six times a week and twice on Sundays Jenny decided to give up on Raelene.

She'd got a lift back to town with a trio of bikies, and Jenny scared stiff she'd come back pregnant. Not street smart Raelene. She was on the pill.

Jenny had prayed in her youth for such a pill. She didn't need it now. She'd wanted to have babies to Jim. It hadn't happened, and if it had, it wouldn't have been another Jimmy – probably another Lorna.

Her mind travelled while she drained the silverbeet, added a dash of cream, grated in a little cheese, added pepper, then left it to sit while she drained beans, mashed the potatoes and wondered where Margot was eating tonight, what she was eating.

She blamed herself for the mess Margot had become. She didn't blame herself for Raelene. She'd shared her bed with that kid for seven years, had sewn her the prettiest frocks, bought her the prettiest shoes. Homemade was no longer good enough for Raelene. She wanted Georgie's green top.

She'd unwrapped it, had it in her hands again.

Take your eyes off it, Georgie, and she'll have it, Jenny thought.

Losing her father too young could have had something to do with the way she was. Developing young had pushed her too fast towards boys. She wouldn't turn sixteen till next November.

'Run out and tell Daddy his dinner is ready, Trudy,' she said and Trudy ran.

Give me a child to the age of seven and I will show you the man, someone had once written. It hadn't applied to Raelene – or maybe it had. She'd been close to seven when Ray had been killed.

She glanced at Georgie who had wrapped her top again and this time stuffed the parcel into her handbag and not a comment out of her.

Her early life had been as disrupted as Raelene's. What she'd seen of marriage as a kid had probably put her off it for good. She'd lost her brother, lost her grandmother, and look at her.

'Daddy said can he please have five minutes' more.' Trudy was back.

'Tell him four and a half and not one second more,' Jenny said, and that little kid ran again to do her bidding.

Why?

How?

Born of Margot, cut from her two months early, her first weeks of life spent in an oxygen crib, handled only by nurses. What did I do with her that I didn't do with Raelene? Or is it the compatibility or incompatibility of blood lines? Do some click, find their missing links and join in perfect harmony, and others fight in the womb and pop out problem children?

And Cara, conceived of rape, her father any one of five drunken Yankee sailors.

The experts said environment was seventy-five per cent of the child. She'd stayed at school, was a schoolteacher, still called Amberley home.

But didn't live there.

Who was she beneath the surface? Why had she come to Woody Creek, and how had she known Georgie's date of birth?

THE LETTER

*C*ara had been attempting to work out who she was since she'd learnt she wasn't who she'd been raised to think she was. She hadn't touched her typewriter since returning from Woody Creek. On the day Morrie and his parents flew home, she'd buried it beneath an ex-Amberley sheeting shroud. In the months since, she'd buried her dreams of marrying Morrie and living happily ever after.

She'd tried to cremate her manuscript. The burning of one page in the sink had caused so much smoke she'd given up that idea fast and sealed it into its giant envelope with yards and more yards of sticky tape, then kicked it deep beneath her bed. So much for magnificent dreams.

An account she'd opened so she might one day buy a car paid for a twelve-inch-screen television with a rabbit's-ear aerial. She'd spent a lot of nights twisting those rabbit ears and ended up connecting wires to them, then connecting the wires to metal coathangers she looped over the top of the sitting room's venetian blind. It didn't look great but she now received a clean picture, or did on two channels – and not a lot worth watching on either of them.

She hadn't told Myrtle and Robert she'd bought it. Hadn't told them she'd been up to Woody Creek either. She went to work, came home, ate what she could be bothered preparing while the television attempted to convince her that one brand of coffee, one brand of soap, one brand of washing detergent was superior to another. She bought what was on special.

Called home on Sunday nights from the box on the corner. Rarely extended her calls beyond the allocated three minutes. Nothing to say. She wrote letters and posted them to England. Morrie wrote back.

Marion swore he had a girlfriend or fiancée in England. Cathy said he didn't. She said his mother had been in hospital again, that they'd removed her second breast, that she was currently having X-ray treatment.

She said that James Collins was being given early release – for good behaviour. And when had that swine's behaviour been good? In January '64 he'd been sentenced to five years. He'd served three, plus the months he was in jail prior to the trial. Apparently they counted, and they shouldn't have counted. And he should have been given twenty years anyway.

She'd returned to the classroom with a new batch of nine year olds and, determined to start out as she planned to continue, she'd worked their little socks off them. On her first day back the office woman had handed her an envelope, her name on it in large black block print. She'd seen *HATE* in that block print, seen the tattoo on Dino Collins's knuckles and known he'd found her. Hadn't wanted to touch it. Hadn't opened it until she was home, in her flat, the door locked, the safety chain on.

And it had been from Georgie, a cute Christmas card, two little girls seated on a chubby Santa's lap, and ten words. *To Cara. Hope Santa was good to you. Love Georgie*

Relief and a different form of fear. She'd understood its message. Given different circumstances, she and Georgie may well have sat together on Santa's lap.

She'd put it away. Knew she should have tossed it away. Hadn't.

Some things are fated, even if we don't recognise fate's hand at the time. On the Saturday morning after receiving the card, she'd found that green top amid a pile of shop-soiled garments on a table at the Melbourne market and, recognising its quality, she'd bought it and handwashed it in her sink. The stain came out.

She never wore green, but every time she'd looked at it, every time she'd sighted that Christmas card in her desk drawer, she'd known who should wear green.

Then in late February, given the job of searching old school files, she'd unearthed her half-siblings, Georgina, Margot and James Morrison-King. Their dates of birth were there, their Armadale address.

So she'd posted the top to reach Georgie on or near to her birthday.

*

On Friday 30 March, the office woman handed her a second envelope, similarly addressed in large black capitals, a smaller, but chubbier envelope. She had no fear in opening that one. Ripped her way into it before she left the building, read two pages at the tram stop and the rest on the tram, four pages, with little wasted space on any one of them.

Dear Cara,

I'm not much of a letter writer, more familiar with docket books, but today has been one of those days you hope you'll never repeat, so you're about to cop its overflow.

Charlie is in hospital and they say that his kidneys have shut down. He's in his nineties. I know people don't live forever but I was convinced Charlie would. I took him down to the hospital this morning, and when I got back, the health inspector was waiting for me. He spent an hour or so sniffing out Charlie's pet plague of mice and his longjohns, then gave me a week to basically remodel the shop or he'll close us down. The fact that Charlie is dying was water off a duck's, and when I rang Charlie's daughter, it didn't concern her a whole lot more. She's no doubt looking forward to inheriting his mice and his longjohns. Then your present turned up. I don't know how you knew it was my birthday, but that top is absolutely fabulous, so I thought I'd let you know that you managed to turn the worst day of my life into something a whole lot better. I was convinced you took one look at us the night you came up to Woody Creek and decided to keep your distance.

I've got a fair idea of what you were hoping to find. I've been imagining finding my father since I was four years old – when I found out I actually had one. Jenny gave me a framed newspaper photograph of him and I thought because he'd been in the newspapers he was a famous movie star. I used to show it to everyone and tell them that when I grew up I was going to be a famous movie star like my daddy. I was about seven when I took the newspaper out of its frame and read what he'd been famous for. They called him the redheaded water-pistol bandit. He robbed banks, jewellers, you name it, with a worn-out water pistol – wouldn't even shoot water. Cops in two or three States had been after him.

Jenny met him when she was fifteen, or he ran her down in one of his stolen cars then gave her a job cleaning his classy house – which turned out to be someone else's classy house he'd decided to borrow. Nine or so months later I turned up, but by then, he was in jail. Most crims reoffend, or so a cop told me once, so I'd probably find him easy enough – if I had the guts to go looking.

I'm sitting in the kitchen, Granny's clock is telling me it's almost half past eleven. It may be right but usually isn't. My watch tells me it's three o'clock – I haven't found time to wind it today and tonight I don't want to. My mind won't stay away from Charlie. I know he's not going to make it this time, so I'm drinking his Christmas wine and sort of wishing him a safe trip. I might add that tonight's bottle is a vast improvement on the one we shared, so it's no punishment emptying it.

I think this must be Granny's old writing pad. I didn't buy it. I never write letters. No one to write to. The last time I used this one was to write to Jenny when she was in Frankston. I can almost feel Granny in it, telling me not to go wasting all of her writing pad. Too late now. I've got one page left.

Margot is in Melbourne, in a psych hospital. Her old boyfriend got engaged and she went off her head and attacked her grandmother with a broomstick. Maisy drove into town to get one of her sons – one of them is Margot's father – anyhow, I'd better stop airing the family's dirty linen or you'll put on your running shoes. Blame Charlie – or his wine. I think I've had a glass too much – too many. There is a definite difference between having had enough and having had too much. Have too much and you do something about it, having enough forces you to persist in bashing your head against brick walls until more than enough becomes too much . . .

I'd finish on that note, except for Granny. Waste not, want not, she used to drum into us when we were kids, so I need to finish this page. She was the town midwife for years. People would come looking for her at all hours. She'd had enough, but she'd saddle up her horse, pick up her basket and off she'd go.

Before I sign off, one more thing. When we were kids we had Granny and Jenny, which I know is a lot more than some have, but Margot also had Nana Maisy and the Macdonalds. Jimmy had Grandpa Hooper and his aunties. I had Granny and Jenny and nothing more. So, to get to the point of what I'm attempting to say, there is plenty of unfilled space in my life for another blood relative. All written applications for this position

will be replied to, though I can't guarantee the same goes for
telephone applications. Once Charlie has gone, then I'm gone.
Love Georgie
P.S. Jen and I both want to know how you knew my birth date.
G

*

Cara folded the pages and slid them back into the envelope. She was
going out tonight. Wished she'd known her horseriding midwife
granny, instead of Gran Norris. Wished she was going out with
Morrie. Wasn't.

She had a date with Chris Marino, a solicitor she'd met at one of
Helen's dinner parties – Helen, a new teacher, or new to Armadale,
enjoyed showing off her cooking skills. Chris, one of her husband's
colleagues, had offered Cara a lift home and she'd accepted. Then
a week later he'd called her at school and said he had two tickets to
a show on Friday night and would she like to see it with him.

She wanted to see it. He was probably the type who would
expect payment in bed after the show, but if he was, he was doomed
to disappointment. There was only one man she'd be willing to
hop into bed with.

*

The show was not spectacular, nor was the company. His car
was. He was punctual. She shouldn't have worn high heels. They
made her taller than her date. He had a pleasant face, was pleasant
enough company. He expected to be invited up for coffee, but
took her refusal well. In points out of ten, she'd give Chris Marino
five. She'd give Morrie ten plus – then delete a point for distance
and two more for his sick mother.

Late when she got in. Shoes off, frock off, dressing-gown on,
she made coffee and took it to the table where Georgie's letter
tempted her to read it again.

There is plenty of unfilled space in my life for another blood relative. All written applications for this position will be replied to . . .

Cara glanced at her sheet-shrouded typewriter, a white useless lump on the landscape, and considered unshrouding it and writing a fast application for the job of blood relative. Georgie had few. Cara had none.

I can't get further involved. I don't want to get further involved. I knew that posting that top would say more than I meant it to say.

Had it said more than she meant?

I was convinced you took one look at us that night and decided to keep your distance . . .

Which was pretty much how she had felt. She'd got off the bus at the city depot feeling desolate, and desperate enough to spend money on a taxi home where she'd washed that town out of her hair. She'd been desolate enough to consider spending the September holidays at Amberley. Then Morrie came back from Perth and she'd put Woody Creek away.

Everyone she knew was either married or getting married, or had been married, and those who weren't were bed hopping. He'd never said he loved her. He'd kissed her, but never once had he stepped over some line he'd drawn across their relationship.

He either had a fiancée at home, or a boyfriend. Marion had suggested that too.

It was after midnight before she removed the sheeting shroud and wound paper into the carriage, not to write a letter, or an application, but to make a copy of Georgie's letter and to somehow trap her voice on paper.

It became much more. Eight pages she wound into the carriage, fast pages. Words she'd been denying for too long were pouring out from some place deep within. Two o'clock when she read what she'd written. It was the beginning of something.

THE MOUSE NEST

Sunday, and Charlie still hanging on to life, or just hiding in there, planning to do the impossible again – or maybe hanging on long enough to make peace with his daughter. Hilda had said over the phone that she wasn't a well woman but would try to get down at the weekend. She hadn't yesterday.

Jenny had. They'd sat by Charlie's bed for two hours, waiting for him to leave. A couple of times they'd thought he'd stopped breathing, but he'd got in a breath and slept on.

Robert and Mrs Fulton were driving down this afternoon to sit with Charlie – their relationship was more friends than tenant and landlord. Georgie couldn't sit with him today. Mick Boyle senior was only free on Sundays and he'd offered to take a few loads of junk to the tip.

Everyone in town knew the health inspector was threatening to close the store. The locals may not miss Charlie but they'd miss his shop and the Friday deliveries if those green doors were locked. Several had offered their assistance, Emma Fulton amongst them. Georgie had accepted her offer. They'd worked together on Sunday morning, with buckets, mops and scrubbing brush. Mick Boyle arrived after midday, loading anything the women pitched out the rear door. There was plenty.

Two o'clock now, Emma Fulton gone home, the last of the crates from the yard loaded, the last rusting tins, old stock Charlie would never toss, tossed. And his easy chair, its springs bursting through the fabric. It was all loaded.

Back in the fifties, Mick had moved an old iron bed from Charlie's house to his storeroom and helped put it together. Today he pulled it apart and added its pieces to the load.

There was an old wooden crate pushed in deep beneath the bed. Georgie picked it up, and beneath it found one of the old foot-square tins biscuits used to come in to be weighed out by the pound. They came wrapped in individual packets now, and had for years. She pitched both crate and tin, then scrambled onto the truck's tray to retrieve the tin, Mick watching her.

'What is it?'

She lifted the lid before jumping down. 'Some sort of photos,' she said.

The tin placed inside the rear door she assisted Mick in roping down the load, thanked him for his help, then watched him out onto the road. Retrieved that biscuit tin then and lifted the lid again. Photographs of Queen Lizzie in that tin.

It rode home with her, on her passenger seat.

Another bottle of Charlie's Christmas wine bit the dust that afternoon. Its wired-down cork suggested it contained something fizzy, and when she got it uncapped, she wasn't disappointed. Drank its bubbles as they gushed out, wished she'd thought to chill it, but she wasn't drinking for pleasure, not today. She needed its hit.

Too much adrenalin flooding her system for it to hit. She took another dose then several more, understanding Shakey Lewis's need for grog, wondering if Laurie Morgan had been an alcoholic, if he'd primed himself before he'd gone out to rob a bank.

That's what she was planning to do – or to rob Hilda, Charlie's daughter.

Lit a cigarette, placed it down on the ashtray, placed the bottle beside it, then picked up the biscuit tin, emptied its contents onto the table and stood looking at it, her internal organs shaking.

Didn't know if she was shaking because she'd found Charlie's stash or because she'd almost missed finding it. She'd always known he had his own pool of money hidden somewhere in the store-room, that he could put his hand on a hundred pound if he'd needed it. She hadn't known what he'd stored it in, where he'd kept whatever he'd stored it in. All week she'd been cleaning. Every night after work when she'd dropped off a uteload to the tip, she'd hoped she hadn't tossed Charlie's stash. She'd checked beneath the weighty old chair, wondering if Charlie had padded it with his filched notes. It hadn't been moved since she'd started working at the shop. Nor had the iron bed. She'd changed the sheets on it, swept around it, swiped beneath it, swiped out a lost shoe or sock on occasions, but never his crate or biscuit tin.

Alarm bells should have rung when she picked it up. Perhaps on a subconscious level they had. The instant the biscuit tin left her hand a warning siren had gone off in her brain.

'Just counting my bickies,' he'd said once when she'd caught him on his knees beside his bed.

Big bickies, wads of it. There had to be years of his filching on the table, and probably his rent money from Miss Blunt. She'd always paid him in cash. Mrs Fulton had at one time paid him in cash.

Until a few years ago he'd spent his ill-gotten gains on packets of shares. When his hearing had let him down, he'd accused his city broker of mumbling and stopped calling him. He hadn't stopped filching any old note that landed in his cash drawer. Real money, he'd called it. The plastic notes he'd considered play money had been safe. There would be no play money in his stash.

She stood shaking her head, staring at rolls of it, green, blue, red. Hilda's once Charlie was gone. Everything would go to her. He had no one else – other than his granddaughter.

And right or wrong, they were not getting their hands on these wads.

'Blame the water-pistol bandit, Charlie. It's in the blood,' she said.

Perished rubber bands no longer bound a few of the wads, but paper notes too long bound retained their curl. String had done a better job. She picked up a string-tied wad and felt its weight on her palm, picked up another, weighing each before tossing it down. She didn't know where to start, if she should start, what she'd do once she started, so she took another sip of wine, then two more.

A small vegetable knife cut the strings from half-a-dozen wads of varying weights. She removed rubber bands, bits of old rubber bands, then swept them and the strings and the mouse dirt into her palm. The mess went into the stove. Rubber stinks. Burning string and mouse dirt stink. The notes on the table stank.

How much was there? Two thousand? Three?

Nothing to be done about a few of the notes. A few genera- tions of mice must have given birth in that biscuit tin, chewed on Charlie's money, shat on it. She fetched the hearth shovel and brush and swept around the clusters of notes, swept up confetti which appeared to be a mutilated fiver. It went into the stove.

'Money to burn, Granny,' she said, then washed her hands, wiped them on the seat of her slacks and lit another cigarette.

She'd have to sort it by colour. That was the only way to go. Stood then, smoke in her left hand, her right tossing curled notes to three corners of the table, red to the right corner, blue to the left, green to her left. And the smell of mouse grew strong.

'Launder it,' she advised, and handful by handful she trans- ferred Charlie's ill-gotten gains to the sink, added water, Rinso, a dash of Dettol.

'Just floating a loan, Charlie,' she said, attempting to sink the mess of paper with her palms, to agitate the blue, red and green pudding through the suds. Left them to soak while she wiped the table with Dettol and drank a little more wine.

Margot liked white towels. What you can't cure, you find a way to live with. She didn't need them at the moment, so Georgie spread four to cover the table, then prepared a bucket of rinsing water, well laced with vinegar.

Charlie had helped himself to a lot of red but more of blue. She rinsed the red first, placing each carefully on a towel, hoping Elsie or Harry didn't decide to pop over, that Jenny didn't take it into her head to drive down, or Raelene ride down. The thought of any one of them arriving suggested she prop chairs beneath the doorknobs.

She worked on, rinsing, shaking excess water, flattening each note, her mind wandering until it was time to spread another towel. The old clock donged three, and too soon four, but she'd emptied the sink, found two escapees beneath the table and given them an individual wash and rinse. The last of the notes were on tea towels, over the seats of the chairs. Towards the end, Charlie hadn't allowed any old note to get away. He'd even filched brown ten-bob notes.

To Georgie, it had gone beyond money. She had five towels' worth of red, eight of blue, forget the green and brown. It was obvious without needing to count that there were riches in this kitchen. She'd placed the notes carefully, nine lengthwise along the towels, and nine widthwise, Margot's white towels made to measure for the job. Granny's raggedy old towels were crowded, the notes overlapping, but religiously Georgie had stuck to nines.

Back in kindergarten she'd discovered the magic of that number, had learnt her nine times tables to disprove Mrs McPherson's theory that the total of all multiplications by nine added up to nine. Amy McPherson had been right.

Nine times nine was eighty-one, multiply that by red ten-pound notes and it totalled eight hundred and ten. Multiply that by five towels and it totalled four thousand and fifty – and that was only the red. She had eight towels' worth of fivers. $81 \times 5 = 405 \times 8 = 3240 + 4050 = 7290$. Now change that into dollars. She had

$14,580 in that kitchen – plus the green and the brown. And she had to sit down. Her wine bottle was almost empty.

Five o'clock when she fetched the ironing board and plugged in the iron. A quick press dried and flattened paper. It made a few of those notes look brand new. She stacked them, by colour, on dry chairs, rubber-banding them when the piles threatened to topple. Steam filled the room, steam smelling of Rinso and vinegar, with overtones of hot mouse, but by seven she was done, the notes were packed into a plastic bag, sealed with sticky tape and the bag slid deep beneath her mattress. No one entered her bedroom. No one was likely to lift her mattress if they did enter her bedroom.

A mountain of soggy towels on the floor, fifty per cent of them fit for the rubbish heap. Tossed the rest into the bath and lit the chip heater, gave them a decent dose of Dettol then left them to soak overnight, which should eradicate the mouse stink.

Charlie was still hanging in there on Monday. He was still hanging in there on Tuesday. Then Wednesday, and the phone ringing when she unlocked the doors. She knew it was the hospital to tell her Charlie had gone.

It was his daughter.

'A chap will be arriving there around midday to do a valuation on the stock and building,' she said.

'Has he gone?' Georgie asked.

He hadn't, or not to Hilda's knowledge. Georgie didn't bother to claim a phantom customer. She hung up on her, picked up her keys and relocked the door. If her chap arrived to do his valuation, he wouldn't be getting in, not today.

She was at the hospital by ten, holding Charlie's hand and telling him about Hilda's chap, about the health inspector, and asking him why he'd bothered helping himself to the ten-bob notes. She told him she'd gone into the money-laundering business, that she was looking on her ill-gotten gains as a bonus for thirteen years of faithful service. He'd heard little of what anyone had said to him these past five years and he hadn't regained consciousness since she'd found him on the storeroom floor. Sleeping his way to death, a sister told her.

At two o'clock that afternoon Charlie wandered off to join his Jeany, and he did it so silently that for a moment Georgie was unaware he'd gone. Kissed him then for the second time in her life and got out of that ward, not wanting to know what happened next. Walked fast to his old ute, telling herself how ridiculous it would be to weep for him – and she didn't. She still couldn't believe he'd done it, had all but convinced herself that he'd beat the odds again, that she'd kidnap him again from the old fogies' home. Couldn't imagine Woody Creek without him, or that shop.

Had her mind been on the job of driving, she may have noticed the motor's first complaint. Her mind wasn't on the job, and fifteen miles from home Charlie's ute decided to follow its master to the graveyard. It did the right thing by her, as had its old master. With its last breath, it panted over to the verge of the road, sighed, and that was that. She sat on its running board, smoking and staring at a dry paddock, at dusty sheep, until a truckie stopped to offer her a lift into town.

Told Teddy Hall that Charlie had gone. Told him where the old ute might be found. He told her it could be the fuel pump. She told him to give it a good funeral, then walked around to the shop and let herself in through the rear door where she wrote a note, wrote it large on the lid of a cardboard carton she sticky-taped in the window.

CHARLIE GOT HIS WINGS TODAY. SHOP CLOSED UNTIL FURTHER NOTICE.

*

Folk can outlive their time, their old contemporaries. The town had stood still for Vern Hooper, for Gertrude. Charlie slept his way to death at two on Wednesday and Hilda got rid of the body at four-thirty on Thursday.

Had he died three years ago, a dozen of the brigade would have been there. All bar two had beaten him in the race for the cemetery.

Few shops closed for him. Miss Blunt closed her doors, and Robert Fulton. That's all. Had George Macdonald been alive, he might have silenced his mill for Charlie. Maybe he'd shake Charlie's hand on the other side. Maybe he wouldn't. They'd never got on in life.

Teddy Hall was at the funeral, wearing a suit. Vonnie had chosen it. She'd told him he had to go, that he was a business owner and the right thing to do was to pay his respects to another business owner. Charlie had always found a job or two for Shakey Lewis. He was there, cleaned up for the day. Enough were there. A few extras came to the wake at the pub where mouse money, the green and brown of it, was shouting two free beers plus sandwiches and tea. To the last, Charlie had enjoyed a couple of cold beers at six.

Hilda and her daughter, who must have had that funeral director lined up before Charlie drew his final breath, turned up for their cup of tea, still dabbing at crocodile tears. Georgie couldn't look at them. She gave the shop keys and a handful of mail to Maisy to give to them. She'd called into the post office on her way to the funeral.

One letter amongst them hadn't been addressed to Mr C.J. White, proprietor. She read it at the wake.

Dear Georgie,
I've been fighting an internal battle since I left Woody Creek. One day I decide to go back and ask Jenny every question I've ever wanted to ask. The next, I don't want to know the answers.

I thought I was an only child until I turned fifteen. That's when Mum and Dad told me about Jenny, that she'd had three other children. Sometime later I found photos of Jimmy in Mum's album. He became very real to me. I used to tell myself that if I'd grown up with my big brother, he would have looked after me. She had no photograph of Jenny's girls and no memory of their names. You and Margot were never quite real to me. Mum told me I looked like Jenny, but I could never raise an image of her in my mind, other than a shadow sighted from the corner of my eye.

Mum and Dad were in their forties when they adopted me. They've been wonderful parents, but they have families they can trace back to England. I always felt like an alien who landed on their doorstep.

There has always been a blank wall behind me. I know now who lives behind that wall, that you live there, that behind you there are grandparents, a horseriding midwife, and Archie Foote.

I'd like to see you again, but on neutral ground. If you ever find yourself in Melbourne, give me a call at the above number, during school hours, and we'll have dinner somewhere and get to know each other.

How did I know the date of your birthday? That comes under the heading of coincidence. One of the teachers is having a retirement party in June. We had the old records out attempting to trace a few of her ex-students. And there you all were, Georgie, Margot and James Morrison-King, with your dates of birth.

Best wishes,
Cara

THE VISITOR

*G*roups of mothers congregated at the school gate at three-thirty, their kids cluttering the footpath. Cara walked around them, dodging a few missile kids, her interest on a tram she was intent on catching. Had she been looking at the mothers she may have noticed a tall one with long copper hair.

'The old school hasn't changed much,' Georgie said, falling into step beside her.

Now look what you've done, was Cara's first thought. Her second, I could have at least combed my hair. No time for a third. A response was necessary.

'You're about the last person I expected to see today.'

'Charlie died. I'm out of a job – out of wheels too. I came down to buy a new ute –and buy you dinner if you're doing nothing better.'

Was she pleased to see her? Yes. No. More yes than no – except she looked like a frumpy schoolmarm shaking hands with Miss Universe, and she was going to miss her tram. Except nothing. There'd be another tram.

Could she bear to go out to dinner with her, looking like a frump? Did she dare take her to the flat?

Plenty more flats too.

'My flat's only a couple of stops away. I need a shower. School-kids shed germs like dogs shed fleas.'

'If you tell me you only use white towels, the deal's off,' Georgie said.

Loading schoolkids onto a tram took time. They caught it then, Miss Norris and Miss Universe sitting side by side, school-kids and their mothers staring, Cara asked what was wrong with white towels.

'I just saw Margot,' Georgie said. 'She's ...' She shrugged. 'She likes white towels and white uniforms. They've got her in blue – she's in a psychiatric place down here.'

Nothing to say to that. Wished she'd worn something decent to school this morning. Wished she'd washed her dishes before she'd gone to school.

'The old trams haven't changed much,' Georgie said.

'Melbourne's bone-shakers. I couldn't live without them. Sydney got rid of theirs.'

'I'm not used to riding in anything I'm not controlling.'

Talk of trams, utes and car yards carried them to Cara's stop and as they walked the last block to the flat Cara apologised in advance for the mess she'd walked away from this morning.

'You're talking to the wrong person about housework. I eat out of a saucepan to save washing up. I fried bread and eggs in a cast-iron frying pan this morning, ate out of it and left it on the hob. Blame our fathers for that. We didn't get it from Jenny,' Georgie said.

'How is she?' Just something to say.

'She went to England a while back.'

'My boyfriend lives in England.'

'A long-distance romance. Probably the way to go.'

They climbed the stairs side by side, Georgie looking around as Cara unlocked her door. 'It was all I could afford when I moved in, now I can't be bothered moving.'

'I could take to living alone, though not down here. The traffic seems worse when you're not driving in it.'

'It gets worse every year. Make yourself a coffee while I shower, Georgie. Open the window if you want to smoke – oh, and my towels are ex-Amberley, white with green stripes.'

'Green's good,' Georgie said.

*

It was easier later, her hair washed, a little makeup applied, clad like Georgie, in jeans and a pretty top.

She made coffee, discussed the school, spoke of the teachers. Only one name was familiar to Georgie, Miss Hadley.

'She's the one retiring in June,' Cara said.

'I thought she was ancient when I knew her. She taught me for a few months. She taught Margot for the best part of two years. I'll guarantee she hasn't forgotten her.'

'Would you be interested in coming down for her party?'

'I could be anywhere by June.'

They didn't go out for dinner. But at six Cara, now asking her questions, learned that Jenny had been adopted by Granny Foote's daughter, and that Archie Foote, the philandering doctor, had been Jenny's father – Itchy-foot, Georgie called him. Granny's itchy-footed quack.

They ate salad sandwiches at seven, and at eight Cara admitted to owning a fold-up bed.

'It's as hard as the hobs. I sleep on it when Mum and Dad come down.'

'Are you shockproofed yet?'

'Against what?'

'You probably ought to know what will be under your fold-up bed before you go offering it.' Georgie had left her zip-up sports bag beside the door. She retrieved it, slid the zip and dug deep to remove a shoe box. 'I need to tell someone anyway. It's screwing up my sleep. Blame the hereditary factor,' she said, lifting the lid.

The mind does a double-take when it's expecting new shoes and it sees a plastic bag full of banknotes. Cara's chair tipped over as she sprang to her feet and stepped back.

'Charlie had been sleeping on it for years.' No reply from Cara. She was having second, third and fifth thoughts. 'The health inspector made me clean out the storeroom,' Georgie explained.

Cara had backed to the stove and could go no further.

'I wish I had a camera,' Georgie said.

'Put it away.'

'Charlie stole it first, then the mice stole it from Charlie. I baited the mice. I suppose that makes it robbery with violence,' she said and lit a cigarette, amused by Cara's reaction.

'How much?'

'A hell of a lot. Fourteen thousand, if I can change it into dollars. 'It's Charlie's black money, his stash – all old money. Want me to get a hotel room?'

'What do you mean by black money?'

'He'd been filching the big notes from the cash drawer since I started working for him. He didn't rob a bank – just the tax department. Some of it would be rent. He owned half-a-dozen properties. At least one of his tenants paid him in cash.' She blew three perfect smoke rings and Cara stood shaking her head and watching them grow.

'He used to buy shares with it, when he could use the phone. He'd reached the stage where he couldn't understand what they said and ended up with shares in some goldmine.' She blew three more rings. 'You're thinking, what the hell have I got myself mixed up with? How the hell do I get myself out of this?'

'I'm thinking, what if someone walked in?'

'Anyone likely to?'

'Put it away.'

'It will still be here,' Georgie said, but she placed the lid on the shoe box, placed the shoe box into her zip-up bag and zipped it. 'All gone,' she said.

'Whose . . . Who does it belong to?'

'Me.'

'You know what I mean, Georgie.'

'Everything he owned will go to his daughter, who he hadn't seen since I was thirteen, when she took off in his car with anything he had of value. Since '58 he's spent weeks in hospital. He was in a coma for a week before he died, and she didn't even come down to kiss him goodbye. She got down soon enough to bury him, though.'

Georgie drew on her smoke and puffed out two more smoke rings.

'How do you do that?'

'Practise. I only started smoking so I could learn how,' she said. 'Do you want me to go?'

'What are you going to do with it?'

'Change it to dollars. I'm doing Charlie's estate a favour by not allowing it to turn up. If I handed it in, the tax mob would go through him to get their due, and I'd probably get the blame for it. I've been fiddling his books for years, covering up for his filching, and I've got a ton of share certificates at the bank that he bought for me with his ill-gotten gains.

'His daughter would go after my blood. I kidnapped Charlie twice from an old folks' home where she'd had him incarcerated. I know he would have wanted me to find it and to be doing what I'm doing. He would have preferred the bloke at the town tip to get it than for it to fall into Hilda's hands. That's my defence anyway and I'm sticking to it. And tomorrow I plan to spend some of it on a brand-new set of wheels. Am I going or staying?'

'I need a coffee.'

'Sit down and I'll make one.'

Near midnight, they dragged the folding bed from its space between wardrobe and window and they set it up between the easy chair and the television.

'I'm not promising you a comfortable night.'

'You get what you pay for, kiddo,' Georgie said.

They drank more coffee, smoked more cigarettes and Cara spoke of Amberley, and the life she'd lived as a kid, then of Traralgon and how she'd loathed that town.

'Raelene's mother lives at Moe. That's on the way to Traralgon, isn't it?'

'I thought her mother must have been dead.'

'It's a long story. Raelene didn't know she wasn't Jenny's until Ray died and Florence turned up, claiming that Ray had stolen both kids.'

'Did he?'

'Probably. He introduced me to electricity and porcelain lavs, and according to Jenny gave me an aversion to marriage. She could be right. Jenny left him in '47, then a few days after we got home, I lost my brother.'

'How?'

'Kidnapped by Lorna Hooper, picked him up from the kitchen while Jenny was getting dressed to take him down to the hospital. Lorna was Jimmy's aunty.'

'Isn't Jenny married to a Hooper?'

'Jim. He's Jimmy's father.'

'Jimmy's father was killed in the war.'

'His family let Jenny think he was dead. He was a prisoner of war for two years. And I've got a date at a car yard in the morning.'

LAUNDERING MONEY

*G*eorgie fried bread and eggs for breakfast. Cara had never eaten fried bread. 'Eat it,' Georgie said. 'It sticks to the ribs.'

No time to draw back from their easy friendship of last night, Cara sat down and ate.

'I had nightmares about your money. It was spread everywhere and two men and a woman came in.'

'Tax collectors?'

'I don't know who they were but the woman had a huge pair of scissors and she was cutting it up. I got Mum's cake tin down and was trying to stuff the uncut notes into it. I don't know where you were, but I was trying to save some of your money for you.'

'The night after I found it, I dreamed I was planting rolls of it in Granny's vegie patch, maybe expecting them to multiply like spuds. We grew buckets of spuds down here one year, all along our fence line.'

'I can't keep a pot plant alive,' Cara admitted.

'Jenny and Jim spend half of their lives in the garden. I like growing things. Granny had half an acre of vegetable garden when we were kids.'

'What was she like?'

'Like Jesus maybe, or him and God rolled into one – or she was to me. She wasn't our blood. Jenny's mother came up to Woody Creek looking for Itchy-foot and ended up dying in childbirth.'

'What were Jenny's parents' names?'

'Norman and Amber Morrison –'

'Amber? Not the Amber Morrison who murdered her husband?'

'Adopted mother. She's our blood though, through Itchy-foot – and I've got to buy my wheels.'

Cara had no interest in utes, but Georgie was orating the book of who she was and Cara wasn't letting her get away. 'I'll come with you.'

The tale of Archie Foote and Juliana Conti was condensed on a tram up to Toorak Road. Georgie had half-a-dozen car yard advertisements she'd cut from newspapers. Dustings was in Toorak Road.

'Granny married Itchy-foot when she was nineteen and left him when she was twenty-seven. I've got his diaries at home. A whole bunch of them were posted up to Jenny when he died, then we found the rest in one of Granny's trunks. I never met him, but I've read his diaries.'

Public transport is not the most convenient means of travel when you're car hunting. They rode half-a-dozen trams that Saturday morning. They found a brand-new red ute in Toorak Road, a '67 HR Holden, hot off the factory floor, but Georgie wanted a white ute.

They found one at a car yard on the Maroondah Highway, a demonstration model with very few miles on the clock, and a quoted price no less than the brand-new red in Toorak Road.

Two pretty girls in a predominantly male environment are considered putty in a good-looking salesman's hands. He charmed them, offered cigarettes, Georgie didn't refuse. She charmed him too, told him to drop his price by a hundred and they'd have a deal. He wouldn't budge on price but offered her new floor mats.

'Where that ute is going, new mats will wear out as fast as old,' Georgie said.

He knew she wanted the ute and went off to talk to his boss, who joined him to seal the deal. With two to deal with, Georgie stopped smiling.

'I've made my offer. Take it or leave it.'

They wouldn't take it, but they had a ute in the workshop, traded in yesterday. They could do her a good deal on that one.

'Same model?'

'Less than twelve months old.'

'Kingpins,' Georgie said. 'I need ball joints.' And she started walking, Cara at her side.

Like a pair of sharks tracking a tasty meal, the men followed, Cara learning that the models to 1966 had kingpins, which weren't a patch on ball joints; she learned too that her half-sister was a hard-headed businesswoman.

They offered a fifty-dollar discount on the white ute. Georgie told them call it pounds and they had a deal. They told her they were giving the ute away at that price.

'I'd hate you to lose money on it,' she said, and this time when she walked she continued on to the tram stop.

The morning was gone before they got back to the Toorak Road showroom where Cara watched wads of red notes taken from Georgie's handbag and counted out to the salesman's desk. She couldn't drive the ute away until Monday so they took the tram back to the city and caught a train out to Flemington.

Never in her life had Cara watched a horserace. Nor had Georgie, but she'd read somewhere that racetracks were the best places to go if you had money to launder.

She was so honestly dishonest. Ask her a question and she replied, and you knew it was the truth. She had a handbag full of money but was no gambler. She cashed a five-pound note to place a fifty-cent bet on a jockey wearing emerald green, and received nine dollars fifty in change.

'Can you keep the new stuff in your bag? It will save sorting it out later.'

A crazy day. The jockey came home in second place, and an elderly punter with flirty eyes told them that if they'd put their money on for a win or a place, they would have got a few bob back. Georgie cashed another fiver and this time backed the jockey for a win or a place. He got lost in the field, but Cara added more new notes to her handbag.

In race three, they backed two jockeys, one wearing royal blue and one wearing black and green. Still no luck, so they split up for race four, Cara armed with her own mouse money. Between them they had four horses running for a win or a place, four chances in a ten-horse race saw one of Cara's come in third.

Georgie's bulk of mouse money didn't appear to shrink, but the wad of plastic in Cara's exploded, and the coinage grew weighty.

It was a day like no other to Cara. She had friends, went out to clubs with Marion, had smoked pot with her twice. She ate fancy meals at Helen's unit, met Cathy in town, though less often these days – but this was different. This was time out from the reality of her life, this was the sort of day when you're glad to be alive.

They started laughing when, in race six, their mouse money on six jockeys and they got a first and a second place and one of the bookies handed back one of their own twice-laundered notes. They were still chuckling when they lined up to again get rid of that note.

They backed the field in the final race, got a first, second and third and walked to the train laughing at stupid jokes, which on a less imbecilic day wouldn't have been funny at all. They laughed on the tram back to the flat, conjuring up an image of the many bookies smelling something mousy when they opened their money bags tonight.

And once off the tram, Georgie smelled a fish and chip shop and made a beeline for it. The proprietor changed a ten-pound note. They bought cigarettes and milk at a café and changed another tenner. Walked home then, stealing scalding chips through a hole finger-poked in the paper. Is there a better way to eat hot chips?

'The first time I ate shop chips was the night Jenny played Snow White in a pantomime,' Georgie said. 'The next time was the night she left Ray.'

'She was in a pantomime?'

'She used to sing. We got free tickets. Ray wouldn't take us but a neighbour did – twice. Wilma Fogarty. She had umpteen kids. Jenny paid for them to go.'

'I knew she used to sing at a club in Sydney.'

'She sang at some sort of club down here every Friday night.'

'Does she sing now?'

'At funerals – which doesn't sound like much of a recommendation, does it? She's good. The McPhersons organise a concert every year or two. She can still do it. Jimmy and Margot took after her – or a bit. I must have inherited my father's voice. My teachers used to ask me not to sing.'

'What's wrong with Margot?'

'Other than a desire to get her own way in all things, not much. She was the runt of the litter. As a kid, everyone gave in to her. She grew up expecting it to continue. Granny stopped, Jenny stopped, Elsie didn't.'

'I thought she must have been . . . slow.'

'Watch her playing cards and you'll change your mind.'

'Do you know anything about my father, Georgie?'

'What do you know about him?'

'Mum said his name was Billy-Bob, that he was an American sailor and that he probably died in the war.'

'We didn't know she'd had you.'

'You don't blame her, do you?'

'What for?'

'For being . . . what she was.'

'A survivor?'

'For having four babies to four different men.'

'I suppose I should. It wasn't a lot of fun having kids call you a bastard before you knew what a bastard was, though I probably blame her more for selling herself to give us a stepfather. She ended up selling his wedding ring to feed us.'

Cara had her key in the door when Georgie told her that Margot had been forced onto Jenny by twin apes when she was a fourteen-year-old schoolkid.

'And they let her keep the baby?'

'She didn't want to keep her. She cleared out and found me. She told me once that she had the name of a doctor who did abortions, that I almost wasn't.'

Jug boiling, shoes off, they sat down, unwrapped the fish and chips and ate with their fingers.

'What's Jim Hooper like?'

'Six foot four, nothing special to look at, but a good bloke.'

'Are they happy?'

'He thinks the sun, moon and stars rise and set in her eyes, and she's the same about him.'

That night, no longer able to keep track of her convoluted family, Cara started taking notes. She had a page for Harry, Elsie and their pile of kids. Lenny the eldest; Teddy, Margot's boyfriend for eight years, now engaged to Vonnie. She had a page for Florence Keating. *Mother of Raelene and Donny. Impregnated at seventeen by Ray King during the years Jenny and Ray were separated.*

'Why did she take him back, Georgie?'

'He turned up in Woody Creek on his motorbike, the Christmas of 1951, Donny zipped in beneath his leather riding jacket, Raelene stuffed into his saddlebag. Donny was around twelve months old, Raelene was three weeks, and both of them filthy and half-starved. I thought he'd murdered their mother.

'After the Hoopers took Jimmy, Jenny had some sort of a breakdown. She functioned but she wasn't Jenny. Elsie and Granny took charge of Ray and his kids, then a few days later Jenny started taking an interest in Raelene, and Granny and Elsie encouraged it. I was about twelve, old enough to know what's what. Jenny slept in Granny's room, Ray slept on a bedroll in the shed. She slept in his bed in Armadale. She dodged him in Woody Creek.

'When he and Harry and his boys built on the two back rooms and Ray moved into one of them, I thought Jenny would move in with him. She didn't. We moved Donny's cot in with him. Until he died Jenny slept in Granny's bedroom.'

They saw Donny on Sunday. Cara tagged along, expecting to see a retarded kid. She saw a man – a boy-man Georgie fed with chocolate buddies. He couldn't speak but he knew what to do with chocolate and he liked Georgie's hair.

'Jenny reckons he can remember my hair.' Gentle Georgie, allowing him to touch her hair, and when he pulled too hard, taking his giant hand and blowing on his palm, making a rude noise and raising a gaping chocolatey smile.

'Swallow it, Donny. You're drooling.'

An odd mixture, that half-sister, gentle as a mother with that boy-man, hard-headed as a lawyer with the car salesman, a laughing girl at the race meeting, and loyal to Jenny.

Cara told her about Morrie, about his sick mother. She told her about Chris, the solicitor.

'I went out with him one night, and the following Monday he sent me a huge bunch of flowers to the school. It was so embarrassing, but sort of nice too. His colleague's wife reckons he's on the hunt for a wife. I'm not on the hunt for a husband – or not him.'

She didn't want the weekend to end, but it did, and on Monday they said goodbye at the tram stop.

*

Georgie found her own way back to Toorak; with brand-new wheels beneath her, she didn't head for home but into the city, to a car park she and Jenny had used when they'd brought Raelene down for her appointments.

She did the rounds of city banks, opening accounts, for Georgie Morrison, and Gina Morrison King, and for Georgina Morgan-Morrison, and into each account she deposited five ten-pound notes which the teller's pen changed into a hundred dollars. She placed a wad of fives and tens into a five-year term investment, with accumulative interest, and as she watched, that two hundred and fifty pound became five hundred dollars. Banks never known for their speedy service, she lost too much of the afternoon, and when Cara returned from school, she found that red ute parked out the front and her visitor sitting in Morrie's place on the concrete steps.

'You're cheaper than the Hilton,' Georgie greeted her.

Later, the tiny kitchen table swamped by bankbooks, seven of them, the small refrigerator crowded with vegetables, fruit, two slabs of scotch fillet steak, Cara considered a larger flat, a two-bedroom flat, she might share with this sister. Knew she could. Her bones knew it.

'I got four per cent on one of my investments. I should have put more into it. Jim's mother's money was invested with a solicitor when he was six years old. It ballooned. I considered spending a bit on shares but I don't know what to buy or how to buy them. I had a peep in at the share-market place, but hotfooted it out. Charlie knew what to buy.'

She'd bought a small leather-covered book, and into it began copying bank names and addresses, the version of her name used there with the amount, a page for each bankbook.

'Have you thought any more about Miss Hadley's party in June?'

'I still don't know where I'll be. Every time I mentioned taking a holiday, Charlie would present me with a batch of shares. I've been nowhere. I might go to England – except I've got no real desire to go there. I'll probably drive off into the sunset and just keep on going.'

'He didn't look rich,' Cara said.

'He wasn't, or not on the books. He had a cheque account for the shop but there was never much in it.' She closed her book and placed it into a zip compartment of a new and larger handbag. 'A few years ago, he had my name added as a signatory to his shop account. I've signed his cheques since someone ran him down and he had no arm to sign with.' Bits and pieces being transferred now from her old handbag to the new. A plastic bag of plastic notes, placed into the shoe box with the mouse money.

'It's gone down,' Cara said, as she may have spoken about a boil on a backside.

'I'll get there,' Georgie said. 'I wonder what Hilda is doing with his shop. I meant to call Jen and ask her if she'd opened it today.'

'There's a phone box on the corner.'

'I'll go home in the morning, see what's been happening.'

She opened another shoe box later. That one contained shoes, beautiful shoes, their price still on the box.

'I'm addicted to shoes – I dare say we crave what we didn't have as kids. We lived in black lace-ups. I've got a dozen pair of high heels at home and rarely go anywhere to wear them.'

'Stay down for a while and wear them, Georgie.'

'I'll try to get back in June – if you'll come to the racetrack with me again.'

'I wouldn't miss it for quids.'

'Charlie was right, you know – that doesn't sound the same if you change the quids to dollars.'

Two shoe boxes was one too many for the bag. She removed the box of notes.

'You can't carry that around in a ute, Georgie?'

'I'd put it into our safety-deposit box, but if I put notes in there, Hilda will consider them hers. I might get my own. I dunno yet what I'll do.'

'Would you trust me with your bankbooks and a bit of it? I could pay some into your accounts each payday. No one comes here, or the few who do are not likely to go poking around in my drawers.'

'Would you?'

'You've got seven books. You'd get rid of seventy pound a week.'

'Multiply that by fifty-two,' Georgie said.

The cake tin of Cara's dream seemed as sensible as anything had this weekend. They loaded it with mouse money and Cara placed it into the rear of her pantry cupboard, then got the giggles imagining Myrtle and Robert turning up one day with their key and opening that cupboard seeking cake.

The couple in the unit next door heard the laughter, a rare sound from Number Ten. They heard movement before daylight on Tuesday morning, heard a door close and footsteps down the stairs.

Then Number Ten was silent again. Silent and lonely, and Number Ten's car space looked lonely.

No laughter that night, only an ongoing rattle, punctuated by the bang of the typewriter carriage, ongoing for hours.

'What the hell is she doing in there?'

*

Rusty, Cara's protagonist, a tall redhead with emerald-green eyes, was as hard-headed as a lawyer, but as gentle as a lamb with her elderly grandfather, Archie. She could work out the accumulative interest on a three-year bond without need for pencil and paper. Her mother, an evil woman, would end up in jail for murdering the elderly grandfather.

Tale of Three Sisters, she named it.

Rusty had been raised by Archie Fleet, her maternal grandfather. Her younger sister, Lena, a spoiled overweight bitch of a girl, had been raised by rich paternal grandparents, and then there was Sarah, the unknown kid sister, raised by her mad mother. The tale was plotless. Cara had no idea where it was going, but it kept on growing.

HAVING A SISTER

Dear Cara,

I swore a dozen or more times that I'd never again unlock Charlie's doors, and where am I writing this? Your lack of telephone forced me to buy a new writing pad. You won't believe what has been going on up here while I've been missing. I don't. I fluctuate between bouts of hysterical laughter and practising arguments for my defence. Don't panic. It's not about the mouse money.

In the late fifties Charlie was in hospital with a broken arm and his daughter signed him into the hospital's geriatric annex, which, to put it mildly, upset Charlie to a point where he should never have been upset.

He spent most of his time absconding, and must have absconded long enough one day to make a six-page will. He left me his shop, its contents and one of his houses — and that was before I'd kidnapped him the first time.

I'm not his only beneficiary. He owned three other shop buildings. Miss Blunt rented one for her drapery business and her father rented it before her. Charlie left it to her. Fulton's hardware shop went to the Fultons, along with the house Mrs

Fulton has been renting for forty-odd years. She's probably paid for it ten times over, but now it's hers. Charles White, justice of the peace, universally described in the past as the meanest old coot in town, has in death become the town philanthropist.

His granddaughter got his shares and the fish and chip shop building. And if you saw her, the snobbiest snob Woody Creek has yet produced, you'd see the justice in that legacy. She'd look good up to her elbows in slimy fish and boiling fat. Hilda, Charlie's daughter, inherited the family home — and a tenant with a five-year lease.

It goes without saying that they are threatening to break the will, which they may well do, though Robert Fulton and his mother will fight them to the death. They've been Charlie's family, and me, according to his will, since Hilda and her dead husband took off with Charlie's car and sundry. There were two pages of sundry listed on his will. He lost his hearing, and much of his sight, but he never lost his marbles. God, how I wish I'd been a fly on the wall the day he made that will. I loved that old man.

Margot is home. Elsie is like a cat who raised a tiger cub — can't or won't see that the kitten she licked clean has grown big enough to eat her. I'm currently sleeping in Charlie's storeroom. Hope Hilda doesn't decide to burn the place down one night.

See you in June.

*

Dear Property Owner,
Miss Hadley remembers you as a bright little redhead with a pain in the posterior sister and a very attractive young mother. We've rounded up thirty-odd students from the forties and fifties. You might meet someone you used to know. Warning. Warning. I've told no one that you're my half-sister. No one, not even Morrie, knows that I'm adopted, so you and I are distantly related through your grandfather.

I think I mentioned Chris Marino to you when you were down. I've been out with him again. He works with one of the teachers' husbands. He called me at school today. He's got tickets to another show and he asked me to go with him, so I'm going. I feel as if I'm two-timing Morrie, which is crazy. He was supposed to fly over in February and didn't make it. I need some sort of order in my life, but the way things are with Morrie, I can't get any order into it.

After the party, I'm going home. I haven't seen Mum and Dad since Christmas. How about flying up with me? We can take a trip out to Long Bay.

See you soon.

Cara

*

Dear Cara,

I've been planning to go up to Sydney since my fourth birthday when Jenny told me my father was up there. I've since learnt that he was in Long Bay Jail when I was born. He's probably still in there, some bald-headed old bruiser, or a poor cowered old con the screws use as a punching bag – which is the round-about way of saying, not this time. Thanks anyway . . .

*

Dino Collins was released at the end of May. Dave told Cathy, Cathy told Cara. She didn't want to know.

Georgie drove to Melbourne on the Friday evening before the party. They went to the races, but you can't recapture a perfect day. They were there to change mouse money for plastic, and they had a time limit. There would be two dozen elderly teachers at the party and elderly teachers preferred to be home at night. The party started at five, and to Cara, it was leaving work to carry bricks. She served tea, passed around sandwiches and sausage rolls, followed by cake.

Miss Hadley had too many hands to shake, and more in common with elderly teachers than old students wearing name tags. Georgie met a Billy Mathews, one of Jimmy's friends, and too hard to explain the facts to him, she didn't.

'Sorry,' Cara said when they got away. 'You could have done without that.'

'I cannot tell a lie,' Georgie said. She left for home at eleven on Sunday.

Morrie phoned two days before school broke up. It was a poor line, every word Cara spoke had to be repeated.

'I wrote to you. I'm flying home for the holidays,' she shouted through the line.

'Can you delay it?'

'I can't keep on delaying my life until you can find a week for me, Morrie.'

'I can't hear you.'

'I know your mother has been sick. You have every ounce of my sympathy. Can you fly into Sydney?'

'I can't hear you.'

'Stay with your mother. I'll be in Sydney for a week.'

'How long?'

'A week. Seven days. If you come, come up there.'

And they lost the line, and she couldn't call him back, not from the school phone. She stood for minutes, expecting him to ring back. He didn't.

*

Rusty's mother bumped off her in-laws that night instead of Archie. Cara was halfway in love with flirty-eyed old Archie. That chapter would lead into a scene where two policemen and Rusty's two half-sisters turn up at his door. Rusty, who hadn't set eyes on her mother since the age of two, was not aware that she had younger sisters. With the grandparents dead and the mad mother in jail, she and Archie would become the guardians of those girls.

She was writing herself into areas she knew nothing about. What happened when a person was arrested? How soon before a long-lost daughter could visit her imprisoned mother? She knew someone who would know. Chris Marino, solicitor, who, according to Helen, Cara could catch by crooking her little finger. Didn't want him. She wanted Morrie.

Her new manuscript accompanied her to Sydney, and when Robert felt the weight of her case, he told her the renovations had been completed, that no more bricks were required. Her brand-new typewriter, which was supposed to be portable but wasn't, was in her case. It left little space for clothing. She wouldn't need much. She planned to spend her ten days at Amberley writing.

The building looked much the same externally. Inside nothing was the same. Walls had disappeared; new bathrooms and kitchens had been installed; external stairways had been constructed, fire escapes for the upper floor units. The old staircase, now a boxed-in entrance foyer, serviced the upstairs units. The lodgers' kitchen had become a communal laundry. No more backyard, back lawn. It had become a bitumen car park, with numbered spaces. The front door was the same door. The leadlight window had survived the transition; the parlour was somewhat shrunken; the big dining-room table had gone to play conference table somewhere.

Mrs Collins and Miss Robertson continued to survive their shared rear unit. Totally different in appearance, interests and personality, Cara had expected one or the other to move on. Not yet – probably never. Robert charged them a ridiculously low rent. The couple in the front upper floor flat had a five year old. A little noise filtered down, though not as much as before. The builders had probably done a good job, though to Cara, Amberley now resembled a staid old Packard with a modern Holden interior.

She gave her parents one day before setting up her typewriter on the kitchen table. Myrtle came in to chat. She moved into the parlour, explaining her pile of pages as a project she was working on. They jumped to the conclusion that it was for school.

'You're on holiday, poppet.'

She set up the typewriter on her dressing table, typing at night and going to bed with a back-, neck- and headache. The light in her bedroom was poor.

Gave it up, packed her manuscript and typewriter away and made a batch of fruit scones which were more like rock buns. Cream and jam disguise most failures.

She was trying her hand at braised chicken, her favourite meal, when Myrtle came to the door to whisper. 'There's a man on the phone asking to speak to you, pet.'

'I told Morrie I was coming up here. Was it long-distance?'

'It sounded local,' Myrtle said.

'You came,' she said, certain it was Morrie.

'Chris Marino speaking,' he said. 'I'm stuck in town for the night and Helen gave me your parents' number. Would you by chance be free for dinner?'

She was cooking dinner, and so disappointed she could have howled. Her first reaction was to refuse. But why should she? There was no reason in the world why she should. She wasn't engaged to Morrie. She hadn't seen him in almost twelve months.

'Where will I meet you?'

'I'll pick you up at seven,' he said.

'Was it Morrie?' Myrtle asked when the phone was down.

'Chris Marino, a solicitor. His firm has got an office up here. He spends his life flitting backward and forward. You'll have to finish cooking dinner, Mummy. I'm going out.'

He rang the new doorbell at seven on the dot. Robert didn't ask his intentions but invited him in for Myrtle to eye as a prospective son-in-law. He charmed them while Cara waited at the front door, clad in black slacks, black sweater and her overcoat.

They ate at a swanky restaurant where the food was good and the wine no doubt expensive. He had her home by ten-thirty, walked her to the door and shook her hand – a very satisfactory conclusion to a pleasant enough evening – and she'd learnt what happened to a prisoner when he was arrested.

Myrtle and Robert asked his age, his genealogy. She knew a little about him.

'He came out from Italy with his parents and sisters sometime after the war. He's the baby of the family – and for the record, I'm not planning to marry him.'

'He has a pleasant face.'

Pleasant, but not exceptional. Morrie was exceptional. Was he in Melbourne?

Footsteps overhead and all three glanced up. 'You wouldn't need them to throw a wild party up there,' Cara said.

'It's better than it used to be. Jenny and Jimmy lived in Number Five and I heard every footstep,' Myrtle said.

Cara nodded, aware that there would never be a more perfect time to come clean – and that it might get their minds off Chris Marino.

'I went up to Woody Creek a while ago. I'm in contact with one of my half-sisters.'

It was not the perfect time. Her admission created a silence.

'And?' Robert asked.

'Her name is Georgie. I've seen her three times, but we write. She's four years older than me, looks nothing like me.'

'Have you seen Jimmy?' Myrtle asked.

'They haven't seen him since he was six. He was raised by his grandfather. Jenny is married to his father, a second marriage.'

'I thought he died in the war,' Robert said.

'According to Georgie, he spent years in a prisoner of war camp. Jenny didn't meet up with him again until '58.'

'My goodness. Do they have other children?' Myrtle said.

'A seven-year-old daughter. They've got Jenny's first husband's daughter living with them. He was killed in a mill accident a few months before she ran into Jim.'

'Is she what you'd hoped she'd be, pet?'

'I didn't get a chance to talk to her, or not alone. I'm the image of her. She lives in a big old house in town, drives a good-looking car. I still don't know who she is – or understand how a woman who already had three illegitimate kids could have a fourth and hand it over to a stranger – and don't take that the wrong way. I thank God every day that she gave me to you, just don't understand why she did it, that's all.'

'I wasn't a stranger, pet. From what I recall, her husband's family hadn't approved of her relationship with Jim and had been attempting to gain custody of Jimmy for some time. She told me she'd lose him if she took another baby home.'

'Then what was she doing having one? Where was Jimmy when she was out sleeping with Billy-Bob and putting him at risk?' Myrtle shook her head. 'Or did she bring him back here? Was I begotten over the parlour?'

Robert, uncomfortable with the conversation, went to bed. Myrtle walked to her sink to dry the cups and put them away, to wipe the table, the bench top.

And Cara gave up and left her to her cleaning.

She was brushing her teeth when Myrtle tapped on the bathroom door.

'I know I'm being silly, but I've been worrying since you told me you were having the phone connected. If he sees your name in the phone book –'

He, Dino Collins, that unspoken, unspeakable name. Cara didn't reply immediately. She spat toothpaste, rinsed her mouth.

'He's been released,' Myrtle added.

'Cathy told me. I'm paying for a silent number.' Or the mouse money was. 'It won't be listed in the phone book.'

Myrtle picked up the toothpaste and replaced the cap; Cara stood, her back to her mother, smoothing on face cream, paying attention to her eyes, looking for the beginning of Jenny's crinkles beside her eyes, Myrtle watching until the lid was back on the cream.

'I received a phone call last week, very late at night. The caller identified himself to me as a police constable and he said there'd been an accident and that I'd need to come down to Melbourne to identify . . .' Myrtle closed her eyes, shook her head. 'I'd been asleep, pet. I was inconsolable. Your father rang the police and it proved to be a cruel hoax. I know it was him.'

That old racing heartbeat, that breath-stealing thumpit-thump-thump. 'How could you know?'

'He has a distinctive voice.'

Cara turned from the mirror, believing, and not wanting to believe. 'You haven't heard his voice in years. You said you were half-asleep.'

'As I was many times in Traralgon when I rose to silence the phone.'

'Did Daddy tell the police who you suspected?'

Myrtle reached out a hand to touch Cara's face. 'He did. He's done the paperwork to alter our number. Be very careful. You're precious to us.' She turned away, then turned back. 'It's wonderful that you've found a sister, but tread lightly there – until you know her better.'

Far too late for that.

JOCKEYS WEARING RED

*T*hat was the beginning, those ten long days in Sydney, and finding a letter from Morrie when she returned, and Chris Marino's perseverance, and his punctuality. If he said he'd pick her up at six, he picked her up at six. And when he brought her home, he saw her to her door and didn't expect to be invited in. He kissed her goodnight. He phoned her some nights, even when he was in Sydney, and he didn't seem to give a damn how much it cost.

Cathy told her that Morrie was flying over to be Gerry's best man at the wedding. He wasn't at the rehearsal. Roger, the university friend, a second groomsman, was driving up. He offered to drive Cara, Cathy's first bridesmaid. She caught the train.

'I'm bringing Chris to the wedding, Cath.'

'Who?'

'Chris Marino.'

'As in sheep. That would make a good author's name, Cara Baah.'

'Shut up.'

'Morrie will be here.'

'Don't bank on it.'

'How would you feel if your mother had cancer?'

'Bad.'

He was there on the day and Cara felt bad, bad for Chris. She introduced him to Morrie, had to dance with Morrie, but she sat with Chris and, determined to prove she was with the one she wanted to be with, clung to his side and drank too much.

Then drove home with him.

*

Morrie's grandmother's engagement ring had crossed the ocean in his wallet. It spent Cathy's wedding day in his breast pocket. As the silver-grey Mercedes backed out, Morrie slid the ring onto the MG keys.

The bride and groom gone, no Cathy to direct him, he drove back to Gerry's house and went to bed. Wrote them a note at dawn, thanked them for their hospitality; then, his case on the passenger seat, he drove.

He got drunk in Adelaide then drove up to Broken Hill and got drunk there. He was out beyond the black stump when he worked out where he wanted to be; it took him two days to get there.

He'd told his mother he intended asking Cara to marry him. She'd given him the ring and, new boyfriend or not, he was determined to get that ring onto her finger before his flight home tomorrow.

Saturday morning, not quite eight when he parked out the front of her block of flats. Too early to knock on her door. He walked down to the corner, to the phone box, where he searched his wallet for the number Cathy had given to him.

Her phone rang umpteen times before her annoyed, 'Hello.'

'Any chance of breakfast?'

'It's eight o'clock.'

'I'll cook?'

'I don't eat breakfast on Saturday mornings. I sleep.'

'Early to bed, early to rise, makes a man healthy, wealthy and wise.'

'It doesn't work for women.'

'I'm in your phone box,' he said and he hung up.

She was pyjama-clad, blue-pyjama-clad, barefoot. She let him in then disappeared into her bedroom. He made toast, made coffee and served her when she came from the shower, jeans-clad, shoes on.

'How's your mum?'

'Good at the moment.'

She ate a slice of toast, drank his coffee. He made good coffee. 'I'll employ you as a butler when I'm rich and famous,' she said.

*

So easy to talk to. They talked until ten-thirty, when she told him she had to leave around eleven.

'Meeting Con?'

'Chris is in Sydney.'

'Two-timing him, eh?'

'Three,' she said. 'You're here.'

'Where are you off to?'

'The racetrack, and I plan to get there for the first race.'

'Mind if I tag along?'

'It's a free world,' she said.

He tagged along, sat close to her on the tram to the city, his mind on the ring, on his key ring, in his pocket.

He tagged behind when she queued to place her bet with a bookmaker and watched her place her money on two rank outsiders.

'I've got more chance of winning,' he said.

'I get nothing back if a favourite wins,' she said.

She didn't win, not on the first or the second race, but she kept queuing up. He started queuing with her, and learned she was placing five-bob bets and cashing five-pound notes to place them. Amused, bemused, he accused her as she made her way back to watch the race.

'You're laundering money.'

'It's been laundered already.'

'Is it his?'

'Whose?'

'Con Baah's.'

'Chris Marino, and he's a solicitor. And if you must know, I'm researching gambling, attempting to work out how much an inveterate gambler might lose in a day.'

'Not much if he only places five-bob bets. And why keep changing fivers if you're not laundering money?'

'That's none of your business – and if every cent was a dollar, he'd lose plenty.'

'Why do you want him to lose?'

'Because that's who Archie Fleet is.'

'Archie who?'

'*Fleet* – as in fleet of foot. The publishers didn't want *Angel* so I'm working on a new one – having fun murdering people, so watch out.'

She got a second in race four and a first in race six, an outsider who paid her twenty-five to one.

'Told you so.'

He watched, impressed, as she collected her winnings, watched her place those notes into a separate purse. Watched her lose on the next race, then win on the last, and on another outsider.

'It's not working today,' she said. 'You're willing them to win.'

'Praise me, don't blame me.'

'Archie's granddaughter inherited her murdered maternal grandparents' house and fortune. She's under-age, so he ends up her guardian, and guardian of her money. He's supposed to embezzle it and lose it at the racetrack.'

'Does he eat out?'

'Why?'

'He could blow his winnings on French champagne.'

'I'm going home,' she said.

He sat beside her on the tram, a crowded tram, sat too close, tried to hold her hand. She removed it. She said goodbye to him in the drive, but he followed her upstairs.

'Go home, Morrie.'

'I make good sandwiches.'

'I'm involved with Chris.'

'I still make good sandwiches.'

He did. Maybe she wanted one. There'd been little tension between them at the racetrack; dodging around each other in the handkerchief-sized kitchen created tension, and the table was too small.

At eight she told him to leave. He told her he was going home in the morning but until then her flat was the next best place.

'And that's the crux of our problem, Morrie. I'm no longer interested in being the next best thing.' She stood, placing distance between them. 'I need you to leave now.'

'I love you.'

The magic words, and he'd said them, and he tried to hold her, but she shoved him away.

'Why didn't you say that at the wedding, or last year, or two bloody years ago?'

'I was two years younger two years ago.'

'Me too,' she said. 'It's too late now. I'm with Chris.'

'You've been with me longer.'

'I'm *with* Chris – in every sense of the word.' And in case he didn't understand that, she added, 'I slept with him the night of Cathy's wedding.'

'That's too much information,' he said.

'Then go before you learn more.'

'I've got nowhere to go,' he said, and he raised a demon in her.

'Exactly,' she said. 'Good old convenient Cara. Tell her you'll be here in February, then change your mind; tell her April, June, and change your mind again. She's always available. You couldn't put off flying over for Cathy's wedding, could you, and that's the only reason you're here now, and if they weren't on their honeymoon, you'd be in Ballarat with them. Sorry, but I'm no longer available.'

'Except to your mafia man –'

'And you're so bloody unfair. My bed has been available to you for two years – and I let you know it too. Now that I'm involved with him, you suddenly decide you want me. You're a dog in the manger, Morrie. You never wanted me. You just don't want someone else to have me.'

'I thought he had – the night of Cathy's wedding.'

'Get your smart Pommy mouth out of my flat. Now!'

'I'll bet he held a loaded gun to your head – your money or your virginity.'

'I hate you. I loathe the sight of you –'

'I love you.'

She was crying, trapped between bench and sink, and he reached out again to hold her, but she snatched for her breadboard and held it as a shield before her.

'Get out, or by God I'll flatten you with it.'

He left.

*

She took two aspros, set her alarm clock for seven and went to bed. Three times she went to bed that night. Couldn't force her bones to still. Couldn't get him out of her head. Hated him, loathed the sight of him. And how dare he come here and . . . and screw up her head.

At one-thirty she emptied her handbag to the table, forcing head and hands into occupation, sorting change from Georgie's mouse money, totalling it, working out how much she'd spent, how much she'd won. The winnings she claimed as her own and placed into her handbag, poured the coins into a screw-top jam jar, then rubber-banded Georgie's share and placed it into the cake tin. Not a lot of mouse money left. One more round of the banks, one more trip to the racetrack should do it.

In the wee small hours of morning, she rewrote the Archie chapter, or rewrote three pages of it. Archie still embezzled his brat granddaughter's trust fund, but Cara now allowed him to win at the racetrack. Readers preferred to read about winners.

Two or three times she'd attempted to alter his name. She'd tried Ernie, Herb, but no other name worked. Initially he'd been placed into the novel as a background character, doomed to die fast at his daughter's hand. Then he'd opened his mouth and she'd realised that Archie was nobody's victim. Given his head, he'd damn near taken over the novel. All three sisters now lived with him, in the in-laws' mansion. She'd chopped a few years from their ages. Still hadn't written the jail scene, or not more than sketched it in.

She was at her desk when her alarm clock started jangling.

Seven o'clock? She went to her bedroom to silence it and to pick up her new jogging shoes, purchased for her by Chris, and probably expensive. He was into running, and so fit. He could run six kilometres and not break out in a sweat. The first morning she'd gone with him, she'd caved in after a hundred yards. She did a few blocks most mornings now, had stopped smoking and was a lot fitter for it.

Not this morning, though. Chris was in Sydney and she was going to bed.

SWIMMING AT PORTSEA

She didn't want to go to Chris's birthday dinner. His family always made her welcome then conversed around her, or his parents did. Chris did when he spoke to them.

His nieces and nephews were bilingual. They swapped from Italian to native-born Aussie mid sentence, even a tiny girl, who adopted Cara. Kids everywhere. Chris's eldest sister had six and his youngest had four, the middle sister had limited herself to two.

She learned Chris's age that day. He was thirty-four, an early Christmas present, his mother said.

'You teaching. You like many children?'

Easier to nod than to shake her head then explain why she'd shaken it.

December the seventeenth, a long and noisy day, Cara lost amid the adult Marinos gravitated towards the kids. One of the older boys had a transistor radio. She heard the news flash.

'Chris,' she called. He didn't like interruptions. Harold Holt, prime minister of Australia, had gone for a swim at Portsea and he hadn't swum back to shore. 'Harold Holt is missing,' she added.

That got his attention. It got everyone's attention, got the older sister translating for her parents.

John McEwen was sworn in as prime minister. He held the fort until January of '68 when John Gorton landed the top job.

Cara flew home for a weekend in January. Chris was working from his company's Sydney office. He ate dinner at Amberley, and he told Myrtle and Robert he wanted to marry their daughter. Their response to his proposal was classic.

Cara's wasn't. 'I'm not ready to make a lifetime commitment yet,' she said.

She had a novel to finish. She'd found a sister she could never introduce to him as her sister.

She'd told him about her novel. She picked his brain for information if he was in the mood. He'd explained to her one night, as he might to a child, that thousands of novels landed each year on a publisher's table but very few made it to publication.

In April he asked when she might be ready to make a lifetime commitment. She was watching the news.

'Shush,' she said. Martin Luther King, a gentle man, awarded the Nobel Peace Prize for his nonviolent campaign to gain rights for American Negroes, had been murdered, shot dead on the balcony of his second-floor motel room. Violence was erupting across the United States, the blacks looting, burning what they could.

That was the week Cathy told her that Morrie and his parents were thinking about moving to Australia.

'They're looking for a house they can rent in Ballarat.'

Bobby Kennedy was assassinated in June and Chris wanted to book a flight for two to Italy, a honeymoon trip.

Do it. Before Morrie comes back. What more could you want in a husband? Say you will. He's got a good job, he's reliable, punctual to a fault. Myrtle is damn near in love with him.

And I'm not.

Love grows if it's given a chance.

And what if it doesn't?

Chris flew away alone in August. Morrie's boat docked before he flew home and every time the phone rang, she was sure it was Morrie. He didn't ring.

Chris came home and he wanted to fly Myrtle and Robert down for Cara's birthday. She'd be twenty-four in October. Robert's knee was playing up and Myrtle wouldn't fly. They sent a card and a woolly dressing-gown.

Everyone of Cara's age was engaged or married. Helen was expecting a baby. She offered the news at Cara's birthday dinner at a city restaurant, and Chris ordered a bottle of French champagne to celebrate.

The bill was huge. He paid it – then added a tip. That's the way he lived, the way she'd live if she married him. He worked long hours, flew backward and forward to Sydney, flew overseas at the drop of a hat.

He'd bought her a pair of diamond earrings for her birthday and not tiny diamonds either. She felt so bad. Felt so old. Felt so . . .

'It's too much, Chris.'

'A pre-engagement gift,' he said.

'They're gorgeous.' They were. She'd had her ears pierced six months ago. His sisters and nieces had pierced ears. She removed the small gold rings she wore to keep the holes open and he watched while she fitted his diamonds in their place.

'They're beautiful. I love them,' she said.

'And me?'

Sometimes you have to lie.

They rang Myrtle and Robert the following morning, or he rang them. He rang his parents. She had to ring someone so she rang Cathy.

'Morrie's mother has got lung cancer now. He said that's why she wanted to move over here.'

'For the better air?' Cara asked.

'Because she knows she's dying and that he's crazy about you, you moron. And you go and do a thing like th—'

Cara hung up the phone. She was engaged to be married. It was supposed to be a time of celebration, of congratulation not castigation.

In November Rain Lover won the Melbourne Cup and Cara watched the race. She had more than fifty cents riding on his back, and was the only one in Chris's party who had a win. The others weren't there to win or to watch horses run in circles; they were there for the social event and to be seen, and Cara wasn't one of them – or with them, not in mind. She was back with Georgie on that first day, when they'd backed the jockeys because they liked their shirts. She was back with the laughter of that day, and the comfortable shoes and jeans.

Not dressed for comfort today. Her heels were too high, and her hat felt ridiculous and she couldn't take off. Hats had never had a happy relationship with her hair. Wished she was wearing jeans and flatties. Wished she was changing Georgie's mouse money for dollars.

No more mouse money to play with.

No more true laughter either, except at night when Georgie called late and spoke long.

THAT FINAL INCH

Yards of aged and faded Christmas decorations removed from cardboard cartons stored all year beneath the town hall stage were unpacked, untangled, shaken into shape and hung once more in the streets of Woody Creek, hung from light pole to light pole. Those employed to do it had done it all before. They hung lights from veranda post to veranda post. A few new globes got them working. By day they looked tatty but they brightened up the old town by night – or some said so. Some said, 'Bloody Christmas again.'

At the post office they said, 'Bloody Christmas cards.'

Jenny and Jim received a few. They posted a few.

Jenny was packing cases when Florence and Clarrie Keating's card arrived, with a letter enclosed.

Dear Jenny and Jim,
You'll think I'm the most terrible mother in the world writing this about my own daughter at Christmas time. I know that it's my fault that she's gone the way she has and that we never should have disrupted her life when she seemed so happy with

you, but for your own good you need to know what's been going on down here with her.

She's got herself into big trouble this time. Our next-door neighbours, who we always got on with so well, kept a full set of the old money, and it was stolen, and they are telling everyone that the police have got proof that Raelene and her boyfriend stole it.

We offered to pay back the cost of it, but they say they can't replace what they had, and they'll see her locked up this time. And now they won't speak to us and the police keep coming here thinking that we know where she is, and we don't.

She's with a chap who has been in jail. He rides one of those Harley motorbikes. Her father used to ride a bike when I knew him and probably still did when he was with you, and I'm wondering if she is seeing Dino as her father. He's far too old for her to be mixed up with.

It's probably not news to you that she's been stealing. She has from us since she was nine or ten, just little things, but lately it's got worse. She took our television a while back, which she couldn't have done by herself. We know that bikie is mainly to blame.

Anyway, Jenny, why I'm writing all this is to let you know that we've sold Clarrie's mother's house and that we'll be moving in the New Year. Neither of us wants to. Clarrie has a good paying job down here, but as he says, we have to think of the other children, who we both love dearly, and want to give them a decent life.

I'm so sorry that everything turned out like it did and I hope one day you can forgive me and that you have a good Christmas.

Yours sincerely, Florence Keating

There wasn't much in that letter Jenny didn't already know about, other than their selling up. Suffice to say that Juliana's brooch was now locked in Georgie's safety-deposit box, that new locks had been fitted to Vern Hooper's doors and windows. They, too, were tired of strange police knocking at their locked doors.

They knew all about Dino, her bikie. They knew the mob shacked up on Monk's land smoked grass, knew that he and Raelene had been shacked up with them until a month ago.

There must have been two dozen grass smokers living out there, males, females and kids, camping in huts, sheds, tents, old caravans.

Jenny had given up on Raelene. Sometimes that's all you can do. *You can't do better than your best*, Granny used to say. She'd done her best and now she was doing her best for Trudy.

She'd turn ten next April. She was too young to send away to boarding school, but that's where she was going in the new year. They had to get her out of this town before she was old enough to understand what was going on with Raelene – if she didn't already know.

Jenny would have sold up and moved to Melbourne tomorrow. Jim didn't want to sell. He'd made a life for himself in Woody Creek. He was the local historian, and currently working on a big project with John McPherson. Woody Creek would celebrate its centenary in twelve months' time. Maybe the town council might shout some new Christmas decorations. They'd already started slapping a bit of paint around.

*

Morrie's father had packed his case for home. His wife unpacked it. She was well at Christmas time.

She remained well through summer, but summer ended in February, and by April '69 she was dying by the inch, though not yet prepared to give up that final inch.

'What happened to Cathy's little friend you were so fond of?'

'She's fond of another,' Morrie said.

'I'd hoped to see you married.'

'Want me to put an ad in the paper – *Unemployed bachelor seeking wife*?'

'Nonsensical boy. What's your father doing?'

Packing his case for the flight home. He did it regularly. To use Cathy's terminology, he was losing his marbles. Gerry's diagnosis was kinder, but whichever way you put it, it was hard to live with. Morrie spent a bit of time unpacking that case now. His mother rarely left her bed, and when she did it was in his arms. He carried her to the couch at night if there was a show worth watching on television. He drove the streets, searching for his father and manhandling him into the car.

His father's loss of memory hadn't been obvious six months ago, not to Morrie – perhaps to his mother. It was obvious to most now. He required supervision to dress, or ended up with his shirt on inside out and claiming that the buttons had come off in the wash. He couldn't remember eating a meal five minutes after he'd eaten it, but that cut both ways. He couldn't remember not eating it either. Morrie fed him when he remembered.

'Did you sign those papers, Morrie?'

'I'll get around to it.'

Power of attorney papers he didn't want to sign. Signing them would be admitting to something he wasn't yet ready to admit to.

'Has the postman been today?'

'Yep.'

'Nothing?'

'Nothing for you to worry about.'

Hope of a reply to a letter was keeping her alive and alert. The letter he'd posted for her a month ago had been returned last week, unopened, as had its predecessors. He'd burnt it, as he'd burnt its predecessors, needing his mother to hold on to hope.

She did through May, then June swept in with a sleety slush that wasn't quite rain and not yet snow. Cruel June. Month of the district nurses coming by twice a day. Month of Gerry coming in each night, and of Cathy, constant Cathy, popping in at all hours, with her gran, always armed with soups, stews, biscuits.

He managed. He unpacked his father's case, chased him down, fed him donated soups and stews at all hours. He poured him whisky too. Enough of it seemed to clear his foggy mind, or fogged up the unfogged parts sufficiently to create an acceptable balance.

Cathy popped in one foggy morning and caught him and his father sipping their breakfast – just another nightcap to Morrie. He'd spent his night sipping beside his mother's bed, willing her to live until morning.

And she had.

'He's bad enough without you pickling what's left of his mind,' Cathy lectured. Then she rang Gerry to dob on him. Gerry knew a retired matron who specialised in easing the dying to their death. She'd move into the house – and Morrie's bed.

'I've got two nurses who don't need my bed, Cath.'

'She'll make sure you don't feed your father whisky for breakfast,' she said and she went to his room to strip his bed and make it up for her nurse. She packed him a case, and slid it beneath the dining-room table, tossed sheets, pillows and a quilt over the couch. His knees would hang over the edge, but he could watch television all night.

The retired matron arrived that afternoon. She looked a fit seventy, and was super efficient. Morrie's father left home. She watched Morrie manhandle him inside, to the couch, watched him turn on the television and pour two drinks.

She dobbed, and by nightfall, Morrie's father was taken to the hospital. Cathy and Gerry caught him while his case was packed. He thought they were taking him to the airport.

'Incidentally,' Cathy said, once she and her ex-army major general had organised the house to their liking. 'I rang Cara half an hour ago. She's becoming Mrs Baah in September, in Sydney, and I'll be six months pregnant, and I'm not being a six-month-pregnant bridesmaid.'

'You're no maid, Cath.'

'I'm not being her six-month-pregnant matron of honour either. She doesn't love him.'

'Isn't ruling my world enough for you?'

'Well she doesn't. She doesn't even sound as if she likes him. And he forces her to go running with him, in this weather, and just thinking about her being married to him makes me want to vomit.'

'Go home and do it, Cath.'

'You'll drink if I go home, so I'm staying until Gerry gets home, then you're coming over to our place for the night and you're going to ring her up and talk some sense into her.'

'Did I tell you the joke about the solicitor?'

'I'm too sick for your jokes, and you're both stark raving mad. I knew you were made for each other the minute I set eyes on you.'

Eventually she went home. He could have taken his sheets and quilt to his father's bed. Didn't want to sleep in that bed, in that room, his mother's room until two months ago. He spent the night on the couch and when he rose at six to check on his mother, the efficient retiree had beat him to it.

Made redundant by that old dame, he went back to bed – to couch – and when he rose again at seven, the major general asked if he wanted cereal or a cooked breakfast.

He picked up his car keys. 'I'll eat on the road,' he said. 'Thanks.'

The MG found its own way to Melbourne, to Cara's street. Uncertain if the day was Friday, Saturday or Sunday, he parked out the front and sat for a time, wondering if Con Baah slept in her bed.

He walked down to the rear of the flats. No silver-grey Merc parked in her bay. He walked back, checking the cars on the street. No Merc – which didn't mean he wasn't in there. He could have taken a taxi, caught a tram.

Phone box on the corner in use, and by the look of the occupant's mouth, she was not to be tangled with.

He had two choices. He could walk up those steps and knock, or he could get into his car and go. If he walked up those stairs and her fiancé opened the door, he had two choices. He could sock him in the jaw, or make his excuses and go. The fiancé was a runner, not a boxer, and he might have come up to Morrie's shoulder. Aware that choosing the first option would be like taking candy from a baby, he walked back to his car. Then remembered he had a third option, under the driver's seat, a small bottle of Johnny Walker. He sat then, looking at her kitchen window and drinking his breakfast. It took the edge off his hunger, but made taking candy off a baby look like a better option.

And he was out again, the bottle slid into his hip pocket, and before he could start tossing up more options, he was climbing those concrete stairs.

'Who is it?'

'A redundant indigent,' he said.

'God Almighty,' she said, but she opened the door.

'He has arisen,' he said.

'It's not even eight o'clock, you idiot!'

'If I hadn't got out, nursie would have had a bib on me and been force-feeding me Weet-Bix mush.'

And the safety chain was off. 'Cathy told me about your parents,' she said.

'She hired an ex-army major general I feel obligated to salute,' he said.

She filled the jug and set it to boil, measured coffee and sugar into matching mugs. He took his bottle from his pocket and added a dash to one mug. She poured it down the sink and, without a word, commenced the process again.

'That cost money!'

'As does coffee. Put it in the fridge or it will go down the sink.'

'That's schoolteaching for you,' he said. 'You're as domineering as your friend, who incidentally said you can't get married in

September because she'll be six months pregnant.'

'She told me.' He allowed her to take his bottle.

*

She knew him so well, knew how he took his coffee, how much sugar. Knew the way his hands held his coffee mug. Yet she'd seen so little of him. If she totalled up the weeks they'd spent face to face they may have added up to six. Met him on New Year's Eve in 1964.

But seeing him this morning was good. He looked as if he'd been drinking all night, maybe all week, looked as if he'd slept in his shirt and trousers.

He was a boy, an irresponsible boy. Chris was a man, well established in his profession.

'Where's your engagement ring?'

'Earrings,' she said, showing her studded lobes.

'Do they count?'

'They're diamonds.'

'Hey, why do they bury dead solicitors twelve foot down instead of the usual six?' She raised her eyebrows. 'Because, deep down, they're all good blokes,' he said.

She smiled, shouldn't have, but it tickled her funny bone. Solicitor, along with estate agent, would never make the list of most honourable professions.

'Did you ever qualify for anything at university – other than drinking?'

'Slinging hamburgers.'

'You worked your way through.'

'Drank,' he corrected.

'What did you study?'

'Law for a while, until I realised I wasn't a good bloke – even deep down. I had a go at medicine, but the buggers gave me a knife and expected me to use it. Con still in bed?'

'Chris is on a big case up in Sydney. He's spent most of the last month up there.' She placed his bottle into the fridge and removed eggs. 'One or two?'

'Two. Got your novel published yet?'

'I sent it to a publisher. They sent it back.' Pan on the hotplate, heating, bread in the toaster. 'I need someone honest to tell me that I'm wasting my time.'

'Cathy not honest enough for you?' He knew she'd read it. She'd told him it was brilliant.

'Cathy's taste in reading material isn't everyone's.'

She broke two eggs into the pan then went to her desk, selected twelve pages and tossed them to the table. 'Read it if you like, but only if you'll be scrupulously honest,' she said and turned again to the eggs.

Familiar working around him, watching him place one page face down and start on the next. She buttered his toast, slid his eggs from the pan. He lifted the pages so she might place his meal down, but continued reading, eating and reading.

There was surprise in his voice when he turned the final page face down. 'Please, miss, I want some more.'

'That's all I've retyped. The rest is messy. When it was returned, I attacked it with a red pen.'

'I'll read around the red.'

'You're just saying that so I won't evict you.'

'I'm saying it because I want to know what happens to Archie.'

'Do you know anything about jails?'

'I'm working on it. Why?'

'Rusty visits her mother in jail and it's an important scene and I don't know enough about jails to make it believable.'

'I saw a prison show on the box a while back.'

'I watched it, but Chris says that Australian jails are different from American jails. I've tried to pick his brains, but he doesn't visit prisoners as a prison visitor. They're his clients. He speaks to them in private rooms.'

'That's why you hooked up with him? Research?'

'I hooked up with him because he turns up when he says he'll turn up.'

'You're supposed to say, Because I love him.'

'That goes without saying.'

'Not for us, it didn't,' he said.

'Stop that or go, Morrie.'

'Then give me the rest of your book. You've left Archie dangling.'

She picked up the rest of her manuscript and dumped it on the table, with a pencil. 'Edit it while you're about it,' she said, then leaving him to it, she went to the bathroom.

He'd made more coffee when she returned. She checked his bottle. It was in the fridge where she'd placed it.

Washed his dishes, the pan, watching him turning pages, occasionally glancing back at a page before reading on. She watched his pencil make corrections, write comments in the margin, then at ten-thirty he stood, stretched, and asked if he could call Ballarat.

She gave him privacy. She took a bag of rubbish down to the bins, and when she returned, he was back at the table, reading. She watched him for a moment, trusting his pencil, trusting him to give her an honest opinion too. Went to her desk then to write to Georgie and ask her to be a bridesmaid in September. What would Myrtle and Robert think of her? And Chris. She'd need to tell him she was adopted and had a half-sister.

Five pages later, one page filled with Morrie, with his parents, she sealed the letter into an envelope, then walked down to the postbox and sent it on its way.

He was still reading when she returned. The least she could do was to feed him. Fried ham and cheese sandwiches, opened a can of tomato soup – and felt Chris's disapproval. He rarely ate bread. Fried bread oozing cheese! He'd be aghast.

Morrie dispatched his share. 'What does Con think of your novel?'

'He's not into fiction.'

'Have you got anything in common with him?'

'Change the subject, Morrie.'

'Cathy says you don't.'

'Cathy only thinks she knows everything.'

He moved from the table to the lone easy chair after lunch, a pile of pages on the floor, on either side of the chair. He read until seven, then again phoned home, just briefly.

'How is she?' Cara asked.

'Sleeping,' he said. 'She's . . . they're keeping her pain-free with injections. She would have wanted . . .'

'They know what they're doing, Morrie. You have to trust them.'

They shared a tin of spaghetti at eight, on toast. She opened her last bottle of milk for their coffee.

Ten-fifteen before he placed the final page down, when he placed his pencil down and sat looking at her.

'You hate it?'

'It's good,' he said. 'Your characters are good. Your ending wasn't what I expected, but to use Cathy's word, it's brilliant. You've got a novel.'

'True?'

'Fair dinkum.'

'That sounds silly coming from a Pom, but thanks.'

'I've served my time here.'

'Fair dinkum?' she said. 'I can't say I noticed much of it. Now you have to go.'

'The major general will be in my bed.'

'Chris will call me before he goes to bed. You can't be here when he calls.'

'He checks up on you, eh?'

'He calls to say goodnight.'

'And to check up on you.'

'It's been a good day, Morrie. Let it end on a good note.'

'Going,' he said.

She opened the door and he, stepping by her, changed his mind before he was by and drew her to him. Kissed her. She didn't fight him.

'Don't take it personally,' he said. 'It was for the one inside you, capable of writing that novel.'

'I'll . . . pass it on to her.'

'You might tell her I love her while you're about it.'

'That would have been enough to win her heart back when she believed that parents live forever, that publishers fought over every would-be writer's scribble.'

'They'll fight over *Rusty*.' Long arms still holding her, and where anyone coming up the stairs could see them. What if Chris had decided to fly home? What if he walked up those stairs?

He kissed her again.

And why did his kiss reach down to the one deep inside?

Because he's bad for me. Because I'm like Jenny, and if not for Myrtle and Robert, I probably would have ended up pregnant at fifteen and had four kids by the time I was twenty. Whoever I was supposed to be might want to drag him into my bedroom, but the one I became knows better.

She shook off her genetics, shook him off too, then stepped back, closing the door between them. Stood behind it, listened for his footsteps on the stairs.

He didn't leave immediately. Perhaps he was waiting for her to leave the door. She walked heavily to the kitchenette window, and a minute later he walked by, just a shadowy figure walking in the rain. She watched him to his car, stood watching until his toy pulled away from the kerb.

Plates, mugs stacked beside the sink, *Rusty* on the table. She glanced at a page or two where his pencil had been busy – and knew, knew without a doubt that with him at her side, with his belief in her, she'd get it published.

Turned back to her sink, full of plates and coffee mugs. Not once in her life had Myrtle gone to bed before the last dish was washed, the last cup placed away. Chris's sink was used, but every time she went to his flat, it looked unused. He paid a cleaner.

Myrtle approved unreservedly of him. For the past two months he'd spent half of his life in Sydney defending someone big – and courting Myrtle and Robert, eating with them, taking them out to restaurants. Robert got on well with him.

She hadn't planned for the relationship to escalate. The first time she'd gone out with him, he'd expected to follow her inside. She'd come straight out with it, told him she didn't sleep around, that she had a long-term boyfriend in England. Thought she'd got rid of him. Hadn't. He sent her a beautiful bouquet of flowers, to the school. Who doesn't appreciate a huge bouquet of flowers?

Then in Sydney, long days, long nights, no television, nowhere to write in peace, her highlight cooking badly in Myrtle's kitchen. When he'd asked her out to dinner, she'd gone with him, just to break the monotony.

He'd pursued her thereafter and she'd stopped dodging him. Taking him to Cathy's wedding had been a huge mistake. She'd only taken him up there to show Morrie that other men were prepared to spend time with her. It had backfired. Determined to prove how happy she was, she'd emptied too many wine glasses and ended the night in Chris's bed.

Research, she'd named it. A final shedding of childhood, she'd named it. Hadn't planned to repeat it. Hadn't for over a month. For Chris, that night had meant more than research.

She was in love with his bedroom and his palatial bathroom. He took her to all of the new shows, drove her there in his expensive car. He'd got her fit. She ran with him on Sunday mornings, and could keep up now – if she was in the mood to keep up.

He drank grapefruit juice when he returned from his morning run. She squeezed his grapefruit on Sunday mornings. No bread for toast in his kitchen. He lived on steak, seafood, salad.

She knew why. She'd eaten several times at his mother's table, beautiful food, beautiful cakes. His father weighed half a ton, his mother not a whole lot less, and two of his sisters were attempting to outdo their parents.

Dark hair, dark eyes, no more height than she, a pleasant face. Short legs, not bandy, but somehow not quite right when exposed in his running shorts.

Nor was his name quite right. Cara Marino sounded like a breed of sheep, not an author. He wanted four children. If Cara Marino had four children she wouldn't have a lot of time left to worry about prize sheep or writing.

And she couldn't stand grapefruit juice – or his yoghurt and grain breakfasts. She'd tried yoghurt and grain one Sunday morning, after he'd put forward his case for its defence, with scientific proof to back up his claims. Lacing on her running shoes was sufficient self-inflicted punishment.

He ate oysters, ate them raw from their shells. He'd eaten snails one night in Sydney, had taken her and her parents to a French restaurant, and when they'd brought his roasted, buttered snail entree, she'd left the table. Twelve hours later, the smell of roasted snails had remained in her nostrils.

He could afford to pay the bill. He knew which wine to order. She didn't know one bottle from the next. He dressed well, wore imported shoes – and ultra-short running shorts and oversized, overpriced runners. And an ankle-length bathrobe and slippers after his shower. And nothing more.

Cara had seen an identical pair of those slippers in a city store, and when she'd looked at the price, she'd dropped the slipper. She could have paid a month's rent with what they cost.

She didn't own a pair of slippers. Old scuffs sufficed. They'd come off a bargain-basement table three or four years ago. Her favourite high-heeled shoes had come off a bargain-basement table, and were prohibited in his flat – their black fake leather soles had a bad habit of marking floors.

His floors were white, white tiles in the kitchen, white deep pile carpet in lounge and bedroom. Always shoes off at his place. Always cold stockinged feet at his place. And so pleased to return to her beige dog-box squat, to its threadbare carpet where she could put a pair of shoes on in the morning and not take them off until she went to bed, where she could always find bread, butter, eggs, cheese.

Absolutely adored his bedroom. The bedhead wall was black, the others white, his bedcover was fake zebra hide. The entire room had been done in black and white with touches of a rich jade green, and he had a pair of the most beautiful black and jade bedside lamps which he'd found somewhere in Italy. He'd been over there twice before she'd known him. He had a grandmother still living in Italy and cousins. He had cousins everywhere.

She'd fly with him next time, see the world with him.

Not when she had four kids she wouldn't –

So delay the kids –

She didn't want four. She'd had her fill of kids. One maybe, but not yet. Her writing was her unborn baby and tonight it was kicking to get out.

John and Beth had a pile of grandkids. Myrtle and Robert would be over the moon if she gave them one, if they lived close by, like John and Beth's grandkids. Chris had mentioned to them that he might buy in Sydney, after the wedding.

Bet he wouldn't. His family lived in Doncaster, lived in a cluster there. Years ago his father had bought a two-acre block, and through the years four houses had been built on it. There was space waiting empty for one more. Cara knew she'd end up in that space – with four bandy-legged kids.

Stop. He's a good man. And you sleep with him. And you're marrying him on 27 September – and will probably be pregnant by your birthday.

He used condoms, making sure there'd be no little accidents before the wedding. An only son, the baby of the family, they wanted a big white wedding, as did Myrtle. The two families agreed on that, if not on the church. Chris's family was Catholic. Myrtle wanted Cara to marry in her own church. They'd work it out, or she'd end up getting two wears out of her wedding gown – if she was prepared to swear to raise her children Catholic. Myrtle hadn't agreed to that either. It mattered little to Cara, who hadn't been inside any church, other than for weddings, since . . . she couldn't remember since when, maybe since Traralgon when she'd asked God to let Dino have a head-on with a loaded transport.

She couldn't see herself as a married woman, in maternity clothes, spending her days like Cathy, head over the toilet bowl as she blew up like a balloon. Definitely could not see herself splitting her bones apart in attempting to push a giant grapefruit through the eye of a needle.

How did she see herself if she dared to peek into the future?

Easy, that one. She was in a bookshop, holding a copy of *Rusty* in her hand.

What else?

This flat.

What else, and be honest.

Morrie beside her.

'Satisfied?'

He hasn't got a job. He lives in a rented house.

He's got a house in England.

His aunt's house.

She thought of his solicitor joke, thought of telling it to Chris. He'd smile, then tell her a long and detailed tale of an amusing incident in his day. She'd feign interest – as he'd feigned interest when she'd told him the publishers had sent back her novel – then he'd told her a long tale of a would-be Sydney writer his colleague had represented, who had become convinced that a Hollywood producer had stolen his plot.

He may have been in love with the teacher, the exterior, the created Cara. Whatever Myrtle and Robert had raised her to be fitted very nicely into his image of the wife of an up-and-coming solicitor. She spoke well, had socially acceptable parents, who may have been more acceptable had they not turned Amberley into units. He'd been ultra-impressed by Amberley's externals, by its position, if unimpressed by its modern renovations – the one thing he and Cara agreed on.

He knew nothing about the inner Cara, the one Morrie had kissed. Didn't want to know her.

Wondered if he'd still consider her an acceptable wife when she told him how Myrtle and Jenny had pulled their swiftie. He'd explain the illegalities, the possible repercussions of that switch.

If I told Morrie, he'd laugh, she thought. If I introduced Georgie to him as my half-sister, he'd want all of the juicy details.

And I love him.

Love on the poverty line erodes fast. I'm flying to Italy via New York on my honeymoon. Chris had two uncles and multiple cousins in New York.

None of his relatives had migrated to England. She wanted to see England, Ireland.

Morrie should be home by now. If he'd gone home. She had his phone number somewhere. Cathy had given it to her months ago.

She went to her bedroom, opened the top drawer of her bedside unit, and was confronted by Georgie's plethora of bankbooks but no phone number. Chris spent little time in her flat, but she wouldn't have left that number lying around where he'd see it.

And she wasn't going to call it even if she found it.

She sat on her bed, sorting through the bankbooks, each one wearing a version of Georgie's name. Morrison, Morrison King, Morgan, Morgan-Morrison, Georgina, Gina, Georgie. For weeks she'd deposited mouse money into each account. She'd got rid of it, and would need to get rid of those books before September. Georgie kept promising to come down for a weekend but she had a shop to run. If she came up to Sydney in September . . .

Bet she wouldn't.

This flat would need to be emptied by September. Little in it was fit to take with her. Her typewriter, television and clothing, and that was about all. Her linen and blankets were ex-boarding-house, old before she'd inherited them. The Salvos might find a use for them, and for her fridge, easy chair, battered coffee table.

She loved her old desk but Chris wouldn't give it floor space. She loved her bed too, bought secondhand and dirt cheap, but the most comfortable bed she'd ever slept in. Loved her reliable alarm clock, bought at Coles the week she'd started work. Its numbers glowed green in the night, and at any given time she could rise up on her elbow and instantly know the hour. What more do you need from a clock? Chris owned a squarish lump of glass wall-clock, more decorative than functional. It lacked readable numbers. He'd bought it in Japan, or someplace.

She picked up her alarm clock and wound its butterfly key, as she did every night, adjusted her watch to match its hands, as she did every night. The watch, bought for her twenty-first birthday by Myrtle and Robert, may have been expensive but was no longer a reliable timekeeper. Overdue for a clean, maybe.

Morrie would definitely be home by now – if he hadn't been picked up for speeding and thrown into jail.

I'd be able to visit him.

She smiled, knowing what she'd say to him if they tossed him into jail, if she visited him.

Greater love hath no man, that he would sully his reputation in the name of research. That's what she'd say and, in prison uniform or not, he'd laugh.

Back when she'd lived at the Windsor boarding house, when he'd driven home late to Ballarat, she'd sat by the phone until he'd called her to let her know he'd got there. He knew this number. He might call her.

It had been a good day, uplifting, relaxing and productive, and it hadn't cost a penny. She'd live a frenetic life with Chris, always out somewhere, running, eating, visiting, seeing the most recent shows, or in bed.

'Go to bed,' she said.

Brushed her teeth, washed her face, smoothed on cream, looked for wrinkles. Looked at her lobes and wondered if earlobe engagements counted. She had no proof that his diamonds were still there unless she checked with her fingers or looked in a mirror.

What else was there but marriage and a house and kids? Marion was going after what she wanted. Everyone was married – Cathy, Michelle, Helen. Marion wasn't. She'd had three bit parts in television shows recently, and would be in a play in July, not at a big theatre, but she had a big role in it. She'd get to where she wanted to be one day and bless her fiancé for dumping her. Fiancés stole time, stole . . . self.

Pyjama-clad, she returned to her tiny sitting room to turn off the heater. Melbourne's weighty phone books were beside it, on her coffee table.

She'd been on the phone when Cathy had given her Morrie's number. Knew where she'd written it too. It was in the margin of the emergency numbers page, a big M beside it.

It wouldn't hurt to give him a quick call. It was a miserable night. The roads would be greasy. She was making sure he'd got home safely, that's all.

It would disturb his mother. Probably wouldn't. It would disturb the nurse – who no doubt was accustomed to being disturbed.

She reached for the phone, dialled the first three digits, then placed it down again.

What will you say if he isn't there?

What will you say if he is?

'Something.' And she dialled the number, and maybe he'd been about to pick up the phone. It barely rang.

'Just checking that you got home,' she said.

'I turn into a pumpkin at midnight.'

'It's not midnight yet. I thought I might be able to visit you in jail tomorrow.'

'I did my best for you but there wasn't a cop on the road.'

'Such is life,' she said. And heard liquid being poured. 'What are you drinking now?'

'It's red, and bottled in South Australia. Not a bad drop either.'

'Drinking makes us less capable of dealing with our problems, Morrie, and creates its own. Go to bed and get some sleep.'

'The major general is in it, and if you saw her, you wouldn't suggest that. Who is in your bed, Norris?'

'Just a couple of tramps I found camped on the stairs. I couldn't leave them out there on a night like this. Sleep tight.'

He didn't hang up. She heard more of something red, bottled in South Australia, glugging into a glass.

'You're still there,' he said.

'You know my number if you need to talk.'

'I need, so talk,' he said.

'My phone bill was through the roof last quarter.'

'Hang up and I'll call back.'

'I have to go to work in the morning. Bye now.'

'It's Saturday.'

'It's Sunday, and getting ready to flick over to Monday. Goodnight.'

*

She was dreaming, her arms loaded with books, dream-walking into a relic of a house she'd won in a lottery, and it had no windows. And why would anyone buy a ticket in a lottery to win a blind house? Someone was knocking. In her dream she knew it was the removalists with the Traralgon furniture. She dream-walked a narrow passage, the house longer than it had seemed. And how had she walked so far from the front door? And it wasn't the front door. It opening into another room, a huge room, claret-red velvet curtains, tall bookshelves.

More insistent knocking washed that room away. And she wanted that room. Wanted to see *Rusty* on those bookshelves.

Clock ticking on her bedside table, its ghostly green hands telling her it was a quarter past one. Dino Collins had found her.

He wouldn't knock on her door. He'd knock it down.

The flat freezing cold, she slid from her bed and, without light, crept to the door.

'I'm calling the police,' she said.

'Desperation calls for desperate remedies,' Morrie said.

'You bloody fool of a man!' She removed her safety chain and flung the door wide. 'You half-witted idiot of an imbecile.'

He needed someone to hold him up. She was handy, and in the doorway she held him up while he kissed her. And he had something sharp between his teeth.

She could have swallowed it. She spat it instead, thinking it was glass, that he'd bitten the top off his bottle of something red bottled in South Australia. Had to turn on the light to see what she'd spat.

A ring. Three diamonds in an old-fashioned setting. A beautiful ring.

'Mum's,' he said. 'And Grandma's.'

'I could have swallowed it, you maniac.'

'But you love me anyway –'

She loved him. The relief of his arms told her so, and his mouth, without the ring, though wine-tainted. And what came next told her so. The unembarrassed shedding of her baggy blue pyjamas, and her mindless lack of care for tomorrow.

She didn't name it research, but learned something anyway. She learned why the human race kept on multiplying.

They had no say in the matter.

REPERCUSSIONS

*H*is ring was too large for her wedding finger but a fine fit on her middle finger where it spent the night. She slept warm beside him until the alarm demanded she arise and prepare for her day ahead. His encircling arm held her back from the morning chill, and his kiss was enough to change her mind about rising.

She'd slept with Chris in a finer room, a wider bed, where even the sheets oozed affluence. She made love with Morrie between wrinkled ex-boarding-house sheets, in a box of a room – and therein lay the difference between lovemaking and sleeping with.

'I'm probably pregnant,' she said.

'I'll demand blood tests,' he said.

And for the first time she thought about Chris, responsible, reliable, his packets of condoms in his bedside drawer. The thought of his condoms moved her from the bed.

Morrie cooked and served her breakfast when she came from the shower clad for the schoolroom.

'It still feels like Sunday,' he said.

'It's not.'

'Is a week's engagement long enough for you?'

'What? You want your ring back next Sunday?'

'Mum came back here to get me married off. Cathy won't be showing by next Saturday.'

'My parents would have forty fits.' They'd have them anyway.

'It might give Mum reason to live until Saturday.'

'You're not doing it for her, are you?'

'Now she asks.'

And no more time to ask anything. Dishes left on the sink, late to her classroom, and breathlessly happy when she got there. Loved his ring, loved him, and he wasn't a Catholic, which might take the sting out of it for Myrtle.

Chris would be in court. She had to call him, but couldn't yet. Myrtle and Robert would need to be told. They'd probably booked the church, were probably pricing caterers, printers for the invitations. Couldn't call them until she called Chris. Didn't want to call anyone.

No one noticed her ring at morning recess, or if they did, they didn't comment.

At lunchtime, she counted coins, then ran down to a phone box where she dialled Chris's Sydney office. He was in court. She shrugged and used more coins to call Amberley.

'Is anything wrong, pet?'

Didn't tell her why. Told her the wedding was off and not to book anything and that she'd call her tonight.

'What happened?'

'I'm out of coins, Mum. I'll talk to you at home. Wait until I call you.'

She reached Chris at four-thirty, after minutes spent on hold, and a phone call to Sydney at that time of day would cost a small fortune. And when his voice came on the line, it's tone told her he didn't need the interruption.

'Can your concerns wait, Cara? I'm in a meeting.'

'I need to tell you that I'm breaking the engagement, Chris. I'm sorry.' Silence, a long empty silence.

'This . . . cannot be discussed at a distance.'

'There's nothing to discuss. I'm sorry, but I'm back with Morrie.'

He'd met Morrie at Cathy's wedding, had suggested after she'd slept with him that a few of those pretty boys leaned a little left of centre. A lengthy half-minute of silence, Telecom's adding machine ticking over while he shuffled papers.

Then. 'I'll call you tonight, Cara.'

'I wanted you to . . .' but the connection had been cut . . . to be the first to know. She stood over the phone, wanting to vomit. Almost did when it rang.

Only Cathy, wanting every detail, and Cara in no mood to give her the details, and no sooner was the phone down than it rang again.

Myrtle.

Told her. Told her that there was nothing to be done about it. Told her Morrie's parents were Church of England. It cut no ice with Myrtle, so she told her that they were getting married on Saturday, if Morrie could arrange it.

Myrtle jumped to the natural conclusion. 'Are you certain Morrie is the father?'

'Not to my knowledge, Mummy. His mother is dying. He wants her to see him married. That's the only reason for haste.'

'Have you told Chris?'

'Yes.'

'What on earth did he say?'

'He was in a meeting.'

He wasn't at five-thirty. 'Have you come to your senses, Cara?'

'I'm so sorry, Chris. I've known Morrie since I was nineteen. I told you about him before we started going out. I'm sorry I let things go so far with us.'

He made a very concise argument while the prisoner in the dock removed the diamonds from her lobes and allowed him to get it out of his system. She owed him that much – and the earrings. Where had she put their box? She'd have to post them back. Couldn't face him. He was too good with words.

He commenced his closing statement, and maybe she knew why he was unmarried. He could cut with his tongue when roused. She'd never seen him roused.

Not a word could she raise in her defence, only, 'I'm sorry, Chris. I'm so sorry.' Like a cracked record, she repeated those words each time he gave her a gap in which to repeat them. Willed him to hang up, but not concerned about the cost, he wouldn't, so she stood and took her punishment, determined not to hang up on him, and she looked at Morrie's ring, his mother's, his grandmother's, now her own, and she loved the continuity of it, the depth of family behind it.

And remembered where she'd put the earrings box.

'I'm sorry, Chris,' she said one final time. 'I'll post the earrings –'

He hung up and she walked to her desk and opened the middle drawer, found the velvet box beneath her bills to pay, placed his earrings into it. Set in gold, they looked new. The box looked new – and too small to post. Have to put it in a solid envelope, send it registered mail.

She left it on her desk, on *Rusty*, then made coffee, made it strong – and no milk in the fridge. Contrary to popular belief, two can't live as cheaply as one, not when both like too much milk in their coffee. Opened her pantry cupboard to search for a can of Carnation milk. Myrtle always kept an emergency can in her pantry. Not a lot of her habits had become Cara's own. She was pleased that one had.

She drank her coffee at the window, watching for his toy car to drive in. He'd come when he could – or call her if he couldn't. At six-thirty she took her coffee to her desk to retype a few pages of *Rusty*.

He came at eight. He'd spoken to his mother's minister, who was prepared to marry them on Saturday, beside his mother's bed.

'Okay,' she said.

She didn't go to work on Tuesday. Rang in with a bad throat.

They bought wedding rings, and left the engagement ring with the jeweller to clean and adjust to size. She bought a new dress, pale blue and pretty.

Myrtle called at five. She and Robert were driving down to prevent Cara from throwing aside a fine young man for a boy, a boy who had been leading her a dance for years. Cara knew from her description of Morrie as *boy* that she'd spoken to Chris. Probably invited him to dinner last night.

'Three against one isn't fair, Mummy.'

'We'll see you on Thursday.'

'Make it Saturday, and drive straight through to Ballarat. We're getting married there at two,' Cara said.

'Don't rush into something you'll regret all of your life, pet.'

'I won't. Love you, Mummy.' And she hung up.

On the Thursday night at five, Chris knocked at her door. Morrie was there. Cara picked up the earrings before removing the safety chain. She didn't invite him in but stepped out to the landing.

He didn't like losing. His face told her how much he didn't like losing. There was nothing more she could say to him, nothing to do but keep offering the small velvet box.

He took it. 'You've made your bed, Cara. I hope you can lie in it,' he said.

*

Jenny was where she usually was at ten to six, in the kitchen, cooking up something for dinner.

'How long have you been doing that for, Jen?' Georgie asked, entering through the rear door. It was always open for her. Most nights she called in on her way home from work.

'Peeling dirty spuds?' Jenny asked, selecting another.

'Feeding a mob?'

'Since I was sixteen. Granny's idea of cooking was a frying pan and a lot of dripping.'

'That's where I got it from,' Georgie said. She sat then at the kitchen table. 'If I ever met a bloke who could cook, I might marry him – incidentally, it looks as if my trip to Sydney is off again.'

'Why?' Georgie shared Cara's letters with Jenny. She'd read the latest and had been planning a beautiful dress for Georgie. She'd told Georgie to tell Cara she'd make her wedding gown.

'She rang me this afternoon to tell me to ignore most of what was in her letter, that she's broken her engagement to the solicitor and is marrying her Pom with the hyphenated name on Saturday.'

'Is she pregnant?'

'I doubt it. She hasn't had much to do with him for the past year or two. She said his mother is dying of cancer and she wants to see Morrie married before she dies.'

'That's no good reason to be racing into marriage!'

'I can't see any good reason, racing or not – unless he can cook.'

'You wouldn't be hinting for dinner, of course.'

'Depends on what you're offering?' Georgie said. 'She's known the bloke, Morrie, since she was at college. He's her girlfriend's husband's mate. I think she was in love with him years ago, but got sick of waiting.'

'Will I peel another potato or not?'

'What are you offering with your potato?'

'Sausages.'

'How rare,' Georgie said.

And Jenny laughed. She'd been hearing Georgie's 'How rare' since that kid was twelve years old. And Georgie had heard her reply to it as many times. 'They're Willama sausages.'

'Oh, a different matter entirely – if you do them in flour with spices.'

'You can. They're in the fridge – and pass me that medium-sized saucepan – the one with the red lid.'

Georgie passed the saucepan. She found the sausages. 'Have you heard anything from Raelene?'

'I never hear from her. One of the commune girls said she was in Sydney.'

'Everyone goes to Sydney bar me. Do you reckon he's still up there?'

'Laurie?'

Georgie was separating sausages with a pair of scissors. 'Who else.'

'He could be anywhere. He'd be hitting sixty now. He was twenty-six when I was fifteen.' She watched Georgie's war with a string of sausages wanting to take them from her hands. Still reminded her of Granny – not in appearance, but in every move she made. Still sounded like her too.

She looked like Laurie, or what Jenny could remember of him, his red hair, his green eyes. She had his kindness too. She could handle Margot. Jenny couldn't – never had been able to.

'Use a plastic bag, love. Toss in a few spoonfuls of plain flour, not too much curry, a bit of salt and pepper and a pinch of ground ginger, then toss the sausages in and give them a shake, and make sure the bag is closed or I'll have flour all over the kitchen . . .'

THE WEDDING

*E*ach day Morrie commuted, east at night to Cara, and west each morning to be with his mother, the sun always behind him.

Cara drove west with him on Saturday morning. No Myrtle and Robert waiting to greet her. She hadn't expected them to be there.

She'd met Morrie's mother at the hospital, briefly, after the lump had been cut from her breast. The woman in that hired hospital bed didn't look like the one she'd met. His father she met for the first time, a frowning little man who told her she had pretty hair, told her five times in as many minutes.

Morrie's retired army nurse chose the mother of the groom's outfit, a pink shawl to drape over her nightgown, a hat to cover her sparse white hair. She propped her up with pillows for the ten minutes it took for the words to be said, the rings exchanged, the papers signed.

Then no more Cara half-Morrison, half-Billy-Bob Someone, Norris by default. Cara Langdon walked out of the bedroom, Cara Langdon-Grenville. And C.J. Langdon-Grenville sounded like an author's name.

There would be no honeymoon. The bride had to work on Monday, but Gerry and Cathy's wedding gift was dinner at a posh Melbourne hotel and one night in the honeymoon suite.

A uniformed porter carried their small cases. Two waiters served them in their suite. All paid for. Champagne paid for. They drank it at the window while looking down on the lights of Melbourne.

When the meal was cleared away, Morrie tested the ridiculously wide bed, bounced on it.

'Who else have you invited?' he asked.

'I thought I'd call down and take what's available,' she said.

'Male or female?'

'Couldn't we fit in one of each?' She sat with him then, and later they lay, with room for two more between them, her hand lifted so the light caught her diamonds.

'I could only see my earrings when I looked in the mirror. It's sort of narcissistic, isn't it, admiring engagement earrings. I prefer them on my finger.'

'I feel branded,' he said.

'You branded me. I branded you.'

'I think it's cutting off the blood supply.'

'It will turn black before it falls off.'

He moved across to share her pillow, and they lay together then, his arm over her, her arm over him.

She asked about England. 'It rains,' he said.

'What are English winters like?'

'Wet.'

'People who have long engagements know every detail of their partner's life by the time they get to the bed,' she said. 'I didn't even know if you were Catholic or Protestant. And how come you're so long and your father is so short?'

'Rain,' he said. 'He shrank.'

'It didn't affect you.'

'Mum chased me with raincoats.'

'We've had a hit-and-run relationship, haven't we?'

'I hit that first night and you ran – climbed a drainpipe.'

'I bought a black lace nightgown, planning to seduce you if you'd flown over that February.'

'I like your baggy pyjamas.'

He won the toss for first use of the bathroom. She took her black lace nightgown from her case and changed into it after showering, and he laughed when she emerged, and told her it was a bit too late to seduce him, and she loved his laughter, and one thing led to another and he won the fight for the nightgown.

'It prickled anyway,' she said.

Lovemaking, still so new, was a breathtaking treasure she'd almost passed up for security. To hell with security. He was a rare and beautiful thing, though not the pretty boy Chris named him. He was beautiful in a manly way. Loved the shape of his mouth, his eyes, hands, his long legs. Her sons would grow tall. Her daughters would be beautiful.

'I should go on the pill for a few months, I suppose,' she said. 'If it's not already too late.'

'Aunt Letty has got ten bedrooms. She'll feed them – if we live in England.'

'Two is my limit. Teaching has put me off large families.'

'I was one of three at one time,' he said.

'Truly? What happened?'

'A flu epidemic. I had two sisters. According to Mum, I almost died of it. I remember the nightmares – rats with giant teeth eating my feet.' And he played the rat with giant snarling teeth, and she laughed at his game.

'I didn't catch anything until I started school. Mum kept me in a glass case, and when she had to let me out, I brought home every disease known to common man.'

'In Sydney?'

'Yep. We lived there until I was thirteen, then Dad transferred to Traralgon.'

'Why?'

'It's a long story. That first book I was writing in Ballarat, *Angel At My Door*, is sort of my search for identity. This is for your ears only, but I'm sort of adopted.'

'How can you be sort of adopted?'

'You can if your mother and one of her lodgers pulled a swiftie – thus the angel at my door. Mum couldn't have kids. The lodger had too many. Her husband went missing in the war. She got pregnant to a Yankee sailor and couldn't take a dead Yank's baby home, so Mum took me.'

'How about that,' he said.

'Want a divorce?'

'I'm thinking about it. Is your other one – *Angel* – finished?'

'Only about six times. I started it when I was fifteen, which is when I found out what they'd done. Parts of it still read like a fifteen-year-old kid's view of life and I got everything wrong.'

'How wrong?'

'My other family. I created a whole family, a town.'

'How do you know you got it wrong?'

'I went up there one crazy day, walked into an ancient old grocery shop and found my half-sister working behind the counter.'

'Just like that.'

'Not quite, but almost. It killed my writing for a long time.'

'What was wrong with her?'

'Nothing. She's gorgeous, tall, regal, with a mane of burnished copper hair.'

'Your Rusty,' he said.

'Yep. She came down here for a long weekend and when she went home I started *Rusty*. It poured out of me like water through an unblocked tap. Incidentally, you did a good job of editing it. If you could type, you'd be perfect.'

'How did you know where to find them? Your other family?'

'Mum knew.'

'Cathy doesn't know you're adopted?'

'I don't tell Cathy everything. She talks before she thinks.'

'You think before you talk.'

'I've learnt it's safer to. That could be why I write. I can dive into the lives of others and let them do the thinking. Tell me something Cathy doesn't know about you.'

'Cathy demands. I obey,' he said.

'Not one skeleton in your family closet?'

'Uncle Henry's ghost lives in an upstairs wardrobe.'

'I don't believe in ghosts.'

'You'll believe in Henry.'

'Your father's brother?'

'Pops is Letty's brother. She's eighteen years his senior. Their own kids kept dying, so she and Henry took Pops in when his mother died. He was a Grenville but old Henry needed an heir, so Pops tacked on the Langdon.'

'What did he do for a living?'

'Not much,' Morrie said. 'An artist.'

'A good one?'

'He sold a few. He had a bit of success over here in the fifties.'

'What was he doing over here in the fifties?'

'Mum is an Aussie,' he said. 'She wouldn't admit it over there, but I think she knew she didn't have long to live and she had unfinished business over here which is why she wanted to come back.'

'Why didn't you tell me?'

'It never came up. I spent my first sixteen years here, went to school here. Here's a skeleton for you. Pops came out from England to marry Mum's sister, old Henry's niece, and Mum stole him from under her nose – anything under Aunt Lorna's nose was in shadow anyway.'

'That almost tops mine. It would make a good story.'

'Lorna wouldn't raise a lot of empathy in your readers. Mum has been writing to her since before Christmas, wanting to make peace with her, and the hard old bugger sends the letters back unopened.'

'Not devoted sisters.'

'She's why we moved to England.'

'Will we live over there?'

He reached for the light switch, and the small light died. 'We'll take Pops home, then rethink our options.'

'Tell me about your manor house.'

'It's overrun by Letty's dogs.'

'I like your Aunt Letty. I've wanted a border collie pup since I was old enough to say puppy.'

'She breeds King Charles spaniels.'

'Of course she would. She lives in a manor house.'

His arm was beneath her shoulder, her arm over him, holding him close, so . . . so safe. She was Cara Langdon-Grenville and she was going to fly to England, live in a manor house and write a hundred novels.

'How tall are you, Morrie?'

'Six-two and a bit.'

'My favourite cousin is six foot two. He was a weed at sixteen. After we moved down to Traralgon, I only saw him once or twice a year, and I honestly didn't recognise him one Christmas when we went up there. He must have grown a foot in twelve months. I haven't grown since I was twelve or thirteen, haven't changed much in shape either.'

'Precocious brat.'

'My real mother must have been. She had her first baby at fifteen, her second at sixteen, her third at eighteen and me at twenty. My half-sisters look nothing like her but I do. It's as if God pointed his finger when she gave me away, and said, "Don't think you're getting away with it that easily."'

'Do you know who your father was?'

'Billy-Bob Someone – a Yank sailor.'

'He sounds more like a firewater distiller.'

'Mum says he probably died in the war. My half-brother's father was in a Japanese prisoner of war camp for two years. According to

Georgie, had the war lasted for a few more days he wouldn't have made it home.'

'Georgie?' he asked.

'Rusty. The old grocer she worked for called her Rusty.'

He didn't reply. She heard him swallow. Knew he was thinking of his mother, so she lay beside him, allowing him time to think.

He broke the silence. 'Do you know your birth mother's name?'

'Jenny. Jennifer Morrison, now Jennifer Hooper.'

The arm beneath her shoulder stiffened, then he freed it and moved away. Too much space in that bed, she moved with him to place her arm again across his chest.

And his heart was racing.

'What's wrong, Morrie?'

He lay on his back, swallowing, attempting to swallow something he couldn't get down. Then he stopped trying to get it down and rolled his feet from the bed.

'What's wrong?' She reached again to draw him back to her side but he removed her hand. 'I asked what was wrong?'

'You talk too much,' he said.

'You were the one asking questions.' But he was off the bed and at the window, looking down. 'Are you thinking about your mother?'

'My mother is a liar,' he said.

'You can stop this right now and tell me what's wrong.'

'You're wrong,' he said. 'I'm wrong. Everything is wrong. Get dressed.'

'Talk sense, for God's sake!'

'You captured her in the first paragraph of *Rusty*,' he said. 'Captured her as an adult. Hair like flame, you wrote, sparking embers beneath the naked globe, a spill of molten copper. It's Georgie,' he said. '*They've all gone to live with the angels*, my mother said. She lied to me.'

'Please stop this. You're making me scared.'

And he turned from the window. 'Jim Hooper is my father.'

She heard him. He was a great one for jokes, and that wasn't a joke – and it wasn't meant to be. She could hear it in his breathing, in his voice. Knew then why his voice wasn't Morrie's. He wasn't Morrie. Jim Hooper was his father. He was . . .

Out of that wide bed then, dragging the sheets, the blanket with her, dragging them as far as the bathroom door, where she shed them and ran to vomit expensive champagne into the toilet bowl.

Couldn't stop vomiting. Even when there was nothing left inside her, she couldn't stop. Her hands gripping cold white porcelain, her stomach heaving, while in the bedroom he found the bedside light switch, not a lot of light, but enough to share a little with the bathroom, enough for him to see her naked form cowering over the toilet.

He came to the door, no further, breathing short, breathing fast until she turned to face him. No words. Two faces, similar in construction, disbelieving eyes staring wordlessly into similar eyes.

You're a perfect match, Cathy had said.

Too perfect.

And the bile rose again in Cara's throat.

He came then to offer a wet cloth, a towel. He didn't touch her.

'I could write my name when I was four,' he said. 'They turned it around when I was six, put the Morrison in the middle, the Hooper on the end. I told them it should have been the other way around. I told them it was James Hooper Morrison, not James Morrison Hooper. She said my daddy's name was Jim Hooper and my grandpa's name was Vern Hooper and they'd like it so very much if my last name was the same as theirs, and wasn't Morrison such a nice middle name.'

She cried then, for the loss of Morrie's voice, for the loss of his big farmer's hands, and the loss of him. Someone stood three feet from her, watching her heaving shoulders, staring at the shape of her crouching over the bowl. Someone picked up the sheet to drape over her nakedness. She dared not name that someone. Then he went away and she removed Morrie's rings, placed them on the vanity unit, and vomited again for their loss.

He returned clothed to the doorway. She tried to stand, but as in any nightmare, her legs had no strength to raise her.

'I used to dream about them,' he said. 'The lost-boy dreams I called them. Little Jimmy always trying to find his way home. Back when they started, I knew he was me. They never stopped, but home changed too often for my dreams to keep up, and after a while he wasn't me but Peter Pan. He could run like the wind, ride his bike at a hundred miles an hour. He could fly. I loved my lost-boy dreams.'

His voice was ripping holes in her heart. Her head on the toilet bowl, she bawled for him, and for her. Wanted him to hold her, and was revolted by what she wanted.

And by what they'd done, in that bed, in her bed. Couldn't live with it. Didn't want to live if she couldn't live with him. Wanted him to go, to stay. Wanted to scream at him to shut up and make love to her. Wanted to scream at him to get out of her sight.

'Mum told me they'd gone to live with the angels. I never doubted her. Jenny used to tell me that my daddy had gone up to live in the stars, and that I'd never forget him because he'd been given the job of painting all of the rainbows, and that every time I saw a rainbow, I'd know he was up there waving his paintbrush to me. I saw him too.

'I worked out my own way not to forget Jenny. She was the scent of lemons. There was a plant in the Balwyn garden that had lemon-scented leaves. For years, every pair of trousers Mum washed, she found a few of those leaves in the pockets. I still do it, crush lemon leaves, pick lemon verbena, lemon-scented geraniums.'

His sigh was a deep sob of a sigh, his voice breaking when he tried to speak of Georgie. But he swallowed, breathed deep and continued.

'Granny used to say Georgie's hair looked like a spill of new-minted pennies. I didn't know what a new-minted penny was, but shiny pennies became Georgie. I had a jar full. Mum and Grandpa used to save me the shiniest ones. I never spent them. I'd sit in the sun, pouring pennies backward and forward from the jar to a little beach bucket, chanting, "Georgie, Georgie, Georgie.'"

'Stop it. Please God, stop it.'

He walked around her, swept the two rings into his hand, then dropped them into his pocket.

'I'd forgotten what Jenny looked like, forgotten her hair. I loved the scent of your shampoo. It's your hair. Her scent is all over you. I should have known.'

'Please God, Morrie.'

He couldn't stop. 'I put them away in England. Everything stopped over there, the dreams, the moving, the changing faces. I took my middle name when I went to university, determined to be someone brand new, called myself Morrison Langdon, became the son of an Englishman, living in a five-hundred-year-old manor house, its roots so deep in the soil, a bomb couldn't move it. I'll take Pops home. I'll . . . . I'll undo it.'

And he picked up his case, his car keys, and he left her, left her kneeling on cold tiles on the bathroom floor, left her alone to howl.

MORE BESTSELLING FICTION BY
JOY DETTMAN

Pearl in a Cage

The first novel in Joy Dettman's sensational Woody Creek series.

On a balmy midsummer's evening in 1923, a young woman – foreign, dishevelled and heavily pregnant – is found unconscious just off the railway tracks in the tiny logging community of Woody Creek.

The town midwife, Gertrude Foote, is roused from her bed when the woman is brought to her door. Try as she might, Gertrude is unable to save her – but the baby lives.

When no relatives come forth to claim the infant, Gertrude's daughter Amber – who has recently lost a son in childbirth – and her husband Norman take the child in. In the ensuing weeks, Norman becomes convinced that God has sent the baby to their door, and in an act of reckless compassion, he names the baby Jennifer and registers her in place of his son.

Loved by some but scorned by more – including her stepmother and stepsister who resent the interloper – Jenny survives her childhood and grows into an exquisite and talented young woman. But who were her parents? Why does she so strongly resemble an old photograph of Gertrude's philandering husband? And will she one day fulfil her potential?

Spanning two momentous decades and capturing rural Australia's complex and mysterious heart, *Pearl in a Cage* is an unputdownable novel by one of our most talented storytellers.

Thorn on the Rose

It is 1939 and Jenny Morrison, distraught and just fifteen years of age, has fled the tiny logging community of Woody Creek for a new life in the big smoke.

But four months later she is back – wiser, with an expensive new wardrobe, and bearing another dark secret . . .

She takes refuge with Gertrude, her dependable granny and Woody Creek's indomitable midwife, and settles into a routine in the ever-expanding and chaotic household.

But can she ever put the trauma of her past behind her and realise her dream of becoming a famous singer? Or is she doomed to follow in the footsteps of her tragic and mysterious mother?

Spanning a momentous wartime decade and filled with the joys and heartaches of life in rural Australia, *Thorn on the Rose* is the spellbinding sequel to *Pearl in a Cage*.

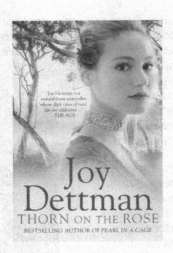

Moth to the Flame

In *Moth to the Flame*, Joy Dettman returns with another dazzling tale of the unforgettable characters of Woody Creek.

The year is 1946. The war ended five months ago. Jim Hooper, Jenny Morrison's only love, was lost to that war. And if not for Jenny, he would never have gone.

'An eye for an eye,' Vern Hooper says. An unforgiving man, Vern wants custody of Jenny's son, his only grandson, and is quietly planning his day in court.

Then Jenny's father Archie Foote swoops back into town. Archie offers Jenny a tantalising chance at fame and fortune; one way or another he is determined to play a part in her life.

Is Jenny's luck about to change, or is she drawn to trouble like a moth is drawn to the flame?

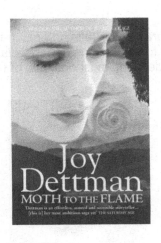

Ripples on a Pond

The old timber town of Woody Creek has a way of getting under people's skin . . .

Woody Creek is preparing for its centenary celebrations – but for many of its townspeople it's just another reminder of the old days, when life was more simple, before so-called progress roared through the town, altering everything in its wake.

Not for Georgie though. As the clock ticks over to 1970, she's determined that the new decade will be the one that sees her finally break free.

For Cara, Woody Creek will forever be tied to a devastating mistake that cannot be undone. She's vowed never to set foot in the place again.

Meanwhile, Jenny's estranged son, Jim, has inherited an estate in the United Kingdom and is trying to make a new life for himself. If only he could shake off his one terrible attachment to Australia.

As Woody Creek draws Joy Dettman's much-loved cast of characters back into its grip, confessions, discoveries and truths seem set to explode in the most dramatic of showdowns . . .

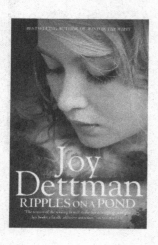